Isobel Neill grew up in Renfrewshire. At an
early age she picked up a [illegible] m
her choirboy [illegible] [develop]ed
over the [year] [langu]ages and
drama, her [interests]. After teaching
music for a number of years, she attended
drama school as a mature student. Family
commitments prevented her working away
from home, but she played many small parts
on TV and commercial radio. She is now
widowed and lives in Edinburgh.

ISOBEL NEILL

After Many Days

This edition published for Diamond Books, 2000

Diamond Books is an imprint of
HarperCollins*Publishers*
77-85 Fulham Palace Road,
Hammersmith, London W6 8JB

This edition first published in 1994

1 3 5 7 9 10 8 6 4 2

Copyright © Isobel Neill 1994

The Author asserts the moral right
to be identified as the author of this work

ISBN 0 26 167384 X

Set in Linotron Palatino
by Rowland Phototypesetting Ltd
Bury St Edmunds, Suffolk

Printed in Great Britain by
Caledonian International Book Manufacturing Ltd, Glasgow

All rights reserved. No part of this publication may be
reproduced, stored in a retrieval system, or transmitted,
in any form or by any means, electronic, mechanical,
photocopying, recording or otherwise, without the prior
permission of the publishers.

This book is sold subject to the condition that it shall not,
by way of trade or otherwise, be lent, re-sold, hired out or
otherwise circulated without the publisher's prior consent
in any form of binding or cover other than that in which it
is published and without a similar condition including this
condition being imposed on the subsequent purchaser.

ACKNOWLEDGEMENTS

The author wishes to thank the following: Robin Bell; the staff of Paisley Library and Edinburgh Central Library; Emeritus Professor Alan Steele and Professor Ian Campbell of Edinburgh University.

Chapter 1

'Puis-je vous aider, Madame?'

I couldn't believe it. There was I, Jessie Forbes, speaking French at ten o'clock on a fine August morning in Paisley and in Moss Street of all places.

Because most Paisley folk are away at the coast during the first fortnight in August, the town was quieter than usual. The river was low and stinking. To get to the post office beside the station I had to pass the jail and the municipal buildings. There were some coaches there and just as I was passing, a train gave a piercing whistle and set off a blast of steam. One of the horses reared. That set others tippeting around. The drivers were swearing like troopers. I decided it was no place for a lady and started to cross the square. Because of that I couldn't help noticing a crowd gathered round something or someone just at the foot of the Dirty Steps in Moss Street. I really should say Meetinghouse Lane but Paisley Buddies call them the Dirty Steps because all the rubbish seems to get whisked there by the wind. Had the whistle that startled the horse upset somebody with a weak heart?

'Plenty folk there,' I thought. 'No need for me to concern myself.' But my step slowed just the same – partly curiosity, I suppose, but partly a kind of guilty feeling about passing by on the other side. Two women broke away from the crowd when I was half-way across the square. Like me they were making for the

1

post office. As we drew level I heard one say, 'All the way from France, too. It must be awful to be no' weel in a strange country.' I stopped, considering. I could still speak a bit of French. My brother Dougie had started me off when I was very young and Beth, my eldest girl, had helped me keep it up. I turned my steps to Moss Street.

The woman stood leaning almost defensively against the wall. She reminded me of *The Stag at Bay*. 'They're killing her with kindness,' I thought, looking at the tight ring of concerned faces. 'She must get away from this.' I edged my way through, took a deep breath and '*Puis-je vous aider*?' There! I'd said it!

Her hand went up to move her veil while she dabbed her eyes. The gesture reminded me of something . . . what was it? Then a memory flashed back – my sister Elsie in our weaving shed in Kilbarchan all these years ago, trying on a kirking shawl . . . the same curve of the wrist . . . tilt of the head. The stranger lowered her handkerchief and murmured, '*Vous êtes très gentille, Madame . . . je serai bien . . .*' I looked at the tawny eyes, the straight eyebrows . . . of course there were lines . . . there would be . . .

'Elsie!' I whispered.

She crumpled suddenly and several people rushed to help me hold her. 'Sixpence when you bring a cab from the station,' I called to a wee barefoot lad at the edge of the crowd. He was off in a flash but it seemed ages before I heard the clatter of hooves and then the driver was helping me hand Elsie into the welcome privacy of the cab. She lay back among the cushions while I chafed the blood back into her hands. All the time pictures were forming in my mind. That day so many years ago when I read out Elsie's farewell note

2

to the others; Dougie's comment when he came in and read it, 'The bitch': that was Dougie who never swore! Mam looking so ill we thought she might have another heart attack . . .

I had made no effort to draw Elsie into conversation, but when the cab slowed down at our gate, she said, 'My luggage is at the hotel in Glasgow.'

'Don't worry,' I said. 'One of the family will fetch it.'

The front door was open by this time. Maggie, the maid, was standing open-mouthed. Then Beth came rattling down the stairs, 'What is it, Mother?'

'Help me get the lady up to the spare room,' I said, 'and Maggie, hot bottles for the spare-room bed, please, and then a nice pot of tea.'

It took a long time to walk poor Elsie up those stairs. Then she collapsed on the edge of the bed, quite helpless.

'Light the gas fire, Beth,' I said, 'while I look out some night clothes. Once she's settled I'll phone Doctor Walker.'

Elsie stirred. 'I do not need a doctor, please, I am quite well – just a little *crise de nerfs* . . . I've forgotten the English.'

'Aye. We understand fine but we'll see later. You look as if it's rest you're needing and Doctor Walker could give you something to make you sleep.'

'You know the lady, Mother?' Beth was puzzled.

'Aye! but we'll talk about that later, too,' I said. 'It's quietness she needs now, a nice warm bed, some hot tea then peace.'

Maggie appeared with the hot bottles. I could see her nose was bothering her but I had no intention of launching into explanations then. Beth went down to help her with the tray while I got Elsie undressed. It wasn't easy. She seemed absolutely helpless and her beautiful clothes had so many fiddly fastenings to complicate matters. I propped her up with pillows while we waited. Soon Beth appeared alone with the heavy tray.

Weak tears were flowing down Elsie's cheeks. Her hands were so shaky that I had to hold the cup to her lips, but she drank gratefully and I even coaxed her to have a wee scone. Though a little colour came to her face the helpless tears were still gathering. So, when she was finished, I slipped the pillows down and drew the blinds while Beth got the things back on the tray. We closed the door behind us quietly and Beth said, 'What now?'

'Send Maggie out to get some vegetables for soup. I'm going to make a phone call.'

'Dr Walker?'

'No. Nancy.'

Nancy Walker, the doctor's wife, is one of my closest friends. We're always involved in raising money for the infirmary. I knew I could trust her not to blether. The doctor nips into the house sometimes for a quick cup of tea in the middle of his rounds. She would tell him what had happened and he would drop in on us, I knew. And with Maggie out of earshot I could fill in some details for Beth.

'Nancy, I've got something to tell you. It'll be a bit of a shock,' I began, then sketched in the rest. Her reaction was not what I had expected.

'Fancy a douce wee body like you having a sister who could run away with a French artist! . . . You can trust me, of course. I'll tell Bill as soon as he comes in. Will he be safe with La Belle Elsie, d'you think?'

4

Though I laughed with her, I had some misgivings. Would this be the view other people would take of what had been a heartache to all the rest of the family, particularly Mam? I wasn't sure that I liked being described as a douce body, either. It sounded pretty dull. Then I shook myself and prepared to get on with practical things. Instinct told me that the fewer people who knew about Elsie, the better; that is, till we had sorted things out. But of course the folk in the house would have to know. Even Maggie would have to be told part of it. First, I would have to tell Beth. She must be eaten up by curiosity by this time.

But Beth forestalled me. 'Is that French woman by any chance the sister who became the favourite of Mrs Hyphen-something at the big house and ran away from Kilbarchan with a devil of an artist who'd been staying there?'

'Who told you?'

'Aunt Bella.'

I might have known. We had all agreed to tell the younger generation a modified version of the story but, of course, my sister Bella never could keep quiet for long about anything.

'Fancy a bad apple in your barrel, Mother. And you used to tell us what good little girls you had been . . . doing what Mam told you . . .'

'Elsie was not a bad apple,' I said furiously. 'She was different from the rest of us . . . more dreamy . . . imaginative . . . but she was a genius with a needle . . . taught us younger ones how to sew. That fellow took advantage of her.'

'Ooh, la la,' said Beth.

'You can forget that,' I said. 'Our Elsie allowed no liberties before they were married. She wrote and told

5

Mam that.' My face clouded at the memory of that awful time, Mam and Faither visibly ageing under the disgrace . . . the gibes and chants of my fellow pupils at school . . .

> *Elsie Allen, quack, quack, quack.*
> *The Frenchman's got her on her back.*

Beth put a quick arm round my shoulder. 'Sorry, Mother, I didn't mean to upset you. I'll keep quiet, don't worry. See if you can keep her here for a while – it would help my French.'

I had to smile. Beth so often reminded me of Dougie and his thirst for education. Of course I had followed my big brother like a shadow and absorbed a lot of his ideas, I suppose. It thrilled me to see Beth getting the chance I missed.

'Well . . . we'll see about that,' I said. 'We don't know what her plans are . . . why she made for Paisley. None of us lived here when she left . . .'

We heard the sound of the back door slamming as Maggie returned with the vegetables. 'I'll help her, Mother,' Beth said. 'What about taking your hat off before the doctor comes?' I hadn't realized it was still on!

Doctor Walker said more or less what we had expected. 'Nervous prostration. Could be quite serious. I get the impression it's a sort of delayed shock she's had. You've done the right thing in getting her to bed. I've given her enough dope to make sure she drops off now. She'll probably wake late in the evening if not before. Let her have any light food she fancies but don't ask her to talk. It's difficult to tell how it may go. If she asks *you* any questions, answer them simply but don't expect her to remember your answers.

6

There's something causing her anxiety and until she can shed that, we won't see any progress. I'll come back after surgery tomorrow.'

That evening I found I was shaking when my husband Sandy's key turned in the lock and I heard my two big sons laughing at something he said to them over his shoulder. As usual I went into his arms and immediately felt steadier. Alex gave a teasing whistle while Allen, quiet, serious Allen, said, 'Behold the lovebirds!'

'I hope you're as lucky, lads,' Sandy said. While he spoke he was easing me towards the snug and asking, 'Did you remember to post your letters?'

Out of the corner of my eye I saw Beth motion to her brothers to follow her. The snug door closed behind us. 'What's wrong?' Sandy asked.

'What makes you think anything's wrong?'

'You were trembling like a leaf when I put my arms round you. What's wrong?'

'I don't think something's wrong, but . . . prepare for a shock, Sandy.'

He pulled me on to his knee in the big chair and I galloped through my story. Sandy listened calmly.

'Well . . . well . . . quite a day, wee Jessie! And now, is there any supper for three hungry men?'

'Sandy Forbes, does nothing excite you?' I asked as he shooed me out of the snug.

Thanks to the dope the doctor was giving her, Elsie hardly surfaced. I would coax her to have a little soup or a little bit of toast but her eyes would get heavy or the slow tears would start and I would be glad to see her settle down again to sleep. As Beth had forecast, Sandy told me to keep quiet about Elsie till the doctor advised otherwise.

7

Beth took it upon herself to inform Maggie. 'It would have been awkward for you, Mother. Keep calm. I just told her that the lady was a member of your family you hadn't seen since childhood; she'd gone abroad and had a sad time there.'

It was on the fifth day, I think, that things changed. Elsie's eyes were shut when I went into her room and started dusting quietly. I had just picked up the lovely handmirror that was one of our silver wedding presents when Elsie spoke from the bed. 'Your hair hasn't darkened at all, Jessie. I was afraid it might.' I dropped the mirror with a clatter and ran to hug her. This time I was the one who was crying.

It was quite some time before I could say anything coherent; then, in spite of Bill's warning, I started on the question which had been uppermost in my mind: 'Why did you not get in touch all these years?'

'Oh Jessie,' she said, her voice breaking, 'if only you knew . . . I can't . . . not yet.' She was shaking with sobs again.

I hugged her tight. 'All right, Elsie. I won't make you talk. Just relax . . . there . . . you'll be fine. We'll look after you. What about a wee cup of tea, eh?'

'Now I know I am in Scotland.' She was half laughing and half crying.

I carried the tray up myself. These first few moments of real communication were too precious to share with anyone. 'Don't worry,' I said as I poured the tea. 'I shan't ask you to tell me anything. Just you get yourself well. When you feel like it, I'll be happy to listen.'

'Tell me, Jessie . . . the family . . . . Mam and Faither?'

'Mam died a long time ago, Elsie. Allen, my eldest,

was two and I was expecting Alex . . . that would be May 1881 . . . aye, the lilac was out at the funeral, I mind. She had been sitting out in the garden for a wee while and went in to start the dinner: the pain hit her. It was a shock to us all. She had seemed to be getting on fine.'

'What about Faither?'

I hesitated, remembering. We had all waited on for a long time after the funeral, worn out with a grief that could be shared only with our siblings. Then when our menfolk started to urge us homewards, Faither had made a husky wee speech, thanking us all for being good to Mam. He turned to Dougie's framed certificates. 'Dougie did us proud at university and did more than his share in every way. He died saving another's life. That's a sweet sorrow. But I'll never forgive our bonnie Elsie for the heartache she caused your Mam.' That was one memory I would not be sharing with Elsie!

'Jean and Tam left their house in Johnstone and moved into the cottage with Faither. You know that Jean's cure for everything is work, work and more work . . .'

'I remember,' Elsie said ruefully.

'Faither died at his loom which was just the way he would have wanted it.'

Then came the question I had dreaded. 'And Dougie?' Elsie prompted. 'I expect he had plenty to say when I left.'

I was saved from replying by Maggie's tap on the door; there was a lady to see me; she'd put her in the dining-room. The collector for the mission I supported in the north end of the town must have been surprised at the enthusiasm of my smile. Never had an interrup-

9

tion been more welcome. I remembered Dougie's bitter face as he whispered to me, 'Don't worry. I'll bring her back if I have to drag her by her hair.'

On my way back upstairs I worked out how to avoid that answer. Elsie was going to hear about Dougie's death sooner or later so now was the time to tell her. I took a deep breath as I settled in my chair. 'This will be a shock, Elsie. Dougie was killed . . . in Moss Street . . . twenty-seven years ago next month.'

'Oh, no, not Dougie too.' Elsie was shattered.

'We were all shocked, Elsie; I miscarried my first baby. He was saving a wee boy who fell from a window. He would have been all right but the bairn was wearing tackety boots and one caught Dougie on the temple . . .'

'Poor Mam . . . her only son . . .' Elsie's voice broke.

I looked at Elsie. Her face was drawn and trembling. I kicked myself for being so stupid. 'I'm sorry, love. This is too much for you, getting it thrown at you all at once. I was hoping you'd come down to dinner tonight . . . meet Allen and Alex . . . no, I think we'd better get you back to bed. I'll bring up a nice tray; then you can have one of the pills the doctor left.' She didn't argue.

Elsie had met Beth, of course, right at the beginning. Sandy had – rather reluctantly, I think – come into her room with me for a few minutes one night. I watched my darling man as he clasped her hands in his big strong ones.

'You're welcome, lass. There's no need to hurry. Just you take your time and do what my bossy wee wife tells you. I always do!'

'And the band played "Believe it if you like",' said I as he made his escape. The tears had welled up in

Elsie's lovely tawny eyes as he spoke to her. When he was gone she just sat dabbing gently with her handkerchief for a while. Then she said, 'You're a lucky lass, Jessie.' It was the first time she had sounded the least Scottish. I answered in kind, 'I dinna need remindin',' and we took another step back to the intimacy of childhood.

For the next few days Elsie still felt unable to tell me any of her story, nor did she want to meet anyone. The rest of the family were all on holiday up north with the young folk.

'You all have such big families,' Elsie said.

'Well, we're married . . .' I began, not knowing how to meet this.

'Ah, the Frenchwomen have a few tricks,' she said. 'The intelligent ones choose.'

I was none too pleased at being bracketed with the unintelligent.

'I wouldn't be without one of them,' I began indignantly.

'Of course you wouldn't,' she soothed me, 'and if Beth is an example, I think you are the most fortunate woman in the world.'

I calmed down then. What she said had intrigued me. What sort of tricks? It was true, of course, that I wouldn't be without one of them but I could remember Sandy's groan of concern when I announced my first pregnancy. At that time he was worried that I was so young. Later we had accepted the knowledge each time with a rueful resignation. Now we were comfortably off with a nice big house and I had Maggie to help me. But in the early days when every penny had to be watched, I knew that each birth set back Sandy's plans for the business. What tricks? Before Elsie went back, I would find out by hook or by crook.

Elsie was quiet for a long time then. I began to wonder if she was wishing me far enough; felt I was prying and was regretting her little bit of confidence. I was just thinking of making an excuse to leave her when she spoke, almost in a whisper. 'I had a little boy. I called him Alain. It was near enough to "Allen" to remind me of home.'

The tears were welling up in her lovely eyes again. I moved to take her in my arms. 'What happened to him, Elsie? Don't upset yourself, please. You're safe here with us. You can stay as long as you like. Let me fetch you one of your pills. Then you can rest.'

'There is no rest for me, Jessie, ever.' Her voice was rising again and she clung to me feverishly. I wondered desperately what to do. Then I heard Sandy's step on the landing. He tapped on the door and I eased myself out of Elsie's grasp to open it.

'Is everything all right?' he asked anxiously. I drew the door to behind me and quickly told him what had happened.

'Let me speak to her,' he said, opening the door and walking in.

Sandy sat down calmly beside Elsie, took her hands in his and said, 'Now lass, I think you've reached breaking point. It's time you got it all off your chest. And what better person to tell than Jessie, eh? I tell you what I'll do. I'll bring up a tray with the spirit kettle, your cups and a tin of biscuits. You can sit there all night if you like – there's the gas fire if you need it – and just blether till the cows come home. You've been bottling it all up too long by the look of you. What d'you say, lass?'

Elsie lifted her head with the grace that had characterized her as a girl. 'I think you are an angel, Sandy.' Then she spoiled it with an unladylike hiccough which sent him off laughing.

The little flame of the spirit kettle fascinated us both for a while. In silence I infused the tea and waited for it to strengthen. It was only when we sat back in the comfortable armchairs that had been moved to Elsie's room that she spoke. 'I do not know where to begin, Jessie . . . You will be shocked . . . upset . . .'

'Don't worry about me. I'll be fine.'

'Yes,' she said reflectively, 'you have a deep well of joy to draw on.'

'What a nice way of putting it, Elsie,' I said.

'It's difficult, Jessie, when I think back . . . a lot of scenes jumbled up, really, and I'm acting in them.'

'Well, tell me any way you like,' I said.

Chapter 2

Elsie waited for a moment or two, then her voice came from far away.

'I knew that everyone would realize that we had planned our escape. That would hurt them. But though I was aware of it at the time, everything melted when Michel turned on the charm. And oh how charming he could be! His delicious accent and the odd little French phrase creeping in . . . I felt so flattered, so beautiful and so important. I wasn't the third daughter of a weaver any more. I was an elegant lady who could hold her head up in any company. And Michel would lead me to the sort of company that I craved – I was sure of that. I wonder that Mrs Nisbet-Brown never saw the danger: leaving us together in that beautiful room with the sun glancing on the rich brocades and the scent of the hothouse flowers making me feel romantic, desirable. And Michel's eyes, before he even tried his pretty speeches, had told me he found me that – desirable. I suppose I was at the age when any healthy girl is attractive to a certain degree. I was so used to hiding my daydreams. Oh, Jessie, can't you imagine how Jean would have poured scorn on some of them . . . and Dougie!

'When he started to coax me to elope I would have none of it. That had not been part of my daydreams. I had expected him to go to my father and say, "Sir, I wish to marry your lovely daughter." We were to have a wedding that Kilbarchan would never forget and Mrs Nisbet-Brown was to insist on holding the reception at Barlochan. There would be a big marquee on the lawn. Michel would do some sketches and afterwards he would paint some beautiful pictures of the scene which would hang in famous galleries in Paris. But Michel kept reminding me how much more thrilling it was to keep things secret . . . "We do not need the rest of the world, my darling. We are complete in ourselves in our own magic world. I want to take you away from this dull village – to introduce my beautiful Madame Blanchard to the most important people in Paris where you deserve to belong." One arm would be creeping round my waist while the other tilted my chin for his kiss. His touch always affected me. I could feel my breasts quicken and felt that he must know what was happening to me. As he got bolder I would be crushed against him while he murmured how he longed to call me his own, to have the right . . .

'He was clever all right, *cet diable*! He knew how to work me up and then leave me longing. Mam's little lectures to Bella and me always came to mind and I would try to be strict with myself. "It is up to the girl to keep a man right," had been her favourite ending. She hadn't said how much the girl would long to do just what the man wanted. Perhaps most girls didn't. Perhaps Bella and I were different from Mam. Or perhaps Mam just saw something we were too young to appreciate and knew that our passions needed reining in. When you're young you just don't think that the oldest grandmother has been through it all and can maybe see things more clearly from her distance.

'It was a lovely summer that year, or maybe I was just more attuned to it. The scents of the flowers

15

affected me strongly. On the May evenings as I strolled through our wee garden at the cottage I would soak up the scent of wallflowers and lilac till they were almost suffocating. I couldn't get to bed quickly enough to dream about Michel; to feel my body which he assured me was perfectly proportioned and to fondle the soft skin of my breasts, all the while feeling the pulse of longing that kept sleep from coming though my eyes were closed on my secret world. During the early hot days of June the roses drove me to distraction and I knew that I would give in to Michel's pleading. He assured me it would be easy to find a Protestant church in France; he didn't mind at all; though he had been christened a Catholic he no longer went to church. "People are not so grim about religion in La Belle France, my darling. I think it is your cold climate that makes people so serious." He made a comical wry face then and had me laughing. Michel was giving me a picture of a different world, a world he assured me was more suited to me than a dull Scottish village. And I believed the *bâtard*!

'Once I had agreed to run away, the next thing was to plan our escape. In a place like Kilbarchan there's not much goes on without someone noticing. Then we heard that Michael Dick, the flautist, had died. Remember him, Jessie?'

I nodded. I had no wish to stop the flow of speech that seemed to be giving Elsie release.

'Mam said there would be a big turn-out for sure and I knew that every man in the village would be following the coffin. The women would be out watching the procession and then they would spend a long time afterwards discussing Mrs Dick's loss over cups of tea. They would assume I was at the big house and nobody would think of it till the coach did not arrive in the evening. It was the ideal plan. Michel was delighted with me. "One Michel by dying will give life to another Michel," he said, sweeping me into his arms. And I swallowed that nonsense!

'Even the early part of the journey was a thrill to me because I had never been further than Glasgow or Greenock. I hadn't realized the extent of the farmlands that stretched for miles and miles not long after we left the big city. I would turn to Michel to remark on something and find his eyes glued on my face with an amused smile curving his lips. I knew that my colour always rose at his intent look. It seemed to excite him.

'When the border hills reared up in the summer sunshine, I thought I had never seen anything so grand. I clutched at Michel's arm. Before I knew it he had my hand in his and was stroking my palm. The other travellers were bound to notice, I felt. I glanced round in panic, wresting my hand out of his grip. Michel shook with laughter but he did not say anything. Behaviour in Paris must be very different from Kilbarchan, I thought. Could you imagine anyone doing that on the Greenock train? No! Neither can I. Michel moved in the finest circles and yet he did things like that. The people in our family never drew attention to themselves in public. I was going to find it very confusing!

'The farmhouses didn't seem strange – mostly a plain Georgian like many of the ones at home. The cottages were not much different either; perhaps not so tightly clustered as ours were. Then we reached the border and not long after that I saw brick houses. "Isn't that funny?" I said to Michel. "Houses made of brick. It's just factories that are made of brick at home."

17

' "We are not far from your home and yet you find so many things strange. I cannot wait to see what you think of Paris: the Champs Elysées, La Tour Eiffel, Notre Dame . . ." He was on familiar territory and I was staring at him starry-eyed. They were getting rapidly nearer, all those wonders he had been teasing me with for so long. I firmly suppressed the guilt feelings that threatened now and again to bubble up. This was life, life as experienced by the privileged; something that the dull spirits of Kilbarchan would never sample. I was to be Madame Blanchard, acquainted with the finest of Parisian society. I drifted off into a daydream while the rails sang, "Soon you'll be there, soon you'll be there."

'When we reached the south coast Michel said that we should rest for a couple of days before I faced the crossing. Then I found that he expected me to share a room. "What's the difference?" he said, "We're going to be married as soon as we reach France." I would have none of it, of course. Mam's little lectures were ringing in my ears again. I saw that he was angry but then he decided to turn on the charm and oh, he could be so charming. His hands were caressing me till I felt I would melt away. When he saw I wouldn't give in, we just spent one night on this side of the channel.

'The crossing was calm. I stayed up on deck all night, watching the stars, and my spirits rose as we approached the French coast. Michel's eyes were always on me. I felt loved, desired. It was a heady experience for a romantic dreamer like me. When we reached harbour it was all such a bewildering bustle. Everyone was speaking so fast. Though Michel had been tutoring me and I was so keen to learn, I couldn't make out a word of it. The smells were different too:

fish, woodsmoke, tobacco. The clothes were different – particularly the men. I stuck close by Michel. He had soon engaged a young lad to carry my trunk. I thought we were making for the Paris train, but Michel started picking his way through all the bustle at the end of the pier and making his way to a coach halt.

'"Aren't we going to Paris?" I asked him.

'"No, not yet," he said. "I know a quiet little inn along the coast. It will be a better introduction for you to La Belle France."

'I climbed aboard. We had to wait some time before the coachman was satisfied that he had packed in as many passengers as his vehicle would hold; then we were off. The roads were rough and the carriage none too well sprung, but it was such an adventure to me. Michel was watching me possessively and with an amused smile on his face. At length we drew up in a quaint little fishing village. White cottages were clustered in little groups off the main road which curved round the bay. In the heart of it all was a solid white church with lots of coloured tiles round the porch, and statues in niches round the walls. Near that, a sprawling inn with lots of outbuildings and a wide entrance to a yard where several other coaches were drawn up. There was a lot of shouting of orders as we stepped down . . . I was glad to escape from the bustle and the smell of horse into the dark cool entrance of the inn.

'Michel soon commanded attention from the landlady, and a wee boy with a striped waistcoat which made him look like a wasp grabbed my trunk. He couldn't have been more than twelve. I felt awful watching him struggle under its weight. Then he showed us into a room with a big bed that took up most of the floor. Michel was tipping the boy and dismissing him. "But we need two rooms," I started to say.

'"We'll be married by nightfall," he said. "You *did* bring your birth certificate, didn't you?"

'"Yes, of course," I said, "but is there a Huguenot church here? And could it be done at such short notice?"

'"Don't worry, my darling," he said, turning on his charm. "Perhaps in the next village is your kind of church. I shall ask. And would it matter? The words are the same anyway. It is the one God who will bless us." I *still* insisted that I wanted a Protestant church, knowing how Faither would feel. Michel shrugged, suggested I might like some coffee; then I could sit in the shade while he went off to make the arrangements.

'The coffee was strong, bitter but so wonderfully French. I felt like a woman of the world, sitting there with my adoring would-be husband. He gathered our papers and disappeared. After a while I found myself nodding off on the hard chair. My sleepless night was catching up on me so I decided to go back to the inn and rest. After all, if I was to be a bride before nightfall . . .

'I went off into one of my lovely daydreams. I woke with Michel stumbling over the step into our room and sprang up with a fright. He looked flushed as if he had been drinking. I looked at my watch. Two'clock. "You've been a long time," I said.

'"Yes; had to do a bit of coaxing, grease a few palms, buy a few drinks but we're all set. Half past four this afternoon and you will be Mme Blanchard and we can share this lovely bed." He lunged at me and I moved quickly away. "Ha-ha, little Miss Modesty," he

20

mocked. "Let's go and eat some lunch, some decent French food to keep your strength up."

'The food *was* lovely. The casement windows were open on to a rather scrappy garden but the smell of carnations came drifting in, the bees were humming, the seagulls calling and I was in La Belle France. I waited till we were washing it down with the bitter coffee. "Where is the church?" I asked.

' "Next door."

' "But that's not Huguenot," I said.

' "No, the nearest one is 60 kilometres away,' he said.

' "Oh, no." I was shattered.

' "Look, Elsie, don't be so silly," he coaxed. "I've fixed the mayor, the priest, the notary, the witnesses, and what would the landlady think? First we book a double room, then you say you are not going to marry me . . ."

'I was in a dilemma then, far out of my depth. "The priest is doing this as a special favour," he went on in an aggrieved tone. "He's conducting a funeral at half past two and is hurrying back from the jollifications in time to marry us. A funeral in this part of the world means unlimited drinking. He's making a real sacrifice, you know."

'I burst out laughing. It was all so ridiculous when I thought of the contrast between home and there. Michel cheered up as soon as I laughed and for the next few hours put himself out to reassure me. He dressed early and vacated the room for me to dress in my wedding finery.

'The church was cool and quiet. I tried so hard to recapture the atmosphere of Meg's wedding but it was difficult. The witnesses Michel had press-ganged were

21

half drunk. The priest smiled rather vacantly at me and then started to gabble. It didn't seem to mean much to him. I remembered Meg floating down the aisle with us younger ones behind her; everyone in that church admiring and loving her . . . I had designed and planned the dresses. I had read about weddings like that, with the bride in a veil and all the bridesmaids in matching outfits . . . And after all, Meg was marrying Duncan. His parents had a big house. It was a good chance for us to get out of the Kilbarchan rut where most girls just got married in a good silk dress which they wore for Sunday best afterwards. It would have been better perhaps if I had settled for what I had.'

She paused then. I wondered if I should suggest that she could leave the rest for another time. Instead, I started up the spirit kettle again. Elsie didn't seem to notice me. She spoke as if in a dream.

'That first week was a strange mixture. All my passionate longings were being satisfied; Michel kept telling me I was looking beautiful and the mirror seemed to say to me, "He's right! You are." Yet there was a queer – what's the word I want? – split . . . Dougie would say "dichotomy". That's it. My dreams were being answered. I had my Prince Charming but I belonged to him now; he kept telling me so and I wasn't sure that I liked belonging to anyone! My body had been my own, inviolate. All these years my daft dreams had brought me a sort of freedom, a detachment from reality. Now they were being fulfilled I had to live with reality.

'Michel never went anywhere without his sketch pad. I was flattered that he kept making sketches of me but absolutely refused to let him paint me in the nude as he desperately wanted to do. Though you jib at many things in your upbringing, Jessie, I think there must always be some that you accept as right. The thought of the world seeing me mother-naked appalled me.

'"I could do it from memory," he would tease me and laugh at my blushes.

'I had expected he would be as eager as I was to get to Paris but he kept putting it off. "The sea air is good for you," he would say. I used to watch him sketch the fishermen mending their nets and then show the result to them. Sometimes I saw him offer the sketch and money changed hands. Then he started painting a picture of the inn.

'"How long will that take you?" I asked.

'"Three days, then another three to dry," he said shortly.

'"But that will delay us," I began.

'"How do you expect to pay the bill here and then the fares to Paris, you little fool?" he said roughly.

'"D'you mean to say you have no money?" I was shattered.

'"A fat dowry you brought," he said bitterly.

'My world turned upside down. This was how he had been thinking of me all along . . . no dowry! All his tales about introducing his beautiful Mme Blanchard to important people in Paris had been based on nothing. I felt numb, frozen in spite of the hot sun. I knew with a horrible certainty that Mme Blanchard would not be meeting important people in Paris; that all he had wanted was my body. The fact that I had refused to give myself before marriage had whetted his appetite; he had had no intention of marrying me. In bitterness I remembered what Mam used to say about me: "Born to be a lady and not needed". I had secretly thought that was true. The rest of the family could be content with the cottage and the weaving shed but my rightful place was in the big house. Instead of that I was stranded in France with a penniless husband who had only wanted one thing of me.

'And he made sure he got that one thing, though I shuddered at his touch that night. "Let's have none of that," he said. "You were the one who wanted to get married, remember?" I suppose I could not hide my loathing. It seemed to drive him to a frenzy. I dreaded being in the room with him from then on. I had married him, so he could do what he liked with my body, was his attitude. Sometimes I would try to fend him off but it just made him more cruel than ever. I was scared the other people in the inn would see my bruises.

'"O God, let my period come," I prayed, thinking that this might give me a respite from his attentions. But the days went by. I thought that the sea voyage might have upset me . . .

'One day Michel questioned me about it. I had been scared to tell him what I guessed would be unwelcome news; also I had been feverishly trying to think up a plan to earn some money on my own and save up for my fare home. When I admitted I was late, he started to curse and swear. Then he ordered me to pack; we were leaving for Paris . . . he knew a chemist . . .

'The train was crowded; children were crying all over the place. I kept feeling sick, partly nerves, I think. Michel snapped a few words at me now and again. I saw people look at us curiously when I answered in English because the extra effort was beyond me.

'When we got near Paris I *did* feel a stirring of

interest. This was the place I had daydreamed about for so long. But in those daydreams there had been a handsome, adoring escort in my elegant stroll down the boulevard. Now that I had been stripped of all illusions, I could see that those lines I had considered masterful were lines of cruelty. And this man was my husband. I had taken him for better or worse, or whatever that priest had said.

'He grunted at me to lift his painting equipment while he stuck my trunk on his shoulder and bundled his valise under his arm. People protested angrily as he forced his way out, calling to me to get a move on or all the porters would be engaged. I came in for my share of the abuse as I desperately tried to keep up with him. It was probably a good thing I couldn't understand it all!

'After some raucous shouting we *did* get a porter and a cab. "At least we're going to arrive in some sort of style," I thought, trying to picture the spacious, airy studio with the marvellous view Michel described. The traffic was so bewildering – much busier than Glasgow. No sooner had I glimpsed a building I wanted to ask Michel about than it was blotted out by a highly piled cart. The journey was much longer than I had anticipated. The streets got narrower till we often had difficulty getting past carts which were loading and unloading. Plaster was peeling off buildings high enough to blot out most of the sunlight. I saw with disgust the debris-strewn pavements.

'I remembered how in Kilbarchan the shopkeepers not only swept but scrubbed the area in front of their premises. Here no effort had been made whatsoever. Here, children were playing amid piles of dust and swarms of flies. In spite of the stuffy cab I shivered.

Michel looked at me angrily as if to say, "What next?" Then he was speaking to the cabman and we stopped in front of one of the dingy buildings. I had time to notice brown shutters, some of them askew, before Michel was urging me to be more careful of his painting stuff. Then he was arguing with the driver – I suppose about the price. It wasn't the beautiful French I had heard him speak in Kilbarchan when he was trying to charm me. The words were beyond me, but not only that, his voice was harsh and guttural. I shivered again while I waited in the dark entrance. At last the driver cracked his whip and moved off, still shouting insults. Michel pushed past me up some steps and shouldered open a door.

'We were in a sort of entrance lobby with cracked tiles on the floor. Several doors with flaking paint opened off it. One of those opened suddenly and a woman I took to be the concierge came out. What a bosom! And it was emphasized with squiggles and twists of braid which trembled in the most comical fashion every time she drew breath. Her grisled hair was anchored with enormous pins in a bun at the back and they wiggled too as she spoke. And she spoke! Michel couldn't get a word in. Her voice was loud and clear, and in spite of the speed I picked up quite a lot of it. I had assumed that Michel owned the studio he had told me about, but that was just another illusion to shed. According to Mme Boucher, there had been no rent paid for six months and not a foot would he set in her studio till he had paid it. He told her if she would let him settle his wife in, he would get her her something money. "Wife!" she exclaimed. "God help the stupid girl." At that, Michel started stamping up the stairs. I followed as well as I could with Madame on our heels, her tongue going like a clapper. When we reached the top, Michel started cursing. The door had been boarded up with several planks firmly nailed across.

'I felt I was in a nightmare with Michel standing there cursing; that woman full of righteous indignation, talking, talking, talking. Everything went black. I heard a terrible noise as I fell. I found out later that some of Michel's painting stuff had gone hurtling down the stairs, narrowly missing Madame. I don't know how long I was unconscious.

'When I came to, I was lying in a strange bed staring at a screen. I saw that a skylight window beyond it was open, allowing the street sounds to float in. I watched the dust motes dancing for a while before I tried to lift my head. The sheets were grey and smelled of stale sweat. The screen was round three sides of the bed and I couldn't see much. A rickety bamboo table with a jug and a cup on it was within reach. I managed to pour myself some water and sip it gratefully.

'There was no sound in the room. I wondered at that. If Michel had fallen asleep in a chair, surely I would hear his breathing! Eventually I risked my feet over the bed. I was fully dressed apart from my shoes.

'The studio bore no resemblance to the one I had imagined from Michel's talk. It was nothing but a big dusty attic, with what looked to me like junk in every corner. Apart from one grimy rug by the bed, the boards were bare and hadn't seen a scrubbing brush for many years. Cobwebs were hanging in every corner. A stone sink had a few dusty shelves round about it with a battered kettle and a few pans. Nearby there was a makeshift table with a rusty gas ring. A card table covered with oilcloth seemed to be used as a dining table.

'It was among the clutter on it that I found Michel's note. It was in French – he hadn't bothered to speak one word in English after we reached Paris. I had great difficulty in making out his writing and some of the words were strange but the gist of it was that he was off to sell a painting to pay the bitch downstairs. I could pick out the ending. "Don't know when I shall be back." I was completely alone in that strange country, without a sou, without a bite to eat . . . he had left me in a dead faint . . . not a word of comfort . . .'

I ran to take her in my arms.

Chapter 3

I was not sure if Elsie would feel like carrying on. She seemed exhausted, but Dr Walker had said she needed to be rid of whatever was worrying her so I waited patiently. I felt her ease herself out of my arms and went back to my post beside the spirit kettle.

She began softly. 'It was getting dark. I had cried myself into a stupor by then. "My God, you look a mess," was his greeting. "I've got the stuff: it'll just take a minute to mix it. Wine is the best disguise for the taste!" He was busily opening a bottle as he spoke. "I can't drink on an empty stomach," I said. He indicated a bundle he had dropped on the table. "You'll find bread there and butter and cheese."

'I ate like a wolf. I think there was anger as well as hunger there, Jessie. I had reached the depths of desolation. Out of that had come bitterness and a determination to get the better of this devil. I think the way we were brought up gave us a funny sort of pride. In our little world of Kilbarchan, self-respect was all. Don't you agree?

'The muck he mixed up for me tasted foul but he insisted I drain the glass. It was no sooner down than I started to retch. "Eat a bit more bread," he said, "to absorb it. Then, for God's sake make yourself presentable and I'll take you to see the Champs Elysées. The fresh air will steady you."

'I couldn't imagine a more back-handed invitation,

but I was desperate to get out of that filthy attic. It hadn't taken me long to find that the wonderful view he had told me about was obtained by standing on the highest chair and sticking your head through the skylight. I suppose a slater might have found it interesting. Apart from a few towers in the distance, all I could see were millions of tiles.

'Well, I *did* try to improve my appearance though I felt horribly queasy. Michel was not going to drag me down to his level. The surliness which had made him stop using English to me would be turned to my advantage. The sooner I learned French, the sooner I would be independent. I would stop thinking of the baby that might have been, that I would have loved and cared for. I had married a devil, a fiend who had no wish to be a father, no thought for anyone but himself. As soon as I could, I would escape from his clutches.

'As we reached the front door I heard a creaking sound and guessed that Madame was watching us. Michel used a few swear words I did not understand. "That bitch never misses a thing," he said.

'"Doesn't she ever go out herself then?" I asked.

'"I've seen her with another old bitch on a Sunday afternoon," he said, "sitting in a café and criticizing everyone who goes by."

'So, I would have to be careful with Madame, I decided. But perhaps even that noseyness could be turned to an advantage if I were clever. I didn't know how. But the cold determination that was my self-defence now told me to note every detail, forget nothing.

'After the series of disappointments I had suffered, I had ceased to expect anything wonderful from the

Champs Elysées, but the first sight of it took my breath away. Even now, after all these years, I still see that picture as I saw it then with my wondering eyes, the grandeur, the space, the lovely trees . . . and all the cafés with people enjoying themselves, chattering in groups or sitting quietly watching the world go by. And the fashions – my clothes seemed worlds apart from them . . . well . . . perhaps that's an exaggeration. It wasn't that everyone was beautifully dressed. There were quite a number of poor folk and some hideous old women shuffling along with dirty scarves tied round their heads . . . but the elegant ones *were* elegant. They seemed to carry themselves so differently from even the smartest women I had seen on the other side of the Channel. Dougie would have described it as a "gentle arrogance" I think. Words were always so important to Dougie. How he coached and corrected us!

'Michel had said the stuff would take anything between twelve and twenty-four hours to work. When waves of nausea and pain had gripped me on the long walk from our suburb, he had assured me that the best way to make it work was exercise. By the time we got to the Champs Elysées I was exhausted and very relieved to find that he was glad to sit in a café with me.

'As usual, he had a sketch pad in his pocket and amused himself by drawing a few of the young girls sitting nearby. I sipped the drink he bought me because I was thirsty, but it did nothing to stop the awful churning in my stomach. I gazed at the rows of lamps. They were like pearls against the trees, and they went on as far as the eye could see. I was fascinated by the sight. But every now and again, a wave of sickness would hit me and the lamps disappeared in a red blur while I shivered.

'I was horrified to find that Michel expected me to walk all the way back again; it must have been nearly three miles. But when I protested, his face set in those bitter lines again and he assured me we had got through the money he had made from the sale of the picture, paying that bitch. He would have to sell another one the next morning. "Old Marcel says it's nudes the market's after just now," he told me. "That was the only one I had. So you'll have to be sensible and take your clothes off. I can't afford another model."

'The next morning he grumbled and cursed as he picked over the piles of canvases and went off with three small ones to Marcel, his dealer. I was glad to hear the door shut behind him. Though exhausted to the point of collapse the night before, I had been unable to sleep because of constant nausea and pain. Michel had snored on, quite oblivious. I had let him too, glad to be left alone.

'"Anything happened?" he asked me as he was leaving.

"I'm losing blood," I said.

'"Good." One word and he slammed the door. I was alone again in that strange city, but this time I felt too worn out to cry. I drank some hot water, nibbled some horribly dry bread, lay down thankfully and got some rest.

'It was nearly two o'clock when I woke. After my previous experience I wasn't too surprised to find Michel still missing. I had no doubt he would be drinking as soon as he had money in his pocket. The attic was unbearably stuffy in spite of the open skylight. I

32

started trying to sweep up but the dust made me sneeze and waves of sickness made bending impossible. I was still losing blood but had no idea what I was looking for or what to expect. Suddenly I *had* to get out of that stinking attic, see something green and shady. As far as I knew, there was only one key and Michel had it. He hadn't locked the door when he went out. Madame would be watching but she would assume I had the key. Anyway, she probably had one of her own. If Michel came back . . . that was the danger. I *had* to get out. I was suddenly desperate.

'Madame's door creaked as I had expected, then I opened the outer door and the heat hit me like an oven. Everything started to swim in front of me. I staggered towards the railings and held on. As the mist cleared, I saw a sharp-faced girl of about my own age staring at me. There was something familiar about her . . . she must remind me of someone back home, I thought. Then I realized. When Michel was picking over his canvases I had seen that sparrow-like look. It was the girl who had modelled for him.

'I watched her trim little figure disappear down the street and wished I could walk away from Michel as easily. Then I pulled myself together and willed myself to walk steadily, though slowly, towards the nearest trees. The trouble was that they seemed to get further and further away. With all the sickness, I suppose I had lost what little food I had eaten. A strong pulse began to beat in my head and unbearable heat washed over me. I reached for the nearest railings. It was the entrance to a church. A few people glanced at me curiously as they came and went. Then an elderly gentleman approached – such a courtly manner. He asked if Madame was having difficulty with the stairs. I replied that Madame was feeling the heat and Madame would soon be recovered. I think he assumed I was pregnant. Anyway, he courteously offered me his arm and assured me the coolness of the church would help me. I was in a fix. I hadn't a sou and didn't know whether I would be expected to put in a collection. I'd had no intention of going into the church. It was an effort to speak at all, let alone work it out in French. It was easier just to let him support me up the few steps and into the blessed coolness. Having placed me in a pew right at the back, the old man made his way down to the front. I watched him put money in a box and then lift a candle. I reckoned that if they paid for candles, it maybe meant there would be no collection and I could relax. It seemed dark there after the glare outside. The church was long and narrow and the footsteps seemed to go on for a long time when anyone came in. I was anonymous and that suited me.

'The place had a peculiar smell, rather musty . . . candlegrease chiefly, incense, wool – that would probably be from the hassocks. There was a feeling of permanence which soothed me. It was years before I saw a Protestant church in Paris and I had walked past it not realizing it *was* a church, only a plain building stuck in the middle of other things. That day, I was just grateful for the peace and the freedom to come and go at any time. Nobody seemed to pay any attention to me but the church was available to anyone.

'I sat for a long time, thinking of nothing. My breathing became slower and steadier. I was having a blessed respite from the sickness. A nun who had been in and out twice looked at me rather sharply, I thought, but no one else paid any attention. It was only the thought that Michel might return that made me get up eventu-

34

ally and face the blinding heat of the pavements.

'The studio was as I had left it. But now I felt a little steadier, I *did* manage to make some impression on the clearing up. Apart from being weak and slow, I felt awkward. What did you do with a heap of dust, high up in a town attic? There was no compost heap in the garden to welcome it. Madame was not the sort of person you would query about these things. I had the impression that La Boucher's main concern in life was raking in the money. Maybe I'm being unfair. She *was* a widow after all. Maybe in that area the rents wouldn't be very high. I suppose a few tenants like Michel would make you take a tougher approach to humanity. I never got to know any of the people who came and went. They were mostly men anyway.

'I knew by the noise he made coming upstairs that Michel was drunk and braced myself. He kicked the door and called for me to open it. I hesitated and he kicked it again. But when he staggered in, his arms full of bottles, he was in quite a good mood. He leaned awkwardly across the table with his burden. I hastily transferred the bottles one by one to a shelf I had cleared. "Come on," he announced. "We're going out to dinner."

'"Aren't you going to change your shirt?" I asked him. He was looking a mess.

'"My shirt is fine. We'll have none of your Mrs Nisbet-Brown stuff – dressing up for all that hogwash they call food in your country," was his answer.

'I wasn't sure if he *had* a clean shirt. That was another thing I was going to have to cope with – washing clothes in a shallow sink with no boiler or anything. I pictured the back kitchen in the cottage at Kilbarchan with its big bubbling boiler; the line from the birch tree

35

in the garden with its array of snowy washing and the larks singing overhead. Suddenly it seemed the most desirable place on earth.

'This time it was not a very long walk. Michel grew impatient when I couldn't keep up with him. "Get a move on. I'm starving," he would say. His voice was too loud after his drinking. And it was still too loud when he led me into a dimly lit café.

'My heart sank when I saw the tables covered in oilcloth with candles stuck in bottles. Then I began to smell the food and I realized how long it was since I had had a meal. I'd never felt as hungry as that in all my life. Though Michel seemed to know the waiter, the man's face never relaxed its grim expression. Michel didn't bother to ask me what I would like, simply ordered. I was just so grateful to have food coming that I didn't resent his high-handedness. There was a basket of crisp rolls on the table. I looked at their lovely golden whorls; I got a sniff of them and my mouth filled with saliva. I didn't know how I was going to wait till the soup arrived. Then Michel stretched out and took one. He just broke bits off as he ate, letting the crumbs drop on the oilcloth. The waiter who was opening our bottle paid not the slightest attention, so I took one too. It was difficult not to choke, I was so hungry.

'I found out later that they don't bother with side plates unless they have butter. Everything was so upside down. I had expected Paris to be such an elegant place – away beyond anything I'd ever seen at home. Well, certainly that applied to the Champs Elysées, but when I looked round the shabby restaurant and remembered how Mam spread a snowy damask cloth for our meals . . . and nobody at home would stick bread on to the cover . . . it was very diffi-cult to balance it all up.

'I was so hungry that any food would have been wonderful but that mushroom soup was . . . oh, Dougie would have said ambrosia. Then there was some veal cordon bleu – I'd never seen veal cooked with cheese before. Anyway, we seldom ate veal at home. Remember, Faither always said it was daft to eat an anaemic calf when you could have one wi' guid red blood in it! I learned later that all the chefs have their own ideas about how that dish should be done, but I've never enjoyed any so much as I did that night. I could feel the colour coming back to my cheeks as I ate. I was blessedly free of the sickness and Michel, though drunk, was not abusing me. He emptied the bottle of wine and was about to order another when he changed his mind, grumbling about what the swines would charge for it. "We've plenty at home," he said. I knew it would be useless to point out he'd already had more than plenty.

'On the way back he started telling me about the pictures he had sold that day. His usual dealer, Marcel, wouldn't touch them, told him to bring some nudes. Then he had gone to old Tournier, got him in a good mood, short of stock, and done quite a good deal. But Tournier, too, had asked him if he didn't have any nudes. "So tomorrow, my lady wife, you take your clothes off or I burn the lot of them. It's time you made yourself useful."

'The next morning I was still losing blood and feeling squeamish again but he had not the slightest sympathy. I had to pose naked for hours on a dais he set up near the skylight while he whistled and grunted at the easel. If I made the slightest move, he snarled at me to keep still. It was so different from the way he had behaved at Mrs Nisbet-Brown's, cajoling and flattering me till I felt like a princess. I thought I had lost the baby but I don't remember feeling guilty. Maybe it was because I was penniless and dependent on that fiend. You see, I was determined to get away. But it seems odd now that I didn't feel vexed or guilty . . .

'But, as it turned out, I just *thought* I had lost the baby. And I thought that for several months because I kept losing blood from time to time. I was feeling awful, spasmodically sick and weak. Michel claimed his conjugal rights regardless. I longed for him to finish the picture so that I could get some rest, but when he did, he went off on a drunken binge for a few days, then came back and started another one. Instead of gaining weight, I lost it for the first four or five months. Then I began to notice a bulge and, one day, I felt the baby kicking. For most women that's one of the happiest moments of their lives. The thrill I felt, however, was nearer to horror. I didn't know what to do. There was guilt then, you can be sure. What if that poison Michel had made me drink had harmed the baby? What if it knew the hatred I had for its father? Knew that I hadn't wanted it?

'My maternal instinct was aroused with a vengeance. The baby was there and I would protect it from the world. I would be ruthless. I remembered that first meal in the shabby restaurant. Michel had been helplessly drunk when he got to bed. He had thrown his trousers carelessly over the chair at the edge of the rug and I thought I heard coins drop from his pocket. In the morning, before he was awake I had a look and there *were* some on the rug half-way under the chair.

It was just possible he knew how much he should have, so I didn't dare pick them up. But I gently moved the chair a little so that they were in shadow. He didn't notice anything but I left the coins there all day just in case. By nighttime nothing had been said so I knew what to do. After that, I waited every night till he was snoring then slipped out and took some money from his pocket – never too much – and put it on the rug under the chair or under the bed.

'Only once did he notice he was short. I had rehearsed well and said quite casually that he had been drunk the night before and it had probably dropped out of his pocket on the way home or maybe he had holes . . . He cursed for a moment or two then got down on the floor. He found the ones under the chair but not the one under the bed. It became quite a game, the only fun I had.

'Hiding the money was quite a problem too. Then I hit on the idea of unpicking trimmings from my hats and resewing them with the more valuable coins inside. I buttoned a little bag into my corsets. Sometimes I kept a few under the rug where it was fixed under the bed. I never had my hoard in one place. I was determined not to be left penniless. Sometimes after he had been painting for hours he would suddenly swear and throw down his brushes and say, "I'm going for a bottle of wine." He would wipe the paint off his hands and stamp out. I soon learned that it took him at least a couple of hours to return so I would dress quickly and nip out. It didn't take me long to find a good baker and a market. I would buy croissants and fruit, then make for the little park where I could sit in the shade and enjoy them. The children would be playing on the swings. At first I couldn't understand their quick chatter, but gradually I would detach a phrase here and there and give myself a pat on the back for progress.

'The morning that first nude painting left the house I was filled with dismay – my face was quite recognizable, you see. I imagined horrible men drooling over it and that was all. You see, Jessie, we never really learned anything about art at home . . . except Dougie, that is. He had such a thirst for knowledge, that boy. He was right, too, that girls should get a good education. I had reason to be grateful for the efforts he made to help us. Where was I . . . ? Oh, yes, that first nude was on show in Marcel's window for quite some time. Michel grumbled that the miserly devil was asking four times what he had given him for it. The last thing I had wanted was to see myself like that in a shop window but gradually I became curious. Just how much *had* Michel got for it? He had never offered me a penny. Certainly we had gone out to dinner a few times, to that same café with the grim waiter, but I had depended on him bringing food home the rest of the time. Usually it was just the most basic stuff: bread, cheese, apples and sometimes paté. He was obviously not used to cooking. But as the colder weather set in, I longed for hot food every night, not just when Michel felt like celebrating.

'The bleeding and sickness stopped when I was about five months and I felt much steadier. It was just then of course I realized I had kept the baby. I was aware of the growing bulge and wondered when Michel would notice. I didn't dare to think of his reaction. But I was determined my baby would have its rights. I would get Michel to face up to his responsibilities somehow or other. Judging by the times he could go out drinking, he still had plenty of money. At last he had stopped pestering me in bed. I was pretty sure that he was indulging himself elsewhere. That would be costing money. Also, I had the feeling that he was eating as well as drinking outside. Sometimes he would hardly touch the bread and cheese he brought home to me. But I would have to be clever, very clever, or the sudden anger would flare up and make him stubborn as a mule.

'"If you gave me some money, Michel, I could get fresh bread in the morning," I said. "I'm always awake before you." He considered it for a moment and then gave me directions as to where to find a baker. It was the same one I had been using on my secret trips! "One step at a time," I thought. So we enjoyed our hot coffee and fresh bread every morning while I planned my next move. If I went to the market I would need a basket to carry things home in, but he would be unlikely to fork out for that. To disarm suspicion I had always given him the change from my trips to the baker but my secret hoard continued to grow slowly. Out of it I bought a crochet hook and some cotton yarn.

'Next day my time in the shelter was spent crocheting a shopping bag. Some of the mothers oohed and aahed at the speed of my work. One of them leaned across. "How I wish I could do that, Madame. There's a little dress in a shop in the Rue Richelieu . . . it's a dream and would suit my Marguerite but oh! it's very expensive . . . the lovely ones always are!" I kept her chatting for a while till I found out where the shop was. I made up my mind to have a look.

'It wasn't difficult to find. The dress *was* beautiful, a fairly firm background with little raised flowers in Irish crochet appliquéd later. I memorized it, then stood swithering. Should I go in to the shop and offer to crochet for them? Perhaps it would be better to show them my finished work. I had done plenty of things for Lilias and knew what I was about. Without a machine, I couldn't do the sort of sewing Mrs Nisbet-Brown had paid me for (to Dougie's disgust), but a crochet hook . . . well . . . I'd never realized before, what magic lay in that simple little piece of bent metal. It was going to be my key to freedom.'

Chapter 4

'The next morning I made up my mind. I would offer to make a dress for Marguerite's mother at a third of the price the shop was charging. If she didn't take up the offer, I would make a sample garment and hawk it.

'I needn't have worried; she jumped at the offer. In fact, she was prepared to give me the money there and then. The French aren't usually so trusting. They referred to me as l'anglaise, of course, and I didn't bother to put them right. I couldn't make any firm arrangements, anyway. My trips to the park depended on Michel being out. Sometimes he got enthusiastic about his work and wouldn't stop for lunch, just nibbled dry bread. I would be stiff and sick and cold before he let me leave the dais. His reaction when he finished was always to get out, with or without me, depending on his mood. He never asked me what I had been doing while he was out. As I always heard him clearly on the wooden stair, I knew it wouldn't be difficult to hide my work before he got in.

'The fresh bread in the morning had been routine for a couple of weeks when I felt bold enough to suggest that if he gave me some money, I could go to the market and get some food for a meal . . . eggs, for example. He made a few insulting remarks about Scottish cooking. I pretended to be amused. In a little while, he relented, slammed some money on the table, saying that it would probably be wasted, and stamped out. I sighed with relief as his footsteps faded on the stairs; then started planning again. I had to have nourishing food for my baby's sake.

'For the next few weeks, things went well. I was no longer hungry half the time. My breasts started to swell and my face lost its terribly drawn look. But, inevitably the bulge got bigger and the day I dreaded came. Michel had warned me to keep dead still and then noticed the convulsive movement across my stomach as the baby kicked me. A few sharp questions gave him the answer he least wanted to hear. He went mad then, cursing and swearing at the top of his voice. Then he said something about a woman, illegal of course, but she'd keep quiet. I realized with horror what he was suggesting.

'I think I went hysterical then; I heard my voice screaming and he was slapping me cruelly, blow upon blow. He lifted me up, threw me on the bed and, oh, Jessie! . . . Even now I can hardly bear to think of it. It's been pushed far to the back of my mind all these years. He forced me then and said that if he couldn't get rid of it one way, he would get rid of it by another. I soon got his meaning. It was a nightmare. I dreaded seeing him sober. The only time I got any peace was when he was dead drunk.

'Then one night he didn't come home at all. All I felt was relief. If he had found someone who would put up with him, I would get some peace. The shop in rue de Richelieu was giving me commissions now. With Michel out of the way, I could lie down whenever my back ached without him leaping on me. When it was snowing, I sat by the pot-bellied stove and crocheted furiously.

'He'd been gone three days when the bleeding started again. I felt scared suddenly, on my own. I *had* to get out. Of course I'd had no money from Michel those three days, either directly or indirectly. My own earnings were dedicated religiously to the baby and our escape from Michel. I would be starving before I touched them. It was *his* responsibility to feed me, I told myself: I had married him in good faith. I knew that I was probably going wrong in the head with my obsession about the baby but I couldn't help it.

'I threw on all the warm clothes I could muster – and that wasn't many – and made for the market place. I'd had nothing to eat but dry bread that morning and the cold was making me catch my breath. All the women there were shrouded to the eyebrows. It was difficult to recognize them. I *did* see the little model. She looked lively and fetching in her fur hood and red wool cape. She was looking at me, not just a quick glance, but staring. Then she came towards me. I hadn't realized till then that I was leaning against the wall of a booth. I straightened up but everything started spinning round about me. She ran the last few steps and gripped me.

'"Are you ill, Mademoiselle?" she asked anxiously.

'"A little sick and giddy," I murmured.

'"You are pregnant, Mademoiselle?"

'I nodded.

'"What is your name?"

'"Madame Blanchard."

'She gasped and stared at me wide-eyed. "Michel *married* you?" she whispered, amazed. "And he is letting you have a baby?"

'I was feeling so miserable, and nearly at the end of my tether or I don't suppose I would have told her,

45

but it all came tumbling out . . . the tales he had told me . . . the long journey . . . the fishing village . . . the studio boarded up . . . the landlady . . .

'"She's a terror, that one," she agreed, "but with a devil like Michel to deal with, can you blame her?" She gave that shrug that is so French. "I am surprised he married you," she said. "He promised me but just kept putting it off. I thought when I was unlucky and became pregnant he would change, but no! He was off to that criminal of a chemist and made me drink that foul stuff . . ."

'"He gave me it too," I told her.

'"And you have not lost the baby?" There was something more than surprise in her look, and I felt a sudden unease.

'"I lost the baby and will never have another, the bastard," she said bitterly, then drew herself together. "Your baby is probably very strong and will survive."

'I shivered with the fear that was nagging at me constantly. Would my baby be damaged?

'"Is he at the studio now?" she asked.

'I told her I hadn't seen him for three days . . . he hadn't given me any money . . . I could die in this strange land for all he cared. I was beginning to get hysterical.

'"I'll help you get home," she said.

'As soon as I started walking, a pain shot through me. Then everything was going black round me. Then I saw the nun, that one I had seen in church; the model, Lou, was calling her "Sister" and, before I could stop her, Lou started telling her the whole horrifying story, including the muck Michel made me drink. Pain was carving me in two by then. The nun muttered something about a long way but Lariboisière would be

46

best . . . then she got busy, calling to a stallholder to
fetch a chair . . . telling somebody to put a blanket
round me and warning Lou to stay with Madame. A
group gathered round me. They were all speaking too
fast, or maybe my brain wasn't working in the pain. I
was being jolted in the middle of a contraction; there
was the smell of horse, the noise of traffic. I was being
undressed, washed. There was a horrible smell of
strong soap . . . I was being urged to lie back and then
I split in two and there was a moment of blessed relief.
Then a voice said, "Il est mort, le pauvre." "Non, non,
non," said another. "We must try."

'After what seemed ages, I heard a faint wailing
sound like a kitten mewing; a nurse was bending over
me and asking, "What is the baby's name?" I said,
"Alain". In a few minutes a priest was there. They
were rattling away in Latin and French while I kept
slipping in and out of consciousness.

'Once when I had been awake long enough to take
a drink of bouillon, they put the baby to my breast but
I had nothing to give him. I wept, of course. The kind
nursing sister said to me, "Do not despair, Madame,
we will keep trying. It will come. Pray to the kind
Mother of Our Lord . . . but no, you are not a Catholic?
Then we will say the Our Father together."' They are
so unselfconscious about praying out loud, Jessie. I
found it quite embarrassing. And yet I was praying for
my poor wee bairn all the time . . . but inside.

'The first few hours they had somebody watching
the baby all the time, stroking his back sometimes and
dropping a few drops of some concoction into his wee
dry mouth. He looked like a tiny, tiny version of an
old man, not like a baby at all. Every time I looked at
him, my heart filled with dread. And I saw my dread

47

reflected in the eyes of the young model, Lou, when she turned up on her way to the theatre where she worked. I hadn't expected to see her again after I was carted off to hospital, but seemingly she hadn't wasted her time. She knew which bar – Faither would have said "howff" – Michel favoured and made straight for it. Her description was so funny that even the nursing sister gave a quiet little laugh. Seemingly Michel was half-seas over and she had to tell him several times that he had a son before he took the news in. The other men in the bar were all laughing at Michel and the landlord said there would be free drinks all round to celebrate. Lou pointed out that his poor wife hadn't much to celebrate: he'd left her without a sou and now she, a beautiful English lady, was among strangers in Lariboisière, and with no money to contribute to the good nuns . . . By this time she had her bonnet off and was going round the tables. The landlord didn't get off without the sharp edge of her tongue . . . she reckoned he'd had more of Michel's earnings than the poor wife and baby would ever see . . . etc . . . etc . . . In a short time she'd managed to coax a considerable sum out of that bunch and made them promise to sober Michel up and see that he found his way to the Lariboisière.

'She dashed off then to her work and I was left to await Michel's arrival. It's funny when I think of it: I had been adamant all along that it was his duty to support this baby, now I didn't want him anywhere near the poor wee mite. Alain was mine . . . mine . . . mine . . . and all I wanted was the milk to feed him with . . . and if the kind Mother of Our Lord could do it quicker, I'd become a Catholic there and then. You're shocked, Jessie. I *did* stop to wonder what the family in Kilbarchan would think of that one, but I was quite sure that my sisters would do anything for their babies. The difference was that none of you would be stupid enough to run away with a lying bastard of a French artist.

'I was staggering under a load of guilt and I'm still not free of it to this day. I'll bet none of my sisters has that to face up to. I felt that if Alain died it would be to pay me for my sins. Michel hadn't wanted him, hadn't wanted me except for my body; had treated me the way he had treated Lou and possibly many others. I wasn't looking forward to his visit, sober or no!

'When he *did* arrive, his face pink with scrubbing, he looked a mess. The nurse who had been at my bedside slipped quietly away. He rocked on his heels just staring at me. I was relieved to find there was to be no Judas kiss. Then he leaned over Alain's little basket. I don't know what I expected, Jessie. I knew how tiny and wrinkled he was; anyone would have felt pity – anyone normal that is. Michel straightened up, then staggered about laughing, "My God, there's been a monkey in your bed before I ever got near you," he gasped. He didn't notice the nun who had approached quietly till she tapped him on the shoulder. Her voice was low but incisive: when Monsieur's visit ended, he was to come to the end of the corridor. The priest wished to speak to him.

'Michel gaped after her retreating figure then he sobered up instantly. He came close to me and hissed, "Did you tell them about the chemist?" I shook my head. I *hadn't* of course, but Lou had. "You did, you bitch, I can tell," he snarled at me. "If that miserable brat dies they'll have the law on me and if *they* don't, the chemist has his own methods . . . you stupid, stupid bitch!" He was glancing round in desperation. A door at the opposite end of the ward had been left open when a nurse went out with a pile of laundry. He made a sudden dash for it. I was crying by this time, of course, and when the nun came back looking for Michel, I wasn't in a fit state to tell her much. That was the last I was to see of my precious husband, though I didn't know that at the time.

'I had more important things to think about and in spite of the upset Michel had caused, was delighted to find my breasts prickling. Poor little Alain was too weak to fasten on, but they sent for the sister who was supposed to be the expert. She put me in mind of Rab Shaw, up at the farm in Kilbarchan, remember? – the same big brawny arms with enormous freckles. You couldn't imagine a less likely nurse for a tiny infant. But she held Alain in one huge freckled hand while she grabbed me anything but gently and forced the drops which gathered into his wee mouth. That performance was repeated umpteen times in the next two days before he managed to suck at all. After that, I was able to lift him every time he gave a little cry. He had so little strength! It was pathetic to watch but I willed him to feed, to survive.

'These nurses were angels, the way they encouraged me. They worked long, long hours and were sometimes drawn and exhausted but they always managed a gentle word. I envied them their composure, their assurance. In fact, I was very reluctant to leave when they judged me fit. There had been no sign of Michel, of course; nor any sign of Lou, whom I looked on as my rescuer. I guessed she would have no wish to renew her acquaintance with Michel.

'The fare back to the studio ate into the precious sum she had raised for me in that bar. I prayed that Michel had not uncovered any of my clever hoards during my absence. However there was no sign of him when I got back. The studio was as I had left it, only the stove was out and dust had gathered on all the surfaces. The picture, *Summer*, was dry. I was surprised Michel hadn't collected it after all his ranting and raving about how much it was worth. I tucked Alain up as warmly as I could while I got on with raking and lighting the stove. That's why I didn't hear footsteps on the stairs and jumped when there was a loud knock on the door. There was nothing for it; he was probably drunk but I would have to let him in or he would start kicking.

'Madame Boucher stood there; not a smile, not a word of welcome; one quick glance over to the bundle on the bed and she launched into her speech. Did I know that the rent was overdue; that a widow had to live and those who couldn't pay would have to make way for those who could. She hoped I knew where my good-for-nothing husband was because he hadn't been near. In her opinion he was the sort who would do a bunk. Perhaps Madame had money of her own?

'I answered in my best Mrs Nisbet-Brown manner that Madame *had* money of her own and would certainly come down to pay the landlady as soon as *that* person did her the courtesy of allowing her to warm the studio for her helpless infant. She retreated in disorder with all her braid quivering. I felt that I had given her no more than she deserved but actually she got a bit more than she deserved, though I'll come to that later.

'I had no idea how much the rent would be. And I had no notion of the fuel bills, either. The weather was bitterly cold and Alain would have to be kept warm night and day. Pride made me hide these worries as I knocked on Madame Boucher's door and demanded to know the reckoning. My knees turned to jelly when she named the figure. It was nearly three times my worst imaginings! I was pretty sure she was taking advantage of me but there was nothing I could do about it. I kept my face calm and haughty and demanded a receipt. When I got back upstairs I sat down and tried to work things out. All the money I had left was sewn into my hats. If Michel didn't come back . . . how long would it last? I had crocheted several little blankets for Alain; he was so tiny that most of them were folded several times, so that wasn't too bad. But I had brought no winter clothes. If I made myself a large shawl, I could tuck him inside when I went to market and keep myself warm at the same time. How I longed for one of the lovely cashmere shawls that Dougie designed!

'I knew that I had to feed myself to keep the milk going for Alain, but it would have to be the cheapest food possible. With the constant interruptions for feeding him, I would not be able to turn out so many garments for the shop in rue de Richelieu. Also, I would be at a disadvantage. I couldn't explain it, really, but I felt they liked dealing with a superior English lady and I would no longer fit the image with a baby in my arms. I gave myself a shake; decided that time was too precious to waste; short trips to market and to buy wool were priorities. When the weather got milder, Alain would be able to spend more time in the open air; his little yellow wrinkled cheeks would fill out, see if they didn't!

'Well, I gritted my teeth and got on with it for a month or so. The wool for the shawl had run away with money I could ill afford; the weather stayed bitterly cold and the stove gobbled up fuel. I was living on soup and bread. Alain had stopped crying and seemed to sleep quite a lot. Normally that would be a good sign but he was still a weak feeder and that worried me. There was no money coming in towards the rent and I had no idea where Michel was. Though I had managed to amass quite a pile of little garments for the shop, I still felt reluctant to visit them with Alain in my arms.

'It was all running through my head as I walked through the market one morning. That's why I didn't see Lou till she was right beside me and peering into the bundle to see Alain. "He's coming on, Elise," she said – she always got my name wrong – "but you don't look too well, yourself."

'I assured her I was all right but she wasn't convinced. "You haven't seen Michel?" she asked. I shook my head. "No, I thought not," she said. "Come along, I'll buy you a hot drink and we can talk." She led me to a small dark café frequented by porters and the like. It wasn't the sort of place I would ever have thought of entering but she made her way to a cosy corner where we were out of the draughts. One flick of her wrist and the young waiter forgot his other clients. "Hot onion soup for Madame," she said. "Hot chocolate and croissants for me."

'The soup was still bubbling from the pot. I warmed my hands on the side of the thick bowl before I took my first spoonful. Lou had taken Alain on her knee, saying that she could manage perfectly well with one hand. It was a while before I realized what she was doing. She'd moved her cup aside, put some sugar on the saucer and spooned some hot chocolate over it. Now she was dipping her little finger in the saucer and offering it to Alain. I stopped to watch . . . yes, his little lips were moving . . . again, and he responded; a third time and there was a distinct smacking sound as he

53

fastened on. She laughed delightedly, "See, he likes it."

' "I'm not sure if it's good for him," I began.

'She laughed again. "Nonsense! That was always a treat for the babies in our house," she said. "There were twelve of them when I ran away to Paris. I wonder how many Maman has now, stupid bitch."

'I gazed at her, aghast. And then I began to think. Here was I, shocked at Lou, and she had only done what I had done. It was a sobering thought. And it's never left me, Jessie. You see why I must do penance at Mam's grave?'

I squeezed Elsie's hand for a little while and then infused some more tea. Elsie's thoughts were far away. When she had handed me her cup she lay back on the pillow. I waited quietly till she started again.

'Lou noticed when I had finished my soup and, without consulting me, summoned the waiter again and ordered chocolate for Madame. It was delicious. I felt a lovely warmth steal over me – not just the food and drink but the feeling that this rough diamond of a wee lass cared. Apart from the nuns – and they were angels to me – I hadn't had a kind word since I arrived in Paris. Pride and determination had kept me going – and the knowledge that I had only myself to blame for the fix I was in. But all of a sudden it all welled up in me . . . what I was missing . . . home and a loving family . . . all the things I had thrown away for a foolish dream. I felt the tears begin to flow.

' "Here, here, here, no tears, Elise, please," said Lou. "He will be a big strong boy; you will see. I was the eldest in our family. I know all about babies; they are tough little savages, believe me!" It was so ridiculous, when I thought of how we had all cosseted our baby sister, remember? But it cheered Lou up to see

54

me laugh and I felt I owed her something so I pulled myself together.

' "Good! Now I wish to speak seriously," she said. "You say you have not seen Michel?" I nodded. "Does that mean he has not collected his last picture? It is still in the studio?" Again I nodded. "Well, that will bring you in a tidy sum." I assured her it would be needed with the rent so high. She asked me what Madame had charged and whistled when I told her.

' "She is a robber, that one," she said. "A cruel bandit. Michel would never pay her that much, I assure you. But we will play her at her own game. I have a little plan, Elise, for you and the little one. First, there is something I have not told you. About three weeks after Alain was born I was passing the shop of Marcel – the art dealer, you know. He ran after me and asked if I knew anything of Michel. Seemingly that bold fellow had gone to Marcel after he visited you in Lariboisière, told him he needed money urgently for you and the baby and borrowed on the strength of his masterpiece which wasn't yet dry. Marcel, the mean devil, had made a tidy profit on *Spring*, though he didn't put it to me that way, of course. So, against his better judgement, he gave your dear Michel an advance on the sale of *Summer*. I took it on myself to pay a visit to that bar I told you about, and flirted with one of the regular customers. He said that Michel had gone there after he saw you in Lariboisière. This will hurt, Elise. He told them all that you had given birth to a monkey; he was going to drown his sorrows; he was fed up with Paris and was going to make for the Dordogne. I gather he was pretty drunk when he left them and he hasn't been back.

' "Now, here is my plan, Elise. I have just moved to

a much better flat . . . it is far from here – the other side of the Seine – near St Lazare."

'"Are you a leading actress, then, Lou?" I asked.

'She started laughing then. "Ah, you are so deliciously innocent, my dear Elise. It is not the money we get from the theatre . . . That is . . . pouff!" She laughed again. "Ah, it is difficult for you to understand, I see. I am shocking you. But, anyway the flat has two big rooms and a little kitchen and bathroom. Monsieur Henri only comes late in the evenings, you understand. I will take him straight to the bedrooom. The flat is warm. It will be good for little Alain. Perhaps you will teach English . . ."

'I interrupted her then to tell her about the shop in rue de Richelieu, and my stock of crochet things and also a little silk dress I've been sewing, and how I didn't wish to go there with Alain in my arms.

'"That is easy,' she said. "I shall look after Alain. See, you will make plenty of money from the picture and your handwork. Then you can save for a flat of your own, if you wish. Now, our plan! Madame goes out every Sunday afternoon on the dot of three with another old sourpuss. You will be seen making for the park with Alain in your arms just before she leaves. I know a fellow with a handcart; he's big and willing. He'll wait round the corner till I give him the signal. You will have packed all the things you wish to bring in bundles. I'll see to the pictures myself. Jean-Jo and I will do it in fifteen minutes. He'll push the cart to my flat – it's a long way. I shall meet you in the little park and we shall travel like ladies in a cab. Non?"

'"But the rent" . . . I began.

'"Rent! Rent! after the way she robbed you, that bitch! Not a filthy sou will she have."''

Chapter 5

'Really, Jessie, it was dreadful of me when I think of it, but it was funny too. Lou was such a little rascal and she egged me on. I was shaking as I wandered round the park that day with Alain in my arms – it was far too cold to sit. When I saw Lou hurrying towards me with a wide grin on her face, I felt such a rush of love for her. She had ordered a cabman to come round to a side gate on the principle that the fewer people saw us the better.

'I was half laughing and half crying as we jolted along – not sure whether I was engaged in a criminal act or a childish escapade. Lou kept exploding into laughter as she thought of Madame Big Bosom's reaction when she found the birds flown. I found it so difficult to equate her kindness to me with her complete lack of concern for other people – even her own mother.

'I soon found out that she was a domestic disaster but because she had taken such a shine to me, she was willing to copy everything I did. The flat that "Henri" was subsidizing for her was in a quiet residential district. Lou assured me that more than half of the surrounding ones were occupied by what we would have called "kept women". She didn't mind people knowing her non-marital status in the least, but she had ambition – not to marry one of these men, but to be considered a high-class mistress. "Perhaps I could teach you English," I said to her that first night when we were sitting on the elaborate couch which dominated her salon. She didn't answer immediately. I thought she was wondering how to refuse me without hurting my feelings. "It was only an idea," I added, looking at her flushed face.

'"Elise . . . Elise . . ." she was stammering, "you would teach me to speak English . . . is it not very difficult? . . . could I be a lady like you?"

'That took the breath from me. To think that I had been down and out and this little street waif had saved me. If she hadn't got me to hospital, Alain would never have been born alive. She was willing to share this flat which was meant to be a lovenest with a stranger and a baby. And now she sat there, flushed and wide-eyed, looking at me with something like adoration. I've never forgotten that moment, and I never will. Nothing I can do will ever repay the gift she gave me then. The courage and self-respect I needed to get through the next five years were built on that.

'At first, of course, it was simply a case of keeping Alain alive. I had to feed him so often because he would get tired within a few minutes of starting. Miraculously his crying stopped almost completely as soon as we moved to Lou's place. Perhaps I was less tired and he felt secure. Lou was delighted to leave the cooking and other chores to me. She would hardly take anything for my food – assuring me that she was getting a wonderful bargain – English lessons and a housekeeper who was a great lady! Of course Henri was paying the rent and keeping her supplied with expensive gew-gaws into the bargain.

'The shop in the rue de Richelieu was pleased to renew my acquaintance. I explained that I had been away. My manner to them had always been a Mrs Nisbet-Brown one so they did not ask questions. One little dress design had been a great favourite and they wanted more. The silk dress – a new departure – drew a lot of "oohs" and "aahs". It was made of chrysanthemum bronze silk Michel had bought for a backcloth and I still had plenty. I managed to extract a tidy sum for it and resolved to buy a sewing machine as soon as possible.

'We had been in the flat only about three weeks when Lou came home from rehearsal in great excitement. "Can you work a sewing machine?" she gasped.

' "Yes, of course," I said.

' "Thank God! I assured them you could and prayed to the Mother of Our Lord that I was right. Listen! There's a rush on in the wardrobe room. That pig of a Bernard is complaining about everything and has changed his mind about our costumes for the new play which opens in three weeks. The wardrobe mistress says she will need extra help. They are bringing in another sewing machine. They want somebody good. I told them you were marvellous, a superior English lady and, if the pay was right, I'd bring you tomorrow."

' "But what about Alain?" I asked.

' "He will come along in his little basket. The wardrobe room is kept quite clean. You can stop and feed him any time. I said your husband had died and the baby had been born prematurely so you fed it often." I was stunned, Jessie. I couldn't say a word. Lou lied so glibly and yet she meant so well. And when I examined my conscience . . . well . . . I had never gone the length of wishing Michel dead, but I was hoping that I would never see him again. She was really only extending my thought in her own kind of way.

'The pay they were offering for this emergency work was good; I would have access to a sewing machine; I would learn the French terms for all the sewing processes. And I might learn some short cuts which would be useful.

'In the event, I didn't just learn short cuts. I learned about a world I couldn't have believed existed. The theatre, which I had imagined to be so glamorous – I had watched the elegantly dressed patrons drive there on our rare evenings out – was anything but glamorous behind the scenes. The wardrobe room which Lou thought was clean would certainly not have passed Jean's inspection. In addition, the walls, or what you could see of them behind the clutter, were dingy and had some damp patches near the windows. I stared at one which was the shape of the map of Africa and reminded myself that I was there to earn money for Alain. He lay quite contentedly in his little basket. The young actresses flitting in and out made complimentary remarks about his pillows and covers. I knew better than to expect anyone to say he was a beautiful boy. I searched their faces for traces of the amusement with which Michel reacted, but found none. Of course, as time went on I realized that most of these girls were self-obsessed; it was easy for them to turn on a glib charm when it suited them, but none of them would put herself out for a moment. Except Lou! And she was behaving completely out of character in her care for Alain and me.

'The wardrobe mistress was relieved that I could speak French. Lou's description of a superior English lady had not included this rather important item. Though I had reckoned myself pretty fluent by then, I did find my first few days working under Mathilde pretty difficult. She had rather a guttural voice and, of course, so many of the terms were new to me. I'd had the sense to keep paper and pencil handy to note them down. It would have been easy to get confused when so many were being thrown at me at once. It was anything but peaceful in the room. Her noisy arguments with the actresses were startling to say the least. I could have been terrified, especially if Alain had been upset, but he seemed to sleep quite calmly through it all. She never shouted at me. Though it must have puzzled her that a superior English lady should have to demean herself by working in these squalid surroundings, I did seem to retain some sort of elevated status.

'So many of the dresses for the dancers were frothy in character. The offcuts from the filmy fabrics were just thrown into a big waste basket. Short lengths of trimmings were discarded too because it was quicker to machine long lengths freehand than to try piecing them. Hats were trimmed with made-up flowers and rosettes because Mathilde had no time to do the fiddly work herself. I noted all this waste. After the life of penury I had been leading, it seemed wicked. I enquired casually about what happened to the basket and found that, as I thought, it was simply emptied and the stuff thrown away. So, I would watch for the times when Mathilde grabbed a finished dress and made for a dressing-room. Then I would sneak out the choicest bits and slip them under Alain's mattress. My desperate poverty had made me like a squirrel. I wasn't quite sure how I was going to use all these up, but I couldn't bear to see them go.

'By the time my stint at the theatre had ended, I'd filled several large boxes with a tremendous variety of pieces. Sometimes at night I took them out to finger them – just for sheer pleasure.

'Then I thought of a use for some of these scraps. Easter was approaching. I had seven weeks. If I spent some of my earnings on children's cheap straw hats, I could remove the tawdry trimmings and replace them with more tasteful ones.

'Lou laughed like mad when I staggered in with a bundle of hat boxes which I had persuaded the friendly shopgirl to let me have with my purchases. She was fascinated when I started to experiment with making little flowers. I explained that we had always had a goffering iron at home for our frilled blouses. She thought our "bonne" did our blouses. I didn't disillusion her. I can see you disapprove, Jessie. That's understandable: but *there* it didn't seem wrong. Lou was happy to see me as a fine English lady; the prices I got at the rue de Richelieu also partly depended on that; and Alain depended on my ability to make money, simply to keep him alive. In a funny way, keeping up the illusion helped me too. Lou asked me several times in the next few days what the name of that fancy iron was. Of course I had learned it from Mathilde so had no doubt about it and couldn't understand Lou's persistence. I got the answer when she came home from a morning call at the theatre proudly bearing a heavy box tied with ribbon. She presented it to me with one of these lovely curtseys that only a trained dancer can do.

'"I had to ask Mathilde where I could get one," she said, "and I had to be sure I got the word right. Mathilde was puzzled. I told her I remembered my mother using one on my frills when I was a child and it looked easy. She didn't believe me but she couldn't very well call me a liar either. While she was looking out the address of the shop, I pinched a bit of ribbon for the bow."

' "Lou, you shouldn't have," I said, not quite sure what I meant.

' "She'll soon cut off another length," Lou said. "She has enough to bandage a few mummies on that shelf."

'I started to laugh and Lou beamed at me with satisfaction. She wouldn't dream of taking any money for the iron, telling me that I ironed her clothes so beautifully, I deserved the best.

'The performance at the theatre seemed to be going pretty smoothly and Lou was spared rehearsals. This allowed me to make quick forays to the shops while she wandered around in her robe, half asleep in the morning. Then, as soon as she had made her toilette she would slip out while I was busy with Alain. I couldn't understand this. It didn't seem in character for her to disappear without a word or seeking my approval for her outfit as she had been in the habit of doing.

'She was off on one of these mysterious trips one morning when a delivery boy handed in a heavy parcel. Gifts from Henri had occasionally arrived in elegant boxes from the more famous dress shops, but usually he brought his love tokens personally and Lou would proudly show me her latest bracelet or fine gloves in the morning. This was far too heavy to be a silk négligé or anything like that. My curiosity mounted as I waited, knowing that she would open it in front of me. When she *did* get in, she was looking very pleased with herself. I remember it crossed my mind that Henri might have a rival.

' "Ah! Good old Henri. He asked me if I would like some earrings. I said I would prefer . . . just you wait . . . you will see . . ." She was tearing at the wrappings like a dog worrying a rat. "*Voilà*," she said. And

63

there was a shining out-of-this-world sewing machine! It could quilt and Dear knows what – quite put Mrs Nisbet-Brown's in the shade. "It is for you, my dear Elise. You will be able to make things more quickly and make more money."

'"But Henri meant it for you . . . you can't," I began.

'"Pouff! I told Henri that my maid can do magic with a sewing machine. He thinks you will be doing things for me . . . oh, Elise, please do not be offended that I call you my maid. To Henri . . ."'

'"I'm glad you did," I said. "It's safer for me not to be recognized." Her face cleared instantly.

'On one of my morning forays I had seen some beautiful brown velvet, greatly reduced in price. I expect they would be needing space for their new summer stock. I thought it over then decided to take the plunge and the next morning I bought quite a lot of it. That chrysanthemum silk dress had caused quite a stir in the rue de Richelieu. I had been curious to find out how much they would charge for it but didn't want to be seen noseying. Lou took it upon herself, however, and found they were asking nearly three times what they had paid me for it and I thought *that* was a good price. When Lou went back a couple of days later it had gone. Obviously it was someone very rich who had got it. I went off into a little dream. I could see that dress with a brown velvet cloak and a ruched muff – both lined in chrysanthemum silk; a straw bonnet with a brown velvet band and little gold flowers trailing on to the brim.

'So, the evening I got the velvet, I worked out a shape for the cloak – a little longer than the dress – with a stand-up ruched collar which would be held together by tortoiseshell clasps.

'The lovely fabric was a delight to work with and I had quite a lot of it done by the end of the first evening. It was the next day that Henri's sewing machine arrived. (We always called it that.) I was able to use it for the ruching on the muff and the collar. After only three days and nights I had the whole outfit complete. Lou waved me off with admonitions about screwing the last sou out of the rich . . . well, she used a word that I certainly won't be repeating before my little sister!

'I walked in full of calm confidence, demanded a high figure and got it. Lou, of course, went scouting afterwards but was disappointed to find it was not on display. Even she had been impressed by the sum I had managed to raise. Of course, Lou's idea was that I would be saving for a flat of my own. Perhaps she had a notion that I would become a great courtesan, the height of her ambition. My secret plan was far different. I would make as much money as I could and when Alain was strong enough I would take him home. Mam would surely forgive me when she saw my wee bairn and heard my story . . .

'You see, when things were at their worst, Jessie, I didn't have a ha'penny to pay for writing paper or postage. When I began to make a little money, Alain was too weak to think of travelling but I kept telling myself he was bound to get stronger . . . I made myself believe that . . . I had to . . . In Lou's flat he was warm and safe. My earnings would improve once I had that goffering iron and a sewing machine. Eagerly I started on those little Easter bonnets.

'I decided to treat myself to a new bonnet at the same time. Lou was charmed by my confection. So was the cabman who drove me to the rue de Richelieu and then offered to carry the pile of boxes in for me. Every one of those boxes had five little hats in it and no two alike! At first the buyer looked doubtful. "It seems a great number," she muttered. Then, when she examined some, her face lit up. "I shall put an advertisement in the newspaper," she said. "I am sure that word will go round. They are so charming."

'I looked round her shop. "The velvet cloak and muff are sold, Madame?"

'"Oh yes, Madame, I did not put them on display. I telephoned Madame Wallach who bought the little silk dress. They had five sons, you see, before the little daughter was born. The good doctor just dotes on his little Marianne. When you brought the cloak I telephoned Madame. She came the following morning and bought it without hesitation. They are having the child's portrait painted before her teeth start falling out. She is five . . . almost six . . . such a charmer. Her hair is silky golden brown and her eyes are dark. I expect the hair will darken as she gets older . . ."

'She rambled on and I half-listened, smiling politely. Then I heard her say, "Of course the doctor is so good with children. He specializes in children's diseases. His reputation is . . ." She lifted her hands to show me how high. "Rich people come from far and near to have their children cured."

'"Does he live on Avenue . . . ?" I can't remember which one I named. It was only to get her reply, you see. "No, no, Madame. It is one of the big houses as you approach the Tuileries. On the right side from here. He is from Germany, I believe, but has lived in Paris many years now."

'I walked slowly back though I knew Lou would be dying to know if I had sold all the hats. Another idea was forming. When I had enough money I would take Alain to the good doctor. He would know how to make a poor premature little baby strong. Alain would be a fine sturdy boy when I returned to Kilbarchan. My mind made up, I hurried back to Lou.

'Her reaction was to burst into sobs. At first I had no idea what was wrong. I just cradled her in my arms and stroked her hair. Then I began to make out the words . . . she would be desolated if her dear friend Elise went away and the poor little Alain who smiled at her every time she went near his cradle and liked a share of her hot chocolate. Then suddenly she sat up, sniffed, and the tears stopped as abruptly as they had begun. "Of course you must see the famous doctor," she said, "as soon as possible. Then when he makes Alain strong, you may not wish to leave Paris and your poor little Lou." I hugged her impulsively but hastened to assure her that it would be a long time before I had enough money to visit the famous doctor who might order some expensive treatment.

'She sat quietly then. I wasn't sure what she was thinking so I just waited. "Elise," she said, "you have more money than you know. I was waiting till you were ready to take the first step . . ." She stopped. Her hands were twisting a brooch – Henri's latest gift – so fiercely that I could see the fabric of her bodice about to tear. "What on earth do you mean, Lou? Is something wrong?" A thought occurred to me. "You haven't been stealing . . . or anything like that?"

'"No, no, no," she said, "but I have a plan, a good plan, but first, we get Alain strong, then I will make you ready."

'"Ready for what?" I asked.

'"How shall I begin . . . ?" she hesitated. I tried to

be patient. This was not like Lou at all. "Yes", I said encouragingly.

'"Elise," she said, "remember when you left that awful place there were lots of pictures . . ."

"Yes," I said, "but Michel said something about them not being in fashion . . . they were memories of a wonderful year."

"Yes, a wonderful year! He was lucky to escape from the Dordogne with his life. He boasted to me once when he was drunk that at least three fathers had been after him with shotguns for getting their daughters pregnant. At the time, I just laughed, Elise, thinking he had been young and wild but I was his real love, his little Lou whom he would adore for ever."

'She mimicked Michel at his most persuasive. It was bitterly accurate.

'"But what has that to do with the picture, with me, with Alain and the doctor?" I asked.

'"Elise, it is confusing, yes? Listen! I told you that the dealer, Marcel, stopped me that day and wanted to know what had become of the picture *Summer*: he had given Michel good money on the strength of it. Well, a few weeks later he stopped me again. This time he was really anxious, I can tell you. Seemingly the Dutch dealer who bought *Spring* was calling on him every time he was in Paris, desperate to get his hands on the follow up . . ."

'My heart seemed to stop for a moment. I can still remember the relief, the blessed relief I felt when I realized that the nude picture had gone to Holland . . . there would be no danger that people would recognize me in the street . . . nudge each other . . .

'Lou seemed to be unsure what to say next to me about it . . . she kept starting and stopping. I couldn't understand her difficulty. In the end I got exasperated and said, "Look, Lou, I've got the bit about Marcel having given Michel an advance on *Summer*, the Dutch dealer who bought *Spring* would like to have *Summer* too. What else is there?"

'She gulped, "Quite a lot, Elise. I will try to tell you in order. There was another dealer, Tournier, who used to take Michel's work. I think Michel fell out with him and switched to Marcel. Well, I worked it out that this Dutch man probably looks at all the galleries when he is here. He may have asked Tournier if he ever had any of Michel's work. So, these mornings when you have been busy with Alain, I have been taking the odd little picture round to Tournier. The first one was one I modelled, and I made out that Michel had given me them instead of money. So far he has bought three at quite a good price. He may be doing what I am trying to do – tempt that Dutch dealer. So, Elise, already you have money! But if my plan comes off, you will be rich, rich, rich!"

'"What do you mean?"

'"Well, Elise, when I have sold a few more and the Dutch dealer knows that Tournier sometimes has Michel's work, you will play your part!"

'"And what exactly is that?" I asked.

'"You must learn to tell lies calmly. I shall teach you. And when you have learned your part, I shall borrow a blonde wig and make you up till you would not recognize yourself. You will drive to Tournier's in a cab. Jean-Jo – the fellow with the hand cart, remember? – will be a servant, in a uniform I shall borrow from wardrobe, carrying the picture for the English lady who has come back to clear up some business. If he hesitates over the price you will tell him that friends in London have given you a list of dealers and if you can't get the price you want in Paris, you will take the picture off to London with you."

' "But, Lou," I said. "What if Michel comes back and finds his picture sold?"

' "But he can't, Elise. Oh, Mother of God forgive me, I should have told you that first, perhaps." She crossed herself. "He is dead. You are truly a widow."

'I was numb. I just sat staring at her.

' "Elise. Elise, I am stupid," she gabbled. "I had been telling people he was dead and I think I believed it before I knew . . ." She was twisting her brooch again.

"Tell me, Lou," I said.

' "The second time Marcel spoke to me I said that I heard you had gone back to England with the baby. But I didn't say Michel was dead. No, it was to the theatre I said he was dead, when you were sewing, remember? Then I went back again to visit that bar. I thought it was better to know as much as possible about the devil's movements. Oh!" She crossed herself hastily. "The one I flirted with that time knew a lot more; he said that two days after Michel had told them all he was going off to the Dordogne, the body of a man with paint-stained clothes had been found behind a wall not far from the bar. He had obviously been drinking and the authorities made enquiries. One of the regulars was brave enough to view the corpse and identified it as Michel. This fellow told me the police wanted to speak to his widow. I told him that I'd heard you'd gone back to England as soon as you were fit to travel. They'll have given up, Elise, do not worry. It would not interest them very much."

'I found the tears welling up in my eyes. Lou put her arms round me. "Do not weep for him, Elise. He

70

was not worthy of a lady like you." But I couldn't help weeping when I thought of the sordid ending to the beautiful life we'd planned. Alain stirred then and I lifted him. While he was feeding Lou told me what I must say to Tournier. "But just a minute, Lou," I said. "Michel borrowed from Marcel on the strength of that picture. I can't just sell it to Tournier."

'"Elise, Elise, you are too good for this world. Marcel cheated Michel. Michel cheated you. Tournier has probably cheated the Dutch dealer and will cheat you too, given the chance. They are all cheating buggers and we will be the same."

'I laughed so much that Alain came off and the milk was spraying all over him. He put up his wee fists to rub his eyes. It looked so comical that Lou started hooting too. After Alain had settled down again, she started to give me her idea of the script. I was not to speak French too well; to sound a little more English – that would disarm him; I was to tell him I had come back to Paris only to settle my affairs; if I could not get a good enough price I would sell the picture in London; I did not want to be delayed.

'"I will show you how to act," she said, then hesitated. "No, perhaps not. It would be better if you could just make yourself believe the story, then you will be just right."

'The money she had already gathered for me was almost enough, I felt, to risk going to the famous doctor and paying for any treatment he might order. But Lou had been saving it all up for the grand gesture. Sudden riches seemed to appeal to her. She was watching me intently.

'"I'll do it Lou," I said.'

71

Chapter 6

'Lou was right, I knew. I had to believe the story myself if I was to play the part without embarrassment. Well, my daydreams had seemed real enough to me. For Alain's sake – and my life was dedicated to Alain now – I would carry this thing through successfully. I was well enough practised in appearing to be what I was not. Lou was determined that I should do the thing perfectly. As she put it, there was no harm in keeping the buggers waiting; they would be all the more eager.

'Meantime, she would try to sell the rest of the pictures to Tournier. There was a sketchbook of Michel's, all done in the Dordogne. Tournier had said, "What could I do with that?" so she wondered would she just throw it out. Perhaps Alain would like to look at the châteaux and the pretty flowers? I got her to fetch it.

'Something changed when I looked at that book, Jessie. I had been filled with hatred for Michel . . . I had wanted to protect Alain from his wicked father . . . but these pictures altered my ideas. What was I going to tell Alain about Michel when he grew up? A boy should be proud of his father, identify with him. These sketches – some of them pencil drawings and some, little details in watercolour – were a delight to the eye. Whatever we might think of his character, Michel was an artist of skill and taste. I decided I would guard that book for Alain. He would have something

I could honestly praise. I told Lou I would keep it for Alain without telling her my reasons. I think she saw it as his picture book. I started reading up the history of the various *châteaux*. There hadn't been much time for reading when every spare moment was spent earning money. The reading itself comforted me – took me back to Kilbarchan and Dougie coaching his sisters in Latin and French: ahead of his time, our brother Dougie, wasn't he?

'After that Lou insisted on a rehearsal every day. She was a relentless critic. You should have heard her! "Not English enough. Not proud enough . . . That's it . . . but keep him hoping . . . You will do well . . . yes." She was determined on the sum I would get for the picture. It seemed astronomical to me. "Elise, remember you are a rich lady," she said; "You married far, far beneath you; you are not worried if Tournier does not give you what you ask; you will easily get that sum in London! You must believe it . . . must . . . must . . . must! Only then will he believe you."

'A sudden thought struck me. "Lou, he *won't* believe me," I said. "Michel probably told him that I was his model for *Spring* and *Summer*. If I'm made up to look different . . ."

'"He'll just think Michel was lying. Tournier knows he was a bloody liar. Can't you see? It's your word against that bastard's and Tournier will take the word of a fine English lady."

'I still feel like laughing, Jessie, when I remember her sitting there, waving her arms in encouragement at me, but every time she referred to Michel she crossed herself without her expression changing by one flicker. I suddenly hooted and she looked abashed. "What is wrong, Elise? I do not understand." I threw my arms around her just the way we used to do with our baby sister. There was something so like . . . the young earnestness . . . something touching and ridiculous at the same time. There was no way I could explain it to her.

' "Lou, you are marvellous," I said. She cheered up instantly.

' "Right! we rehearse again, Elise; you are walking into his dark little shop. Jean-Jo has held the door open for you; he carries the painting but stands well behind you. You do not speak French too well but are too proud to care. Begin!"

'Well, that was the way it went on, Jessie, as spring merged into summer. The chestnuts were out and the boulevards were breathtakingly beautiful in their fresh greenery. My walks were a joy, or would have been if I had been more confident of Alain's health. He seemed to be holding his own but had little strength. He made no effort to pull himself up but would smile happily when I propped him up on cushions where he could see us. Lou showed an uncharacteristic patience with him. She knew as I did that his development was far from normal. He never showed any of the signs of temper and frustration you would expect, especially from a boy. The time had come to see that doctor and it would be better to get the transaction of the picture completed first.

'So the day arrived. I had spent the previous evening parading in my borrowed plumes before Lou. She assured me she had rehearsed Jean-Jo at his own home. "He thinks you are a great lady who can no longer afford a servant. When we cleared Michel's flat, I let him think I was taking the pictures because Michel had not paid me my wages. That makes good sense to him. So, you see, he cannot give you away." I knew she was right. I *had* to believe the story myself and with all her careful rehearsals, I did!

'Tournier was shorter than I am. That helped. I could look down on him as I spoke; at his balding head with its tufts of black and grey hair; his waxed moustache with one side slightly higher than the other; the prominent veins on his temple and the little red flecks in the white of his eyes. He was thrown off balance by my manner, I could see. Though his initial response was more or less what I expected . . . "Such a price is impossible, Madame. No London dealer will give you anything like that. In fact, it is only in Paris that a comparatively unknown painter . . ." I cut him short, assuring him that knowledgeable friends took a completely different view; that Dutch dealers were paying high prices in London these days. I nodded imperiously to Jean-Jo, who prepared to lift the canvas. I watched Tournier carefully. Something shot through his beady dark eyes. His hand stretched out to detain Jean-Jo and I knew I had won. "Madame, if you could leave the picture with me for a few days . . ."

'I assured him I had no wish to linger in Paris and again nodded to Jean-Jo. Tournier began, "Your price, Madame, is extremely . . ." I cut him short by restating it firmly. His Adam's apple was jumping up and down, and sweat began trickling down his brow. He was thinking of that Dutch dealer. I kept my expression firm and slightly stern. Then I took one step towards the door and he capitulated. Suddenly, a wave of sickness swept over me. After all, there was so much at stake and I'd felt all along that Lou could be wrong in her daring estimate. But, thanks to her training, I was able to tell myself that I was a grand lady who was receiving the sum she would have obtained in London.

'Lou was getting ready for the theatre when I returned in triumph. We had to contain ourselves while she paid off Jean-Jo with a generous tip above his promised fee. I thanked him graciously, still playing my part. Lou asked him to take care of his borrowed uniform; she would collect it in the morning. As soon as the door closed behind him she grabbed me and we started dancing round the salon. Alain chuckled at this unusual entertainment. "You will not go to bed tonight," she said. "We will drink champagne until we are drunk . . . drunk . . . drunk."

'"But what about Henri?" I asked.

'"Henri? He can go to the devil. If he doesn't like it, I shall get someone else. It is easy now I speak a little English and behave like an English lady . . . Well, I see how you look at me, Elise, I behave *almost* like an English lady, I mean." I was helpless with laughter by this time. Though she would be late for a costume call, Lou could not bear to tear herself away till I had described the transaction to her twice over in detail. "Marvellous, marvellous," she kept shouting, clapping her hands. "I never thought the bugger would pay it . . ."

'"But you told me . . ." I said.

'"Yes, and you believed me and made him believe you. You are a great actress, Elise. And you are a rich woman and now you will take Alain to see the famous doctor and he will make him a big strong boy. Please, let me see the money . . . all that gold . . ."

'"But I didn't get gold," I said. "Nobody with any sense would keep all that money in a shop. I got this bill drawn on Coutts Brothers."

'Lou was horrified. "You didn't accept a piece of paper," she said. "He will have cheated you, the bastard." I assured her that Coutts Brothers was a very respectable bank which had started in Scotland and now served merchants all over the Continent. I knew the place where I was to exchange it, Les Deux Anges in the rue du Bac. She accepted my word rather reluctantly. I could see that she would have preferred the chink of gold coins.

'We *did* drink champagne that night. When I enquired about Henri, Lou assured me with a few adjectives that there were as many fish in the sea. "He pays your rent," I pointed out. "Do not worry about that, Elise," she said. "Now that you are teaching me to be a real lady I shall get a richer admirer who will give us a better flat or perhaps a house. The corner of rue Cardinet would suit us beautifully."

'I was touched that she said "us". I had a need to belong. And yet I felt guilty too, for I knew that as soon as the doctor had made Alain fit, I would be packing up and leaving for Kilbarchan. Lou would be hurt desperately, I was sure; she would find it difficult to understand because she wasn't thirled to her family. Oh, Jessie, it's a long time since I used that word . . . but there isn't really an English one that fits exactly.

'Well, the next thing was to get an appointment with the famous doctor. I managed it for a few days later. It gave me time to finish a lovely little silk suit I was making for Alain and to trim a hat for myself. It seemed important then. I don't know why. I get worn out just thinking about it even now.

'It was a beautiful day; the scent of the roses, newly out in the gardens; the round-topped trees in the Tuileries were in full fresh leaf. Children were playing

77

happily. Alain looked so lovely in his little silk suit. I'd embroidered bluebirds on the yoke. I was thinking, "He'll be playing like all these other children once Doctor Wallach treats him."

'The house was big and airy with tiled floors in the hall and the anteroom I was shown into. There were lots of plants in huge china pots and jardinières. The wooden shutters and the dark green linen blinds looked heavy. I didn't have long to wait. The nurse who summoned us wasn't young and reminded me in a funny way of Nurse Duncan in Kilbarchan, though there was little physical resemblance. Perhaps I was looking for reassurance, security. Up till then I'd been trying to work out how much I should edit out of my story to them, but somehow the memory of Nurse Duncan and then the sight of the tall, distinguished doctor himself tore at my defences. While she disappeared into a room beyond, he took my hand firmly, then ushered me into a comfortable chair. He smiled warmly at Alain who instantly smiled back.

'"A happy little fellow, I see," he said. "No fear of strangers."

'"No . . . but . . ." He waited and I couldn't think what to say, then I blurted out, "He's over six months old. He makes no effort to sit up. He never gets cross."

'His expression had changed. I could see he had thought Alain much younger.

'"He was premature, Madame? You had an accident, perhaps?"

'"Perhaps I should just tell you the whole story," I said.

'"I think that would be as well," he replied. He sat back then, as if he had all the time in the world. It's a funny thing to say, but he seemed just like God to me.

I had been tossing about in a rough sea for a long time; people had thrown me lifebelts – those kind nuns . . . Lou – but suddenly I felt I had reached a safe harbour. The uncertainty was over. I could confess! This tall stranger would understand.

'"Take a deep breath, Madame, and begin."

'I went all the way back to Kilbarchan, Jessie: to my elopement, the hurt I had given my own family and Mrs Nisbet-Brown. Then France. The lines deepened round his eyes when I told him about the stuff Michel made me drink and the way he had carried on when it didn't work. Looking at that good man, I found it astounding that I could ever have fallen in love with someone like Michel. I suppose when you're young it's difficult to recognize integrity . . . He heard me through it all – the kind nuns at Lariboisière . . . Michel's first and last look at his son . . . the kindness of little Lou . . . my worries about Alain.

'"Dry your eyes, Madame," he said when I had finished. "Thank you for telling me such a difficult *histoire*. We will put it behind us and see what can be done for the lovely little Alain. When you are composed, Madame, I shall ring for the nurse. She will take baby away to weigh him while I write down some details."

'Alain was underweight for his age, of course. I knew that. The doctor played with him for a little while before he started the examination. Alain chuckled happily. It suddenly struck me that this was the first time he had heard a deep male voice, and also how starved I had been of male company ever since I left home. I remembered how our Lilias liked Faither to play peepbo with her when she was just a wee thing. We thought it was his deep voice.

79

'When Doctor Wallach had finished, he spent quite a long time just looking at me with Alain supported on his knee. I had told him that I wanted to return to Scotland as soon as Alain was fit and he started with that. "The journey you propose, Madame, is a long and difficult one with many changes of temperature. I would not recommend it for this little fellow. You see, his lungs and his heart are not fully formed. He cannot breathe deeply. There is a tremor . . . an uneven beat in the heart. A chill could cause severe complications. It will do him good to be out in the warm sunshine as much as possible, Madame. Spread a rug on the grass and let him crawl if he makes the attempt, but do not encourage him to make more effort than he wishes at any time."

'He saw that I was stunned, and spoke so gently. "I regret, Madame, being the bearer of such sad tidings. I see that you love your baby deeply. He is so well cared for . . . a little suit with bluebirds . . ." I knew he was saying just the first thing that came into his head to give me a chance to draw myself together. I was completely broken or I wouldn't have blurted out that I had made Alain's suit and I had made the dress and cloak for his own little girl and that was how I had heard of him. He looked absolutely amazed. Then he came round the desk, put Alain in my arms and said, "Wait there, please. If Madame Wallach is at home I am sure she will wish to meet you."

'This was something I had never imagined. I had known that Alain was far from normal and I think deep down there had been a fear that even the brilliant doctor would not be able to put him right, though I had suppressed that. I had certainly never thought of divulging the sewing connection and I had not expected to tell him my whole story so frankly. In those days I was so used to presenting a false front to the world that it was hard to believe I could have been stripped of all pretence by one caring doctor. He was soon back and asked me to accompany him to the salon where Madame would like me to drink a cup of chocolate with her.

'Madame Wallach was like a plump little robin with soft brown hair escaping from her chignon. She was energetically plumping cushions on a couch. I got a warm greeting before she took Alain from my arms and propped him up securely with a "There you are my little man . . . plenty of cushions so you can sit up and show off the lovely suit your clever Maman made. There is something I wish to show her before our chocolate arrives. You may look too!"

'She crossed quickly to a corner of the room. "This arrived only this morning, Madame. You are one of the first to see it and rightly so, from what my husband tells me." She turned the heavy picture round and propped it up on a settle where the light caught it. I drew my breath in sharply. The artist had made a superb job. The chrysanthemum silk and brown velvet I had handled so lovingly gleamed to perfection, enhancing the innocent beauty of the young girl. She had a lovely open expression, not shy and yet not bold. The brown eyes shone with hidden laughter – no bored sitter, this one. He'd posed her on a chair with a low table beside her. The velvet muff dangled casually from one hand while the bonnet rested on the table beside a doll. In spite of the elegant clothes the picture had no stiffness about it. The soft curls of golden brown hair round her forehead had not been contrived.

'Tears welled up in my eyes at the sheer beauty of

it, Jessie – maybe they had been due to come anyway. Then Madame Wallach had her handkerchief out too. We were both dabbing our eyes when the maid arrived with the chocolate. She was about to leave the room when Madame Wallach asked her to wait. "You have not a baby carriage, Madame?" I was speechless. I think I just shook my head. She turned to the maid. "The baby carriage is stored in the coachhouse. Ask the garden boy to fetch it out for you and remove the wrappings. The bedding is in the chest by the nursery window. Please arrange it prettily for Madame." As soon as the girl left the room I started crying again. Madame Wallach patted my arm gently. "God is good, Madame. He will take care of your little son, here or above . . . never fear." Her French was funny, very heavily accented. She knew it too, because while I was trying to pull myself together she said, "You speak French so well, Madame, and yet you have been here only a short time. I have been here almost sixteen years but my biggest son he tells me I still speak like an Austrian."

'"I thought you were German," I said.

'She shook her head. "My husband is German. We met when I was a student nurse in Vienna. He came to Vienna to the children's home where I was working . . . he was so tall, so handsome, so kind to our little patients. I think all the nurses were in love with him. I was amazed when he chose me."

'I'm not sure now, Jessie, if I said it out loud, but I remember thinking, "He chose wisely."

'"We were both very young when we married," she went on, "but I was an only child and my parents were able to help us while Albert continued his training."

'I listened, considering her life in this safe happy

haven, complete with healthy children whose father adored them and contrasting it with the time I had endured with Michel and the disaster his treatment had brought on my little Alain. How different things would have been for me with a husband like Albert Wallach.

'I had gone to that house for Alain's sake only, hoping against hope that a miracle could be worked. That miracle had not happened. Alain was never going to be like other boys. Though the doctor had not said it in so many words, I knew that I could not hope to rear my little son. And yet there had been another kind of miracle, a sort of peace that had come to me. I knew the worst now but I had been given the encouragement to carry on caring for my lovely little boy. And he *was* lovely by that time, Jessie, believe me. All the wrinkles had gone. He just looked small-boned and delicate, a little angel. These kind people, so happy in themselves, had inevitably seen a lot of sadness in their work and could urge acceptance because of their sure faith.

'We left by the garden door, Alain comfortably ensconced in the baby carriage. "A long walk will do you good, Madame," my kind hostess said. "There is nothing like it for leaving your worries behind." I had never pushed one of these things before and felt very self-conscious as I set out, but gradually I *did* feel I was shedding a load. Alain looked so happy; he was getting fresh air without any exertion and I was walking in a way I had not walked since I left Kilbarchan. I couldn't help wondering what Lou would say. Her lovely little flat was only meant for one person and certainly not designed for baby carriages. But I needn't have worried. Her first concern was what the doctor had said about Alain. I tried to soften the truth – for myself as well as for her, I think. But I saw the colour leave her face for a moment. Her view of the obstruction in her salon was simple – "Now I will *have* to get a richer lover. Henri's flat is too small for our beautiful baby carriage. You will make me a magnificent hat for Sunday, Elise, and I will see which of them I can charm."

'Though I laughed with her, I began to wonder if it was not time to look for a place of my own. After all, I was comparatively rich. The doctor's fee had been modest; there was to be no expensive treatment for Alain, only a mother's care. Was I being fair to Lou? Yet, when I looked at her playing gently with Alain and heard her eagerly repeat sentence after sentence in English, it was plain to see that we had a sure place in her otherwise rackety life.

'I walked many, many miles with that baby carriage. I soon found that Alain loved the river and the boats, particularly the *bateaux lavoires* with the glass sides open on a good day and the rows of washer women scrubbing away while the wind caught the soap suds and sent them scudding across the Seine. There was a big steam crane called Sophia by the Port Saint Nicholas which fascinated him. We visited it day after day right through summer and autumn.

'When the cold weather set in I could not risk taking him to the damp chill air of the river. Though I spent hours playing with toys and drawing pictures for him, it was obvious he was restless; his eyes would keep turning to the window and he would say "Dodee". This was the nearest he could get to "Sophia". It was heart-breaking to watch him. Day after day the mist drifted up from the river and my efforts to amuse my wee son became more difficult. Then at last, one day in mid-January the sun broke out of the mist half-way through the morning. Alain's head kept turning towards the window. He would screw his eyes against the shafts of sunlight and say "Dodee". Suddenly I could stand it no longer. I warmed all the blankets for the baby carriage, then bundled Alain up in umpteen layers of clothes. I remembered how we wrapped Lilias up the day of Kilbarchan Horse Fair . . . the day I met Mrs Nisbet-Brown. I remembered that as I lifted my rolypoly baby and propped him up in a ring of cushions with rugs pulled up to his chin.

'The sky was a milky blue and an orange sun dazzled me as I stepped out. Everything looked so beautiful . . . the frost sparkling on the tiles and the bare trees. Some boys had made a slide and were tumbling and shouting their way along it. Alain got quite excited, chuckling and turning his head to watch them. It was lovely, yes! But it was bitterly cold too. So much so that when I crossed the place Vendôme and reached the rue de Rivoli I was tempted to turn back. But the thought of all those plaintive little cries of "Dodee" urged me on to let him have a quick look at his beloved crane. At last we reached the wharf. My hands inside my thick gloves were quite cold by then and I began to feel I had been really stupid in risking the outing. As soon as I angled the carriage to let him have a clear view, Alain went daft. For the first time ever, he managed to pull himself up and forward, his eyes sparkling. Then he started waving but soon lost his balance and toppled back against his cushions. I thought it was time to get home but Alain set up a hullabaloo – something that had never happened before.

'My feelings were so mixed up. He was behaving

like a normal boy! Yet the words of the kind doctor were ringing in my ears and I knew I daren't risk letting my baby catch cold. I had to turn about, trying to soothe him with a little song, telling him we would come back when it was warmer. His cheeks were rosy with his feverish crying. He looked healthier than he had ever done and yet . . . I had ignored the doctor's guidance. I prayed that there would be no repercussions.

'Lou remarked on his lovely pink cheeks, I remember, when she kissed him goodnight before leaving for the theatre. I had expected the colour to subside after he had been home for some time and had been watching carefully. Lou's remark did nothing to ease my worries, which I kept to myself. He fell asleep with his thumb in his mouth not long after I laid him down for the night and I began to relax. The salon was cosy, the lamp shone on my crochet, leaving Alain in a shadowed corner. Everything seemed normal. I was just packing up my work and thinking of preparing for bed when I heard a little cough followed by a whimper. I was over by his bed in an instant. I could see he was fevered before I even touched him. Terror caught at me. "A chill could cause severe complications," the doctor had said. What exactly did he mean by that? Then I remembered Mam's pleurisy; how Jean had insisted that everything for the bed must be warm and dry. I rushed to build up the stove which I had just damped down for the night. While I raked and riddled I could hear Alain turning and tossing. The whimpering was becoming a wail. I spoke soothingly to him as I rushed to get spare bedding and nightclothes round the fire. Then I lifted him in his blanket over to my chair. Perhaps a feed would soothe him, I thought.

But he turned from the breast, his nails scratching me as the tiny arms flailed. Panic was rising in me all the time. His curls were plastered to his head with sweat. His cheeks were two fiery spots. I dabbed at him with a warm towel, not daring to strip him till the room was back up to temperature. Then I heard Lou. Was Henri with her? He had never heard a sound from Alain. What would he think of his flat being a home for refugees? It's funny how anything so unimportant could run through my head at a time like that.

'She burst into the room, saying, "Damn all men," then stopped when she saw Alain. "Oh, no," she said, sinking on her knees before him.

'"I should never have taken him out today," I said. She offered to make him chocolate but I told her he had refused the breast. Then as we watched, his wailing changed to a sort of snoring sound. I looked at her in panic.

'Lou jumped up then. "There's a doctor just round the corner," she said and was off. I tried propping Alain against my shoulder to see if that would let him breathe more easily but he slumped there; the snoring against my ear got louder; then it became a sort of rattle; then suddenly there was silence. It took me a second or two to realize what the meaning of that quietness was. Oh, Jessie! My wee boy was in my arms but he was dead!'

Chapter 7

Elsie wept in my arms for a long time. I wasn't much better myself. I couldn't help putting myself in her place. When her sobs ended I wondered if I should suggest it was time to take a rest; but her body still gave convulsive jerks. I compromised by lighting the spirit kettle again. There was something compelling about the little blue flame. We both watched it in silence. Elsie's hands were shaking badly when I handed her the cup and saucer, but as she sipped the hot liquid I saw her face begin to ease a little.

'I'm keeping you out of your bed, Jessie,' she said.

'Don't worry about that. I'll be fine. Beth and Maggie will see the menfolk out in the morning. You've been bottling so much terrible stuff up for so long. We could never have guessed what you were going through. Mind you, I remember Jean saying once that if you were happy you would be writing to Mam to tell her about it.'

'Aye, Jessie. She was right about that. How I wished that some of my ain folk were nearer! I had no idea where to begin. It was Lou who took over because I was numb; just couldn't think things out for myself. Luckily for me she was free. The night Alain died she had barged in saying, "Damn all men." Well, I got the answer to that later. Seemingly she had been reprimanded by the producer for something that happened on stage – I'm not sure what now: her cheeky answers have just become more sophisticated over the years. Of course, she will say that it's since I taught her how to be an English lady. That's a laugh! Where was I? She gave him a cheeky answer and he threatened her with dismissal, whereupon the bold Lou told him what he could do with his job. There was a reaction later, of course, and when she burst into angry tears outside her dressing-room, one of the actors took her into his arms and comforted her in the extravagant way they did. She had already torn off half her costume on the way – these girls had no modesty. I used to wonder what Mam would say about it all when I was sitting at that sewing machine and watching their bold antics with the men.

'Well, according to Lou, Henri came on them like that with her half-naked and the fellow kissing and stroking her. He went up in a blue light. So that was the end of that romance. I think she was getting tired of him anyway and now that I had money we were not depending on him to pay the rent so she felt reckless. Of course, I didn't realize it at the time but it all worked in my favour. She was free to consult Jean-Jo's mother, who had buried more than one child; then she led me from one place to the other, repeating things slowly when my numbed brain could not follow the rapid and sometimes guttural speech of the officials. We paid out at the municipal offices, the undertaker and the church.

'Then came the funeral. It was so different from ours in Kilbarchan where everyone knew everyone else and the whole village turned out. In fact, I thought there would just be Lou and myself, but Jean-Jo in his best Sunday clothes came along, supervised by his mother, who obviously thought she had a hand in this funeral.

'I stared out of the carriage feeling that I was in some sort of play. It all seemed so unreal. Some of the buildings still showed signs of the siege barely five years earlier; some which had been destroyed were being rebuilt. I watched the dust caught in the frosty sunlight. We rolled through the place de Clichy heading north, our wheels clanking on the frosty cobbles. I shivered when I saw the name avenue de St Ouen, for that was the name of the cemetery we were heading for. It was a new one and nicknamed "Cayennne" by Jean-Jo and his like. We stopped at a little church for a short service. That seemed unreal too, I'm afraid. Lou and the others crossed themselves at the appropriate points but I felt completely numb. That was probably a mercy. Then we were back in the carriage and rolling into the cemetery. There was nothing very peaceful about it; just a vast plain, really. We could hear the sound of the trains clanking and shunting nearby and the frosty air brought the more distant sound of buildings in construction . . . the chink, chink, chink of countless chisels. The graves in the children's part of the cemetery were a shock – so different from anything I had ever seen – decorated mostly in blue and white with ornaments made out of beads. It was winter, of course, and real flowers would not be growing out of doors. The priest was kind, but on such a bitterly cold day I could see he was not inclined to linger. Though he had been paid for his services, I slipped him some money suggesting that a bottle of whisky from my native Scotland would warm him up. I don't know if it was obtainable. I never saw any. He probably preferred mulled wine or something anyway.

'We took Jean-Jo and his mother to lunch in a restaurant of Lou's choice. I've no idea now where it was but the food was good. I had to go through the motions of sampling each dish for fear of embarrassing them. Lou, skinny little thing that she was, had the peasant's approach to food – if it was there you ate it – while Jean-Jo and his mother were built on the generous lines that always suggest good appetite. I had to numb myself for their sakes while planning an orgy of grief once I got the flat to myself. I was afraid it might not be easy now that Lou had no job and no Henri.

'I was still shivering when I returned with her to her cosy nest, having said good-bye and thank you to Jean-Jo and his mother. "Elise," she said, "I think the best thing for you is to go to bed and get drunk. You will sleep and forget for a little while. It is the only way. I do not like to leave you, but I learned the other day that one of the big shops is looking for a model. I have to dress and go soon. Perhaps the post is already filled but, if not, I have a good chance now that I speak a little English and behave like a lady." I hurried her off, wishing her luck but telling her not to worry if the post was filled; we had plenty of money to pay the rent.

'I can still remember the long sigh of relief and despair that I gave when the door closed behind her. At last I was alone. A coldness which had nothing to do with the temperature had me in its grip. I wrapped myself in a warm dressing gown, heaped extra blankets on the bed and crawled in. Then I started howling like a wolf. It was a dreadful sound . . . torn from me horribly . . . but such a relief! I could hear it go on and on till I was hoarse. I dozed a little, made myself a cup of tea and dozed some more. By the time Lou returned I was asleep. She was surprised to find me so hoarse when I woke. I suggested I'd maybe caught a chill and she accepted the idea.

'She had been lucky at the big store. Though they had had many applicants for the job, none had seemed quite right. Lou with her well-trained body was always worth a second look, but I think I can take credit for improving her taste in clothes. Under her mantle of soft green, she wore a brown velvet jacket I had made her – the same velvet as little Marianne's cloak. It emphasized her tiny, tiny waist and the graceful sway of her hips. They were impressed by her hat too – one of my confections. Lou, the little minx, told them it was made by a high-class English lady who was very expensive and liked to design for individual clients – never two hats the same. "They're interested, Elise," she said. "I was careful not to say too much – I learn from you, you see. I think they will perhaps ask if you will design for their important clients. It would be good, no?"

'At that moment the last thing I felt like doing was creating hats, but she was so eager to help me in the only way she knew how that I agreed. I let her run on and on about the shop and the people she had met. She was doing it to distract me, I'm sure, but at that stage all I could think of was my wee boy lying all alone in that cold bleak cemetery. I think I had the death wish. I just wanted to be with Alain.

'Lou, as a model, did not have to appear so early as the other shopgirls, but she was used to actress's hours and had a scramble to make herself presentable in time the next morning. This meant she did not have leisure to worry about me. I was glad. Though I would have been dreadfully lonely without her, I knew I had to work out my sorrow my own way and that meant privacy for tears. Tidying the flat was second nature to me and I did it without thinking. Also without thinking I started to get the baby carriage ready for I was going to see Alain. Oh dear, how daft I was, Jessie! When I realized what I was doing, the tears started again of course.

'It took me a while to calm down and remove the traces. I still had my pride, vanity perhaps. But whatever folk like to call it, it has kept me from going under many a time. I set out on foot because I was so used to walking with the baby carriage. The air was bitterly cold and I soon quickened my pace. Madame Wallach was right. There is something about walking that helps you leave your worries behind. But, of course, when I saw that bleak field and all the wee graves, it all washed over me again. There were a few folk there, some of them elderly and, in spite of that, kneeling in the cold by the graves. I stood as long as I could, then was forced to get my blood going again by walking back. The sight of Alain's wee carriage set me off once more, but when I had exhausted my tears I fell asleep in the armchair by the stove.

'I had gone on like that for a few days when Lou came home one night and announced that she had telephoned Madame Wallach. "We are to take the baby carriage on Sunday afternoon at three o'clock to the orphanage beside the convent on the rue St Florentin. She is donating it to them. She will meet us there."

'"But why did she ask you?" I wanted to know.

'"Well, we thought you would feel silly pushing it all that way empty." I guessed that they had fixed it that way so that I wouldn't be vexed at the contrast between my walks with Alain and this last parade with it empty.

'However there was more behind it than that and it wasn't exactly empty. It was Lou who arranged the bedding on the carriage and she took one of the pillows, wrapped a shawl round it and tucked it under the blankets, saying, "See! No one will believe it's empty. We are just out for a brisk walk." I was glad of her foresight for the world and his wife were out enjoying the first fine Sunday of the year and one or two people automatically glanced at the "baby" as we passed.

'The orphanage was a very ancient low building which had obviously been damaged during the siege. The chips in the old grimed stone gave it an incongruous, undignified look. We opened the creaking gate and approached what appeared to be the main entrance, but we had only gone a few steps when Madame Wallach came hurrying round the side of the building followed more sedately by a nun. I was greeted with a warm hug before Madame Wallach turned to Lou. "Thank you so much for telephoning me and telling me of our dear Madame Blanchard. It is good that she has a friend like you." Then she turned to introduce me to Sister Josephine who was in charge of the little ones and would be very glad to have the baby carriage.

'We were urged to go inside and drink tea with the nuns and lay-helpers. I could sense Lou's reluctance and felt I should make some excuse, but Madame Wallach forestalled me. Casually taking Lou's arm, she told her what a treat it would be for these poor little girls to see the lovely demoiselle in her beautiful clothes: the orphanage depended chiefly on the fees from the girls in the convent school next door; as a destitute child was never refused shelter, funds were always stretched. True, the girls from the school sometimes handed in outgrown clothes from their little brothers and sisters, but all the clothes that were made for them were grey. The nuns thought it was more practical.

'It was indeed sad to see so many of the poor wee mites in sombre grey from head to foot. They gazed round-eyed at us as we paraded through. I noticed that a sadly misshapen girl, who seemed to be a helper, was particularly entranced by Lou. When we reached the parlour I mentioned this to Madame Wallach.

' "Yes," she said. "Poor Catherine. She was dropped and left crippled by a drunken father. Her mother died when she was two and she has been here with the good nuns ever since – that's about fourteen years, I think. Most of the children are moved to other homes in the country when they are about eight years old, but Catherine was kept on. She has a very gentle nature and cares very competently for the little ones. Also she loves sewing and helps Sister Agnes who teaches the convent girls to make the clothes for the orphans. I'm afraid Sister Agnes has more good intent than skill, as you may see. Of course, grey is practical."

'I looked at the sad, bedraggled little dresses and the boys' pathetic breeches. Nothing seemed to fit. Sister Agnes obviously had no idea of how to cut a pattern. The young ones seemed to be playing quite happily, so they weren't affected, but how did Catherine feel, I wondered! Her body was twisted and bent over so that her waistline rose almost to the armpit on one side. The rough grey fabric, riding up against her neck, was causing irritation, I could see. "Grey *is* practical," I answered Madame Wallach, "but surely the little ones could wear grey pinafores over something brighter – or even have little coloured collars."

'"Of course you are right," Madame Wallach said. "My dear, I should like to ask you something. I told you that it is the fees from the convent which keep the orphanage going. The nuns, of course, are not paid. I wonder . . . would it be possible for you to come in, perhaps two afternoons, to teach the girls . . . give Sister Agnes the benefit of your undoubted gifts?" I swallowed hastily. I knew that I must visit my little boy every day. That was essential. I was besotted with that idea, you see. But, if I rose a little earlier, perhaps . . .

'Quickly I worked it out. I would be able to walk to St Ouen. Then I could get omnibuses which would take me quite near to rue St Florentin. I could have lunch in a little café. "Yes, Madame," I said, "I should be happy to assist."

'Madame Wallach knew what she was doing. Nobody with my dressmaking skills could look at these children in their sorry outfits and not itch to do something about it. Catherine was given leave to join me as my "helper". This was a cunning way, I think, of getting her free lessons among the fee-paying convent girls who might have resented her. She was a delight to teach, patient and willing. I became her confidante. Her current thrill was the promise that she would be allowed to push the baby carriage in the Bois de Boulogne on a fine day when a nun was free to accompany her. That poor child had seldom been out of the orphanage grounds.

'The only fabric I had to work with at first was that dreadful grey stuff. Seemingly it had been a generous donation from some factory owner. I can just hear Dougie saying, "Fire insurance", can't you?'

We had a good laugh together, remembering our brother's sometimes scathing remarks about those who were less than sincere.

Elsie went on. 'When I was teaching them pattern-cutting, I gave them several different models to work from. This let me measure up Catherine, who would make her own dress. I was determined that even if she had to wear that horrid grey, it would fit her comfortably. And at the back of my mind, I had a plan. When Catherine walked in the Bois de Boulogne, she would have a pretty dress and it would disguise her deformity as well as Elsie Allen could manage it!

'Well, looking back, I think that work at the convent kept me sane. I was giving of my best, freely. I think I saw it as a sort of expiation for all my selfishness. Catherine got a beautiful dress to go walking in – soft blue to show up her brown eyes. I remembered the dress I made for you, Jessie, the New Year you were ten. It was red flannel and Bella crocheted a triple collar. And Dougie was so impressed that he did a painting of his favourite wee sister in it.'

'That painting is in the snug downstairs, Elsie,' I assured her. 'It was Dougie's best piece of work and he presented it to Sandy as a personal gift the night before our wedding.'

'He must have thought a lot of the man who was marrying his wee sister.'

I contented myself with saying, 'Aye'. The time was not ripe for telling Elsie of the emotional adjustments that had had to be made even in our comparatively calm surroundings. 'You were telling me about the wee crippled lass,' I prompted.

97

'Yes. My gift to Catherine caused quite a stir. The emotion was overpowering. I don't think that lass had ever had anything bonnie in her life. I'd graduated all the tucks and gathers – it was quite a job – to try to hide the distortions of her body. The crocheted collar had to be adjusted cleverly too. But what a difference it made to her appearance! I'd made her a bonnet in the same blue – just plain in outline, but with pleated ribbon under the brim and with a nice firm fastening for the ribbons so that it wouldn't tilt. I felt amply repaid for the fiddly work when I saw that girl's face. "It's like being in heaven," she said to me. I started to teach the girls to crochet and got them to bring in any scraps of wool from home. We must have made many dozens of wee collars to cheer up the miserable grey dresses of the orphanage girls. The boys got little bow ties that Catherine buttoned off and on for them. Well, that was the start. Once the ball got rolling, people would hand in cloth and yarn to the convent and by the next year, that grey fabric was reserved for pinafores that covered pretty, bright clothes.

'Lou's firm had asked me if I would be willing to make hats for some special clients. It didn't need Lou's prompting by that time for me to ask a high fee for my work. Of course she found out that the shop was charging the clients almost double that price. In spite of my windfall with the painting, as my brain began to tick over more normally I had the sense to realize that my riches would not last for ever. It came to me that it might not be a bad idea to invest my capital in a milliner's business. To succeed, it would have to be in a high-class area. But then, what if I sank all my money in it, then had an illness which stopped me working for months on end? Insecurity was something I had suffered too long to risk it again.

'The family are bound to ask me why I didn't make for home then when I had plenty of money but, you see, Jessie, I couldn't leave Alain. I had to go to that cemetery every morning. Then they're sure to ask why I didn't write. How can I tell them how often I tried, the tears soaking the paper in front of me? But it was such a long story to put down on paper; I couldn't invite anybody to come and stay – there wasn't room; I didn't know if they all hated me for what I had done. By that time I had lost all my romantic notions and knew what I deserved. Many a time when I was walking to that awful place I would think of Kilbarchan and wonder what was happening there. Mam's health had been so poor after Lilias's birth. What if my elopement had been the last straw! What if it had killed her! Then they *would* all be against me! As time went on, it just seemed more and more difficult and Kilbarchan was further and further away. There's maybe more to it than I have worked out yet. Albert that's Dr Wallach – seems to think that if I am utterly honest to my loving sisters, everything will become clear. He says that the mind builds up barriers against what is too painful to remember.

'I kept up my pilgrimage to St Ouen right through that spring, summer and autumn. Then one miserable day at the end of November when the cold wind was making my eyes water, I found a large bonfire smouldering in a corner of the cemetery. The smoke was horrible and there was a revolting, greasy smell. I passed, coughing and with a handkerchief held over my face. Nearby, an elderly woman rose stiffly from her knees. "You never get used to it, do you?" she said grimly as I approached.

99

' "What is it?" I asked.

' "It's the coffins burning, my dear. Their five-year let is up."

'I must have looked bewildered. Slowly and patiently she explained. "They get buried there, eh? They stay there five years in peace, eh? Then the land is needed for other corpses. They dig up the coffins, eh? The bones go in the ossuary over there." She pointed to a stone erection I had thought was a war memorial. There were always wreaths in front of it. The old lady went on, "And then they have to burn the coffins: and that's the horrid smell, my dear. Are you all right?"

'I was far from all right, as you can guess. I found out later this practice was normal because the city was moving outwards, especially to the north, and land was scarce. Of course I had no idea of that at the time. I turned and stumbled out of that cemetery and I kept walking without seeing a thing till I got to the orphanage; I must have crossed lots of busy roads but I simply don't remember. Sister Josephine was near the back door, unpegging bedlinen which was stiff as boards. I must have looked a sight because she let the sheet she was folding drop on the ground and hurried towards me. "Madame, You are unwell?"

'I could hardly speak. The words came out in the wrong order. It was as if I had never learned French. She got the gist of it as she held my arm firmly and guided me into the little parlour, settling me into the only comfortable chair. "Wait a moment, Madame," she said. "I shall return."

'I was still shivering in spite of the many layers of clothes I was wearing when Sister Josephine came hurrying back. "Catherine will bring you some tea,

Madame. Then we will go to the chapel together." She was chafing my hands as she spoke. The wrinkled old face close to mine was full of concern, but it was a calm, controlled concern. That was something I had noticed about all the nuns in Lariboisière, their control.

'The tea helped and I was able to pull myself together before Sister Josephine led me along what seemed an endless corridor towards the chapel. There was the usual smell – candlegrease, damp stone, damp wool and stale incense. She guided me towards a statue of the Madonna. It looked pathetic and so artificial to me, garishly painted and with chips in the plaster. The infant Jesus was as stiff as a stookie. I concentrated on the beautiful flowers which had been placed at the chipped feet. "We will kneel, Madame," Sister Josephine said, "and ask the mother of our Lord to care for your little son."

'Her words took me back to Madame Wallach, her cheerful kindness, her caring, her steady faith in the goodness of God through it all. Maybe that statue that seemed so tawdry to me was simply a channel for her to something wonderful and sure. As I knelt beside Sister Josephine, I thought myself back to our church in Kilbarchan, the silent solemnity of the communion service; then I thought of Meg's wedding, Duncan's face as he turned to watch her come down the aisle and the waves of love that were all around us; then I was at the twins' christening and I remembered the minister saying that the whole congregation had a share in those two wee boys and we were to pray for them. These nuns were giving up their lives to service and prayers for others. I had been too centred on my own grief. When Sister Josephine rose, I walked with firmer step to the outer door of the chapel. I put my donation in the box and thanked her for her kindness, assuring her that I would be all right on my own. I knew she had plenty of duties awaiting her and I had already stolen a lot of her time.

'I wandered down towards the river, in spite of the cold mist. I had a lot to think about. The river traffic moved sluggishly. I thought of the seamen with stiff fingers handling ropes and cargo. Life had its grim times for most people. Notre Dame suddenly loomed up out of the mist. I had never been inside it. There was nothing to stop me now – no Alain to hurry back to from the rue de Richelieu; no baby carriage with Alain propped up on his cushions; no Alain. The tears were gathering as I crossed the forecourt.

'The height and space of that place just took my breath away. An organ was playing and the sound seemed to fill every nook and cranny. I was used to the idea of side chapels by then, but here there seemed to be so many. Throngs of people were tramping up and down and yet there was plenty of room. People were taking candles and lighting them before kneeling in prayer. Some were whispering, some murmuring and some just stared silently ahead. Being used to the quietness and stillness of the church at home, I couldn't see how anyone could concentrate on prayer in that stir. Then it struck me that was what the candles were for – to help focus their sight and their thoughts. I found a seat and sat there . . . oh, it must have been the best part of an hour. When I rose I felt quite stiff. I made my way to the main doors. The mist had lifted and low shafts of strong sunlight blinded me as I stepped forward. That was why I didn't notice that a man in front of me had stopped to put on his gloves. I crashed right into him, then staggered and fell on the flagstones. It was so embarrassing! He was extremely concerned, helping me up and apologizing profusely. People began to pause and stare. This made me feel worse. He sensed it. "Let me accompany you to a café, Madame. Some cognac or hot coffee might help you." Normally I wouldn't have dreamt of going off with a stranger like that but, as I said, people were staring, I *did* feel a bit shaken, he had a lovely voice and was obviously a gentleman.

'"Thank you, monsieur," I said. "I should be very grateful." And that was how I met Georges.'

Chapter 8

There was a sort of caress in the way Elsie said the name, 'Georges', that alerted me. Though I could see a hint of dawn edging round the spare room curtains, I must confess I was too nosey to urge her to stop. She seemed in a dreamy state as she went on.

'His attitude to me had just the right degree of formality for me to feel safe. The waiters treated him with deference and I gradually relaxed a little. I was aware that there were probably traces of tears on my face and I was far from looking my best, but his voice was low and kind as he sipped his cognac. "I often slip into the cathedral at this time of day to hear the organ and to gaze at that ceiling. I am an architect, you see, Madame. I don't think anyone with my training could fail to be stirred by the magnificence of Notre Dame. Do you find it so, Madame?"

'I had to admit that that was the very first time I had ventured in. He expressed his horror at the idea and asked what I thought of the English cathedrals. Of course, I was stumped. It was tempting to do what Lou had taught me so well – lie my way out of it – but after my experience at the cemetery I was stripped of that sort of falsity. I told him I had been brought up quietly in the country in Scotland and that our little church was simple but beautiful. I expect he pictured me in something like Mrs Nisbet-Brown's house. I hastened to assure him that I had found the cathedral truly wonderful and he seemed satisfied.

'I did not linger when I had finished my coffee and cognac; he rose as soon as I did and offered to call a cab for me. For a second or two I hesitated in case this was some sort of gambit in the game that Lou played so adroitly, but then I looked at his courteous bearing and decided I was safe; and a cab home was exactly what I wanted at that moment.

'That night I tossed and turned. The nightmare of seeing and smelling those burning coffins would switch to the lined kindly face of the nun. And then I would be sitting in the café with Georges – Georges Dutoit – and gaining strength from his low, calm voice. I was starved of male company. Of course I didn't analyse it at the time but my body had been awakened by Michel and in spite of all his cruelty I suppose I could not return to my maiden state.

'I guessed that an attractive man like Georges would probably be married and I was right. I learned all that quite soon. He had . . . has . . . one daughter; his wife had never been strong and her pregnancy was a difficult one. So there were no more. Later on in our relationship he told me that he had worked for his wife's father, who had one of the finest practices in Paris. There was no son to follow the old man on and he was delighted when Georges took up with his Marguerite, a delicate girl who was still at the convent when Georges first started work in the office. She spent a lot of time with her mother in the South of France. As Georges put it, he always met her in the most favourable surroundings – at fashionable assemblies in the city or in the lovely villa which they owned near Nice. Their romance blossomed and in due time Georges asked for her hand. He *did* have one misgiving, when his future father-in-law advised him that it would be better that they shouldn't have children. But Georges was enamoured of the gentle well-bred Marguerite and, not to put too fine a point on it, he was ambitious. His heart drew him to Marguerite, yes! But his mind told him that Papa Durant, a rather elderly parent who intended semi-retirement for himself when Georges married, was looking for security for his beloved daughter and with her hand would go the prospect of inheriting the sort of practice he could only have dreamt of otherwise.

'I gathered that the marriage was a pretty subdued affair. Her parents were anything but pleased when they found that Marguerite was pregnant and Georges was made to feel a monster. The difficult birth didn't help that situation. Though his father-in-law recovered his equilibrium once Marguerite was restored to normal, Georges felt that Madame Durant would never forgive him for the rest of her days. But the little new arrival soon showed that there was nothing delicate about her. Marie-Isabelle took after Georges in appearance and was the sort of lively youngster who kept nursemaids running. George's face always lit up when he was telling me about her. It seemed such a pity that he could not have more children. I remembered Albert Wallach with his happy brood and wished Georges could have shared that sort of happiness. In my secret thoughts I was really wishing that I could be giving him those children. I see I am shocking you, Jessie. I shocked myself but the thoughts kept returning.

'I know now that I was really attracted to him physically right from the first though I wasn't aware of it. Just a few days after that first visit to Notre Dame, I felt drawn to go there again. I suppose I was hoping to see Georges but, of course, I wouldn't admit that to myself at the time.

'I was sitting there. The organ was playing. The music was wonderful. Somehow I felt I was being transported to another plane. It was particularly wonderful because I had little to uplift me at that time. Then suddenly, Georges was at my side. He sat down quietly. After a little while he asked if I would like him to show me the cathedral. I was only too happy to take up his offer. I walked round slowly with him, feeling I was in a trance. He drew my attention to details I would never have noticed; explained . . . explained . . . explained. It was a new world. I'd looked at buildings before and admired them, but this took looking to another dimension. His beautiful voice was full of enthusiasm for this cathedral he loved. He suddenly looked so young. Now and again people glanced at us. They saw us as a couple, I'm sure, and the thought thrilled me. "But Georges is married," I kept telling myself, trying to chase away the wayward thought. There was so much to see and all of it fascinating.

'I glanced at my watch and found that we had been there two hours. "Monsieur, won't your staff be wondering what has happened to you?" I asked.

'"No," he said. "I am the boss. I make my own programme. I have been in the country this morning looking at a site that a very special client has chosen for his house. Now I shall be able to let my imagination take over and sketch a few ideas for him. But a visit to Notre Dame always does me good . . . perhaps it humbles me . . . it certainly inspires me. Now, dear Madame, may we drink coffee together?"

'I knew I should be saying "no" but I had nothing

to go home to – only memories of a baby carriage and a little boy who loved a steam crane and who might still have been alive if I had not taken him out on that bitterly cold day to see his beloved Sophia. Lou would not be home for some time yet; and then she would probably be going out to meet Henri's successor, whom she hadn't brought home so far. I faced a dismal night by the stove with my needlework and my memories, most of them sad and bitter. I'm not making excuses for myself. Yes, I am. Albert said absolute truth would be the simplest and best way to peace for me.

'Instinct told me even then that there could be danger in the pleasant relationship with Georges. But a kind, courteous young man was offering a pleasant half hour in a café with interesting people to watch and a lovely voice to comfort me. I said, "Thank you, monsieur."

'It started like that and it went on – an honourable friendship. In my case it soon deepened into love and through time, I realized that Georges was caught in the same trap. Nothing was said but his eyes glowed as he looked at me; my hand was pressed to his lips on parting. Marguerite spent a lot of time in the south with her parents. Without little Marie-Isabelle, the house seemed deserted to Georges. We were both lonely. Though he did not put things into words at that time, I gathered that Marguerite was afraid of pregnancy and their intimate life had ended. I reckoned that was why she spent so much time away.

'I visited Alain's grave every morning. The long walk which I had continued out of habit kept me healthy. But, more and more, my feet would turn to Notre Dame. And often Georges would be there. We would sit quietly together, absorbing the peace and beauty; then we would automatically make our way to the café where our friendship had begun. Georges had designed the house of his dreams for his wealthy client. It only took a word from me to start him enthusing about it as the work progressed. I heard about all the delays and frustrations; about stupid workmen; suppliers who did not keep their word. Then there would be the triumphs as another stage of the work was completed and a filament of his dream was added.

'One day we had adjourned to the café as usual, but I could feel a change in Georges. I was sitting there on a lovely May day. The chestnut candles were in their full glory. I could smell lilac somewhere near. Women dressed in the paler colours of summer were parading and proudly showing off their new hats. That was the time when the hats were at their most ornamental, I remember . . . flowers, bird's nests, stuffed birds; in short, anything they could get to stay put. Some were comical and I felt my lips curling in amusement at times. Georges was toying with his coffee spoon. He wasn't looking at the passing show; he was looking at me. "You should smile always, my dear Elizabeth," he said. "It shows you at your loveliest. I wish I could take away your pain and sorrow."

'My heart started to pound. I felt full of joy – a joy which I knew to be dangerous. Georges could and did take away my pain and sorrow, but it was wrong that he should feel this way about me. I knew that, yet I gloried in it.

'For a while I said nothing. He was bound to see how affected I was. I had to gain control of the situation before anything damaging was said. "You are a good friend, Georges," I said, "and I hope it may be possible for us to remain friends." He understood immediately and his tone became more brisk.

'"How would you like to see my masterpiece tomorrow? I could get the train from St Lazare at lunchtime. You could join me further up the line and we could get off at St Cloud and have lunch there before travelling on to Vaucresson. It would be a nice change for you, this lovely weather. I'd love to show it to you."

'I hesitated. This was a dangerous path. Yet, the prospect was so alluring: new pastures for me after my restricted years in Paris; a chance to wear one of the lovely outfits I had made and seldom wore; a charming intelligent companion who understood every nuance, one who would never land me in an embarrassing situation. I couldn't resist it!'

'Georges was leaning out of the carriage window. I knew that we could be seen by many people on the train so I was careful to keep my smile cool and ladylike and to walk without undue haste. He greeted me courteously and handed me into a seat opposite himself. I had to control my breathing and found it easier to study the fresh summery landscape than to look at Georges. We alighted at St Cloud. Georges summoned a cab and we were off to a lovely old coaching inn. The countryside had opened out as we progressed and I revelled in the changing vistas. Lunch was served in a sheltered garden. The food was delightfully cooked . . . everything so fresh. The salad looked like a painting. In fact, the whole thing looked like a painting – an arch of early roses nearby, the rough white linen tablecloths, the plump girl in frilled bonnet who served us with a wide smile, the golden crisp rolls in their sturdy baskets. It was all thrilling. And Georges looked so happy. I paraphrased the words he had used to me the day before, "You should smile always, my dear Georges." Only I didn't say them out loud.

'Another cab took us bowling along the country roads to Vaucresson. "We're nearly there," Georges said. "Just round this bend." I gasped when I saw the house, so much bigger than I had imagined and yet so inviting. It curved outwards almost in a semi-circle to make the most of the view. The golden stone shone mellow in the clear light. There were columns – not pretentious, forbidding things but graceful and beautiful in clusters of three at strategic points round the ground floor on to the terrace.

' "Later on you won't see it so clearly from here," Georges was saying. "We'll be planting a screen of trees right at the edge of the property. It's far enough away not to spoil their view." The cabman was instructed to come back for us in an hour and Georges took on his favourite role of guide. A lot of the things he explained that afternoon were far beyond my understanding but it was a joy to watch him expounding his theories and throwing out the odd greeting to the workmen, who obviously respected him.

'The cab took us back to St Cloud. We had tea in a little café, then joined the train for St Lazare. We shook hands formally on parting at the station. We were forming the rules for this game we were playing. It was uncanny how our thoughts seemed to meet. And it stayed that way for several years.

'Lou took to staying out all night. Her ambitions were being fulfilled – she was well on the way to being regarded as a high-class courtesan and that had always been her dearest wish. I would have felt desperately lonely had I not had the thrill of meeting Georges to look forward to. Loyalty to Madame Wallach made me keep up my work for the convent. Mothers of some of the wealthy pupils were now asking me to design clothes and hats for them. I still toyed with the idea of buying a hat shop but a tentative investigation into the prices and legal arrangements had rather scared me. Weeks, months, years drifted by and though I had always had the dread at the back of my mind of the time when Alain's grave would be given up, it seemed to loom nearer all of a sudden. When I was with Georges I did not mention this because I knew that he liked to see me smile, but my sleep was being disturbed and I started to lose weight.

'One day Georges remarked on this. "Are you feeling well, chérie?" he asked. "You seem to me to be thinner than you used to be. Are you sitting up at nights working for these nuns? Perhaps you do too much, hein? You walk a great deal to that cemetery." My resolution to keep smiling suddenly failed me and I started to pour out my tale of horror. We were sitting in our usual café at the time. Georges quickly paid off the waiter then rose and offered me his arm. "I think we should walk, Madame," he said. We headed towards the deserted part of the Champs Elysées. A keen wind was whipping my skirts and I had to hold on to my hat carefully. Georges kept patting my hand. At the end he asked a few gentle questions about the date of the funeral. "How I wish I could take away your dreadful fears, my dear Elizabeth," he said. His eyes were bright with tears of pity and it took me all my time not to throw myself into his arms. A few weeks later, I found him waiting for me in a cab outside the cemetery. He was there every day after that. Then came the morning I had dreaded. The awful smell was there again. I hurried past with my handkerchief up to my nose . . . Oh God!

'There was a gaping hole. Nothing! Just a gaping hole. My baby's bones were in the ossuary as if he were worthless. I was shattered, absolutely shattered. I started to run and kept on running through the cemetery gates and down the road though I heard someone shout. I couldn't think of anything. Then Georges was by my side, panting, and the cabman was trying to still his horse. Then Georges was handing me up, throwing directions at the driver and asking him to hurry. As we clip-clopped along Georges took me in his arms, murmuring endearments. I clung to him desperately, forgetting all propriety. After a while, he murmured that we were nearly at the restaurant and I might like to tidy myself.

'"But I don't want to eat," I said.

'"No, but you will have privacy, some brandy to warm you and then perhaps a little coffee or something." His arm was still round me and I felt him willing his strength to me. I dug out some remnants of pride and made myself look respectable. When he handed me down, I walked erect into the restaurant which was in a district I had never visited before. Georges murmured something and we were asked to follow a soft-spoken waiter upstairs. The room we were shown into was partly panelled in oak but the general impression was of a warm, rich red. The damask which covered the remaining panels of the wall was repeated in a sumptuous couch and two large armchairs. In a corner a small table was laid elegantly for a meal. It was the sight of the stove which gave me most comfort at that moment. I was experiencing a return to the intense cold that had hit me after Alain's funeral and felt I would never be warm again.

'Georges ordered brandy and hot chocolate. Then he drew one of the armchairs towards the stove, opened the firedoors and gently chafed my fingers. When the waiter returned he drew a small table towards us, laid out our cups, uncorked the brandy and quietly left. Georges crossed to the door and locked it behind him. This surprised me. Locking a door in a restaurant seemed a funny idea. Georges said, "You will not wish anyone to see you so distressed, my dear." That made sense but it still seemed funny that there should be a lock there at all.

'Georges poured some brandy into my steaming drink, then held the cup to my lips. With encouraging murmurs he managed to get quite a lot of that firewater inside me. He encouraged me to cry freely while he alternately rubbed my hands and kissed them. At last I finished sobbing. The brandy was untying the knot in my stomach. I began to think what I must look like and murmured something about it to Georges. He put his arm gently round me. "You are beautiful as ever, my dear. Let me help you to the couch."

'He took off my shoes, then started stroking my feet. I felt the warm blood rush to my face. There was something very sensual about it which made me feel bewildered and light-headed. Georges was murmuring, "How I wish I could comfort you, my little treasure." He had never put his feelings into words so plainly before. At that moment I was desperately in need of comfort. What happened next was inevitable . . . I knew it was wrong, Jessie – of course I did – but I could not control my desperate longing for love: nothing less than love taken to its utmost would satisfy me. And

Georges felt the same. It was a long time before he unlocked the door quietly then rang for the waiter. We had a meal brought up to us – I can't remember what we ate but it took a lot of discipline for me to hide my feelings when the waiter was around.

'Well, that was the start of our new relationship.'

Chapter 9

I wondered if that was to be the end of the story but Elsie was sitting quietly, watching me. 'D'you want to go on?' I asked.

'If you're not too shocked,' she said. 'It's such a relief . . .'

'I'm not a silly wee schoolgirl, Elsie,' I said. 'I've got eight bairns and the postman didna bring them.'

She chuckled then sat quietly again for a wee while before starting. 'We found it impossible to return to the restrictions which had bound us before. Georges found me a shop in a good district. The flat above it was delightfully appointed and he visited me there, always discreetly and outwardly observing the proprieties.

'Of course I felt guilty, Jessie, especially when I was with the Wallachs. I had become almost one of the family there and I knew how shocked they would be if they ever found out about Georges. My everyday life was a mixture of hard-won success in business and steady friendship with the people at the orphanage and especially Anna Wallach. I watched little Marianne grow into a lanky schoolgirl and then a lovely young woman.

'Then Paul Auclair arrived on the scene. He was a young doctor who had been a student at Albert's lectures and soon showed a special interest in Marianne. Though she was still so young and had been rather

116

sheltered as the youngest of the family, Albert and Anna could find no fault with Paul. I was a frequent dinner guest and had many opportunities of observing the two young people together. It was lovely to watch them, shy and tentative at first, then becoming more glowingly aware of each other till the most casual observer would recognize their affection.

'There was one fly in the ointment, however. Paul was the only child of rather elderly parents who owned a prosperous vineyard in the Bordeaux area. It had been inherited by Madame Auclair from her mother. Madame Auclair . . . well, sister Jean would say she had a guid conceit o' hersel'. She had been born in that château as had her mother before her and she certainly let people know about it.

'It seemed nearly all the villagers worked for the Auclair family and no one dared cross her. That is, no one but Paul. When he decided that he wished to be a doctor, his mother had done all she could to dissuade him: what did he want with a job when the vineyards were there for him to take over – vineyards that had been in her family for two hundred years? How many young men were given the start in life that he had?

'Paul had listened patiently to her tirades which really affected him less than his father's silent disappointment. Then his father died suddenly. Madame Auclair was sure that now Paul would see where his duty lay. The young fellow returned from the funeral looking a wreck. He was not long in seeking out Albert to ask for his advice.

'"You still feel you wish to be a doctor . . . it is the only thing that will satisfy you?" Albert asked, knowing well the answer. "And you say that there is a well-trained staff quite capable of running the estate?"

' "Many of them have worked in our vineyards for more than forty years," said Paul.

' "I can understand your parents' disappointment," said Albert. "After all, none of *our* sons has chosen a career in medicine, but neither Madame Wallach nor I would think of trying to influence them in that matter. Each man must choose and, having chosen, give of his best. I think you will do that. In time, your mother will grow used to the idea."

'Paul was delighted to have his own wishes endorsed by Albert. After that his visits to their home became more frequent. Anna confided in me that Albert hoped to take Paul on as his assistant. "He is specially interested in paediatrics and Albert will be delighted to help him progress," she said.

'It wasn't long before the young couple begged to be allowed to marry. "What could we say?" Anna asked me. "We were very young ourselves and so much in love. We have no regrets." I must confess, Jessie, that for a moment I felt a sharp pang of jealousy. My leap in the dark into matrimony had resulted in disaster and a dead baby. Though I had won through to a consuming happiness with Georges, I had never had any right to display that happiness.

'But I threw myself into the wedding preparations – almost the way I did for our Meg – remember? Marianne took it for granted that Tante Elise would design her wedding dress and it really was a delight. Marianne had been one of my favourite pupils at the convent – keen and skilful but always ready to laugh at herself when things went wrong. During those discussions over the dress I learned quite a few things about the newly grown-up Marianne. For one thing, she was terrified of her future mother-in-law. "Don't tell Maman," she said, "or it will upset her. I'll just have to get used to it. Poor Paul, he hates to see her treat me so coldly. I have to make light of it for his sake."

'"I'd like to tell that old lady a thing or two," I said. "It's a pity she doesn't live nearer."

'"Paul's upset because she says she won't come to our wedding," Marianne continued. "I know how he feels, but in a way I'm quite glad. Maman thinks it's an insult to Papa – after all, he *is* the most famous paediatrician in Paris."

'"Not just that," I said. "I'm sure there isn't a finer man in Paris." She hugged me then. "Oh, Tante Elsie, you are such a comfort."

'"Well," I said, "if the old witch turns up breathing fire and brimstone, just send for me."

'"I'll remember," said Marianne, laughing.'

Elsie stopped for a sip of water before continuing. I had noticed her voice becoming hoarse but she seemed happy to go on.

'It was the day before the wedding. I was giving Lou instructions about one rather difficult client who would be calling for her hat that morning. The phone rang. Lou answered it. "It's Marianne," she said. "Sounds in a stew."

'The girl's voice was high as she babbled, "Nothing pleases her and she has upset Maman; brought her maid too, even though she said she wouldn't be coming. If Papa comes home – he is lecturing today – and finds she has upset Maman, he will be angry. You have never seen Papa angry. He admires you so much; but he can be dreadfully angry at times if he thinks someone is being unfair. Poor Paul will suffer all the more if Papa tells Madame what he thinks of her behaviour."

'"Calm down," I said. "Go back to the salon and smile sweetly. You are Paul's bride tomorrow, remember. She is a twisted jealous old lady but I shall handle her. Lou will fetch me a cab and I shall be with you soon."

'Lou had turned towards the stairs when she heard me talk about the cab. "Just a moment," I said. "Help me into my new green dress."

'Lou gave a little whistle when she fastened the last hook and I ran my fingers down some folds. "That should silence her," she said, adding a word or two that I pretended not to understand. That sent her off chuckling. I rearranged my coiffure to suit the new green creation which I would be wearing for the first time. Not even Lou had seen it.

'"Oh, Elise," she gasped, when I descended the stairs, "you are *formidable*." Lou can be such a comfort.

'My confidence was at its peak when I was shown into the Wallach drawing-room. Anna was looking quite fraught and leaned against me as I embraced her warmly. Then I was introduced to Madame Auclair. The thin gnarled hands barely touched mine as she muttered her response. Then her nostrils flared angrily as she turned to Anna again. "I would have thought, Madame, that the day before the wedding would have been reserved for the family." Anna gasped at her rudeness. It was the sweet little bride whom I had cautioned to stay calm who rounded on her future mother-in-law. "Tante Elise is my favourite aunt and the most famous milliner in Paris. She has designed my wedding dress." She didn't say, "So there", but it hung in the air. I summoned all my cunning. A lot depended on the next few minutes.

'"I have heard of your beautiful château, Madame," I said. "My late husband was particularly interested in the very old ones. What age is yours exactly?" She muttered a figure I could not make out, but I smiled and nodded appreciatively. "And it has been in your family, I believe, all that time." Her answer came reluctantly. I gathered that it had been in another branch of the family originally but had crossed to hers over two hundred years before.

'"It must be a wrench to leave the beautiful countryside to come all this way to the noisy city," I went on. She gave no reply. "These long journeys can be so exhausting. They *do* fret the spirits and make one feel cross."

'She looked at me sharply then. I saw her raise herself a little in her seat. I went on. "I do hope you will have recovered by tomorrow. You will have the most beautiful bride in Paris for your daughter-in-law. I have had only my best workers engaged on the dress. Of course, it is supposed to be kept secret till we see our lovely Marianne in church but I am sure that you, as the most honoured guest, would love to have a little preview and I shall explain all my ideas about the detail . . ." I was offering her my arm as I spoke. She would be sure to notice my expensive perfume. She gave her head a little shake and then we were off. I burbled on, "Because of Marianne's lovely brown eyes I chose ivory silk rather than pure white; and then I imposed the soft gleam of pearls – so rich, I always think, don't you? They gleam against the gold thread of the embroidered leaves; you shall see!"

'I talked all the way up the stairs and gradually she

came to. I couldn't say she was sweetness and light exactly but she *did* become more manageable and we got her through the wedding day without any disasters. Marianne was the vision of loveliness I had planned. Both Albert and Anna had tears in their eyes when they saw her walk towards them. Yes, I think I can pat myself on the back for that one, Jessie.

'After the wedding I didn't see very much of the Wallach family for some time. Anna and Albert went off on a round of family visits and, of course, the young couple were absorbed in themselves. My reputation as a milliner was building up. The much-reported wedding had not done that any harm. Many of Marianne's friends had been directed towards me for that important final touch to their wedding outfits.

'Marianne and Paul were living in a small house in the Auteuil district. The beauty of it was that it had a little garden. In due course I was designing a christening robe for Annette. She was followed eighteen months later by Marthe. I couldn't help contrasting the happy prosperous life that these two young people enjoyed with the horror that had been my lot. I yearned for the beauty of young love that would never be mine. In some ways, Jessie, I think I have never fully grown up in spite of all my experience. On my visits I was always greeted warmly and invited to cuddle a baby if I wished. But even that, though comforting in its way, gave me a pang. I longed for Alain.

'Before very long, Lou joined me in the business. At first it was her modelling ability I found valuable. My prices were high, and an elegant model plus the exclusive tag that I had won encouraged people to pay them. Soon I found that her peasant shrewdness had developed into a keen business acumen. She knew about Georges' visits but, of course, could see nothing to disapprove of in them. Lou and I had formed a bond that could not easily be broken. We were both prospering and life ran very smoothly, though our approach to love was so different.

'One night when Georges arrived I noticed a mischievous smile playing round his lips. He was longing to tell me something, I could see. I decided not to spoil his pleasure by asking questions but waited calmly till our dinner was over and we were sharing the comfortable sofa.

'"I have a surprise for you, my darling Elizabeth," he began. "You won't let me buy you jewellery but I think you will accept this gift. You see, I intend to share it with you." The sort of discretion we practised would seem to rule out anything I could think of in the sharing line. I looked at him, puzzled.

'"I got the idea that night you showed me your husband's sketchbook. Remember how you told me that you had read up the history of all those châteaux and I said it was sad that you hadn't seen any of them? Well, a client of mine had asked me to look out for a holiday home for him – somewhere quiet and sheltered, he said. The Dordogne seemed a likely area so I made several trips there. It didn't take long to find the sort of property he was looking for – he was prepared to cough up quite a considerable sum – but while I was there I looked for something else and found it. Are you going to ask me what?"

'I paused for a moment to tease him and said, "Should I?"

'"Oh, my dear Elizabeth, I hope you will like it." He began to look rather anxious so I gave in and asked, "What is it?"

123

' "I've made a little sketch, chérie, here it is. It is yours. I have bought it in your name. You will have to sign some papers, of course, but I give it you with all my love for the happiness you have brought me these last years."

'As he spoke Georges was smoothing out a sheet of thick paper and offering it to me. I gazed at the drawing of a little cottage, almost smothered in roses. The steep tiled roof was divided by three dormer windows. It was like something out of a child's story book . . . enchanting. I longed to step inside.

' "But I cannot allow you to give me an expensive gift like this, Georges," I protested.

'He shook his head, ruefully. "My dear Elizabeth, I know that it is not the custom in your country for a well brought up girl to accept expensive gifts from a man who is not her husband or fiancé. You have explained. I admire that strictness in a way. But, this is France. We see things differently. You have given me such joy. We could have more. Don't you find it irksome to have to be so discreet all the time? When we visit this tiny little lovenest, there will be no one who knows us. Think of it, my darling. I have thought of nothing else since I bought it. We will have a little kingdom all to ourselves. The garden is overgrown – so much the better. We will make love there – ah, you blush so prettily!" He had taken my coffee cup and laid it aside and his arms were enfolding me, his lips drowning my protests. The truth is that I *had* been finding our restraint in public a bit of a strain though I had been punctilious in observing it for both our sakes. The cottage did seem like paradise.

' "You will see those castles which you have studied in books," he went on. "I shall be your guide. It will be a delight to me and we will love and love and love in our little cottage with the bees humming among the flowers. Please, please, my darling, accept my gift and the gratitude that goes with it."

'He was fondling me. I imagined that garden and the scent of the flowers. It took me back for a moment to Kilbarchan. I remembered how the flower scents there would send me into a daydream of longing for a handsome hero . . . Georges was that handsome hero. He was offering to make me Queen in our own kingdom – a small one, certainly, but a kingdom where we could be free of restrictions and let our passions have full sway. I agreed to go with him for a few days as soon as I could arrange things with Lou. Though we had a well-trained staff by that time, I still felt happier when I knew that she was in command.

'Despite his delirious happiness at my acceptance, Georges still planned our journey carefully to avoid suspicion. We would be on the same train but we would not travel together. When we alighted Georges would make sure that no one who knew him was around before he joined me. "Once that bit is over," he said, "we shall simply get a coach to our own little lovenest. Oh, my darling, how I am longing . . ." The rest of that evening was spent in dreaming of delights to come while Georges, sensing my joy, took his share in full measure, tearing himself away reluctantly just before midnight.

'I was still in a dream of delight in the morning. I found myself stroking my body as I remembered Georges' hands . . . Lou noticed. "Ah-hah, my cool English lady, you were not so cool last night, I think!" Then she laughed heartily at my blushes. "Me! I have forgotten how to blush, chère Elise." She went off into fits of laughter again. Of course I told her about Georges' gift. She fully approved.

'"I have always said you are foolish to refuse his offerings. A man feels important when he gives you expensive gifts. That is good for him. And besides," she said, her peasant shrewdness showing through, "when he leaves you, you will have something worthwhile – not just pretty speeches and worn sheets. Ah, you are shocked again!" She was off in more gales of laughter.

'I spent that day in a dream, planning my wardrobe. In our lovenest we could relax but I would relax prettily. For the journey I would be elegant but comfortable, as befitted the wife of a man like Georges. For the first time I felt I could afford to pretend that was the true position. I dug out Michel's sketchbook and tried to decide which château we would visit first. I had often wished to see them and now the best of all possible solutions to that problem was near. Georges would be a willing and competent guide. And after each visit we would return to our darling little cottage *"et demeure . . . et demeure . . . et demeure . . ."* That was the end of a little verse I saw once on a sundial. Isn't it lovely, Jessie? Suggests bees humming quietly – *"et demeure . . . et demeure . . . et demeure."*

'Those first few days in the Dordogne were the honeymoon of my dreams. Georges adored me with his eyes and I responded eagerly to his caresses. Sometimes when we lay replete under a shady tree in our little garden I would see a tear trickle down his face. He had murmured once, "This has been denied me, my darling. I have never known such joy. Indeed I had given up all hope of ever knowing it. My little Marie-Isabelle was the only compensation." He never blamed Marguerite, and I was glad of that. It would have lessened my respect for him. I think, too, he realized as I did that he had entered into the marriage guided a little more by his head than his heart. He had accepted the disappointment philosophically and channelled his affections towards Marie-Isabelle.

The châteaux, seen through Georges' eyes, were as fascinating as I had dreamed. I had hesitated many times over Michel's drawings without making up my mind which I would like to see first. In the end I left it to Georges to decide. He too hesitated for a little. "Well, the entrance to Domme is certainly stunning but I think we shall visit Hautefort first."

'"That one has a long history," I said.

'"Certainly, but that is not my reason for choosing it first. It is the wonderful view we will have long before we reach it. We will come out of a wooded stretch on a hill to find ourselves looking at this dream of a château perched proudly on a rise across the shimmering valley. Your husband has captured it beautifully."

'I didn't know whether to laugh or cry. Georges was paying Michel a compliment. He expected me to feel gratified and in a funny way, I did. I wondered what he would have thought if he had known the details of my life with Michel. When Georges met me I was completely engrossed in my baby's death. So, I suppose he did not like to ask questions about my dead husband. My information, even as our intimacy progressed, had been sketchy: I had met Michel when he was visiting my friend, Mrs Nisbet-Brown; she had wanted him to paint my portrait; my family would have disapproved of any alliance so we had eloped. I implied that pride had kept us apart. It suited me to

127

leave him under a false impression of my background. Perhaps that tells something of my relationship with Georges. Neither of us was being honest. He was cheating his wife. I was cheating . . . I don't know . . . it's difficult to say.

'Georges noticed my distraction. "You are tired, my love. Let us rest. I shall tell you about each castle as we travel there."

'Since our visits to the Dordogne had to be of short duration, Georges decided that we would visit one castle on each occasion. I was in a dream of love and love-making and happily agreed. I suppose all our sight-seeing trips were memorable in one way or another but a first venture tends to have most impact. We had held hands in silent contentment while the horse trotted along the winding roads. But though Georges had prepared me for the view that would greet us when we emerged from the woods, I still gasped in wonder.

'Georges was smiling delightedly. "I knew you would not be disappointed, chérie. Now, I shall tell you about the castle. You knew that it has a very long history. Yes, that is true but it has been out of the hands of the historic family for some time now. When I last visited it one of the locals declared that it was now in the hands of parvenues. His grandfather worked for the 'real' family. Of course there's nobody more fussy about social distinctions than your ancient retainer. The château is built on the site of an ancient fortress, of course. Many of them are."

'"They would see the enemy coming in the old days," I volunteered.

'"Yes, and get time to warn the local people who would throng into the fortress for shelter, taking what animals they could with them. They would have their own well, of course. A pure water supply was essential in a long siege. There would be a sizeable grain store and an even more sizeable ammunition store. The contents of that altered over the centuries . . ."

'I watched Georges' animated face, his expressive hands which were helping shape the scene for me. What a pity he had no son to wonder at all these war preparations, to ask the questions a boy would be bound to ask. "The first château," Georges was saying, "was built on the site of a mediaeval fortress. It was besieged by Richard the Lionheart in 1183. That siege lasted only a week. In 1630 or thereabouts the Marquis de Hautefort decided to extend it and build a 'proper' château because that one was primarily a fortress. It took nearly forty years to complete. The old retainer I spoke about told me that there is a long underground passage connecting those towers. It was an exhausting walk at times. Of course, in a siege it might be possible to keep the horses in a place like that. But just think, my love, how dreadful it must have been for people who were old and rheumatic. Away from the blazing fireplaces these buildings would be freezing cold."

'I gave a shudder. Cold for me would forever be associated with my desperate struggle to keep my little Alain alive and with the bleak despair of my visits to his grave.

'"Ah, I have been describing it too well for my gentle Elizabeth," said Georges, tucking my arm fondly in his.

'That was our first château visit. I looked forward eagerly to each one and was never disappointed. Everything was a wonder to me, the rolling countryside and the wide peaceful rivers. The wildflowers too were different from those I had known at home. It was only then that I realized I had missed the country. Paris with all its wonders had satisfied me for a long time, but now I looked eagerly forward to each visit to my beloved Dordogne.

'There came the day when we had almost exhausted our list. "That is the last of the châteaux in this vicinity," said Georges, "but next time you will not be disappointed because we shall visit the village of Rocamadour. See! your husband has coloured it. In the sunshine that village positively sings with colour. We shall leave our little cottage early to give us plenty of time to climb the steep roads and lanes. It clings to the hillside, you see. Everything grows so well and the colours . . . well, you don't have to be an artist to appreciate those colours. That is for next time; back to Paris tomorrow and now, the best part of our day, my darling, we return to our little cottage . . . just you and me and the quiet night with the scent of the flowers . . ."

'We returned to our little cottage. I didn't know it was going to be the last time – the end of a long, happy dream. Georges' love had been the driving force of my life. All the work and the other duties had been coloured by it. In his arms I knew delirious happiness, the magic I had been searching for all through my girlhood and, after the Michel fiasco, had never expected to find.

'Now I come to the really difficult bit. One night when Georges arrived at the flat I could see he looked different. After fifteen years, I had got to know him as well as any wife possibly could. First of all, he asked for some brandy.

'"Are you ill?" I asked.

'"No . . . not ill," he said and stopped.

'I waited for a long time while he sipped the brandy and said nothing. His eyes were dead, staring in front of him. There was a pause which seemed to go on for ever, then he cleared his throat.

'"Marie-Isabelle came to me today. She begged me to give you up."

'"But how did she know about us?" I asked, shocked.

'"I expect her mother told her," he said numbly.

'"D'you mean to say she knows?" I was flabbergasted.

'"She's known for a long time. There's always someone who sees you. Marguerite didn't mind. She heard that you were a lady and would be discreet." He went on without realizing what a blow he had dealt me. "Marie-Isabelle wants to get married. The uncle of the young man is a bishop. Word has filtered through and he does not approve of the alliance. Marguerite thinks the young fellow very suitable and Marie-Isabelle is hopelessly in love . . . she begged me. Oh, my dear Elizabeth, what can we do? I can refuse that child nothing but I shall be desolated without you." He started heaving with dry sobs. I stared, sharing his despair but unable to offer him any comfort. I knew that this break would be final – it would have to be. My pride was shattered to learn that our relationship had been observed, assessed and accepted by Marguerite. I felt cheapened. All these years I had considered myself Georges' *real* love, his wife in all but title. But in the eyes of the world which he inhabited I was his mistress, a kept woman.

'My joy had not been built on a sure foundation; that joy which had filled my heart, my mind, my body and my soul. It had been specious. Suddenly I wanted rid of him. With a dry mouth I pointed out that there was no use in delay, assured him I understood all about the lease of the shop and flat and practically shooed him out.'

Elsie had been crying during the last bit of her story and I found it difficult to make out the words. I wondered if I should insist on her having a rest – I was beginning to feel worn-out myself – but she seemed to want to go on.

'For a long time I seemed to feel nothing,' she said. 'Then a dreadful tiredness came over me. All I wanted was to pull the blankets over my head. I bathed automatically and put myself to bed though the evening was only half gone. In the morning I made myself some tea and crawled back into bed. I heard the shopgirl who always opened up the shop bustling about her duties. Important clients seldom arrived before eleven a.m. and Lou usually dashed in a few minutes before that. If I was not down in the shop when she arrived she would nip up to the flat and we'd often have a cup of coffee together while she kept a wary eye on the roadway for any likely carriages.

'That morning I was still in bed when she appeared. Lou was instant concern. "What is wrong, Elise? You have stomach-ache . . . chill?" I murmured that I was just tired, hadn't slept well. She looked dubious but assured me she could manage in the shop and would send for me if anyone important arrived. It was a relief not to have to embark on explanations. At that stage I felt I never wanted to speak of Georges again, especially to Lou, who thought he was just the perfect gentleman for her Elise; what did a sexless wife matter? She did not deserve Georges. Lou's opinions were never moderate, I fear.

'I was still in bed when the shop closed late afternoon and Lou looked really worried. Though her culinary skills had never improved, she insisted that she was going to make me a meal . . . I must eat. The omelette she produced was anything but light, but she sat on my bed till I was forced to eat it to the last forkful. She was cudgelling her brains as to what else she could give me when I found the tears start to trickle down my face.

'"You are ill. I must fetch a doctor," said Lou, alarmed.

'"No, no, a doctor can't cure *my* trouble, Lou," I muttered. After that, of course, she had to get the whole story. Her indignation knew no bounds and she started to call Georges names. I would have none of it.

'"He is just the victim of circumstance, Lou. We both are. There is nothing can be done. I am being punished for what I did to my parents all those years ago."

'Lou shook her head in amazement at that one though it was a thought which had always lain buried at the back of my mind even in my calm, happy days with Georges. It was odd how one could live with someone as I had done so contentedly with him and not understand how different his attitudes were. It had not upset him that his wife knew of our relationship. Such situations were common in his society. How different the outlook would have been in Kilbarchan! The gap between us was almost unbelievable.

'Lou was out of her depth when it came to emotional upsets. *Her* solution had always been to rant and rave for a little while then find someone else. My lethargy, which went on for several days, stumped her, though she continued to urge me to rest and assured me she could manage everything. She phoned the convent for me, too. I can't remember what excuse she made for my absence but she probably sinned her immortal soul quite happily. I think it was seeing her bewildered concern at my inactivity that finally made me pull myself together. There was bitterness mixed with my sadness. Was every dream to be snatched away from me? But the pride which helped me deal with Michel's landlady and the people in the rue de Richelieu came to my rescue again. I was determined that no one would know the disaster which had hit me. I would be the English lady who made glorious hats and who was a patroness of the orphanage.

'But it was far from easy. There was always the danger of meeting Georges. That kept me out of Notre Dame. I was haunted by the feeling that if Marguerite had known of our liaison, then probably many other people had too. Had they been sneering at me behind my back? How far did such information travel? I was pretty sure that the Wallach family knew nothing of it. During the day I could keep myself busy and pre-pare to deal with any embarrassments. It was the nights I dreaded. My body had become tuned to Georges' skilful lovemaking. It was impossible not to crave that glorious fulfilment. I writhed for hours, glad that I had the flat to myself and no one could hear my groans of despair and longing.'

Chapter 10

Elsie's voice was practically gone. I knew by the light filtering through the curtains that Sandy and the boys would soon be up and moving. In fact, I was pretty sure that I had heard a slight creak on the stairs. That meant that Beth was probably downstairs already.

'Now, Elsie,' I said, 'it's time you settled down for a wee rest. Your voice is worn out. I'll hear the rest later.'

'I'm being selfish,' she said. 'It's just so lovely to have you there beside me, Jessie.'

'Look!' I said. 'Would you like me to come in to bed beside you?' I saw by her face that she would, so I went on. 'You take the bathroom next door. Help yourself from anything you like in the cupboards . . . toothbrushes, etc. We're well stocked with spares. I'll use the bathroom on the half-landing.'

'Two bathrooms, Jessie!' she croaked.

'I married a plumber,' I reminded her.

I was not sorry to snuggle down by that time though I felt that it was unlikely that I would be able to sleep. Elsie's arms were round me. I listened to her breathing. It was slowing a little and getting deeper . . .

I woke at midday. Elsie was fast asleep. Gently I eased myself out of the bed and slipped on the clothes I had been wearing the previous day. When I reached the kitchen, Beth was there. 'Aha!' she said. 'The sleeper awakes! Dr Walker was here, but when I told him that there were two sleeping beauties upstairs he said he would come back about three o'clock. What's happening?'

I gave her an edited account of what Elsie had told me, ending with, 'Her voice was giving out so I thought it was time to call it a day.'

'D'you think she has more to tell?' asked Beth.

'Oh, yes. She seems to find it helpful to have me listening.'

'And just how much sleep have you had, little Mother?' she asked, putting a playful arm round me.

'Not enough! But it will have to do,' I said, 'if the doctor is coming at three.'

'Right! I'm in charge. Maggie's away off for some messages. She's apt to be noisy so I thought she would be better out of the way. Lunch is à la carte and the chef is willing.' My tall daughter was smiling down at me encouragingly.

'Lunch!' I said. 'I haven't had breakfast, chef.'

It was pleasant to be back in the normal surroundings of my home – the smell of cooking, the warm sun streaming in the windows and my geraniums smiling at me. I had been in another world, listening to Elsie. It was certainly fascinating, but it was nice to be home again for a little while.

'Is this going to be a Scheherezade business – a thousand and one nights?' asked Beth.

'Well, I don't know,' I said, 'she seems to want to go on but I've no idea how much more she has to say. From what I've heard already, she has lived through more than most and suffered more than most too.'

'Father's worried that she'll knock the stuffing out of you with her troubles.'

'Oh, your father!' I said.

'Aye, my father – sensible fellow, remember? Doesn't say much, but sees a lot. If I were you I'd be back in my own bed tonight.'

I had to smile. Beth had taken to bossing me – for my own good, of course. It was funny how she reminded me of my big brother at times. But I'd better change and be smart for the doctor coming. I listened at Elsie's door on the way by, but there was no sound. She had had two of her pills with the last cup of tea early in the morning and they seemed to have taken effect.

'Ah, the walking wounded!' was Dr Walker's greeting. 'Right! What's been happening?'

We were in the snug so I was able to give him a pretty full account of Elsie's doings.

'Makes our home life seem rather dull, eh?' He ventured. 'Do you think she has much more to tell?'

'That's what Beth asked, but I don't know,' I said. 'She just seems to want to keep me beside her.'

Bill Walker sat with his fingertips meeting as he did when he was trying to diagnose. 'All these things you've told me have happened some time ago. I know they could have been bubbling away below the surface but something recent must have brought them to a head. She was in a terrible state when I saw her. I know you said she had mentioned something then about doing penance. I suppose she means in Kilbarchan at the graveside or something. Worrying about that, I suppose . . . No! I still think there's something worse to come! Don't look like that now. It's not your worry. Whatever it is has happened. Your sister is here safe with you. You'll have to keep yourself as detached as possible while giving her your support. I don't want an extra patient on my hands. Now, I'd better go up and look at her.'

Elsie stirred as we entered the bedroom. She gave an enormous yawn. 'That's what I like to see,' said Doctor Walker. 'Nothing like sleep for making you feel better.'

Elsie's smile was hazy. 'Still far away?' said the doctor, taking her pulse. He watched her carefully for a few moments. 'All I can suggest is more of the same,' he said. 'A light meal when you feel like it. I'm told that your little sister is an excellent cook. She appears to be a good nurse too. I'll look in tomorrow,' he said, patting her arm gently as he turned to go.

'That sleep is doing her good,' he said as we walked downstairs. 'Of course the pills could give us a false idea of just how calm she is, but I think we're winning.' To Beth who was waiting for us he added, 'See that your mother keeps her strength up.'

I went back up to Elsie's room but she was fast asleep again. 'What about having a little seat in the garden, Mother,' Beth said. 'I'll listen for Aunt Elsie while I get on with the cooking. Father's golfing tonight so he wants something light, early.'

My favourite corner of the garden was really warm. I sat down thankfully in the deep teak chair and tucked a cushion under my head. With my eyes closed I could sniff the roses, the honeysuckle and the little pansies which were in the urns beside my chair. It was all so soothing. I woke with Sandy kissing me. 'What . . . ?' I said.

'Beth said I was to go and wake the sleeping beauty. She came out with a cup of tea a while ago and you were fast asleep. She thinks you've been in the sun long enough. You've to come and eat something with me. Come on, up you get!'

'Elsie . . .' I started.

'She woke up not long ago and Beth took her a cup of tea and a bit of sponge cake. That was all she fancied. Beth says she'll try her with some soup later.'

I smiled ruefully. Not only was I to be supplanted as cook but as nurse too. Still, I was the only one Elsie would tell her story to; I knew that!

When I next went up to her room Elsie was washed and tidied. I hesitated about asking her to begin again and then I thought how awkward it was for her if she thought I was reluctant to listen. Then I reasoned that she could always say 'no'. 'Do you feel like going on, Elsie?' I asked.

'If you can put up with me . . . ?'

'Surely. What's a sister for?'

She smiled wanly. 'I haven't been much of a sister . . .' I put my finger gently on her lips. She lay back on her pillows. 'Where had I got to, Jessie?'

'Georges had left you but you were determined that people wouldn't get a chance to laugh at you. Lou was being supportive. You were being very brave though you missed him so much.'

Elsie swallowed. 'Yes . . . I had a well-trained team of cutters and sempstresses by then so I could devote myself to the designing side but I was beginning to feel that the premises were far too small. The workrooms at the back of the shop were overflowing so that I had had to use one of the bedrooms upstairs for some of the hand-embroidery work. There was a complication. If I moved to larger premises, it was unlikely that there would be a suitable flat upstairs. I had furnished that one to my taste and for Georges' comfort. Then I began to wonder if it would not be better to be in different surroundings, away from all the associations, to make a fresh start, but where?

'I had not been near the Dordogne since Georges left. Lou had urged me to sell the cottage. "Get some money in your palm," she said. "It will take away the sting." I knew that it wouldn't – not for me – but I couldn't explain that to Lou. Nevertheless I found myself confiding in her one day when I felt my step dragging and inspiration lacking.

' "Yes, this place is too small," she said. "Let's buy that house at the corner of rue Cardinet that we always promised ourselves." I started laughing, then saw that she was serious. "Why not?" she asked. "I seldom take gentlemen home nowadays anyway, and I certainly would not disgrace you. In fact, I find the life of a businesswoman much more interesting. I use these silly men when I wish a visit to the theatre or the opera. Then they must take me to the most expensive hotel. That way I advertise our lovely designs to the people who have the money to pay our silly prices, *non*? Do you know how much money we are making, my dear Elise? We could keep this shop and use the entire flat for workrooms. The present workrooms downstairs could be divided and made into elegant intimate rooms for the clients to study our designs . . . choose . . . try for effect . . . They could bring their husbands – or better still, their protectors. *They* spend more money. We could offer them an elegant glass of champagne too, if they had enough money to make it worth our while."

'The little *piaf* who came to my rescue all these years ago is a force to be reckoned with now. Though I flatter myself that I taught her many things, all my teaching would have got us nowhere without her natural gifts.

'"If the price for the house we wish is too high, there's always that cottage in the Dordogne which is stupidly empty and eating up money for taxes. You could sell it or rent it out," she persisted.

'"Lou,"' I said, "you don't know what you are asking of me. The thought of going back there . . . where we were so happy . . ."

'She was full of contrition. "Look, my chère Elise, I shall go down there and see to everything. I shall bring the papers here for you to sign."

'"I don't think the lawyers will allow that," I said.

'"Not even when I have flirted with them? Ah, you do not think much of me . . . *non*? Come, now. You will write to those dusty old lawyers this minute. Tell them that your charming friend is coming to sell the cottage for you. If they are nice to her, who knows how much pleasure the transaction could bring . . . Ah! You laugh. That is an improvement. Now, you will brace yourself. You will not let the world see that one man can cause you so much sorrow – you who are a fine English lady, the most elegant woman in Paris and the cleverest designer. If they insist that you must sign the deeds after I have sold the cottage for you, then we will close the shop, declare a holiday and travel on to Nice with their big, fat cheque in your pocket."

'She stood over me while I wrote that letter. There was no doubt about it, I *did* feel better once I had put pen to paper. Lou's words had stirred me. They showed that I had not been so clever at hiding my grief after all. I had been neglecting my friends and had been poor company for those I had visited. I would

141

call on that proud grandmother, Anna Wallach, that afternoon and show her a bright face.

'Anna was indeed delighted to see me. "Ah, you are looking much better today, my dear," she said. "Albert and I have been worried about you. Even away back at the wedding we thought you looked a little tired, though so elegant. We felt you had made such a tremendous effort for our Marianne. Since then you seem to be working even harder, so hard that you never have time for pleasure. You have decided to change, I think." My guard slipped for an instant. "Yes, Lou has persuaded me to sell the cottage and we are going to have a holiday in Nice." The last three words came out slowly for I realized I had let the cat out of the bag. I wondered how Lou would redeem that sort of slip but no inspiration came.

'"Cottage?" she asked. I looked at her calm, honest face and the loving smile. A tissue of lies would be a poor reward for all her family's kindness to me.

'"I'm afraid you will be shocked," I started. "Perhaps we should sit down." She obeyed, looking puzzled.

'I told my story simply: my meeting with Georges when I had learned that my darling baby would be removed from his last resting place and thrown into the ossuary; Georges' kindness; his imperfect marriage; my shock at finding the grave empty; my desperate loneliness and need for comfort. The whole sorry story came out. She never said a word but I saw by the way that her hands tensed in her lap that she was fighting with her disapproval, just as you have had to do, Jessie. At the end I saw that there were tears in her eyes, but she made no move to comfort me.

' "Surely, my dear," she said, "you were not brought up to such . . . how shall I put it? . . ."

' "Disgraceful behaviour," I supplied. "No, indeed. My parents had very high standards. I have betrayed them twice over . . . running away with Michel and then associating with Georges. All I can say is that I have indeed been punished."

' "No wonder you have looked so haunted these last months . . . or is it years?" she said. "It is a pity you are not a Catholic. You could go to confession and then do penance; rid your soul of that blot which is making you so unhappy. Were your parents so set against our religion?"

' "I had never known anything about your church till I came here," I said. "There were no Catholics in my village. I had never met any. Once in Glasgow, a big city, I saw a group of nuns. I felt afraid. They looked so strange. My brother-in-law, who is a pastor, said that I should not be afraid of them; that they did very good work among the poor."

' "Indeed. You have seen our sisters at the orphanage and, my dear, you have done very fine work there yourself. We are all aware of that. I won't deny that your story has shocked me. Your life has taken many strange and sad turns. I am sure that with your courage you will be able to turn these dreadful experiences into something good. I wish I were cleverer and could advise you, but it may be that simply telling me has rid your soul of a little of its load. Albert said one day that he thought it was soul sickness you were suffering from. Of course, we thought it was still your earlier troubles that were haunting you. Now!" she said, her voice brightening, "let's have some tea, shall we?"

'I knew that she would be bound to tell Albert and

I felt a pang. I remembered Marianne's words, "He admires you so much." If there was one man whose good esteem I valued it was Albert Wallach.

'I wondered if their behaviour towards me would alter now that they knew my secret. It did, but not in the way I had expected. Within a few days of returning from Nice I received a phone call inviting me to a party at the Wallach's house. "Paul is joining Albert here in his practice and we are celebrating," Anna said. "We have decided, Albert and I, that we shall go out more now that Albert is shedding part of his load. A few of Albert's colleagues will be joining us. I'm sure you will find some of them interesting."

'My first feeling was one of relief that the Wallach family had not written me off. Then I began to wonder what I would wear for this happy occasion, the first for many weeks. My bedroom was strewn with outfits and I was humming happily when Lou looked in that evening.

'"Good!" she said. "I have my lovely Elise back, not a haunted stranger." She pointed to a rather showy dress which shimmered from blue to green in the light. "Wear that," she said. "It will make them sit up. There might be a handsome fellow among the colleagues. Remember what I said . . . there are as many fish in the sea . . ."

'In spite of myself I felt a flicker of interest. Georges had turned up out of the blue, after all. Of one thing I was sure, however: there would never be another clandestine relationship. I had burned my fingers twice; that was enough.

'Anna had excelled herself with her flower arrangements and table settings. The happy atmosphere of that home was a balm and a tonic at the same time. I

144

could never quite define it. Anna, looking more like a merry robin than ever, led me through the introductions, throwing names at me at a speed I could not follow, then with a flourish she announced, "Doctor Dommer, who will take you into dinner, my dear. You will have lots to talk about, I'm sure. His two daughters attend the convent." My partner blushed to the roots of his fair hair. Seeing his embarrassment helped me control my desire to laugh at Anna's blatant matchmaking. So this was what I was in for! Anna was going to provide me with distractions. I wondered if Albert had had any hand in it and glanced over to where he stood talking to an elderly couple. He saw me and raised his glass in my direction. "He admires you so much," Marianne had said. The thought came to me suddenly, "Oh, if only it had been Albert . . ." The thought, unfinished as it was, shocked me. This kind couple were doing their best for me in my unhappiness even though they disapproved of its cause. Quickly I turned my attention to Doctor Dommer. He must be a widower or Anna wouldn't be thrusting him at me like that. Probably he had his own share of troubles. I must see what I could do to make his evening a pleasant, unembarrassing one.

'And I believe I managed it. There was much laughter round the table once the wine got flowing. I found myself relaxing when Doctor Dommer joined in. He was forgetting to be afraid of me. I praised his little girls, who were actually very shy and uncommunicative. Catherine, my helper, had told me that they had been like that since they lost their mother. It all fitted the pattern I had guessed at from Anna's introduction. I wondered what I would do if Doctor Dommer should feel bound to invite me out to dinner or something, but he courteously handed me into my cab and that was that! Only a few days later I had a pretty invitation card from Anna.

We are making up a box for the opera and would love to have you join us. Marianne and Paul say that they would come in their cab for you so that you do not arrive alone. I do so hope you are free.
Your affectionate friend,
Anna Wallach

'That was the start of a round of socializing which I was surprised to find myself enjoying. These were well-educated, cultured people. A few of the wives might be on the frumpish side but they made a pleasant change from some of the clients I had to be civil to – spoiled, pampered pets! While my spare time had been monopolized by Georges there had never been time or opportunity for parties. We had been so self-absorbed that our conversation was limited to the things that we both loved – beautiful things . . . old châteaux . . . elegant new buildings . . . lovingly laid-out gardens and, of course, ourselves. I found now that in company I was not very well-versed in the political life of France which seemed to be a conversational topic which never flagged. I had queued up and paid my five centimes for a copy of L'Aurore to read Zola's famous article. Did you hear anything of that here, Jessie?'

'Well, I don't actually remember,' I said, 'but Beth talked about it one day. She tries to help me keep my French up – something about J'accuse wasn't it?'

'That's right. I thought that it was very well written but I had so many other things to think about that the troubles of Dreyfus didn't really mean too much to me.

Here were people arguing furiously over it. I noticed that Albert didn't seem to say much. Then I recollected that he was German and Dreyfus had been accused of selling French Army information to the Germans. It was odd to think that, in a way, we were in the same boat – outsiders in this Paris that we both loved.

'I kept my ears pricked for all the information I could gather about the Dreyfus affair in case I should be asked for my opinion. It was difficult for me to feel really involved. He had been condemned – let me see – yes, 1894, I think, and imprisoned on Devil's Island. Many people thought it was unjust – the work of an anti-Jewish faction. Dreyfus was a Jew, you see. Anyway, Zola put the cat among the pigeons when he wrote *J'accuse*. He was condemned to a year in prison for slandering the army but he managed to escape to England.

'As time went on I found myself being invited not just to the parties got up by Albert and Anna but to those of their friends. It was gratifying to find that I was a social success. I began to feel the disadvantage of not being able to act as hostess myself. Why shouldn't I be a lady with a salon? The small flat was impossible. More and more I began to see the point of Lou's idea of moving to an elegant house if not in the rue Cardinet, then somewhere of similar standing. There I could give brilliant parties, return hospitality and show them what a Scotswoman could do! Only they thought of me as l'anglaise, of course, and it was too late to start disillusioning them now. While I wished to remain anonymous it had been a very useful inaccuracy.

'I often wandered out at lunchtime to look at the fashions in the stylish shops. Somehow it gave me a feel of what was needed in my designs. I prided myself by that time on being a leader of fashion, sensing what women would respond to when they were tired of a current mode. I returned from one of these lunchtime strolls to find Lou in a state of high excitement. "There has been a phone call," she said – "Pierre Lyon. He would like to speak to you. I looked at your engagements and saw you were free. He is coming at four o'clock."

'"What can Pierre Lyon want with us?" I asked. "His stuff is cheap and nasty."

'"Yes, but it sells well," Lou said. "He's reckoned to be worth a fortune. It won't do any harm to speak to him. I'm dying to know what he wants. There was something else I was going to tell you but I think I'll leave it till you have dealt with the Beau Pierre." She rolled her eyes in an alarming fashion.

'"I think you had better sit in on this meeting," I said. "Somehow I have the feeling that two minds will be better than one."

'"What if he doesn't want me butting in?" asked Lou.

'"He can lump it," I said loftily. "You are my co-director, after all. I take no major decisions without you."

'She threw her arms round me. "Ah, my darling Elise. You are so noble. You treat me like a fine English lady."'

'We hustled around getting everything perfect for the "Beau Pierre", as Lou kept calling him. We were both looking rather elegant if somewhat flushed when Monsieur Lyon was ushered in. I had tried to imagine what he would look like, this successful manufacturer of cheap clothes, but nothing had prepared me for the

148

ultra-slim dandy who minced into my little drawing-room. I was at a loss for a second or two, then Lou piped up, "I expect you know Madame Blanchard."

'"Certainly," he said taking my hand. "I have admired you from afar at the opera, my dear Madame."

'"Indeed," I said. "I should like you to meet Mademoiselle Croquelois, my partner in this business."

'"Oh!" he said. Then muttered the usual greetings. "I had not realized that you had a partner."

'I ushered him to a seat then waited, outwardly calm but wondering what in Heaven's name he had come about.

'"Madame Blanchard," he began in rather a high voice, "I have admired your designs and exquisite workmanship for a long time. As you may know, I have been functioning in a different market – success-fully, I may say. At the moment – this is confidential, please, I am considering buying a very large shop in an excellent quarter. No one knows, as yet, that it is for sale. I have an idea which I would like you to con-sider. It involves a large outlay of capital on my part but I am prepared for that. Before long, I think we might both benefit greatly." He paused while I frantic-ally tried to work out all the possible implications of his preamble. There was silence. I raised my eyebrows and he started again.

'"I would still have my inexpensive clothes for sale on the lower floors but what I would like to do is to branch into a much better-class market. There are many women who would like to have good tasteful clothes but cannot afford the exclusive tag and the inevitable high prices which go with it. What I would like you to do is to join me in this business venture. On an upper floor there would be a large department where the clothes were designed by you but made up in numbers – not great numbers – perhaps you could work out simple variations which would not necessitate much adjustment in the machine room. These clothes would still be rather expensive, of course, but not up to the price of the exclusive ones. We could also have a separate department laid out very sumptuously where you could have your custom-made clothes and millinery. You would have a sizeable office and designer room on the top floor. That is the rough idea. Are you interested, Madame, Mademoiselle?"

'I could not think of a thing to say, Jessie. It was the little country girl – turned model – turned actress – turned courtesan – turned businesswoman who spoke first. "We would naturally have to know the financial arrangements before we discussed anything else, Monsieur."

'After that we talked and talked. I vaguely heard my shopgirls locking up. Then Pierre Lyon took out his watch.

'"Mesdames, the time has flown. Could I engage to take you out to dinner, perhaps, so that we may further discuss this affair?"

'Lou had risen. "I regret that I am already engaged for tonight, Monsieur." She drifted round behind his seat.

'He looked at me, "And you, Madame. Would you honour me?" Lou gave me a quick nod.

'"Thank you, Monsieur, I shall be very happy," I said.'

Chapter 11

'"Now what are you up to?" I asked her when we had ushered Pierre Lyon out. "I didn't particularly want to have dinner with a stranger. It could start all sorts of gossip."

'Lou laughed hilariously. "My dear Elise, there will be no gossip. I would swear by the Virgin that he is *tapette*."

'"What do you mean, '*tapette*'?" I asked.

'"You did not see?" She minced across the floor in a good imitation of Monsieur Lyon. "The narrow hips, the high voice . . . ? My dear Elise!"

'I certainly didn't. "He has a funny walk and a not very musical voice but why do you call him a carpet-beater?" I was completely at sea.

'"That is what we call one of *them*," she said.

'"What do you mean, 'one of *them*'?"

'Lou sat down. "Really, Elise. You are being slow. When you invite our dear Pierre to your home, you do not look out for your pretty little sister; you look out for your handsome brother! Now do you understand me?"

'I didn't. Lou stared at me. "Are you teasing me, my clever anglaise? You cannot really be so . . . so . . . You have not been in a convent all your life. No, you must be teasing me!"

'"For pity's sake, Lou," I said. "I've no idea what you are talking about."

'Lou lay back in her chair and laughed till the tears ran down her face. "I would not have believed it," she gasped more than once. Then in a few graphic sentences she gave me some information my education had not prepared me for. "Oh, if you could see your face, Elise," she chortled.

'"I'm not going to dinner with him after that," I said.

'"Oh, yes you will," she said. "He will behave perfectly. You are in no danger." Again she exploded into laughter. "It sounds like a marvellous business opportunity to me. He is filthy rich – must be, with all those factories. We'll have that house on the corner of rue Cardinet. Oh, I forgot to tell you with all this – there is actually one for sale, not on the corner but near. The legal gentleman I shall be entertaining tonight told me about it. With your permission I shall mention the possibilities our dear Pierre has put forward. I shall get free advice, you see. There is one thing I do not doubt, Elise: I can handle men."

'"I don't doubt it either," I said with a weary sigh.

'"Come now, my beautiful anglaise. It is time for you to dress up to meet our benefactor. You will charm him and keep him guessing. We will make sure we get the best terms possible before we put pen to paper, yes?"

'"Shouldn't you be going home to dress?" I asked.

'"There is no hurry. My lawyer has a business meeting," she said.

'"At night?"

'"Yes, they often hold them then. Their wives think they last a long time." She chortled again.

'"Life in Kilbarchan was never like this," I muttered.

' "What do you say?"

' "Nothing. Tell me what will impress our friend to whom it will make no difference," I said.

' "There will be other people in that restaurant," she informed me. "We must always advertise. It is good business." She ran her fingers along the hangers in my wardrobe. "Here! This is right. You will not frighten him, but he will appreciate the difference between that seaming and the stuff on his rags. Do not fear. They are not dangerous, these men. In fact, they are a little more sensitive than the others. There was one in the theatre I used to go to when Bernard was changing his mind all the time about how he wanted a scene played. Dear little Franc used to comfort me. He did not mind if I cried on his shoulder. And there were no complications. Now, tell yourself that tonight, Elise! There will be no complications. I'm sure you have had enough of them."

'There was some truth in that, Jessie, I had to acknowledge, as I hurried to prepare for the carriage coming. Lou's information had given me a funny feeling about this encounter, but I would have to ignore that. This deal could reshape my life, take me into a different sphere where it might be possible to forget Georges with his fascinating talk and his beautiful brown eyes; the bleak despair that clouded them as he told me of Marie-Isabelle's plea. I took a deep breath. An office with room for all my designs! Space to sketch, to try out models; it was exhilarating. And no complications. Lou had understood me pretty well when she emphasized that!

'Pierre Lyon was immaculately dressed. The restaurant was very expensive with tables well spaced. Of course, it hadn't needed Lou's parting advice for

153

me to watch that I didn't commit myself to anything till we had discussed it with a lawyer. "He hasn't made all that money," she said, "without having his wits about him." The food was delicious. I found myself relaxing and beginning to see the humour of the situation. Lou was a minx! She said things in such a crisp way that they stuck in the mind and made one want to laugh at the wrong time. I kept my eyes on his hands as he talked; finely shaped, expressive hands. "The cutting would have to be skilful, of course," he was saying. "When we are dealing in the quantities I deal in, it is important not to throw away three centimetres here and three centimetres there on a tuck. It can make a huge difference in the total amount of material. In your exclusive designs, it does not matter. That deeper tuck makes for comfort and obviates creasing. They are priced accordingly. I expect you use the off-cuts from your expensive dresses in your millinery."

'"Of course," I said.

'He nodded approvingly. "I think, Madame, we have a great deal in common." I thought back to Lou's little lesson and nearly choked. Fortunately he was tucking into his steak by that time.

'I could not fail to be fascinated by the picture he painted as the meal progressed. Repeatedly he emphasized the difference between the sort of merchandise he would be selling on the lower floors and my exclusive domain where the clients would arrive in a little gilt lift. Time flew by as I listened to his plans. When, finally, he handed me down at my door and kissed my hand I was ready for a lovely long dream session in a scented bath. There was much to think about. I hoped I could remember it all for Lou. I began to wonder what she would wheedle out of her lawyer friend. It was a good thing that no important clients were booked for the following morning. Lou and I would have plenty of time to work out our ideas.

'Pierre's factories would make the bulk orders for the things I was designing for him. Even so, I knew I would have to increase my staff, Jessie. That was a move that had been overdue for some time but I had delayed because of lack of space. Now that Lou was my partner, she was an excellent substitute for me when I was closeted with my designs. I would have to keep up the lease on the shop till the new premises were ready, of course, and there must be no interruption for my important clients. In this as in many things, people got into habits. I had quite a few who had been with me for nearly twenty years. They knew that I could disguise a thickening waist, re-fashion a favourite dress to suit a changing figure. Tact had become second nature to me, you see. My years of penury had taught me to think out each move.

'Sleep was impossible for hours that night. I was making plans, discarding them, worrying, exulting. It came to me that I had not seriously thought of turning down Pierre Lyon's offer. Yet, if Lou's lawyer "friend" advised against it, we would certainly have to reconsider. Neither of us knew anything of big business. In our little realm, prices were high and quite a lot of money changed hands but the book-keeping was relatively simple.

'I waited impatiently for Lou's arrival the following morning. "Well, what did he say?" I asked as soon as she entered the flat.

'"About what?" she asked mischievously. "Is there any coffee ready, my darling Elsie? I did not have time

155

for breakfast this morning and I was working hard last night."

'In spite of my long liaison with Georges, I still found Lou's frankness about her personal life disconcerting. At last she was settled with coffee and croissants. "Well, there are many things to consider, of course. Guillaume says that he will investigate the affairs of Pierre Lyon as far as he can. On the face of it, the retail outlets are sound but a word here and there among his business friends may unearth something worth a second look. What Guillaume suggests is that when he has anything to offer in the way of information, he will get in touch with you and you can make an appointment to visit him in his office. If you wish to see him before that – say, if Pierre is pressing for a decision – you should telephone him. One thing he does *not* want is for me to turn up at the office. His wife's brother works there too. Guillaume thinks that his wife may have her suspicions about these business meetings even though the men plan them carefully. They have a sort of code, you see. They say that they will meet at a certain place but they know that that means another place. Oh, dear, it's too early in the morning!! You know what I mean. That Guillaume makes sure he gets his money's worth!"

'"Well, I'd better be getting on with some new designs," I said. "If all goes well, we shall be needing them."

'"It's a good thing that *I* don't have to design anything right now," said Lou, yawning. "I hope nobody wants to see anything displayed today."

'Her words did not worry me in the slightest. I had seen Lou jump to attention at the merest whiff of a sale before. If a client had arrived that very moment needing advice and persuasion, Lou would have been full of encouraging smiles and gentle flattery. She had the born actress's ability to understand a character.

'Though, in a way, the indecision was worrying, I had a sudden rush of energy. The ambitious dreams of my childhood were taking a slightly different form. I was determined that nothing Pierre suggested would be allowed to undermine my reputation for being exclusive. That was what appealed to my clients most and there was always a danger that any suggestion of copying a design for the cheaper factory goods would drive them away. However, he had seemed to understand that and be as anxious as I was to maintain it. I realized that he had a breadth of vision in his work. He wanted money, yes! But he was prepared to get out of the usual rut and patiently build an unusual empire. And I would be Queen of that empire. That sounds vain, but it was true. He was going to build on the reputation I had painstakingly built up and, without it, his new venture would have no credence.

'I set to with a will and soon had a sizeable portfolio of designs. It was important to have a reserve now and also more made-up models for Lou to display. Sometimes I didn't know whether to laugh or cry when I saw Lou with her perfect willowy figure glide along the salon inspiring a rather dumpy woman to think that she would charm all comers in a similar outfit.

'We began seriously to consider the house on the rue Cardinet. When I gave up the lease on the shop my flat would be gone anyway and though I knew that Lou would be happy to put me up temporarily, the urge to feel secure was there. But the house now on the market would have to be bought long before we had any of the enhanced profit from Pierre's enterprise and, perhaps, before we had even accepted his offer. Lou was as determined as I was that every possible precaution would be taken for us on that score by her friend, Guillaume.

'"What if you fall out with Guillaume before this thing goes through?" I asked one day.

'"I am not stupid, Elise. Till the deal goes through I am the most exciting lover for a brilliant, handsome, clever man . . ." She coloured each word as she rolled her eyes. "The day after – pouff!"

'I had another reason for wishing to acquire the house on rue Cardinet. All these parties I had enjoyed since the end of my affair with Georges had been given by other people. I had tried to reciprocate by inviting people to a hotel once or twice but it did not have the right feeling, somehow. With a house in rue Cardinet I could be a lady with a salon. It was something I knew I could do well – like Lou and her man-management! I sometimes wondered if Lou ever thought of the difference Pierre's arrival would make to her role in our business. When I found out how quickly she picked up marketing ideas, I had been happy to leave that side of things to her. She would come back triumphant from a visit to a supplier, "The old bugger wasn't going to budge but I told him there were other firms . . . He said that he had clients with much bigger orders who got the same discount as we did. I said they had nothing like the reputation for quality that we had. Didn't he want his name associated with quality? Also, some day we might decide to branch out and we certainly wouldn't be content with his miserly discount then. He wasn't very happy but we've got it!" She would flourish the papers then and say, "Let's drink the profits, Elise." Of course, she was sure that she could manage any man. That probably included a *tapette*!

'Word came via Guillaume that other people were interested in the house in rue Cardinet and we had better hurry up if we wished to be involved. "You have set your heart on it, my dear Elise?" asked Lou.

'"Well, it would be lovely – of course we haven't seen inside it yet . . . and we haven't earned any extra money towards it . . ." I hesitated.

'"We shall go and see it this afternoon," she said. "We have plenty of money in the bank. We shall see to it that it is Pierre who pays for the new premises. He has probably bought them already anyway or he wouldn't have been approaching you with all these details thought out."'

'Our outing that afternoon reminded me of a much earlier one with Lou. As we stepped into the cab I remembered that park where I had walked to keep myself and my baby warm till Lou arrived with a cab to rescue me from the clutches of Madame Boucher. How we had giggled! And it was the same Lou who had loved my frail little son throughout his brief life and had mourned with me like a sister. I owed Lou a lot. I looked at her bright face. "Isn't this exciting?" she said.

'I couldn't help sharing her excitement when I stepped into the spacious entrance hall and noted the high ceilings, the graceful archways and the good solid woodwork. As we walked from room to room I was mentally refurbishing them to my own taste. While our guide was commenting on the spacious apartments and the quality of the workmanship I caught Lou's eye on me once or twice. She said very little while we were inside but we were no sooner back in a cab than she ventured, "It's exactly what you want, isn't it? I was watching your face, particularly your eyes. I didn't say anything while that fellow was around – it doesn't pay to let them know you are too keen. Let's have it, Elise."

' "I would want to change all the decor," I said.

' "Of course! I saw you doing it. I'd love to hear your plans. But Guillaume said it was urgent. Perhaps you should make an appointment to see him tomorrow morning. He will advise you how to go about things. We must not delay. Haven't we promised ourselves this house for a long, long time?"

'That was the start of a very anxious week but finally we heard that we had won. The house was ours. We invited Anna and Albert to join us that night at a celebration dinner.

'Lou was bubbling over, of course. I couldn't help feeling how thrilled Georges would have been, hearing my plans for the house. There was always that twinge of regret no matter what I did.

' "Well! We have something wonderful to talk about tonight," said Albert. "Anna and I are dying to hear all your plans."

' "What! No *J'accuse*?" I asked.

' "You are tired of hearing of friend Zola?" said Albert.

' "Well, people get so heated . . ." I began.

' "Yes. Sometimes I have to remind myself that I am host when the Ligue de la Patrie faction are sneering at the Droits de l'Homme crew. I think the Ligue followers are biased and ridiculous, but I have to be very careful or they remind me that I am not French – as if I would support Dreyfus simply because I am German."

'"You could remind them how many French children you have helped," I said.

'Anna broke in then. "You weren't at the Duparc dinner last week, Elise. You should have heard my careful husband then. Alfred Moreau and his wife were there. I think you may have met them though they are not on our list and we certainly will never be on theirs!"

'"Cheers!" said Albert.

'"Oh he is naughty," said Anna, smiling fondly at the sinner. "Well, Monsieur Moreau was on his hobby horse. We got a long tirade and he ended up with, 'And if there's money in it, you can be sure the Jews are there.' That man of mine jumped on him right away; told him that some of the finest doctors he knew were Jews and he's never heard one of them demand to know a patient's race or creed before he decided to cure him. I can tell you, Elise, I didn't dare look at my hostess."

'Jessie, you should have seen the four of us. Lou was sitting there applauding Albert like mad – we'd had a few drinks by then – and Albert was bowing low with his hand over his heart. We were really daft with all the excitement. Albert pointed out that Lou was probably not the least bit interested in stories of our political friends and could we please talk about the house in rue Cardinet. Of course I was delighted to oblige.

'We lingered over that dinner for hours till Anna noticed one of the waiters yawning. Just before we left we had got on to the subject of the World Fair for which the preparations were now well under way. That was the subject that returned to my mind when I lay in bed that night. Georges would be bound to be involved, I thought, and yet I had not seen his name mentioned though I scanned the newspapers. One article had declared unequivocally that all Paris's leading architects had been commissioned. There would be considerable rivalry to see which pavilion was most successful, it added. Someone had told Lou that there were to be moving pavements. She said she took that with a pinch of salt. I was inclined to agree with her but I fell asleep dreaming that a pavement was moving, taking Georges away from me: only a few yards separated us and yet I could not reach him; I was exhausted with the effort and lay down: the pavement took me gliding on and I thought I might reach Georges eventually . . .

'I woke a few hours later with tears on my cheeks and murmuring Georges' name. That beautiful home I was about to create lacked the one person needed to make it perfect. I knew it was wrong to feel like that, but all the joy we had been expressing at that daft dinner and all the admiration I had seen in Albert's eyes and those of other men round about – I'm not being vain, Jessie; just trying to paint an accurate picture. As I say, it had all added up to make me feel such a longing to be in Georges' arms, to be caressed.

'I knew it was wrong and I knew that I was condemned to live without that joy for the rest of my days.'

Chapter 12

While Elsie was mopping her eyes I thought I heard Beth's step on the stair. She was walking slowly. That probably meant she was carrying a tray. 'Quick!' I said. 'I think Beth is bringing us something to eat.'

It was amazing how quickly Elsie pulled herself together while I pinned up a stray strand of her hair and straightened the bedclothes round her. My guess had been right. A few moments later Beth was singing out 'Gangway for a naval officer!' and I was opening the door for her. Suddenly I felt hungry. An enticing fragrance rose from two perfect flans with smoked haddock and cheese filling. 'I thought these would be easy to eat, Mother,' Beth said.

'Perfect!' I replied without consulting Elsie. It was time she got some nourishment inside her, I judged. After a little hesitation she *did* lift her knife and fork. I suppose I was setting an example. I hadn't known I was hungry till Beth appeared but I think my reaction to all the strain of Elsie's story was to long for something safe and pleasant. And Beth's flan was just that! It's something I can be proud of, I think, that my three elder daughters can all cook a good meal.

We were just finishing the flans when Beth appeared with two daintily decorated dishes of chocolate mousse and a pot of steaming coffee. 'Oh, doesn't that smell good?' said Elsie. Beth grinned with satisfaction. I wondered if Sandy had been the instigator of that piece of work. I remembered how when I was worried about one of the young ones not eating, he would take me aside and warn me not to say anything. Then when the food appeared Sandy would say 'Yum-Yum' or something daft like that and start eating enthusiastically with never a look near the child. Even when his own plate was cleared and the child had not started on his, Sandy would pay no attention. He would ask, 'Do I get a nice pudding now? I'm still hungry.' And I would play along with him in his daft game and say something about, 'Oh, well, you've cleared your plate. I suppose I'll have to find you something else. Big strong boys need good food.' Before very long the bairn was eating his dinner. That worked nine times out of ten.

I looked at Elsie sipping her coffee. 'Will you feel like going on, love, or are you tired?'

'I'm being awfully selfish, Jessie. You must be tired. You were awake long before me.'

'Don't you worry about me,' I said. 'What I'll do is fetch my night things and then when we're tired I'll slip into bed beside you. How's that?'

'It's such a relief, Jessie. I've been bottling things up for so long . . .'

'Aye. That's bad for you,' I said. 'The doctor thinks you'll feel a lot better when you've got it all off your chest. By the way, you needna worry about him tellin' anybody. His own wife . . . well, she's got a touch of your wee Lou about her . . . she says she knows sometimes that he knows something she would like to find out but he shuts up like a clam; says his patients must be able to trust him. She says he would make a good priest and he tells her she would be in a fix then! They're a fine couple – good fun!' I said.

'Come to think of it,' said Elsie, 'that's something I've never known with a man; a relationship that's good fun. With Michel it was tempestuous and, latterly, vile. With Georges it was all searing passion – tenderly expressed but never much fun about it; we were so intense. But if you're prepared to suffer more of my blethers, Jessie, I would just like to get the story out.'

I opened the bedroom door to call Beth but she was already on her way upstairs. After we had brushed our teeth I got into my slippers, Elsie propped her pillows to her satisfaction and started again.

'The thing I feel worst about now, Jessie, was not getting in touch with Mam; not letting any of you know that I was still alive. From this angle it seems absolutely unforgivable.

'When I was in abject poverty, of course, there was no money for a stamp or writing paper, but when I had the money from the paintings, I could have got in touch. It would have been up to the family then to decide whether they wanted to fetch me home. But Alain wasn't fit to travel. What if he had died on the way to Kilbarchan? I would have been blaming myself then just the way I blame myself now for taking him out that bitterly cold day. No, the right time would have been after Alain died. I could have explained that I wanted to be near his grave. You would all have understood that. If I'm utterly honest, I think I did not want to risk being spurned. I wanted to return home successful and prosperous, not abject.

'Now, Albert – kind soul – has admired me for the success I have attained but he has a way of putting it in perspective, a way that started me thinking. I began to wonder what I was chasing in my desire for success – power? If so, what would power do for me? I suppose what I was really looking for was compensation for the horrors I endured with Michel; for the disappointment of my disastrous marriage; had Alain lived, that would have been gradually forgotten in my plans for my son. Also, I have to confess it, my body craved a man. I suppose I had always been passionate and once my body became geared to it . . . Oh, dear! What a way to be talking to my wee sister. But you've got your nice Sandy. You can understand, I see.

'In Georges I thought I had found the answer, the security of love. But that particular house was built on sand. In many ways now I wish I had never met him. It brought nothing but disaster. Perhaps through time I'll see that there was some meaning, something to be learned; well, I suppose I would never have known anything about architecture if I hadn't met Georges. And that has added another dimension to my life. It would be a pity to live in a beautiful city like Paris and not appreciate its fine buildings to the full. Where was I?

'Yes! We bought the house, Lou and I, and had a grand celebration to hansel it. There I go again – another Scots word. There isn't an English one, is there?'

I thought for a moment. 'I suppose it's similar to the symbolic gifts we take a New Year; a wish for all sorts of blessings on the house – food, drink and fuel and the happiness of fellowship. I wonder how Dougie would have put it?'

Elsie broke in excitedly, 'Isn't that funny? I was just going to say the same thing.' We had a good laugh together but the nearest we could get to an answer was 'hold an inaugural celebration' and that still didn't quite fill the bill.

Elsie started again. 'The business deal with Pierre took some time to arrange but at last I was settled in my lovely office with its large bare windows opening on to the skyline of Paris. My regular clients were delighted to arrive by the little gilded lift and to walk on sumptuous carpets into the elegant showrooms where my creations were shown to full advantage. Lou was in her element. The little *piaf* had gone, and only reappeared now and again in the small drawing-room of our own fine house where we put our feet up after an exhausting evening's entertaining. While our maids cleared up the public rooms, Lou would give me a fine imitation of some of our guests. I couldn't help laughing even when her efforts bordered on the unkind.

'Not only did we achieve a fair amount of immediate success in the mass-market clothes but I found my private clientele steadily increasing. Now that I had no longer to worry if we had bitten off more than we could chew, ideas flowed freely and I approached my drawing board with joy. There I could shut out Georges completely. Remember how sister Jean's cure for any trouble was work, work, work?'

'I remember, ' I said ruefully.

'Well, Jessie, the social evenings continued. At dinner parties I still had to listen to a lot about the Dreyfus affair, but by that time I had to avoid Albert and Anna's eyes or we would all have betrayed our amusement as we remembered Albert's social trespass. When the talk turned to the World Fair and the marvellous buildings that were taking shape round the Tour Eiffel it was a different matter. I longed and yet dreaded to hear Georges' name but it never came up. Albert and Anna, relieved of family responsibilities, indulged their love of opera and theatre to the full. At first I had dreaded bumping into Georges but as time went on and our paths never seemed to cross, the fear gradually diminished.

'So, I was off my guard as I walked on Albert's arm during the interval parade one night, behind Anna and her principal male guest. They turned a corner and we followed, talking enthusiastically about the performance and came face to face with Georges and his wife. We both coloured with the shock, then bowed stiffly. It was all over in a few seconds but not before I had seen the naked misery on his face and caught the sudden suspicious glance his wife threw at me and then Albert. I was stunned. My step faltered and Albert steadied me. "Something is wrong, Elise?" he asked. I looked up at him, unable to speak. "I think I understand," he said. "Now, you will remember that you are here to enjoy yourself. You are among friends."

'My instinct was to make for home and hide, but Albert's words helped me to walk on and even to smile to other acquaintances. When we returned to our box after the interval I heard him murmur softly in German to Anna. She glanced at me and then said, "I think Albert would have more room for his long legs if he sat beside you, Elise. If the gentlemen could rearrange the seats . . ." In no time we were settled down again. Albert did not draw any attention to me – his reassuring presence was all I needed at that moment and he knew it. I was filled with gratitude for Anna's thoughtfulness.

'I paid little attention to the music as I gathered my scattered thoughts. My first meeting with Georges would have been a shock anyway but seeing Marguerite made it more so. Georges' description of her delicate health had somehow made me think of a slightly built, frail woman with a pale face. On the contrary, Marguerite was short and podgy and her complexion could only be described as florid. She had what I have always thought of as an "I want" face with deep lines on either side of her nose. Her cheeks and chin wobbled slightly as she jerked along. This was the wife of Georges who loved elegant smooth lines and beautiful proportions. He had paid for his youthful ambitions with a vengeance. Marguerite's glance of suspicion towards me had changed to one of envy when she saw Albert. For one brief moment I wished that she had something to be envious about, then chided myself, remembering Anna's kindness.'

'Once I had overcome the shock of Lou's revelations about Pierre I found his company very interesting. His appreciation of my work at first surprised me. I had assumed that because he sold cheap stuff, he would be blind to the finer points, but that was far, far from the truth. I sensed that, like Lou, he had had little in the way of advantages. The way to money and power had seemed to lie in bulk sales, so he had made for that market. He was sensitive, however, to fashion and to women's reactions.

'Now and again he called at our little kingdom on the top floor, always immaculately dressed. At first I had rather resented this intrusion but had to tell myself that it was his money that was giving me the chance to exploit my talents to the full. Then I gradually found myself discussing things more and more with him. There was a lot in what Lou had said – "no

169

complications". I could talk freely on a subject which interested us both. The success which was now evident was balm to my pride. My feelings for Georges were now of pity rather than longing.

'But there was one area where I was still lost and vulnerable. Whenever I heard a baby cry I thought of Alain. As I cradled Marianne's lovely children in my arms I remembered all the times I had done the same for my own frail little son. During the night I was sometimes haunted by the memory of that morning when I had found his grave empty. I still visited St Ouen to put flowers at the ossuary but it was in the convent chapel that I felt nearest to him. I had never given up on my work there. Somehow it was a debt of honour I owed. The calm faces of the nuns used to break into gentle smiles when I appeared. After the blows I had suffered to my self-esteem over Georges, their constancy was balm. Gradually I found myself visiting their chapel more and more often. I would kneel at the chipped feet of the Virgin and sink into a soft stupor while I prayed for my little boy and asked Her to help me forget Georges. That would certainly have shocked you lot at home. I know that the Good Book says, "Under whom there is none to whom thou shalt pray," but I wasn't praying to the statue, I knew it was just meant for remembrance. I felt *She* had lost her son, too, and would understand. I was sure my family would have some theological objection to that, but it was just the way I felt at the time, Jessie. In my desperation that little chapel with the smiling Virgin gave me some peace.

'I realized that I had been drawn to the Catholic faith for a long time, what with the nuns in Lariboisière and these nuns in the convent, Monsieur and Madame

Wallach and their obvious love for humanity. All of them had a serenity and security that I longed for, so I took instruction and became a Catholic. It has brought me great comfort, Jessie.'

'But surely you could have found comfort in your own church?' I ventured.

'That was far away, Jessie, and linked in my mind with my departure from Kilbarchan. I know this is difficult for you to understand. You see it as defection – they all will! Albert seemed to think that once you knew my whole story all these difficulties would melt away. I hope he's right.'

I put my arms round her. 'You're home. That's the important thing. And when Doctor Walker's got you back to normal I'll be delighted to take you up to meet the others. Oh! I'm looking forward to that. Now, what happened next?'

'Where was I in my story? Yes! The shock of seeing Marguerite. I told Lou about it later. "Serves him damn well right!" or the equivalent was her comment. She had by then dismissed Georges as being unworthy of attention. Yet at one time she was delighted for me.

'A few days after that encounter at the theatre I was in the little corridor leading to my office when I saw Marguerite step out of the lift and move towards the showrooms. I turned quickly before she could see me and bumped into Lou, who was coming out of my office. "Oops! You're in a hurry," she said. I put my fingers to my lips and she followed me in. "What's the mystery?"

'"We have a new client," I said.

'"What's new about that?" she asked.

'"It's Georges' wife. Noseyness, I expect."

'"*Ooh, la, la,*" said Lou, the light of battle in her eye.

171

"Would you like to bet how much I land dear Georges in for?"

'"Now, don't be ridiculous, Lou," I started, but the little minx had gone.

'I sat at my desk for a long while, my pencil idle. Then I remembered. There was an archway between the two salons and once or twice when in one salon I had noticed that by the angle of the mirrors I could see reflections thrown back from there into the other room. Curiosity got the better of me. I closed the office door quietly and walked on the soft carpet into the nearer salon. Not only was Lou the quickest dresser in the business – her years in the theatre were responsible for that – but she could build up a camaraderie with the shop assistants without ever losing her authority over them. They were grouped in admiration as she paraded before Marguerite in a tomato red costume with sable collar. The jacket, pinched into her tiny waist, flared out over her supple hips and rotated sinuously as she walked. It was the most expensive thing I had to offer in the way of day clothes at the time and totally unsuited to anyone with a less than perfect figure. In fact, I didn't really expect to sell that design at all. It was by way of being an eye-catching indulgence on my part. I expected to give the exemplar to Lou, who was now exploiting its possibilities to the full.

'Lou paused and I heard Marguerite's voice. "Don't you think it's a little . . . well . . . bright for me?"

'Lou had that team well trained. One by one they offered their commendations; it would look so warm on a chilly autumn day; it was one of the loveliest things that Madame had ever created; it was so flattering to the figure . . .

172

'"Where is Madame?" asked Marguerite.

'Lou spoke smoothly, "Madame is very busy with some new designs for an important wedding."

'Marguerite looked disappointed. "I am sure," went on Lou, "that you will not find anything more tasteful than this. It is certainly the one I would choose for you, but if you wish to see something less . . . more like your present outfit, I mean." One of the assistants was afflicted with a sudden cough but Marguerite was silent, considering.

'"You think it would suit me?" she asked.

'"It would enhance any woman," said Lou.

'"I've never worn that colour before." Marguerite was hesitant.

'"Sometimes it is a good idea for women to get out of a rut," said Lou daringly. "It makes the husbands sit up and take notice."

'I felt they must hear my indrawn breath. That little minx would ruin our business if she went too far. But Marguerite suddenly squared her shoulders. "I'll have it," she said.

'Lou gave the girls around her a quick warning look. "I'm sure you will be delighted, Madame. Clothilde will measure you, if you'll come this way." I noticed her flash another warning look as she hurried off to remove the model outfit. I made my careful way back to my office and sat waiting for inspiration which wouldn't come. In my mind's eye I kept seeing Marguerite's dumpy figure clothed in tomato red.

'Lou didn't knock. She had been suppressing her wicked mirth too long for that. "You'll never guess," she chortled.

'"I saw you," I said, my voice stern with disapproval. Lou looked startled for a moment. "I was

173

watching through the mirrors in the other salon . . . if you're at the right angle you can see things . . ."

'"Now, I've learned something new," said Lou. "Could be useful. But, Elise, can you imagine her – that rosy skin against tomato red, and those haunches!" She went off into peals of laughter. I tried to keep my face straight. Lou sketched an imaginary figure round herself and started to parade à la Marguerite round my office. It was too much. I found myself doodling my own impression of our latest client. Lou saw what I was up to and came to look. We ended up clutching each other like a couple of silly schoolgirls. When we had sobered up, I tried again to remonstrate with Lou. "You're teaching the assistants the wrong attitude to clients," I said. "They are supposed to be respectful."

'"Ah! Elise, my darling, you have never been a little working girl. I understand what they are thinking of the rich bitches who spend their silly husbands' money on expensive clothes instead of taking some exercise to make themselves look better. But we benefit, you see, from their stupidity. The girls know that well. It's good for them to have a little fun. I train them so they will keep within bounds. Do not fear. But I am wasting your valuable time. The more designs you make, the richer we shall be." She went off humming a cheeky little tune.

'It was a long time before inspiration came, however. Lou and the girls had had their little bit of fun and I couldn't honestly say I felt sorry for Marguerite. But it was Georges who would pay for it – not just in money but in the pain the sight of his unsuitably dressed wife was bound to cause one of his sensibilities. What if he thought I had been the one to inflict the cruel joke? It was a painful revelation to find that, in spite of all the heartache our liaison had cost me, I still needed Georges' good opinion.

'I couldn't help feeling uneasy about Georges in the days that followed, in spite of Lou's assurance that he could well afford the extravagance. Her view of our separation was that he had deserted me and deserved to suffer. Besides, she kept reminding me, it had been such a laugh; who could resist teasing the stupid cow?

'The scope for my work was now pretty well boundless, with Pierre needing more and more designs for his increasing sales. These were much more difficult, I found, than my own individual models. The restrictions were irritating and demanded a great deal of discipline. I found that when I left for home at night I was pretty exhausted. But the sight of my lovely house always comforted and cheered me. By the time I had bathed and changed I was always ready for any entertainment the evening offered.

'That particular night I was to be at the home of a couple who were in Albert and Anna's circle. I could relax with these old friends and there was always the thought of a new encounter. I smiled at the prospect. I was still a romantic at heart – probably always will be, come to that. My maid had been looking out for me and opened the door promptly. I felt a moment's unease. Lou had gone home early for an appointment with a recent conquest but had been feeling off-colour and regretting the arrangement. "Has Mlle Croquelois left?" I asked.

' "Oh, yes, Madame . . . some time ago, but a gentleman is waiting to see you."

'I was puzzled. Pierre always came to the office, naturally. Albert or any of that circle would have spoken on the telephone. "Where is he?" I asked.

'"In the small drawing-room, Madame. I thought that since you have an appointment you will not wish to be detained."

'"Thank you, Monique," I said.

'She opened the door and Georges rose from my favourite armchair. "Thank you, Monique," I said automatically, and the door closed behind me.'

Chapter 13

'My first thought was a stupid one: he had come to scold me for making a fool of Marguerite. Then I realized I was being silly, but still my legs would not move. Georges too stood silent, staring at me. Then he cleared his throat. "I had to come," he croaked. I said nothing. He tried again. "Elizabeth, my darling . . ."

'"Don't!" I said, my voice strangled. "You have no right."

'His arms which had been raised towards me dropped limply by his side. "I have no right. I have no life; no joy; nothing to live for. You taught me what life could be like. You gave me the sort of experience I have always dreamed of but thought was impossible. Now I live in limbo."

'"You have a wife . . ." I started.

'"Yes, I have a wife," he sighed.

'"And a daughter," I added.

'"Marie-Isabelle has gone to live in Italy. Her husband has a post there. I've lost her, too. She is caught up in other things. It is natural. Her mother resents it and demands all my attention. Elizabeth, I should never have given you up – not even for Marie-Isabelle."

'"We were in the wrong," I said. "It was bound to end sometime."

'"As far as I am concerned it will never end." He moved towards me. "Oh, Elizabeth, my dearest, I cannot live like this." He was reaching out for me and I backed away.

'"Don't tell me that it all meant nothing to you; that you can forget me so easily in your trips to the opera; in your business success. My work has gone to pieces. I am worse than useless in the office now. Please! Please!"

'He was trying to take me in his arms again. I felt the tears on my cheeks.

'"Surely these tears mean something. You cannot have forgotten all those heavenly days in the Dordogne . . ."

'"Don't!" I said fiercely. "We mustn't. We were wrong. We were cheating. It was a false joy." I heard the sobs rising in my voice.

'Georges moved quickly. His arms were round me and I was pinioned. He was kissing me passionately. I tried and tried to resist. Then I felt myself melt in his arms. For a moment I was in heaven but only for a moment. I remembered Anna's clenched hands when I told her my story; remembered the faces of the kind nuns who would have been scandalized by my behaviour if they had known; remembered that my passion had once led me into a disastrous marriage and a dead baby. My body was a snare – as harmful to Georges as myself. I tried to push him away but he held me more tightly still, his lips on mine. Then I felt myself go faint.

'I was lying on the settee and Georges was patting my hand when I recovered consciousness. His face close to mine was beaded with sweat, his brown eyes wet. The lock of hair which fell over his brow was quite grey.

'"Oh my darling, my darling," he was murmuring.

"What have I done to you? I swear that in the beginning I only meant to comfort you in your distress. But you took me into another world. Must I be denied it for ever?"

'"We must both be denied it, Georges," I whispered.

'"You are stronger than I am, my darling," he said. "You have gone ahead and made a success of your life. I have dwindled to nothingness without you."

'"But you taught me so much . . ." I began.

'"Yes! I taught you," he said with a sigh, "and I gloried in teaching such a pupil. If only we had met before I knew Marguerite and you your Michel, how different life might have been . . . the heights we might have climbed!"

'There was nothing I could say. We sat in miserable silence. At last he rose stiffly. "I see that I am dismissed," he said. "You are probably in the right, but it is difficult for me to see it. Could I have one last kiss? I swear I shall never trouble you again."

'We moved slowly to the door. I was enfolded gently in his arms, then we clung desperately together for a long time. When we drew apart, tears of despair were running down his cheeks. He mopped them angrily.

'"You mustn't let the maid see you like that," I said. "Do you wish to wait till you have calmed down a little?"

'"No," he said bitterly. "I must get away. Let me go. I want to walk . . . to think . . . Can't you let me out yourself?"

'"Quietly, then," I said. And these were my last words to Georges.'

* * *

'Closing the door softly, I crept back to the little drawing-room to cry my heart out. The chiming of the ormolu clock reminded me that I should have been dressed and ready to leave for the dinner party. I knew that my voice was hoarse with crying. How could I make my excuses? The last thing I wanted to do was to speak to a polite acquaintance. I would telephone to Anna and she could explain to my hostess. What would I say . . . a chill . . . a headache? Both were true. My reaction to sorrow always seemed to be a dreadful coldness. A chill would excuse my sore throat, so I used that.

'Anna was full of concern and kindness as usual and promised she would convey my regrets to her friend.

'Monique tapped on the door, "Aren't you going out tonight, Madame?"

'"No," I said, "I feel I am starting a cold and my eyes are strained. I think I shall rest at home tonight. If you could bring me some tea . . . ?"

'I managed to behave quite calmly when Monique returned with the tea and again when she collected the tray. It was a relief to know then that I could flop. I was worn out with tears. I sat back remembering, remembering my sadness which Georges had done so much to assuage; remembering the joy we had found abandoning ourselves to our love; the cottage which was our lovenest, the overgrown garden with blowsy roses drooping over the smaller flowers and every inch of it blooming just for us, or so it seemed. At night the casements had been open to the heady scent of stocks. I breathed deeply remembering, remembering the lassitude which they induced, which drew Georges towards me, his face shining with a youthful joy; once in his arms I would hear the beat of his heart as his lips took mine; he was an artist in love, I used to think, considerate even in his deepest passion, which was the nearest thing to heaven I could imagine. I knew that I appreciated Georges all the more because of my experience with Michel.

'The evening ticked by. Scenes from the past were alternating with the dismal one I had just been through. I was glad that Lou was off on some adventure. She had said she might not be home till morning. By then I might be able to use the skill she had taught me in dissembling. I had just fed myself with this comforting thought when I heard the sound of a carriage stopping at our door. I looked at the clock. It was too late for callers. The bell jangled and I heard Monique hurry to the door. There was a low murmur of voices.

'"Monsieur and Madame Wallach," Monique announced.

'Anna came to me, arms outstretched. "My dear Elise, are you all right?"

'I started to lie. Then Monique closed the door behind them. I stopped. "What made you come? I said it was just a chill."

'"My dear Elise, I know you so well," she said. "I felt you had been crying and now that I see you I think I was not wrong."

'I hesitated and then asked them to sit down. Albert was wearing his professional look; the keen blue eyes had probably noted the inflamed eyes, the shaky hands . . . but he said nothing.

'"I told Albert that something had happened to upset you – am I right? I know that you are good at concealing your feelings, so we thought it might be something serious and we left the party early. They know that Albert is lecturing tomorrow so nobody

181

would think a thing about that. But I am chattering. If there is anything we can do to help . . ."

' "I do feel shaken," I said. "I had not meant to tell anyone but I know how discreet you are and it would be a comfort – Georges came here tonight. He wanted me to take him back. He is distraught. He regrets giving me up. His daughter is now in Italy. His work has gone to pieces. He looks so much older. Oh, Anna, you would have pitied him if you had seen him. You couldn't have helped it."

'Anna had her arm round me. "I *do* pity him, my dear, and you. What did you say?"

' "I told him that it could not be. We had no right to our happiness. I sent him away. He gave me his solemn word that he would not trouble me again. Even in his misery he was considerate to me, Anna."

' "Oh my dear, what a pity it is you did not meet an honourable man in the first place," she said. "Albert said he only had a glimpse of the couple but he sensed wretchedness that night at the theatre. What was it you said about the wife, my love?"

' "I got the impression of a woman who would get her own way every time and not by being pleasant. Perhaps it is an unkind judgement on such a brief acquaintance, but the lines of the face tell a lot when you are observant. Georges' case is certainly pitiable but the fact remains that he *is* a married man and should not be risking your reputation."

' "That is my fault, of course," I hastened to say. "My mother was fond of giving my younger sister and me little lectures before we went out and she always ended by saying that it was up to the girl to keep the man right."

' "Your mother had fine principles but I think

the responsibility should be shared. Now, my dear Elise, have you anything to make you sleep – a draught?"

'"Yes. There is something in my cabinet. You think I should take it?"

'"Sleep is the kindest healer. You will forget for a little while and distance yourself from this dreadful predicament. Georges has promised to keep away from you, so you will be able to continue your absorbing work. That is a blessing. You have suffered great loss before and behaved bravely. I am sure you will do the same now, my dear. If you feel we can help, just get in touch with Anna. Your volatile little Lou will help you in her way – or won't you tell her?"

'"I expect I shall," I said, "but her relationships never go deep. She won't understand my feelings."

'"No. Perhaps she has schooled herself that way if her early life was unsatisfactory, but she loves and admires you – there is no doubt of that. And of course the nuns at the convent will offer you comfort without knowing the cause of your distress. It is their vocation."

'I was finishing breakfast when Lou arrived. She joined me at coffee. "Ooh, my dear Elise, you have no idea the proposal I have had – a count, no less! And when I say 'proposal' I mean marriage!"

'I gazed in amazement. "That's new," I said. "When did you meet him?"

'"Well, one night when I was at the theatre in a party he was in another party there. They met up and he drifted towards me. I wasn't interested in him because he's quite old, but it never pays to show that, so I expect I flirted a little if that was what he wanted.

183

He invited me out another night. I was ready to trot out an excuse when someone addressed him as 'Monsieur le Conte'. So I thought it might be worthwhile to arrange *one* assignation. After all, a titled companion is not to be sneezed at. I found him harmless company, always courteous but slow in coming forward, if you see what I mean. We went out together a few times. Nothing, but nothing, happened! I couldn't work it out. Then he invited me to go one Sunday recently to his home in the country – I had been late getting home on the Saturday and you were up early, spending the day with Marianne, I think. Anyway somehow I never got round to telling you. I was trying to puzzle things out, as I said. That day while we were walking in the lovely gardens he told me that he was impotent. Well, that's the first time I've heard that one, I can tell you. It should have made me laugh but somehow it didn't. He's such a kind old sod.

'"He says he is madly in love with me and is thinking of buying a house in Paris. Usually he spends most of his time at the manor in the country and just puts up (at *our* favourite hotel, Elise) when he is in town. I gather I'm the magnet which is drawing him to town more frequently. Well, he's always reluctant to part – that's why I've been late so often. He asked me if I would stay with him last night. Well, the idea seemed so funny – I mean, a night with an impotent man! But I thought I might as well. It would be an experience. And I would get some rest. After the way I worked for that Guillaume when we were negotiating for the house, a bit of rest appealed.

'"I felt a little giggly when we got to the bedroom, I can tell you. He wanted to help me undress. When he saw me mother-naked his face flushed and he suddenly looked much younger. Well, we were in bed and, of course, I automatically gave him a little help . . ."

'"Lou," I said, "you shouldn't be telling me all this. How would your count feel?"

'"Robert! I think he would be delighted. You see, he found that he is not impotent at all. He is fifty-nine and last night was the first time!!! Can you believe it? I couldn't get him to stop talking. He was so pleased with himself. From some of the things he said, I gathered that his childhood had been as bad as mine, even though he's filthy rich. He hardly ever saw his parents. He had a nurse who used to treat him cruelly, lock him in a dark cupboard for supposed naughtiness. And then, later, he had a Jesuit tutor who talked a lot about the sins of the flesh and thrashed Robert mercilessly on the slightest excuse. No wonder he found me 'different'. He had been scared of women, he told me, but I had an innocent look and had smiled so sweetly at him. Yes, no wonder you smile, Elise."

'She threw her head back and laughed merrily. I hesitated before speaking, then decided to risk it. "Lou, you say he has proposed to you. But don't you think that now he knows it might be possible for him to father an heir to the title, he might wish to marry a young woman who could give him children?"

'"I thought of that, Elise," she said, "and I haven't made my mind up yet anyway. I'd hate to leave this lovely house. You have made it a dream home. I shall not do anything in a hurry." Her face grew bitter for a moment. "Even if I were twenty-five I could not give him a son – thanks to our charming Michel. But, you see, Elise, after all these years of being scared of women, he thinks I am very special indeed. I'm not boasting when I say that most girls could not work this miracle for him."

'"No, you are right," I said. "I wonder what the correct title for your gift is?"

'That set Lou off again. I tell you, Jessie, some of her suggestions would have shocked any well brought up count! I realized how much I had been absorbed in my work when I had missed hearing a blow-by-blow account of Lou's affairs of the heart. She *was* getting older of course – we both were – she was forty-five and I was forty-nine, no less, and remarks she had dropped while we were negotiating the purchase of the house told me that she was finding a keener interest in business than her flirtations. Her heart had never been engaged anyway. When one lover fell out of the running she had simply got hold of another one. Had her early experience of a deceitful man like Michel embittered her? Knowing that she could never have a child would rule out all thoughts of a normal set-up – that is, what would have seemed normal to me. The idea of becoming a countess must appeal to a girl who had risen from the humblest of beginnings and could now take her place in a fairly high rank of society. I smiled wryly when I thought of her belief that I had made her a "fine English lady". It was her labelling of me as such that had given other people the same attitude to me. I suppose we had helped each other. That was why we made good partners in business. And it would do that business no harm if my partner were to become a countess. The French might proudly claim that they were republicans, but titles were still good for our type of business.

'"We're going to be late," said Lou, bringing me

back to the present. "How did *your* party go last night?"

' "I didn't," I said. "I mean, didn't go. I was rather fevered and thought I had a chill coming on, so I made my apologies and sat by the fire. Anna and Albert left early so they dropped by to check up on me. He told me to take a sleeping draught and I would feel better in the morning."

' "Your eyes look a little inflamed," she said. "Just leave early if you don't feel well. I've nothing much on my plate today and no hungry Guillaume to meet at night, thank God!"

'Sitting at my desk later I felt rather proud of myself that I had managed to hide my troubles from Lou. Of course, if she hadn't been toying with the idea of a title, she would probably have noticed that I was looking subdued. It made it easier not to have to go over the miserable story again. I didn't want to think about Georges. I would concentrate on my work. There was never any shortage of ideas to be worked out, either for my special clients or for Pierre's ready-to-wear "Elegance" lines, as he called them. I saw Lou briefly at lunchtime but went straight back to my desk afterwards. It was about four o'clock when Lou joined me for coffee. "The girls are all of a twitter," she said. "The newsboys are shouting about a man who has thrown himself from the Bordeaux train. They say the two men who were in the carriage with him are suffering from shock."

'I shivered. In spite of my sleeping draught I had been awake early. "You're too sensitive, Elise," she said. "The poor bastard had probably run up gambling debts. Things like that happen. These little sillies next door are enjoying the thrill in spite of all their 'ohs' and 'nos'. Is your chill still troubling you? Perhaps you should get home early."

'I shivered again. "Perhaps I shall do just that, Lou. You'll be here to see to things?"

' "Of course," she said.

' "They didn't know the man's name, did they?"

' "What man? Oh, the train! Nobody said. Why?"

'I shook myself. "Oh, I don't know . . . just a funny feeling . . . someone walking over my grave."

'Lou was looking perplexed. "It's a saying we have," I said. "Don't worry, I'm off."

'There was a knock at the door. Lou made a face and whispered. "Shall I get rid of them?" I shook my head and called, "Enter!"

'As soon as I saw Anna Wallach's face I knew that my unreasoning fear was not so absurd after all. "How are you, my dear?" she asked. "Is your chill still troubling you?"

'Lou answered for me. "I've just advised Elise to go home. She's shivering."

'I was indeed shivering, uncontrollably now. Tears were running down my face.

' "I have a cab at the front of the emporium," said Anna. "Are you free to help me down in the lift with her? No fuss, please. Just tell your staff she is suffering from a feverish chill. Wear your veil, my dear," she said to me. "They'll think it is just vanity because your nose is red." She was the quiet, authoritative nurse. Lou issued her brief instructions and joined us on the way to the lift.

'The cab driver had obviously had his instructions and came forward quickly to assist me into the carriage. I managed to keep my head up till we were safely away from the emporium.

188

'"It was Georges, wasn't it?" I whispered.

'"Yes. How did you know?'

'"Something told me. He was in such despair. Oooo –" My voice was rising and I threw my head back to find relief in a scream. But Anna's left hand clamped over my mouth and her right held my arm in a vice-like grip. She hissed in my ear. "You will control yourself till you are safely in your own bedroom. Do you hear me? I shall be forced to slap you and it will hurt." She would have made a good sergeant major, Jessie. She managed to keep me in control while she issued her orders to Monique and got me up to my room. Monique was sent scurrying to the kitchen. When Anna had helped me undress she started to unpack the capacious bag she was carrying. It held several medicaments. "Some are for you," she said. "The others are to fool Monique. By the time they have done their worst you will be able to cope with any awkward questions that crop up. My dear, this is a dreadful happening, but we must be very careful what we say. Albert says that it is a good thing to play on the feverish chill that will keep you out of the way till you have recovered a little from the shock."

'"How did Albert know?" I asked.

'"He was lecturing at the hospital this morning. Before he left, the body had been brought in. Albert had lunch with some of the specialists who were, of course, discussing the episode. Someone mentioned that the deceased had been the head of a prosperous firm – architects. Albert became alert then and found out the name without drawing any attention, of course. As soon as he got home he asked me to find some excuse to get you safely away before you learned the news."

189

' "You are angels," I said through my tears.

' "Not a bit of it," said Anna briskly. "Just good friends. Look how you helped us out with Paul's difficult mother. You have always been Marianne's favourite aunt. I treasure the lovely portrait of my baby which owes so much to your skill and artistry with the needle. We shall see you through this, never fear! The nuns will help you too. But at this moment what you need is a little pampering. I shall instruct your maid. Do not be alarmed if I imply that your chill is a little more serious than we know it to be. It will excuse my visits – and Albert's. Have you told anyone that Georges was here?"

' "No," I said. "Lou was too full of her own news. She has had a proposal of marriage from a count, no less."

' "What?"

' "Yes. We may have a countess on our staff. Naturally the thought was occupying her mind so much that she did not pay too much attention to me. I told her I had a chill and hadn't gone to the party. That was all."

' "Good! She might have let something slip to the shopgirls if the news had been sprung on her. Albert says we must be careful to keep your name out of this. Only Monique knows then?"

'I murmured agreement and Anna nodded. "I'll see that I keep her so busy treating your chill that she won't notice anything else. Georges had never been here before, had he? Could she have thought him someone connected with your business – say a lawyer?"

' "Perhaps," I said slowly, "but he would give his name; she announced him."

' "Is she likely to remember?"

'"It *is* a common name . . ."

'"Well, we must hope she doesn't. As I said, I'll keep her busy. Now, I expect you will have to tell Lou?"

'"Oh, yes! She's ingenious," I said. "I don't think we'll have anything to worry about there. She will probably help with Monique. I've never seen anyone so quick at inventing a lie when necessary."

'"Someone like that will be valuable to you for the next few days," Anna said. And indeed Lou was.

'When Monique remarked that the man who had thrown himself from the train was a Monsieur Dutoit and the man who had visited Madame the night she had a chill was also Monsieur Dutoit, Lou had said, "They're all over the place, these Dutoits – lecherous devils, the lot of them." This had sent Monique into kinks. Lou had casually added that she must check up; make sure that the lawyer Dutoit who had visited Madame had completed the deal they were anxious to put through. Madame was so feverish that she might not have remembered when she got to the office in the morning.

'Though she dealt with the affair so astutely, Lou had been shocked by Georges' death. I think she felt rather guilty about having dismissed him from the scene so lightly. Her love affairs had certainly never reached those depths. They had been quickly forgotten by her and the sort of men she consorted with. This Robert she had found was different and seemed to be showing her a new aspect of love. I encouraged her to talk about him. It distracted me for a little while and pleased her. Obviously she was feeling a little out of her depth now that an affair was no longer a clandestine or casual one. She had probably given up all thought of marriage, though I sometimes wondered what she planned for her old age. She had kept her wonderful figure so far. The discipline of the ballet class had got her into the habit of exercising. Early on in our relationship she had taken me in hand and made me learn some of the basic ballet exercises too. I had reason to be grateful to Lou for so many things! With skilful make-up she could still look quite young, but seeing her in the morning made me realize the changes that were taking place in her as in myself. Perhaps it was as well that we had a successful business to comfort us!

'Thanks to Anna's frequent visits when she was occasionally accompanied by Albert, I was able to face the world a week later. The shopgirls accepted my drawn face as the result of a severe chill. The nuns at the convent were happy to see me back, though really, Catherine – now Sister Catherine – had absorbed all that was necessary for the work required. Hers was the responsibility for the work the girls turned out. I was the gracious patroness, merely a figurehead to encourage the wealthy parents who sent their girls to the school. It was very much a case of "the end justifying the means" and, knowing the need of the orphanage, I was happy to be instrumental in providing the means. My visits to the chapel were more important to me now than ever. Of course, Georges was always in my mind. It was impossible for it to be otherwise. I had read the newspaper reports of the case anxiously, but nothing I had dreaded transpired. His office staff had said that he was finding difficulty in concentrating; he had complained of sleeplessness; his power of invention seemed to have deserted him. He had said ruefully to a member of the staff, "I haven't had a blessed idea for months." His wife was prostrate with grief. His married daughter had come from Italy for the funeral. It seemed safe to discard that particular worry.

'I threw myself into designing a new collection.'

Chapter 14

'Though I seemed normal, Jessie, and was getting on well with my work, it was difficult for me to think of resuming my social life. There was always the nagging fear that some people were bound to know of the liaison and blame me for Georges' death. When I had voiced this fear to Albert he had pointed out that it was fear of scandal that had made Marie-Isabelle ask Georges to leave me. They were unlikely to wish it leaked out now. He did point out that by staying at home all the time I was more likely to cause comment. "You have been seen as an ornament to the society of Paris, my dear. Don't you think that people will be bound to remark on your absence? You can't go on having chills."

'This brought the laugh he hoped for and, once chewed over, gave me the impetus to resume my partygoing. Lou was quite keen now to invite Robert to our lovely home. "He knows I haven't made up my mind about him," she said. "He's content to wait. He dreads being given up so he'll wait patiently – provided I comfort him, of course. But he's a once-a-night fellow – not like Guillaume – so I don't mind. Oh, Elise, you should see your face. It's such fun shocking you."

'I suppose it *is* funny that I'm still shockable after the life I've led; but not so shockable as some of my sisters, I'm sure. What would Jean make of Lou, d'you think?'

'She'd probably say her mother should have given her a skelpit leathering,' I supplied.

'I'd forgotten that expression,' said Elsie. 'Where was I? Yes! Well, I resumed my social life by giving a grand party. We really worked on it for a solid week, Lou and I, with the help of the maids. Of course, the house in the rue Cardinet is just *made* for parties. Lou, who has never been known for her domestic skills, was anxious to impress her Robert and willingly worked to my instructions.

'"I think we should have a photographer for this," she said. Pierre, who was always keen on any innovation that would enhance his business, had recently paid one to photograph the emporium in its various aspects. We were tripping over light cables in the salons but Lou had patiently modelled several of our most showy evening ensembles and the resulting prints had been very much admired. He had managed to interest one of the top-grade magazines in those and we had a lot of free publicity when they made a feature of our artistic salons. Their descriptive write-up had ended with, "Madame Elise is now one of the most sought-after designers in Paris and well-known for her personal elegance."

'Lou, reading this out to me had added, "And not a word about the lovely model – soon to be La Contesse de Verperies – whose entrancing figure showed these beautiful clothes to the greatest advantage."

'"Shame!" I said. "And are you soon to be La Contesse de Verperies?"

'"In a way, it appeals," she said, "but I'd lose my freedom."

195

'I was looking forward to seeing them together at my home. I had noted that Lou seemed to think marriage would demand a loyalty she had certainly never shown in her other liaisons. This Robert was being viewed in a different light, obviously.

'Only excitement had kept the pair of us from being physical wrecks by the time the grand occasion arrived. I suppose I'm a perfectionist by nature and at that time I had an obsession about something to atone for, to wipe out; by doing something really well, I could be forgiven something I had done badly. I should have "kept Georges right", as my mother had put it, and there would have been no tragedy. I inhaled the scent of many choice blooms, examined for the last time the setting we had planned, and felt a little ease seep into my being. Words from my childhood came to mind, "And God saw that it was good." Then the inapropriateness hit me and I started giggling.

'"What's amusing you, boss?" asked Lou.

'"Just feeling like God," I said.

'For once, Lou couldn't find a reply.

'We did have the photographer and were duly written up in the gossip columns. Once I had withstood my baptism of fire I started to go out to theatres and the opera again. Pierre and Lou's Conte de Verperies had been added to our usual party by then. I was surprised to find just how witty Pierre could be when he shed his "strictly business" attitude. His gossip was quite wicked, but it was impossible not to see the funny side of it. It was women who were usually accused of gossiping. Perhaps these fellows – *tapettes* – had a feminine streak which made them that way. Lou had said they could be sensitive and kind.

'The Conte de Verperies said very little in company

but his eyes were seldom off Lou. I saw how protectively he treated her. It would be a fine thing if she *could* find it in herself to love him enough, I thought. Her sprightliness would be a tonic to him. Perhaps, at his age, he no longer felt the need for children. If his own childhood had been so miserable he might have a less enthusiastic outlook on youth anyway. I noticed how he glowed every time she smiled at him. Lou had said that he longed to take her travelling with him, show her the world. But she had told him that she was a businesswoman and could not take all that time off. It struck me then how we were getting older and perhaps would not be able to keep up this momentum. Of course, our enterprise had taken off very rapidly and, thanks to Pierre's longsightedness and acumen, was liable to continue on that road. Perhaps it was time to think of some way of easing that burden.

'It seemed a coincidence but was probably just a logical development to find that the same thought had been working on Pierre. He asked me to have lunch with him one day about six weeks after my grand party.

'We were no sooner at table than: "You probably haven't time to waste," he said, "so I'll come straight to the point. In my factories and in my offices I am constantly training new people. I think that you train new cutters, machinists and embroiderers in your own workshop. You train new shop assistants too. What you do not train is new models and new designers. I know that the exclusive tag is essential to your most expensive output, and that must remain, but I have a proposition to make. What about getting Lou to train up a model or two – advertise, I mean? The name of Elise would be enough to bring them in in droves. You wouldn't have to pay the earth – the cachet would mean a lot. And now that photography is becoming the new science of the people, there is bound to be scope for those girls. Lou could pick them. A little training in the theatre would be quite a good background. In the beginning they would have to double as shop assistants. You might have to cope with a bit of jealousy there from the others, but I shouldn't think Lou would put up with insurrection in the ranks." I had to smile at that.

'"Now, designers!" Pierre went on. "I've had what I modestly think of as a brilliant idea." He grinned at me. "What about a biennial design award: *The Pierre-Elise Award for Dress Design*? The candidates would have to submit a folio of designs. The requirements would be laid down by you, and you would, of course, adjudicate. The prize would be a money award plus a year's design tuition supervised by you. Now wait! I'm not trying to add to your burdens or disturb your office. There is a room near your workshop which is kept for dress and hatboxes. The bulk of these could be stored in the basement and immediate requirements brought up. I thought that the successful young designer could have that room. His efforts would be for the Elegance label. At the end of his year he could move on, unless he proved to be very valuable. I thought the idea of every second year for the competition would be a good one. It gives us time to draw our breath. If the winner doesn't fit in, we have a year to think up something else or employ someone else. All their designs during their year would be our property. In fact, if some unsuccessful candidates submitted the odd good design, we could buy that too. It would gradually free you from a lot of the Elegance work which, I think, you do not find so thrilling as your own. Am I right?"

'"Yes, I can't deny that I like the freedom to choose the best of everything in the way of materials," I said. "As to your plan, it will need a lot of discussion. And, of course, Lou will have to be included in that. In principle, I think it *would* be wise to make provision for eventualities. I lost a few valuable days with my chill, for example. With someone sharing the Elegance work, I would have had a bigger reserve portfolio . . ."

'"Do you think that your Lou would still want to be here if she became a countess?" he asked.

'"Without a doubt," I said. "This firm is one of the reasons that she has so far failed to come to a decision about her personal life. Lou enjoys commerce and is a very astute businesswoman. She constantly astounds me. I *do* think, however, that she would see the point of training up a new model or two – perhaps one in the generous proportions that most of our clients possess. That way I might sell the model garment instead of just having it for an example in Lou's measurements. Also, if she *does* become a countess, it might be rather *infra dig* for her to be rushing off to change her clothes to display any model. As Madame la Directrice, a countess would be a distinct asset. But, as I said, Lou must be consulted fully on this."

'We parted on that understanding. Before Robert called for Lou that evening, I gave her a rough outline of Pierre's idea. "I told him that you would have to be included in any discussions, of course," I added.

'"How do you feel about it, Elise?" she asked.

'"There's quite a lot to be said for it, if properly handled. It would give us more freedom. You could be off travelling, Madame la Contesse."

'I noticed a hint of a blush as she giggled. Lou blushing! That was something.

'After he had delivered his great idea, Pierre left the subject alone for quite a while. I had said it would need time and consideration and he was giving me just that. His professionalism gained him more respect from me day by day. Lou had asked me if it would be in order for her to mention it to Robert for his opinion.

'"He'll be discreet?" I asked.

'"He'll be anything I ask him to be," she replied, and I could quite believe it!

'It was just a few evenings after that that we had a box at the opera – a sort of family party, as Lou put it. That amused me when I thought back to Lou's comments on her own family. We were walking in the usual parade at the end of the interval. Anna and Albert were in the lead, then Marianne and Paul; Pierre and I came next, and Lou and Robert were dallying in the rear. I saw Albert stop, whisper something to Anna then move swiftly to Paul and mutter something to him. Anna called Marianne to her and they moved forward quickly towards our door with Albert and Paul following as if in discussion. Then a raucous strangled voice rang out, "That's the bitch! It's all her fault. She killed him."

'"Hold her!" said Albert to Paul. They had Marguerite's arms pinioned to her side and were trying to hold her upright while she squirmed this way and that. She started to scream abuse and Albert covered her mouth with his hand. Anna came hurrying to my side while attendants came running from every quarter.

'"Monsieur le Conte," called Albert, "will you see the rest of our party to their box? Doctor Auclair and I will see to this lady."

'"What's wrong with me?" muttered Pierre.

'"No title!" hissed Lou. "Albert knows what he is doing. Come along Elise . . . a little dignity please. I shall show you how to be a real English lady. You have never seen the noisy fishwife before in your life."

'Lou was acting the animated concert-goer while giving me the occasional nudge with her toe. On my other side, Anna sat calmly as usual. It was just before the last scene opened that Paul Auclair slipped into our box. "Face the front," came Lou's warning to me. Then Paul's murmur was relayed. Albert had gone in the ambulance.

'Anna placed her hand gently on my knee. "Albert will have her taken to *his* hospital. He will speak to the doctors in the way they understand. Never fear!" Though her words brought a certain reassurance, I was glad to see the end of that performance and reach the safety of my cab. Lou assured Anna that she and Robert would see to me and be ready to answer the telephone should Albert have anything to report.

'I jumped when it rang. Lou didn't linger but hurried back. "He said that it was as well he went with her. Apart from briefing the doctor in charge, he was able to deal with a newspaper reporter who was hanging around. He thinks the ambulance men must have tipped him off – they do that for a fee! You can never depend on the accuracy of their reports, of course, but Albert took the precaution of asking him to read back his notes, on the pretence that he wanted to be helpful. He thinks the fellow was rather in awe of him and won't do too bad a job."

'I feared to step out of the door the next day till I had read the newspaper. There was the usual lurid headline – SOCIETY LADY ATTACKED AT PARIS OPERA. And underneath:-

Doctor Albert Wallach, the famous paediatrician, was in Madame Elise's party. He and Doctor Paul Auclair were able to restrain the hysterical woman till help arrived. Afterwards Doctor Wallach spoke to our reporter. He said it was common for someone who had been through some crisis, such as bereavement, to wish to lash out in anger. Often their victim was someone in the public eye who was enjoying success and praise. This, temporarily, made the subject feel better but was no long-term solution. This aggression, however, was not so harmful to the patient as another common form which was dejection and self-hate. This could often lead to suicide. 'It is obviously easier to treat someone who is still alive,' said the famous doctor. When asked what treatment he would recommend, Doctor Wallach said, 'Acquire some grandchildren. I am a paediatrician, of course, and specially interested in the study of the young, but I have also observed their wonderful effect on the old and the troubled. It is impossible not to feel some hope for the future when you look into the clear eyes of a child and answer their innocent questions. I hope that the poor lady who lost control tonight has some grandchildren to help in her healing.

'"Good for Albert," I thought. "If anyone passes on that word to Marie-Isabelle she will probably remove her mother to Italy. Even if she doesn't read it, she is very anxious to avoid scandal, as Albert keeps reminding me. A mother like that on the loose is not likely to recommend her to the family she wishes to please."

'It gave me the courage to make for the emporium. Lou had said in her practical fashion that if the press bothered us it was just to be expected, but we couldn't afford to waste time hiding from them. I was surprised to find an attendant on duty beside my lift on the top floor. Pierre was taking no chances. Lou had been watching out for me and followed me into my sanctum. "Glad you're here. Pierre has a reporter in his office downstairs. He made sure you weren't disturbed. Pierre thinks we might as well make use of this publicity to get the idea of the prize launched. He asked if I thought you would approve and I said it would do you good to have something different to think about. He's got a bottle of wine there and seems to have the fellow quite entranced. The idea of being the first to hear of our great plan has gone to the reporter's head, I think. Your presence would be welcome if you feel like it, but Pierre said not to trouble if you'd rather not."

'"Since the word is out, I think it would be better if I lent my presence, added weight . . . how would you put it, Lou?"

'"Dazzled the silly little fellow into swallowing every word from your dulcet lips," said Lou.

'"Aha!" I said. "Methinks the bold Robert reads poetry to his lady love."

'I wouldn't dare repeat Lou's reply to you, little sister, eight bairns or no!

'Pierre was delighted to see me. The reporter, already flushed, coloured up further. I had trouble controlling my twitching lips. Pierre made the introductions, I sat down and he sketched in what he had already told the fellow. I added a few details, then invited questions. I watched his Adam's apple move furiously before he managed something in a hoarse voice. From then on, it was easy. I elaborated on his questions and now and again asked him to check on his notes since I had noticed that his pencil stopped, forgotten, from time to time. I was very helpful, encouraging and, remembering Albert's piece on the theatre débâcle, chose my words with care. "When I have worked out the requirements for their portfolio, we shall certainly be advertising the competition," I ended.

'"And that piece of news will make him popular with his editor," I thought as I made my way upstairs to Lou: Lou who might well become a countess any time in the near future and whose frank remarks would shock a fishwife, let alone my sisters!'

'Though the thought of Georges still returned to haunt me at night it was impossible not to feel bright during the day. There was such an air of gaiety in Paris as the opening of the World Fair drew near. I had taken many a stroll down by the Seine to admire the magnificent pavilions that had sprung up all round. It was really something worth seeing, Jessie. It was spread over 280 acres, I think they said, and all these buildings were lit up at night. And of course the Tour Eiffel, picked out in electric lights, was standing guard over the whole thing. It seemed that so much was happening. After all, it wasn't so long since electric light had been a luxury, and here it was, used on the grand scale! Dreyfus had been pardoned, so we were spared a lot of that stuff at dinner parties. President Loubet seemed to be popular. It's difficult to put it all into words,

Jessie, but there was so much that was new and yet there was an air of stability that hadn't been there before. I couldn't help being affected. Lou was bubbling over most of the time. She always loved excitement and yet she too was happy to go off to the country with her Robert.

'Inevitably the fine buildings made me think of Georges and I found myself judging them with his eyes. I was rather proud to think that by that time my eyes were really informed; there was little of the detail that escaped me. In the fine weather of early summer we would find that our steps turned there inevitably at the end of each dinner party. The lights fascinated everyone. Albert and Anna got up a party one night and chose the British India and Colonial Restaurant – in my honour, they said. I disclaimed any responsibility for the food in advance. I can't remember much about it now, though it certainly wasn't up to the standard of our favourite restaurant in the north of the city, but the view, Jessie!!! We were right on the banks of the Seine, hanging over it in fact, and fairly high up in the building. The pleasure boats constantly passing under us all bore advertisements on their awnings and were filled with brightly dressed passengers. None of us paid much attention to the food.

'Even on the odd wet day, the place was thronged with people enjoying the novelty of the moving pavement or just gazing in wonder at the new world that had sprung up among them. The monumental gate was worth a visit itself. It was on the south west side of the place de la Concorde. The huge archway was crowned by an allegorical scene in the guise of a Parisian lady dressed in the fashion of the day welcoming the guests to her city. Lou was quick to note that the dress she was wearing was not unlike an outfit I had designed the previous year. Being Lou, she capitalized on it by murmuring remarks to our clients, drawing their attention to the statue and suggesting that they would remember seeing it in Madame's collection a few months earlier. Most of them hadn't but were flattered to feel they had inside information and something more to talk about at their dinner parties.'

'Talking about dinner parties, Elsie,' I said, 'I'm beginning to feel that a wee bite before bedtime would be welcome. I think I'll nip down now and see what the chef at the Paisley and Colonial Restaurant has to offer. D'you know, Elsie, that girl bosses me like nobody's business but she's always so logical about it and I have to give in.'

Beth came out of the snug as soon as she heard my step on the stair. 'I thought it was time you had some supper. Father and I had ours half an hour ago.'

'Ah! but you weren't listening to tales of Paris,' I said.

'No, but I'll expect to have them relayed at your leisure, Mother mine,' said my big daughter, making her way to the kitchen.

Sandy drew me into the snug and shut the door quietly. I was in his arms and he murmured in my ear, 'When do I get my little wife back?'

'I don't know,' I said. 'It seems to go on and on. At the moment she's telling me happy things, but the doctor felt that she had suffered something recently and that accounted for the breakdown. I think I've just got to let her carry on.'

'Well, don't let her wear you out. Remember she brought a lot of her troubles on herself.'

'You're being cruel, Sandy.'

'Not a bit of it – just realistic. She will always put herself and her feelings at the heart of everything – no emotional control. Aye . . . aye . . . she's attractive, wee Jessie, and she's talented and she has her good points and she's your big sister . . . But I'll not have her wearing you out. What are you going to do now?'

'The chef is making a little bedtime titbit for us and then I'm going to crawl in beside Elsie and she can talk as long as she likes.'

'Well, I hope you'll be crawling in beside *me* tomorrow night and I'll not waste your time talking,' my dear man said as he released me.

Chapter 15

Later, when Elsie was off to her bath, I carried the supper tray downstairs. 'Scoffed the lot, I see,' said Beth.

'I gather that toasted sultana scones are not a usual bedtime titbit in Paris, but I think she'll be converting them when she goes back. She certainly ate her share,' I said.

'It sounds to me as if she is recovering,' said Beth.

'Aye, it's all happy stuff just now,' I murmured, 'but you saw her when she arrived, Beth. Something serious was eating her up then . . .'

'Girlhood scenes remembered and all that,' said Beth. 'Didn't she say something about doing penance? She'll have to get out of bed for that surely? By the way, Mother, I've finished the work I was preparing for next term, so the sooner you get Aunt Elsie up to scratch, the sooner I'll be off up north.'

'There's nothing to stop you . . .' I began.

'Oh aye there is,' said Beth. 'While you're being kept up half the night you need support and it has to be kept in the family, remember. But we'll feed her up on sultana scones and hope she'll soon be on her tootsies again.'

She was coaxing me to smile, I knew, but there were so many things nagging away at the back of my mind. 'You know,' I said, 'she hasn't let anyone know she is here yet. You'd think that Lou would be worried . . .'

'Have you suggested it to her?'

'No. I've a feeling it would upset her. She seems to have terrible guilt feelings about not writing to Mam.'

'Aye, well, it wouldn't do much good writing to Mam now – there's the address for one thing. Sorry, Mother, you're not in the mood for jokes.' Beth put her arm round me and kissed my cheek. 'How would it do if I wrote to Lou and sketched in the story?'

'But we don't have the address and I wouldna like to ask Elsie in case it starts her off again.'

'Didn't she go on about the house – rue Cardinet, wasn't it?'

'Aye, but we don't know the number,' I said.

'Mother, in that set-up the mail is handed to a servant and you can bet your boots that every servant in the street knows who Elise is. We could put it "chez Madame Elise Blanchard, rue Cardinet" and I'd be very surprised if it doesn't get there.'

'Lou won't know who you are . . .' I began but Beth was getting impatient. 'Mother dear, I *could* begin, "Je suis la nièce de Madame Blanchard . . ."'

'Aye, that would be fine,' I said, vanquished.

Elsie and I were both bathed and scented when we snuggled down together. 'Now where was I?' she asked.

'Well, there was the wee reporter and his Adam's apple I remember,' I said, 'and you were going to use the publicity and the World Fair and Lou was telling stories as usual, the wee minx. My, but she's clever about it too!'

'I think you would like her, Jessie, even if you found a lot to disapprove of in her way of going about things.

'Well . . . having courted all that publicity I had to get my skates on about drawing up the examination requirements. I engaged Lou's help in this. "I expect

they'll all be dying to do eye-catching evening outfits,"
I said, "with feathers sticking out at all angles."

'"Yes! And I know whose bum the feathers will be
sticking into," added Lou.

'"I don't know," I said, "we might give them to
Natalie."

'Natalie was the first of our new acquisitions in the
way of staff – a stately well-upholstered and carefully
preserved matron whose measurements were certainly
nearer those of our usual clientele. My sharp-eyed Lou
had noticed, however, that many of them still preferred the sort of garment that *she* displayed. They had
come for a dream and hoped that money could buy it.

'"Though the evening ensembles are a gift to the photographer and a 'must' for publicity," I said to her,
"what we are really concerned with is someone who has
an eye for line – an instinct for proportion and some new
ideas. For every evening outfit a woman has in her
wardrobe, she has six day outfits, you can be sure."

'"Why not suggest a title for each section," said Lou.
"An Evening at the Opera; A Walk in the Bois; By Train
to the Midi; An Afternoon Reception; things like that!"

'"That's an excellent idea," I said. "I'll have to
give them instructions for how they are to be presented – sketches of details, size of the full-colour
presentation . . ."

'"Right!" said Lou. "That's your department. I'll
toddle along to the workroom. They seem to be taking
a long time with that last country outfit we asked for.
Will you put the advertisement in immediately?"

'"Yes. We might as well get things moving," I said.
"I think I'll put it in general terms and then ask
intending candidates to write in for an application
form. It makes it sound more important."

'I decided not to allow the entrants too long, Jessie. It might make it rather difficult for anyone starting from scratch, but those interested in dress design would probably have some completed work or, at least, rough sketches lying about. If they were really keen, they would manage it in time – even if they *were* starting from scratch. It hadn't done me any harm to have to work against the clock when I was starting up. Besides, the public would lose interest if the results were to be delayed.

'The few days after the advertisement appeared were anxious ones. What if very few applied? What if none of the work was worth considering? We had committed ourselves to a sizeable sum *and* I was expected to coach the winner! What if he – or she – turned out to be the best of a bad lot and unteachable? It was a relief when the first batch of requests arrived.

'It wasn't long before the folios themselves began to trickle in. Lou objected to having her assistants receiving and relaying the packs which the eager contestants delivered by hand, no doubt hoping to get a peep at my office. Pierre, who was at the butt end of her complaint, sent one of his junior staff to be on hand to record details of the candidates.

'I had expected that the task of adjudicating would take up a deal of my time but nothing could have prepared me for the avalanche which descended after a few weeks. Pierre, on learning of this, offered to take first look at the entries and weed out the impossibles to save me time. By then I knew that he had an excellent understanding of what was required. Now and again he would pass something on with a note, "I rather like this but it would take too much material for the 'Elegance' range. Is there any way to get a similar effect by different cutting?"

'Far from being restricted to the best of a bad lot, I began to get excited as the odd little treasure turned up. "Now why didn't I think of that?" I would ask myself, then laugh when I thought that other designers probably had said that about my own work. I began to look forward eagerly to what the day would bring. Marguerite's attack faded into the background. Then one morning the first pack I unfastened made me gasp and then sit speechless. I looked at the name. Franc Rapello. "No one is going to beat this," I thought as I turned drawing after drawing over and then started all over again. Of course, there were mistakes, snags which he could not foresee but experience would tell him . . . those gathers would make that panel fall differently because the material would be heavier there and he would lose that effect . . . but it would only need him to see it made up and he would understand immediately. The colours were interesting. He had married some that would have seemed impossible and made it work. That was a gift the Italians had. "Rapello" . . . there was probably Italian blood there. I felt my face flushing with pleasure. This competition would certainly be no wash-out. Properly handled, it would not only bring the publicity we had anticipated but give us a year's supply of interesting new designs for the "Elegance" range. Something told me that he would learn quickly. I could concentrate more on my exclusive file. Come to that, I'd have to look to my laurels with a promising youngster like Franc Rapello around! Eagerly I lifted the telephone to summon Lou and Pierre.

'"What's up?" asked Lou. "You sound happy."

'"I think we've discovered a genius. Have a look at those!"

'It wasn't long before Pierre appeared. "You wanted me for something?"

'Lou answered for me while I sat back and studied their faces. "Elise thinks she's discovered a genius and I'm inclined to agree with her, though I don't know anything about the cutting, of course."

'"He uses colour so differently," I said to Pierre. "These narrower panels will make for economy in the cutting."

'"I can see that," said Pierre dreamily. "I think you're right. Of course, I insist on taking a little credit myself. I thought this scheme up."

'"Of course, my darling Pierre," said Lou, embracing him in her most exaggerated fashion. "You thought it all up and we shall all be rich and Elise will have a little more time to enjoy herself and maybe this Franc will be handsome and make my poor Robert jealous."

'"He's twenty-two," said Pierre. "His mother is more likely to be jealous, you little cradle-snatcher."

'Lou pouted, then burst out laughing, but I noticed two angry spots on her cheeks. Pierre rose. "Now ladies," he said, "let me take you out to a lovely long lunch. I think we deserve it."

'We attracted a lot of attention in that restaurant but we were too happy to care. I suppose even Pierre had found it difficult to be sure that our prosperity was not just a flash in the pan. In the fashion world particularly, public taste could be fickle, but we seemed to be guiding it and I had the feeling that Franc Rapello was going to enhance that reputation in a way none of us had foreseen. In my mind's eye I could picture "The Rapello collection for the younger woman".

'Pierre lingered over the wine in a way I had never seen him do before. "We shall really make a splash of this presentation," he was saying. "It will need to be a large assembly hall. I think it would be a good idea to invite all the young people who entered the competition."

'Lou's eyebrows shot up. "That will cost us."

'"Yes, but think of all the press reports we shall get out of it. Then, many of the public figures will feel more inclined to come if they think it is not confined to the rich clients. They will be able to pose as supporters of the young. The photographers could make quite a lot of this. It will need Lou, of course, to show his designs."

'"No feathers," I whispered, sending her into gales of laughter. Pierre wanted to know what that was all about and Lou promised with much rolling of the eyes to tell him when he was a little older.

'"Well! When do we announce it to the press?" asked Lou.

'"Wouldn't we be better to let the winner know first?" I asked.

'"Yes. He could have changed his mind," said Pierre, "and you'll have to start all over again." Lou started to make a few indignant suggestions as to what she would do to him if he dared. I kicked her under the table and she muttered softly that when she was a countess I wouldn't dare . . .

'I muttered equally softly that when I had told Robert a few things about her, she would have a snowflake's chance in Hades of being a countess.

'"When you've finished giggling, ladies," said Pierre, "I do think we should get back to see what's happening to our fortunes."

'Franc Rapello didn't change his mind. He was enraptured at the idea of being the first winner of the

214

Pierre-Elise Award and delighted to think that he would have an office of his own to work in. Lou saw him before I did because I was working flat-out on a wedding-dress design that morning. She drifted in to my sanctum. "Oh, Elise. You will fall in love with him. He is beautiful!" She gave a huge sigh. "And he is very slim. You will want to mother him and feed him and cuddle him. Those eyes! And the long, long lashes. The ladies will come just to see him."

'"As long as the husbands pay the bill, I have no objection to all the ladies falling in love with Franc," I said.

'"Ah, my cold anglaise," she moaned. "His skin is smooth and olive and the eyes are so, so brown with the whites so, so white."

'"Lou," I said. "Could you please go elsewhere and rhapsodize? The young demoiselle and her oh-so-demanding mother will be here and I'll have nothing to show them."

'"Just show them our Franc," she said dreamily, then relented. "I'll watch out and waylay them. We have quite a number of very distracting designs made up just now. I'll climb into one and be ready." That was Lou! One whiff of a sale . . .

'We spent many hours, Lou and I, discussing the décor for the award ceremony. After the success of our house-warming and later parties we were reluctant to do less than magnificently. "Go ahead, ladies," said Pierre. "Spend what you like but remember it's your money too that you're throwing away." Since both of us had known poverty there was no likelihood of our throwing money away. Every sou we spent was going to show its worth. The press, too, was helping quite considerably. It was rather a dull time for news now that the World Fair was fading into the background and so our young reporter tended to drop by to hear the latest reports.'

'We looked at a few likely venues before we made up our minds; "Too draughty, people like to be warm," Lou would say; "Too high a ceiling, our flower arrangements would be lost," I would add. Finally we made our decision and I went back to my office to sketch the room in proportion and to decide on the décor. "What about asking Franc to help decide on the setting?" asked Lou.

' "Next time, maybe," I said. "By then you'll be over your infatuation and able to keep your mind on your work."

'In a way, it was a repeat performance of our house-warming party, only this time Pierre was involved too. We were all determined to make the occasion unforgettable and knew that its success could bring a long-lasting benefit to our enterprise. I forced myself not to give in to the exhaustion which constantly threatened me; to put Georges' horrifying death and Marguerite's frightful exhibition behind me. Pierre was certainly right in wishing to increase our staff. That thought came to me oftener and oftener. But I ploughed on beside Lou, whose energy seemed inexhaustible, while our favourite reporter haunted the premises in the hope of hearing more details of the grand occasion. "I shall flop when this is all over," I kept telling myself.

'Of course the excitement of the Great Night itself revived me. Due to our detailed planning, which had provided for every disaster except an earthquake, as Lou put it, everything went swimmingly. The city dignitaries were present in satisfying numbers, largely

216

thanks to the reporting of our well-primed friend. Franc was boyishly pleased with his success and showed it. He was a photographer's delight, as was Lou, of course. When Pierre kissed me goodnight, he summed it all up. "I think we have safely reached the top. If we keep our heads, no one will be able to challenge us after this."

'Of course, there's always a reaction. I felt it keenly next morning. I was tired, yet restless. What I wanted was a spell with Anna and Albert, some homely commonsense and a little time to play with Marianne's children who had been complaining that Tante Elise never came to see them any more. I went in to my office as usual but there was no work done. This was not wholly due to my lassitude. The salesgirls were re-living the events of the night before and Lou, in her best form, was imitating some of the dignitaries who had graced the occasion. She saw my warning look as I passed by. "It is all right, Madame, the girls know that we must be careful outside. We are all in this together." They nodded in assent, but I could not be so sanguine. I could see a lot of our careful work being undone if a hint of this was mouthed beyond the premises. Then I shook myself. I was being the "cold anglaise" that Lou bemoaned so often. Also I knew that the minute a potential client appeared on the scene, Lou's team would respond to her eyebrows and all would be attention and eagerness to please. Not for the first time, I wondered how they would react if or when Lou became a countess. Then I reminded myself that Lou was a born actress. I was worrying quite unnecessarily.

'The quiet of the early morning didn't last long. Once people had had time to read the morning paper, the curious newcomers drifted in along with the fulsome regulars who wanted to congratulate "Madame" and reinforce their connection. Many were anxious for a glimpse of Franc, but he had still a few ends to tie up and farewells to make before he settled in Paris. I had urged him to do this so that he could concentrate solely on his new venture, and he was grateful. Lou, while greeting familiar clients warmly, took the opportunity to display some of our latest models and urged Natalie to do the same. In the relaxed atmosphere, which seemed to be an extension of the night before, several people came to ask my advice. My approach was rather different from Lou's but I knew from experience that it worked. I discussed the problem seriously and then assured them that several items which would be appearing in my next collection would meet their needs. Lou tended to grab the impulse buyer while I drew the more thoughtful client who might well have regretted an unconsidered purchase. "This way they look forward to it, Lou," I had assured her. But Lou wasn't convinced.

'"Get them in the mood and grab their money, is my motto," she maintained. Seeing Marie, our expert from the workrooms, come to measure at least two clients that morning, I could see Lou's point.

'On Sunday morning I phoned Marianne to apologize for not having seen her for so long.

'"Oh, Tante Elise, you won't have heard the news. Papa and Maman are going off on a walking holiday in the mountains of Austria – the Vorarlberg. They have talked so much about it for so long and now Paul is going with them. I had not the heart to say 'No' to him when he asked if I minded, but I am tied, feeding the baby, and I could not go. Then I said to myself, 'Tante Elise will comfort me.'"

'"And so I shall," I assured her.

'"But no! That is all spoiled. Paul's mother wants me to go to her while Paul is away. I said no, no, no, of course. But Maman says that she is an old lady with no one to love but Paul and his family . . . I'm sure she doesn't love me . . . and Papa said that you are very busy and you are making a success of your life in spite of all your difficulties and I must not be a burden to you."

'"You could never be a burden to me, Marianne," I cried.

'"I was right! I said so to Papa. I said that I was nearly a daughter to you. It was only because you were so busy with the competition that you were not visiting me and when the competition was over you would be back."

'"Certainly, and it's over now," I said.

'"But we travel tomorrow, Tante Elise. Papa and Maman have already left for Bordeaux where they will stay with my brother, Heinz, for a few days. Paul will accompany me to his mother's house and then join them there. Oh, I feel so miserable about it all, but Papa says we cannot always do entirely as we want and I must consider Paul's mother; she gave him birth and loves him deeply in her own way. I must give her a chance, he says, to love our little ones too. Maman and he get so much joy from the babies; it is only fair to share that. I know he is right, Tante Elise, but oh, it is so difficult . . ."

'I stirred myself. "Your father is right, of course, Marianne, and if you handle her cleverly the old gorgon isn't really so bad." I knew what I was doing might not be exactly acceptable in Anna's sight, but it produced a reassuring giggle from Marianne. "Butter her

219

up. She responds to flattery. Encourage Annette and Marthe to be nice to her. Bribe them if necessary, but better still, if you can, convince them she is a kind old lady and they have to take care of her. Ask her if little Louis is like Paul at that age. Encourage her to tell you tales of his childhood. Don't get sorry for yourself. Be clever. Treat it as a game. You never know, you might find yourself getting fond of the old trout. Don't tell your dear parents I put it that way, of course."

'Marianne was laughing by then. "Tante Elise, you are a tonic. I *do* wish you could be with me. I could put up with anything, I think, if you were there to make me laugh and see things in proportion."

'"Well, if things get difficult, just conjure me up and you'll manage, I'm sure. May I pay you a short visit today or are you too busy packing?"

'"Oh, come, please. The children will forget what you look like if you don't . . . no, I'm teasing! They keep asking for you. Come as soon as you can, please."

'Those few hours I spent with Marianne and her children were the perfect antidote to all the artifice I had been engaged in for so long. The little gifts I took had been in my house quite a long time, I realized. It seemed almost unbelievable that I could get so wrapped up in the world of fashion to the point of neglecting Marianne – who did indeed seem like a daughter to me now – and those lovely children. As I read to them and they twined their plump little arms round my neck, I could not help thinking of Alain and all I had missed. Anna was so lucky. She had met Albert. Then I found myself blushing. I was coveting Albert, and Anna was the truest friend any woman could wish for. My passionate nature was a snare. It had landed me with Michel. It had put an end to

Georges' marriage and then his life. Quickly I put my own thoughts behind me and started up a singing game with Annette and Marthe.

'As I shook hands with Paul and wished him a happy holiday, I was aware of Marianne's bleak face in the background. "I'm sure Marianne and the children will cheer your mother up," I said. "She must be very lonely."

'He smiled appreciatively. "Yes. I'm hoping that they will keep her busy. Her life is very empty now – nothing but disappointment, it seems."

'"These young people will stir her up," I assured him while Marianne made a face behind his back.

'I did not go straight home. It was a day for getting away from the perfection my work demanded, a work that was by its nature artificial. I found myself making for the convent and the peace I knew I should find there.

'With Albert and Anna away and Lou busy with her Robert, I had little to look forward to in the way of evening entertainment. It did give me a chance, however, to get on with my designing which had suffered from the preparations for the award ceremony. I was careful in my behaviour with Franc Rapello and warned Lou to be the same. "We don't want him to get cocky," I said. "Don't forget that any intimacy would be difficult to retract from when we are working in such close quarters. We are a generation older and that should help to prevent him taking any chances. I think he is serious about his work and will fit in well. Just a little distance, Lou . . ."

'"Ah! my cool anglaise. You are as bad as Pierre but you are probably right," she said, pouting.

'Though I had no great hopes then of Lou's taking

my advice, she seemed to adjust to the situation. In one direction she was certainly changing. No wealthy lover appeared to supplant Robert. While she still managed to amuse the salesgirls when they were off duty, her business sense became more acute every day. I could see how Pierre's attitude had changed towards her and, remembering his initial reluctance to include her in our negotiations, could not help being amused.

'Franc's deference to me was rather amusing too, but gratifying nonetheless. When I showed him some of the flaws in his prize-winning designs, he was eager to make the corrections I suggested. Of course, I was never slow to give praise when he turned out something really remarkable, and that happened often. During his first two weeks he was quite happy to work on into the evening. This suited me as I had nothing else to look forward to. I soon saw that he had the artist's gift of becoming utterly absorbed in his work and I could happily leave him to get on with it.

'I had warned Lou that I would be late next morning as I had an appointment with the hairdresser. I was almost ready to leave when I heard the doorbell.

'Monique's face was enquiring as she held out the telegram, "It's come all the way from Austria, Madame."

'"Oh, no," I gasped.

'"Do you think it is bad news, Madame?"

'I pulled myself together. "I had better open it, hadn't I?"

Madame Wallach has been killed in a fall. Please break the news gently to Marianne. I shall join her

at the château as soon as I can leave. The doctor
has many things to arrange here.

    Paul Auclair

'"No, no, no," I whispered. The room started to
spin round and I held the telegram in the direction of
Monique but she was starting to spin too.

'I came to on the sofa. Monique was holding smelling salts to my lips and a brandy bottle and glass were
on the table beside me. "We must pack immediately,
Monique," I said.

'"But, Madame, you are not fit to travel . . . the
shock . . ."

'"Once I have sipped some brandy I shall recover,"
I said. "Meantime, will you phone Mademoiselle
Croquelois at the emporium – you know the number
– and tell her what has happened and that I shall be
travelling as soon as I can."

'The brandy *did* help, though I still gave enormous
shudders from time to time. Monique returned from
the telephone. "She says I am to pack some warm
clothes for you as shock always chills you."

'"That was all she said?" I asked. Monique nodded.
I felt vaguely disappointed. Lou knew how fond I was
of Anna. Indeed she had always seemed fond of Anna
herself, though maybe a little wary. Of course, Lou
was every inch the businesswoman now, I reflected.

'I moved slowly upstairs to superintend the packing.
It was a frustrating business because I found difficulty
in concentrating. "But Madame, you will need a dressing robe," Monique was prompting when we heard
the front door slam.

'Lou mounted the stairs with an unladylike speed.
Her arms went round me as the tears began and she
issued quick orders to Monique.

'By the time I walked down my elegant steps to the waiting carriage, I was, in appearance at least, the cool anglaise. Lou had worked her own kind of rough magic. "I wish I could come with you," she said, "but I'd probably send the old dragon into fits and that wouldn't help Marianne."

'"You're better here, looking after the business," I said.

'"Mmm," agreed Lou. "It's a good thing we've got Franc. Pierre can start making up some of his designs to keep the public interested. He's talking of taking him round to the factory anyway, just to let him see some of the practical difficulties."

'I knew she was doing her best to distract me. I was grateful, but really, at that moment, the whole empire meant nothing to me. I was up against human loss, the loss I had experienced in its worst form when Alain died. I was going to perform a dreadful task, breaking such news to Marianne. She would need all my strength till Paul got back to comfort her. Who was going to comfort Albert? I supposed there would be all sorts of legal complications to sort out since the death had taken place outside France.

'All the way on the train the thoughts were buzzing round my head. I felt so, so weary but I could not rest. Time seemed to drag and yet I dreaded what was to come. Anxiety for Marianne drove all thoughts of my appearance from my head. I was certainly no longer Lou's "cool anglaise" by the time the coachman handed me down at the château.

'A servant informed me that Madame Paul had driven out with the children to visit a neighbour; Madame Auclair was resting in her sitting-room; did I wish to send a message?

'I hesitated for a moment. "I do not wish to disturb your mistress," I began. Then a bell began to ring. The servant said, "That is my mistress. May I give her your name, please."

'Paul's mother took her time about appearing. My thoughts began to drift to Anna, to the picture she had proudly shown me of Marianne, her quick sympathy when she learned of Alain's health, the immediate offer of the baby carriage. Then I saw her in the convent, her understanding for poor Catherine who had never known the joy of pretty clothes; all the sensible ways in which she had used her gifts and coaxed other people into using theirs. The tears were streaming down my face when I remembered how she had supported me in my sorrow over Georges even though she disapproved of the liaison, the ready way she had lent me Albert's support at the theatre. How many women would have known that all I needed at that moment was his steady presence?

'As the sound of a cane tapping on the mosaic floor reached me, I mopped quickly at my streaming eyes. A large mirror by the door showed me that I was almost unrecognizable with my blotched red face. Then I saw Madame Auclair approaching. She caught sight of me in the mirror and jerked forward, moving almost at a run. Her hand stretched out for the telegram as she gave a strangled cry, "Paul, my baby!"

'"No, Madame," I cried, but she staggered and fell in a heap in front of me. I tugged a nearby bell and servants came hurrying. While I was tucking a cushion under her head, she gave a dreadful shudder; her face twisted violently and her jaw stayed clenched. "We must have a doctor," I said.'

Chapter 16

'Can you picture it, Jessie? I was stuck there . . . waiting . . . waiting . . . waiting. One of the maids was crying and I couldn't think of a word to say to her. When he finally arrived, the doctor could only confirm what I already knew – Madame Auclair had died of shock.

'"I blame myself," I said, "I had been weeping. She misunderstood. I tried . . ."

'"You must not do that, Madame," the doctor said courteously. "This would have happened sometime . . . some people . . ." he waved his hand vaguely. The elderly servant who was standing beside us ventured, "If I may speak, Madame, Sir? . . ."

'"Certainly," I said.

'"Our mistress was very worried about the young master going to the Austrian mountains; said they were dangerous. She worried about many things, especially when they affected her son; she was a lady who found it difficult to be at ease. Those of us who had been with the family a long time understood this. She saw much trouble in this family when she was young. It made her . . . the way she was. Bernadette, her maid, said that she had feared Monsieur Paul would not come back, so it would be easy for her to imagine when she saw you holding a telegram . . ." he tailed off.

'"You see, Madame," the doctor said, "it is just as

226

'"Oh, yes, Madame."

'"Then they can deliver the invitations that way. It is unusual, but I think that when people learn the circumstances they will understand. I shall see Monsieur Paul about the invitations. I have organized many receptions in Paris so I could design the table layout here and see to all the flower arrangements. The cook is going to have the most difficult task."

'"Perhaps not so difficult, Madame." Henri was unbending. "You see, our butcher had expected an order . . . had prepared some things and has been disappointed . . . I could not issue such orders and the young master was absent . . ."

'"Right!" I said. "We have no time to waste. I shall see the young master, if you will consult the cook. If we stick to the pattern of the late master's funeral, we can't go wrong."

'My tiredness fled as I realized so much depended on me. Paul was full of contrition when he heard of the invitations. With the help of the estate books he was able to find the necessary addresses – in fact, he knew many of them already once he brought his mind to bear on it. While Paul was searching for addresses, I had started writing some of the cards in my best script, ready for him to sign. "Is there no end to your resourcefulness, Tante Elise?" he said with the first smile I had seen since his return.'

'The grooms were only too happy to be doing something active next morning. I mentioned their possible worries to Paul.

'"I'd never dream of landing any of them in a fix," he said. "Of course Marianne would like to be rid of

' "Has the priest fixed the time?" I asked.

' "Yes, he had to agree that with the bishop who will perform the ceremony."

' "The bishop is coming?" I asked.

' "Oh, yes, Madame. The late master always saw that a share of the best vintage went to the bishop."

' "And after the burial?" I prompted.

' "Well, normally, Madame, there would have been invitations sent out to all the leading people in the district and they would come to the château for a funeral spread with our best wine – you see, even in sorrow the vintners have their pride."

' "And those invitations were not sent out?" I asked.

' "The young master was not here, Madame, and the young mistress is not well . . ."

' "Is it too late now?" I was speaking brusquely and Henri's tone sharpened too.

' "It could be done – that is if the young master wished."

' "I think he will. It is only because he is distracted, I'm sure. And it is only the leading people who are invited?" I probed. "What about the estate workers?"

'Henri's face brightened a little. "They normally come back too, and a large collation is laid out for them in one of the barns."

' "Well, we've no time to waste, Henri," I said. "The first thing to do is to make sure that the cook can cope. Then we shall have to find some way of getting those invitations out. Lists of addresses . . ."

' "The details of the late master's funeral are recorded in the estate books," said Henri.

' "Excellent!" I had the bit between my teeth by then. "The grooms can all ride, I take it? Are there any other young servants . . . ?"

237

unimaginable loss. I was going to have to step in to a role I had never imagined. The first thing was to consult one of the senior servants. I chose Henri, the one who had spoken up when the doctor was there. I think we would call him the butler, but I was never sure on this point. He seemed to have a thorough knowledge of the procedures at the château. Summoning him to the library, I asked if he could spare me some minutes.

'"The young master and mistress are distraught, Henri," I said, "and I have no knowledge of the style of a family funeral in this part of the world. You would have been here when the late master died?"

'"Yes, Madame, it is not so long ago."

'"No. I understand," I said. "Perhaps you could sit down, Henri, and just tell me, from the beginning, what will happen at the funeral."

'He was faintly disturbed at the idea of sitting down while he was on duty, but I could see how shaken he too had been. The servants must have been worrying about their own futures. Paul had no wish to carry on the business personally. They would worry that he might sell it and be rid of all responsibility. Come to that, I had no idea if this was what might be in Paul's mind. Certainly Marianne had no affection for the place. And yet . . . it had such possibilities . . . some lively damasks instead of all the dreary faded browns . . . but I must concentrate.

'Henri's word picture of what would happen was fascinating, like nothing I had ever experienced. Every male worker on the estate would follow the coffin to the village church. The horses would be decked in funeral plumes. They would take the long circular route so that the very elderly and the young could be by the roadside to pay their last respects to La Dame.

funerals almost immediately in summertime. Had there been any legal problems the body would have had to be moved a considerable distance to a mortuary. The coach was not due till last night. Two of Marianne's brothers managed to get to the funeral by hiring horses in Feldkirch and riding the rest of the way."

'"So, two of her sons managed to get there."

'"Yes."

'"That's good," I said.

'"Marianne doesn't seem to think so," Paul said wearily. "She keeps saying that she should have been there. She should have insisted on getting a wet nurse for the baby."

'"But the doctor feared she might get milk fever," I protested, "and she knew about the travelling difficulties."

'"She never told me that. Oh, Tante Elise. Stay with us, please. Marianne is so upset and I don't seem to be able to help her. We are all worn out and her father will have no strength to spare, either. He has always said that you were brave and strong . . . Can you stay for a little while at least?'

'I told him the position – that I would be able to stay unless something urgent cropped up and I was pretty sure that Lou could cope with most things.

'The funeral of Madame Auclair was to take place the morning of the next day but one. The doctor had taken it upon himself to see to many of the aspects. It was only when I saw one of the senior servants hanging crape over the pictures in the main hall that I realized we were preparing for a much bigger occasion than I had bargained for. Marianne was too immature to deal with this situation even if she had not been suckling the baby and had not just suffered an went on, "And we could stand there and see Switzerland, Germany and Italy as well as a large area of Austria. We were so lucky with the weather. Usually the clouds are threatening even if they don't actually bring rain. We rested for a while after a lovely picnic. We were really reluctant to leave that view. We were going down the long way, which is more gradual, I suppose it would really be goat-tracks. On that side there was quite a lot of vegetation – shrubs and the occasional tree. We had to watch our feet because of scree, of course, especially when you had to step from a higher path to a lower. And that was how the accident happened! Dr Wallach was leading. He had just stepped down and Madame was following. She was stepping on to her right foot and then seemed to change her mind. She swivelled and skidded on the scree. As she slid forward she knocked the doctor off his feet. He fell forward while she rolled slightly to the left and fell down the slope. She hit some small rocks and bounced over them but came down, cracking her head on the sharp edge of a boulder. Tante Elise, I can still hear that dull crack! I think the doctor felt the same foreboding as we hurried down. A climbing party which was just a short way ahead hurried back to join us. The sound of scree always alerts a climber!

'"We knew, the doctor and I, that it was hopeless, though we listened for a pulse, of course. Blood from her ear was staining the grass. Naturally the doctor was upset. I'm afraid I wasn't much help. I was shaking like a jelly, Tante Elise, but don't tell Marianne. Two sturdy young men from the Austrian party carried Madame down the rest of the way. They were used to the paths and made light of their burden. Seemingly it is the custom in those mountain villages to hold expected some communication but, no doubt, there were many things to attend to and we would simply have to wait.'

'It was early evening before Paul arrived. I had warned the servants that no one was to break the news; he was to be taken straight to his wife. After the strain he had been under I knew that he was likely to be unmanned by this further blow. When I heard the carriage I made straight for my own room and stayed there till a servant came seeking me much later.

'"He's lost his boyish look," was my first thought as Paul came towards me, hand outstretched. Neither of us could speak at first. I noticed a little nerve jumping by his eye. I was the one to break the silence. "What is happening . . . there?" I couldn't for the life of me remember the name of the place that Paul's telegram had come from.

'"The funeral took place yesterday afternoon."

'"Oh," I said. "I thought it might be delayed because of legalities."

'"No. The accident was witnessed by another party of climbers so we had no difficulties that way."

'"How did it happen, Paul?" I asked. "She was used to those hills, Marianne said. Didn't her father take her climbing there when she was very young?"

'"Yes. He was brought up there. Oh, Tante Elise, it happened so simply and so quickly. Even now I can't believe it. We were being quite ambitious in the one we tackled that day – the Hohe Kugel – but there was no thought of real danger. We had gone up the direct way, which is quite a steep climb. The view from the top was magic. We could see the Bodensee so clearly."

'That's what they call Lake Constance, Jessie. He

233

'"Didn't the doctor give you something to make you sleep?" I asked.

'"Yes. He put the little maid in charge because I was so upset. He told her I was not to take it till Louis had had his feed. He was late in waking and I had just newly had the medicine when you arrived. Would you be an angel and stay with me till I fall asleep?"

'I stroked her hair gently and she gradually snuggled down. Her breathing steadied and slowed, the little frown lines round her eyes smoothed out. When I was sure she was deeply asleep, I disengaged myself gently, rubbed my stiff joints and slowly made my way to the guest room I had been given. I lay tense for a long time, thinking over the events of the day, then I came to Marianne's tribute, "You're so like Maman, Tante Elise, so comforting." It was a compliment I certainly did not merit, but I fell asleep, happy with the thought.

'The next morning was difficult for us all. The house was in mourning, but the young children knew nothing of this and expected to be kept amused. Marianne longed for Paul's return but there was no news. As the morning wore on little Louis, normally a placid baby, grew fretful. Marianne was tearful as she tried to nurse him. In the end I offered to take all three children out with the nursemaid. At first Marianne objected. "I think he is hungry and I am not able to feed him," she complained.

'"Don't worry," I said. "If the worst comes to the worst the doctor will get a wet nurse. He said so. He is seeing to the practical side of the funeral arrangements meantime. I know it is difficult for you, but do try to rest a little, my dear."

'"If only Paul were here," she said. I too had

I told you. You must not blame yourself." He lifted his head as the sound of carriage wheels was heard. "See that the children are taken straight to the nursery," he said to the servant. "I shall have to break the news to the young mistress."

'"I have worse than that to tell her," I said, and showed him the telegram.

'"This is incredible! The young master and the young mistress . . . both. It is incredible! And it is the reason for your weeping, Madame?"

'"Yes. She is . . . was . . . a very dear friend. Marianne is going to be devastated at the loss of her mother. As you see, I have been asked to break the news."

'"It would seem that I had better stay," he said.

'"Yes," I agreed. "She is still suckling little Louis. This terrible news couldn't have come at a worse time for her. It is almost bound to make her unable . . ."

'"Probably. I can arrange for a wet nurse if it becomes necessary," the doctor said.

'That was something I had not thought of. I was grateful for his practical forethought. Paul was going to return with the intention of comforting Marianne, only to learn of this fresh disaster; there would be the funeral to arrange and Lord knows how many formalities to deal with. The doctor could probably help with that. What would happen about the château? I shook my head. Marianne would be with me in a minute and I had to tell her the most dreadful news she had ever heard in her young life. I had to be strong . . . *had* to be!

'"Aunt Elise!" Marianne's face lit up as she caught sight of me and started to hurry forward, then she paused. "Something is wrong. Paul. He is not used to the hills."

' "No, not Paul," I said, putting my arms round her. "My darling Marianne, you will have to be brave. Your mother has had an accident."

' "Mother? She is used to the hills. She was climbing with her Papa when she was just a little girl. Maman . . . she is not . . ."

'I nodded, unable to speak. Marianne began to shake violently. "I must go to her. Poor Papa, he will be alone. Help me get ready, Tante Elise."

' "My darling," I said, "You remember that Paul said there is only one coach a week to the little village. We do not know how long it took him to reach some place where he could send off these telegrams. I fear the funeral may already be over, unless it is held up by formalities. Besides, you have the baby to feed. You cannot go."

' "He can have a wet nurse. I must go to Papa."

'The doctor broke in. "You might get milk fever, Madame, and you would be no use to anyone if you were ill. Madame Blanchard is right in saying that the funeral may already be over. There will be no mortuary in a place like that and so, in summertime it is usual to hold the funeral very soon. Besides, your husband will need your support here."

' "Why here?" Marianne asked.

'I led her to a chair and held her tightly while the doctor explained his presence. He ended, "Madame Blanchard is inclined to blame herself for what happened as your mother-in-law caught sight of her in that mirror when she had been weeping, but I have assured Madame that such an event could have taken place at any time. Madame Auclair was of a nervous disposition; she worried unnecessarily about many things, found it difficult to believe that all was well with her family. We understood and made allowances, but I am not really surprised that her death should be in this fashion. It is only so dreadful that you and your husband should be bereft in one blow like this . . . so dreadful!''

'Marianne was sobbing now. The doctor nodded wordlessly to me. She had to get release from the horror. I heard him murmur to the old servant that he would like to see Marianne's personal maid. She had travelled with only a nursemaid, I knew, but Madame Auclair would no doubt have allocated someone to her for form's sake. The girl appeared. The doctor spoke for a moment, handed her a box, then asked her to repeat the instructions he had given before dismissing her to her duties.

'After Marianne was in bed and the doctor had departed I sat alone in the sombre little drawing-room. I was worn out emotionally but my brain chugged on. Paul would return in a worn-out state himself. He was extremely fond of Anna, I knew, and hero-worshipped Albert. He would have had many telegrams to send, contacting all five of Anna's sons. Would the funeral be delayed because of inquiries? I had no idea what the legalities would be. I knew nothing of such things even in France, Jessie. Lou had seen to everything for Alain's funeral and there was no question of an accident there. Austrian law could be far different. At least Albert would be speaking his own language. Perhaps the funeral was already over. The doctor seemed to think that was a reasonable assumption. Would any of Anna's boys have got there in time? What would Paul do about the château? Marianne had never been enamoured of the gloomy old place, but that could be because of its association with Paul's mother. Paul was a conscientious fellow. He was going to feel a certain amount of guilt. He had chosen a path in life which his mother deplored. When we had discussed things earlier he had told me that the business could run itself. There were many employees who had been with the family all their working lives. But the château itself! That was a different matter. It must cost a fortune to run. It would be silly if all the money from the wine business were to be eaten up in keeping an empty castle.

'Paul's work with Albert meant so much to him. Earlier Marianne had said, "Papa never books any patients in August, but Paul didn't like to ask if he could join them in Austria in case there should be an emergency in Paris. Papa assured him that the doctor who always stands in for him then would be happy to do so as usual."

'I had arranged for one of the senior servants to send a wire to Lou for me, telling her about the old lady's death and asking her to let me know if there was anything urgent at the office; meantime I would like to stay with Marianne. Her reply had been reassuring and told me that a letter would follow. Meantime there was nothing I could do. It might be wise to go to bed, conserve my energy for what the morrow might bring.

'Slowly I mounted the stairs and moved towards my corridor. Then I changed my mind. I would look in on Marianne; see if the pills the doctor had left had done their work. I knocked softly and the little maid answered the door. "Is Madame asleep?" I whispered.

'"Is that you, Aunt Elise?" came Marianne's voice.

'I moved towards the bed. My lovely, lively little Marianne looked careworn and oh, so vulnerable. She stretched out her arms to me as she had done when she was much younger. I nodded to the maid and she slipped out quietly. Cradling Marianne in my arms, I found myself singing softly to her as you used to do to Lilias, remember? You were always her favourite big sister, Jessie!

'"Your song is sad, Tante Elise, no? Sad, but lovely," she said. "What does it mean?"

'It was the "Iona Boating Song" I was singing and I tried to convey the picture of the Western Isles to her – the blue peaks of Mull with the clouds wreathing them and the monks patiently rowing. "And that is the song they sang as they rowed the dead kings of Scotland over to Iona for burial," I ended. "It is sad but it is also a song of faith and assurance, one your mother would have approved of."

'That brought the tears again and she hugged me more tightly. "D'you know, Aunt Elise," she whispered, "I did what you said. I buttered Paul's mother up and persuaded the children to be tender towards her. Last night when they were ready for bed they put out their arms and kissed her without being told. She smiled proudly as the nursemaid led them away. Then, when I was leaving her at night, I steeled myself to kiss her too. She didn't say anything but I turned a little as I reached the door and saw her wipe away a tear. I felt a bit of a Judas because I didn't really feel like doing it . . . I feel guilty about it now because it was insincere."

'"Don't feel that way, Marianne. You made her happy. We don't always understand these things, but I think God used your gesture for a good purpose."

'"You're so like Maman, Tante Elise, so comforting." She was weeping unashamedly now.

'"Didn't the doctor give you something to make you sleep?" I asked.

'"Yes. He put the little maid in charge because I was so upset. He told her I was not to take it till Louis had had his feed. He was late in waking and I had just newly had the medicine when you arrived. Would you be an angel and stay with me till I fall asleep?"

'I stroked her hair gently and she gradually snuggled down. Her breathing steadied and slowed, the little frown lines round her eyes smoothed out. When I was sure she was deeply asleep, I disengaged myself gently, rubbed my stiff joints and slowly made my way to the guest room I had been given. I lay tense for a long time, thinking over the events of the day, then I came to Marianne's tribute, "You're so like Maman, Tante Elise, so comforting." It was a compliment I certainly did not merit, but I fell asleep, happy with the thought.

'The next morning was difficult for us all. The house was in mourning, but the young children knew nothing of this and expected to be kept amused. Marianne longed for Paul's return but there was no news. As the morning wore on little Louis, normally a placid baby, grew fretful. Marianne was tearful as she tried to nurse him. In the end I offered to take all three children out with the nursemaid. At first Marianne objected. "I think he is hungry and I am not able to feed him," she complained.

'"Don't worry," I said. "If the worst comes to the worst the doctor will get a wet nurse. He said so. He is seeing to the practical side of the funeral arrangements meantime. I know it is difficult for you, but do try to rest a little, my dear."

'"If only Paul were here," she said. I too had

expected some communication but, no doubt, there were many things to attend to and we would simply have to wait.'

'It was early evening before Paul arrived. I had warned the servants that no one was to break the news; he was to be taken straight to his wife. After the strain he had been under I knew that he was likely to be unmanned by this further blow. When I heard the carriage I made straight for my own room and stayed there till a servant came seeking me much later.

'"He's lost his boyish look," was my first thought as Paul came towards me, hand outstretched. Neither of us could speak at first. I noticed a little nerve jumping by his eye. I was the one to break the silence. "What is happening . . . there?" I couldn't for the life of me remember the name of the place that Paul's telegram had come from.

'"The funeral took place yesterday afternoon."

'"Oh," I said. "I thought it might be delayed because of legalities."

'"No. The accident was witnessed by another party of climbers so we had no difficulties that way."

'"How did it happen, Paul?" I asked. "She was used to those hills, Marianne said. Didn't her father take her climbing there when she was very young?"

'"Yes. He was brought up there. Oh, Tante Elise, it happened so simply and so quickly. Even now I can't believe it. We were being quite ambitious in the one we tackled that day – the Hohe Kugel – but there was no thought of real danger. We had gone up the direct way, which is quite a steep climb. The view from the top was magic. We could see the Bodensee so clearly."

'That's what they call Lake Constance, Jessie. He

233

went on, "And we could stand there and see Switzerland, Germany and Italy as well as a large area of Austria. We were so lucky with the weather. Usually the clouds are threatening even if they don't actually bring rain. We rested for a while after a lovely picnic. We were really reluctant to leave that view. We were going down the long way, which is more gradual, I suppose it would really be goat-tracks. On that side there was quite a lot of vegetation – shrubs and the occasional tree. We had to watch our feet because of scree, of course, especially when you had to step from a higher path to a lower. And that was how the accident happened! Dr Wallach was leading. He had just stepped down and Madame was following. She was stepping on to her right foot and then seemed to change her mind. She swivelled and skidded on the scree. As she slid forward she knocked the doctor off his feet. He fell forward while she rolled slightly to the left and fell down the slope. She hit some small rocks and bounced over them but came down, cracking her head on the sharp edge of a boulder. Tante Elise, I can still hear that dull crack! I think the doctor felt the same foreboding as we hurried down. A climbing party which was just a short way ahead hurried back to join us. The sound of scree always alerts a climber!

'"We knew, the doctor and I, that it was hopeless, though we listened for a pulse, of course. Blood from her ear was staining the grass. Naturally the doctor was upset. I'm afraid I wasn't much help. I was shaking like a jelly, Tante Elise, but don't tell Marianne. Two sturdy young men from the Austrian party carried Madame down the rest of the way. They were used to the paths and made light of their burden. Seemingly it is the custom in those mountain villages to hold funerals almost immediately in summertime. Had there been any legal problems the body would have had to be moved a considerable distance to a mortuary. The coach was not due till last night. Two of Marianne's brothers managed to get to the funeral by hiring horses in Feldkirch and riding the rest of the way."

'"So, two of her sons managed to get there."

'"Yes."

'"That's good," I said.

'"Marianne doesn't seem to think so," Paul said wearily. "She keeps saying that she should have been there. She should have insisted on getting a wet nurse for the baby."

'"But the doctor feared she might get milk fever," I protested, "and she knew about the travelling difficulties."

'"She never told me that. Oh, Tante Elise. Stay with us, please. Marianne is so upset and I don't seem to be able to help her. We are all worn out and her father will have no strength to spare, either. He has always said that you were brave and strong . . . Can you stay for a little while at least?"

'I told him the position – that I would be able to stay unless something urgent cropped up and I was pretty sure that Lou could cope with most things.

'The funeral of Madame Auclair was to take place the morning of the next day but one. The doctor had taken it upon himself to see to many of the aspects. It was only when I saw one of the senior servants hanging crape over the pictures in the main hall that I realized we were preparing for a much bigger occasion than I had bargained for. Marianne was too immature to deal with this situation even if she had not been suckling the baby and had not just suffered an unimaginable loss. I was going to have to step in to a role I had never imagined. The first thing was to consult one of the senior servants. I chose Henri, the one who had spoken up when the doctor was there. I think we would call him the butler, but I was never sure on this point. He seemed to have a thorough knowledge of the procedures at the château. Summoning him to the library, I asked if he could spare me some minutes.

' "The young master and mistress are distraught, Henri," I said, "and I have no knowledge of the style of a family funeral in this part of the world. You would have been here when the late master died?"

' "Yes, Madame, it is not so long ago."

' "No. I understand," I said. "Perhaps you could sit down, Henri, and just tell me, from the beginning, what will happen at the funeral."

'He was faintly disturbed at the idea of sitting down while he was on duty, but I could see how shaken he too had been. The servants must have been worrying about their own futures. Paul had no wish to carry on the business personally. They would worry that he might sell it and be rid of all responsibility. Come to that, I had no idea if this was what might be in Paul's mind. Certainly Marianne had no affection for the place. And yet . . . it had such possibilities . . . some lively damasks instead of all the dreary faded browns . . . but I must concentrate.

'Henri's word picture of what would happen was fascinating, like nothing I had ever experienced. Every male worker on the estate would follow the coffin to the village church. The horses would be decked in funeral plumes. They would take the long circular route so that the very elderly and the young could be by the roadside to pay their last respects to La Dame.

236

' "Has the priest fixed the time?" I asked.

' "Yes, he had to agree that with the bishop who will perform the ceremony."

' "The bishop is coming?" I asked.

' "Oh, yes, Madame. The late master always saw that a share of the best vintage went to the bishop."

' "And after the burial?" I prompted.

' "Well, normally, Madame, there would have been invitations sent out to all the leading people in the district and they would come to the château for a funeral spread with our best wine – you see, even in sorrow the vintners have their pride."

' "And those invitations were not sent out?" I asked.

' "The young master was not here, Madame, and the young mistress is not well . . ."

' "Is it too late now?" I was speaking brusquely and Henri's tone sharpened too.

' "It could be done – that is if the young master wished."

' "I think he will. It is only because he is distracted, I'm sure. And it is only the leading people who are invited?" I probed. "What about the estate workers?"

'Henri's face brightened a little. "They normally come back too, and a large collation is laid out for them in one of the barns."

' "Well, we've no time to waste, Henri," I said. "The first thing to do is to make sure that the cook can cope. Then we shall have to find some way of getting those invitations out. Lists of addresses . . ."

' "The details of the late master's funeral are recorded in the estate books," said Henri.

' "Excellent!" I had the bit between my teeth by then. "The grooms can all ride, I take it? Are there any other young servants . . . ?"

' "Oh, yes, Madame."

' "Then they can deliver the invitations that way. It is unusual, but I think that when people learn the circumstances they will understand. I shall see Monsieur Paul about the invitations. I have organized many receptions in Paris so I could design the table layout here and see to all the flower arrangements. The cook is going to have the most difficult task."

' "Perhaps not so difficult, Madame." Henri was unbending. "You see, our butcher had expected an order . . . had prepared some things and has been disappointed . . . I could not issue such orders and the young master was absent . . ."

' "Right!" I said. "We have no time to waste. I shall see the young master, if you will consult the cook. If we stick to the pattern of the late master's funeral, we can't go wrong."

'My tiredness fled as I realized so much depended on me. Paul was full of contrition when he heard of the invitations. With the help of the estate books he was able to find the necessary addresses – in fact, he knew many of them already once he brought his mind to bear on it. While Paul was searching for addresses, I had started writing some of the cards in my best script, ready for him to sign. "Is there no end to your resourcefulness, Tante Elise?" he said with the first smile I had seen since his return.'

'The grooms were only too happy to be doing something active next morning. I mentioned their possible worries to Paul.

' "I'd never dream of landing any of them in a fix," he said. "Of course Marianne would like to be rid of the whole thing, but we don't know how little Louis may feel some day. She is in low spirits anyway and not fit to judge. I loved the château when I was young, though I was never particularly interested in the wine vats. But I didn't have to be. My father and all his staff saw to those things. I don't suppose many children are interested in that sort of thing. It was unnatural for Maman to suppose that I should be. But when some of my young friends visited me we used to have great fun hiding from the adults, particularly when it was time for them to go home. I hope our children will enjoy it as I did."

'"It is a beautiful building," I said, "and could be brightened up considerably with some new wallpaper and curtains."

'"Yes, I quite agree," said Paul. "Papa and I used to say so, but Maman was rather obsessed with the family history and wanted to keep things exactly as they had been. The setting is magnificent. Even Marianne is forced to admit that!"'

'It was late before I reached my bed that night, exhausted but satisfied that the elegant setting would enhance any wine and food that the guests were offered. The difference that the floral arrangements made to the sombre rooms was beyond even my wildest hopes. I've always been very affected by flower scents myself and hoped that other people would feel soothed by the many fragrances I had managed to amass from the extensive gardens. It had taken many hours of effort but was well worth it. The staff had at first been shocked by some of the containers I had seen fit to use – copper shapes from the kitchen and things like that – but, thanks to my experience in the rue Cardinet and at our reception for the Pierre-Elise Award I had every confidence in my own judgement.

'The morning of the funeral found Marianne still low in spirits as we set out for the church. "I *do* wish Papa had managed to get here in time," she said.

'"Perhaps it would have been just too much for him," I suggested, "having to be civil to all these strangers. I think he will be more inclined to wish for quietness. The children will be a comfort to him."

'I knew she was desperately seeking the comfort of a loving father but felt that Albert was going to be sadly in need of sustenance himself, and who was going to give *him* any? His sons would be returning to their own homes; Paul was out of his depth as it was with this funeral and the business adjustments that would follow. Once Albert got back to Paris, he would throw himself into his work. I knew that that would be his salvation as it had been mine. But while he was at the château, I was going to be the only person who could support him in his struggle against grief. I must not fail him!

'It seemed odd to see so many people weeping as the cortège passed. Madame Auclair had always seemed to me to be utterly selfish, unlikely to inspire affection. Yet Paul's father must have thought differently. Paul had said she was obsessed with the family history. Sometimes what can be charming in a young person as an amusing bias, ends up as unlovely bigotry. Perhaps those weeping country people were seeing the end of an era, a safe and secure living where they all knew where they stood. I must urge Paul to assure them that he cared what happened to his tenantry. Albert seemed to think I was strong and I had to live up to that, put my experience to good use.

'Later, as I was introduced to the various notables, it was gratifying to be congratulated so frequently on the transformation I had worked on the old building. I kept a wary eye on Marianne but, though pale, she seemed to be doing her best to act as the young mistress. Anyone hearing of her great loss would be bound to be sympathetic, I felt sure. Several of the older men were making offers of help to Paul too, I noticed. "I might be very grateful for your advice. Thank you, Sir," I heard him say to one near neighbour.

'Gradually they all drifted homewards. Sounds still came from the barn where the workers were congregated, but Paul trusted the senior servants to see that order was maintained. He had made a brief visit earlier to thank them all for their support at the funeral and had taken my advice about assuring them that their future was safe in his hands. Marianne was summoned to feed little Louis; Paul had gone to the library to start on the mound of paperwork that awaited him, when I heard the sound of wheels coming towards the house. Could it be Albert? I felt my pulse race a little at the thought. What was I going to say to him? What words could possibly express my sympathy . . . my understanding? I walked slowly into the main hall. The door from the outer hall was opened and Albert walked through.

'Neither of us said a word as we met. He held my hands in his for some time. I felt the tears gather gently in my eyes as I looked at his ravaged face, then I turned and he followed me into the small drawing-room which was warmed by the late afternoon sun. "Marianne?" he asked.

'"She was called away a short time ago to feed little Louis. She is dreadfully upset, of course."

'"But still managing to suckle? . . . I feared . . ."

'"We *did* have a little trouble. The doctor here sent a wet nurse, but after she had given the baby one feed, Marianne felt she was fit again. I think there was a little pride involved," I risked adding.

'Albert smiled gently. "I imagine there would be. And the funeral?" he asked.

'"This morning," I said, "but the last of the guests is not long gone. It is quite an affair, seemingly, when one is mistress of a château."

'"And my little Marianne, my baby, will be mistress now. It is very difficult to believe. Does she fit the role, Elise?"

'"Not at the moment," I said honestly. "She is too distressed about many things – her mother's death, the fact that she could not be at her funeral. She feels vulnerable yet has responsibilities, conflicting loyalties; she does not like this place and, according to Paul, would like to be rid of it."

'"And what does Paul say to that?" asked Albert.

'"He feels that it is little Louis's inheritance and the child may wish to take it up. Many people here depend on him. If he were to 'get rid of it' it might be impossible to guarantee their security. Though he has little interest in winemaking, he loves the home he was brought up in, so he has many new responsibilities to bear."

'"Without Marianne's support, you are saying?"

'"Yes." I paused. "Please do not think I am blaming Marianne. I understand only too well what she is suffering and I know that, given time, she will cope well, but she is young, she is suckling her baby and I know from my own experience how emotional that can make a girl; she has lost a loving mother when she most

242

needed advice and support. She is longing to see you and be your baby again but feels rather ashamed of her weakness too, I feel."

'"My dearest Elise," Albert said, stretching for my hand, "you have so much understanding and love for our little girl. Some day she will thank you herself but I thank you now for coming here and standing by her. Now I had better go seek her, I think."'

Chapter 17

'For a while after he left I sat thinking, then I drew out the letter which had arrived from Lou. In her hasty uneven script I read,

I hope you don't mind – I told Robert about Paul's dilemma with the château. He had a very good idea and I asked him to write it down – I can't be bothered with these things! You would laugh if you could see how some of our ancient clients just melt if Franc passes by. I fear he will get conceited but at the moment he's quite untouched, just desperate to get on with his work. Perhaps he's one of *them*. Come to think of it, he gets on very well with Pierre!! I'm only teasing you, my cool anglaise. He's got a drawing (his own work, I expect) of a very pretty little country girl pasted up on the inside of his cupboard door. I saw it by accident and he actually blushed! How does a country boy get all these ideas about clothes? His father is a grocer! It doesn't make sense. Of course, if I become a countess it won't make sense either. I'm just trying to cheer you up, my dear Elise. I expect you are running that château beautifully in the absence of the dragon.

'That was Lou, bless her heart! One look at Robert's letter which she enclosed had told me it could be very useful. Once Paul had dealt with some of the papers that awaited him, he'd be able to give it a share of his attention. I read it through again, more carefully than had been possible at the first reading.

Châteaux in the south of France are much sought after by wealthy English people who wish to escape from the cold of winter. They do demand some comfort for their money. I do not know what state of repair Paul's château is in, but if it is sound and well furnished then you, my dear Elise, could advertise it for him in one of the leading London publications. It pays to ask a lot of money. These people tend to think more highly of you if you do. It is, of course, necessary to employ a lawyer and to demand good references . . .

'If Paul chose to consider Robert's idea, I could certainly be a help, I thought. Wording the advertisement was quite important and also showing prospective clients over the premises. It needed someone who understood each little nuance of the language. The state of the château – that was more of a worry. I had managed to make it look inviting with flowers but that was a makeshift, temporary measure. Something more would be required if Paul wished to attract a wealthy guest who was used to a beautiful home. The heavy, old furniture would be no drawback – they would expect that – but these dismal old curtains would have to be replaced; some of the chairs would have to be re-upholstered. Of course, I could see to having the curtains made up in one of Pierre's factories but upholstery would have to be paid for elsewhere. I had no idea how Paul would be placed financially. It could be that old Madame Auclair had clung to the decrepit hangings and furnishings because she did not have the money to replace them! But Paul had not thought so.

'I returned to my bedroom and picked up a measuring tape from my little workbox. Once I knew the yardage involved I could give Paul a better idea of likely expenditure. I would measure the walls too. Some good wallpaper would improve those rooms beyond recognition.

'By the time we gathered for a family meal that night, I had worked out quite a few ideas of my own. Marianne, of course, was monopolizing her father and he was patiently answering her questions and responding to her stories of the children's progress.

'"You have managed to keep them happily unaware of the sorrow round them? That is good," Albert said. "Life goes on and we must not impinge our grief on others, particularly those who depend on us."

'I wondered if Marianne would pick up the message implicit in his words. It was some time before I got the chance to broach the subject of Robert's letter. Paul snapped to attention immediately. "That sounds a good idea," he said. "They would expect the staff to be here?"

'"Oh, I should think so," I said. "They may be proposing to bring the odd personal maid, but that would be all, I should think. It is possible that they would give large houseparties. I take it that there are plentiful supplies of household equipment, dishes, cutlery, bedlinen . . . that sort of thing?"

'Paul laughed. "I've heard my mother boast that some of *her* mother's wedding gifts have not been started on yet."

'"Good! No expense there, then," I said. "The difficulty as I see it is the décor. Some of the rooms desperately need new wallpaper – these log fires in the winter have taken their toll over the years."

'"Over many years, Tante Elise," he said. "Nothing has been changed in my mother's lifetime. I don't know how long before that either."

'"Well, earlier this evening I started measuring up the rooms. You see, I could have the curtains made up in one of Pierre's factories, but the material would be expensive. It would be madness to try to hang cheap material here against all that solid furniture."

'I was interrupted by a little chuckle from Albert. "You see, Paul, I told you that your Tante Elise's advice would be invaluable."

'We went on to discuss some of the decorating possibilities. "There's the question of time, too," I said. "You really want to catch a client before the autumn sets in. By the way, what is the fuel situation? Will it cost a fortune to heat the place if the weather should be unkind?"

'"No, not really," said Paul. "We own the woods on that hill you see to the north-east. That's where our logs come from. I don't know about the charcoal, but I never heard my father complain about fuel expenses."

'"I suggest, then, that you decorate the rooms which have been used most, trying to get them ready to show in, say, five weeks' time. Then, when you have a gap in your let, you could go on gradually improving the place as time and money permit."

'There was a pause after I spoke and I wondered if Paul thought I was being officious, but he was looking at Marianne. "Well," he said, "do you still think we should get rid of it?"

'"If you sold it we could have a beautiful house

in Paris and a holiday home too. The children would have every advantage . . ." she tailed off while Paul watched her steadily. Then she turned to her father, "What do you think, Papa?"

'"It is not my decision, my love. I have never known what it is to have a magnificent place like this as an inheritance. Certainly if I were Paul I should not discard it lightly. You have found the house gloomy, but I think if you were to see it through Tante Elise's eyes, you would see something far different."

'She turned to me then. A voice in my head warned me to go carefully. I must not belittle Marianne. She was feeling lost, bewildered and outflanked. Things were changing too rapidly for her to cope. "Well," I said slowly, "as a businesswoman I'd say that it is a good investment. Once the decorating is done you have a better property to sell if you decide to do so. The wine business will run efficiently with the present personnel, I understand. I take it that it is profitable?" Paul nodded. "You should be able to draw in enough money from the let of the château, I should think, to pay for its upkeep. So I see no reason why you shouldn't be able to have your fine house in Paris in a matter of a few years if all goes well."

'"And little Louis would still have his inheritance," urged Paul.

'Marianne smiled at last. "I wonder if the greedy little rascal cares," she said.

'"He's a healthy boy," said Albert. "I'm so glad you have managed to feed him through this sad time. Well done, my love."

'Marianne, mollified, turned her smile on Paul while Albert gave me a knowing look. We were allies, plotting for these two young people's welfare. The idea warmed my heart.

'I suppose I've done a lot of thinking about Albert ever since then. To begin with, we were both involved a great deal with the young couple and their transactions. As Robert had suggested I drafted an advertisement and placed it in a London journal. Only two people made enquiries but the first party to view the house was enchanted with the whole set-up. It was a gorgeous September day; doors were open on to the terrace. I had filled the house with flowers again and this time there were some elegant curtains to back them up. Even the rooms we had not had time to decorate looked so much more welcoming with their new hangings.

'I had feared that Pierre might be sticky about lending the services of his factory staff for this rush job, but I needn't have worried. I think he had always been pleased that his association with me took him into the Wallachs' circle, and his regard for Albert had increased that night Marguerite made a scene at the opera. When I went to the factory myself to see how things were shaping up, I realized what a difference it made to have vast surfaces for cutting out and also teams of expert sempstresses working on the hand-hemming. At my urging, Pierre was invited down to the château for a weekend before the first guests arrived. He was in his element in those grand surroundings and I think the visit more than compensated for any annoyance he might have felt initially.

'By the beginning of September Albert had thrown himself into his work again. I knew that the little patients who drew his sympathy would also bestow their own kind of healing on him and I was glad of it. My own work had suffered badly with all the interruptions, but Lou had looked into my portfolio and had followed up the notes I had made on certain customers with the result that many of the garments I had been keen to show in our autumn collection were already made up. As I set to work I was aware that my designs were a little more sombre than usual. I knew it was dangerous to let my own mood be reflected too closely, but the warm dark shades appealed to me without a doubt and I could only hope that many of my clients would feel the same. It was comforting to know that Franc's brilliant range would more than compensate.

'Some of the new materials were enchanting. It seemed that the fabric designers had surpassed themselves and when I got to the evening range, which I had left till last, I found my old enthusiasm returning. There were no opera parties to distract me at that time because Albert was in mourning, so I took the opportunity of spending many evenings absorbed over my drawing board. Lou showed no sign of shrugging off Robert. Gradually they spent more time in the house at rue Cardinet. I began to fear that Lou might expect to bring him home with her, as she had done with Henri and so many others in the early days. It seems odd that the idea should shock me but that house has been a real home to me – the only one I have had since I left Kilbarchan. Sharing it with Lou is one thing but . . . with a couple . . . no! But, either Lou has acquired some delicacy or Robert has had a stronger influence on her than appears on the surface; in any case they have continued to conduct their affair elsewhere.

'The weekends were a difficult time for Albert, even

though Marianne was assiduous in inviting him for meals to the little house in Auteuil. "It is all right when the children are there," he said to me once, "but I feel that once they are off to bed, I am imposing on the young couple. It is natural for them to wish for the company of their own generation. After all, Paul works with me. We get on well together – I would not wish anyone to think otherwise – but I think it is better that their life should not be too closely bound up with my consulting rooms."

'After that I started arranging little dinner parties at my home, inviting some of the people who had shared those happy occasions with Anna and Albert. They in turn organized similar intimate social evenings. Lou and Robert were happy to swell the numbers at times. Pierre, too, always seemed glad to be included. I wondered sometimes if these gatherings might not be a strain on Albert. He was always so considerate of other people's feelings that it might be difficult to tell. When I tentatively sounded out Marianne on the subject, she had no doubts. "Papa finds the big house by the Tuileries so lonely now. I offered to arrange some parties there for him but he said that you managed everything so beautifully in your lovely quiet house and he knew that you did not expect him to try to reciprocate – his efforts would be in vain, anyway."

'Sometimes when the other guests had gone, Lou and Robert would be murmuring in one corner of the room and Albert and I sat, saying very little, by the fire. I loved those peaceful, comforting moments.

'I was pretty sure by then that Lou and Robert would marry eventually, but it was a bit of a shock when he told me one night that they were looking for a house in Paris. Lou hadn't said a word and that was most unlike her. "None of them ever pleases this lovely little lady," he said to me. "You have made rue Cardinet a beautiful dream, my dear Elise. She does not wish to wake up."

'"I would have you know," said Lou, "that Elise and I looked for a long time before we found this house. It is her creation. Nothing we have seen could hold a candle to it."

'"I am sure that if we *did* find something remotely possible Elise would advise us how to make it into a home we would enjoy," said Robert. Lou looked slightly annoyed and quickly changed the subject. After that they spent more time at Robert's manor in the country. This sometimes made it awkward for me when I was arranging the guests for my social evenings. Lou and Robert were my home team, as it were; so, I never felt like a lone woman. I knew that many of Albert's circle set great store by etiquette and I tried to be careful to respond to the rules. Yet none of them seemed surprised when Albert sometimes lingered on by the fire when the others departed. I secretly treasured those moments alone with him in a domestic situation but always confined my talk to generalities or to Marianne's children.

'Then I started dreaming – the way I had done when I was a young girl; those dreams that were not quite genuine dreams because I was making them happen while I was still half asleep. And Albert was always there, putting his eager arms round me and saying, "Let me take you home." In the morning I was always ashamed and would tell myself that that was no way to think of an honourable man who was mourning a much-loved wife. But it was impossible to shake the dreams off completely till I got into my office and turned my mind to building up a good stand-by portfolio.

Pierre had come to me one day eager to talk. "I've been thinking, Elise, do we want to lose Franc when his year is up – it's not long now!"

'"No. We certainly don't," I said.

'"I propose that we give him a good salary – he only has pin money now. The lad has a girl in his home village, I understand; may want to marry."

'"Lou will be jealous," I said.

'"What!" said Pierre. "She's making plenty."

'"I meant about Franc getting married," I said.

'"She's mad. The fellow would never think of her that way."

'"Don't be so sure, Pierre," I said. "I've watched the way his eyes follow her and she never misses an opportunity of talking to him."

'Pierre looked troubled in spite of his scorn. "I suppose he's never met her sort before . . . living in a one-horse village . . ." he tailed off. I had a sudden memory of Pierre's first visit and the lesson Lou had given me that night and had to turn away hastily from the sort I had never met before!

'As I drew the drawing block towards me I wondered if Lou's infatuation with Franc had anything to do with her reluctance to settle down with Robert. Pierre was keen to speak to Franc straight away, but I pointed out that we *did* have a partner.

'"Oh, yes," he said impatiently. "Could we have her in now? The sooner we get that lad anchored the better."

'It crossed my mind then that if Pierre got his way Franc would still be with us when the next winner was due to spend his year under my tutelage.

'Lou said, "Oh, yes, he's worth it," without the slightest hesitation. I looked at her keenly. She was flushed. I felt a pang of sympathy for the absent Robert. "Shall I fetch him?" she asked.

'"Might as well get it over and done with," said Pierre. "I'm off to one of the workshops in ten minutes."

'Lou came back with her arm linked in Franc's and laughing up at him in her most flirtatious style. He too was flushed and adoring.

'"Trouble," I thought. "Trouble with a capital T. I'll need to get that girl under control."

'Pierre outlined his proposal. I watched Franc carefully but I needn't have worried. He was over the moon; thanked us all profusely while assuring us that he loved working in the emporium. Pierre went off satisfied. Lou had perched herself on the edge of my desk with a dancer's grace. Franc, wound up, perched beside her. "Jeanne-Marie will be so thrilled. We are longing to get married but I could not afford it. Now it will be possible. I tell her so often of you elegant ladies. She longs to meet you. The older women in our village are all fat – or scraggy. They do not walk proudly like you. I tell Jeanne-Marie how you hold your head and step out, not stump on one foot after another. She wishes to grow old like that and she will be so happy when she can come to meet you."

'I didn't dare look at Lou. "That will be lovely," I assured Franc. "But now, if you don't mind, I must get on with some work. I have lost so much time recently." He jumped to attention and it gave Lou the chance to hurry off.

'Seeing the quantity of stuff that Franc had created

in his time with us made me very aware of my truancy. I made an effort to spend as much time as possible with him as it helped focus my thoughts on dress design which, after all, was what was paying for my lovely home in rue Cardinet, that lovely home which Lou had used as her excuse to Robert.

'Franc's energy was inexhaustible. I could not say the same for mine. Sometimes I wondered if I was expecting too much of myself. Then I remembered how much I had achieved not so long ago. The answer lay elsewhere. The answer lay with Albert and my longing for him and that was something I must cut out of my life entirely if I were to be able to carry on as before. During the day I could school myself to behave like the successful designer, concentrating on her work, but night-time could not be controlled. I would wake from a troubled sleep weeping with a sense of loss. In the early-morning light my thoughts would roam from my future – what did it offer? – to my past. What had my family thought of me when I let them down so badly? Would they have had me back if I had gone in the early days? If I summoned up my courage and wrote to them, would they answer? Where would I write to, anyway? Mam and Faither would be dead. The others? I imagined that Jean *could* still be in her clean, shining little house in Johnstone, but Jean was the member of the family whose retribution I most feared. Meg *could* still be in her manse in Glasgow but that was unlikely. Duncan was a live-wire and his fine preaching had probably brought offers from more desirable areas of the city or beyond. Bella and you, and even baby Lilias were probably married and scattered by then. And Dougie; I didn't dare think of Dougie, who had never quite approved of me anyway. I would shake my head clear of such thoughts and rise to face another day.'

Elsie's body was trembling. I hugged her close for a while, then I suggested a cup of tea.

'It's the middle of the night,' she said.

'The spirit kettle's here,' I said. 'I'd like a cup.'

We both sat staring at the little flame without saying a word. I had had so much to absorb and Elsie must surely be worn out with the memory of all those things that had happened. Yet she was telling me of success; and the doctor thought there had been some blow which had been too much for her. I hoped she wouldn't decide that she had had enough. I was desperate to hear the rest of her tale.

We sipped our tea, still without speaking. Then, when I had tidied away the cups and got back in beside her, Elsie went on again as if there had been no break.

'My visits to the convent had been interrupted by the preparations at the château, but I returned to them now with a deeper interest. In a way I was doing this work for Anna. It was all I could do for her now. All, that is, except comfort Albert and that carried its own dangers. The thought of him alone in the big house which had resounded for years to the laughter of his children filled me with pity. I had wondered at times if Marianne and her family would move in with him, but Albert's remarks about Paul and himself having to spend some time separate from their working environment had cured me of that notion. Also, Albert was older than I was. Though more distinguished-looking than ever, he was bound to have reached the stage of relishing peace and quiet – but not loneliness, I mentally added.

'The nuns enjoyed a great deal of peace and quiet, even working so near the children. They seemed to be able to create an oasis of calm round themselves. Of course, they had nothing to fear for the future. When they became old and incapacitated, they would be looked after in a tranquil environment. What had I to look forward to, I used to ask myself. A certain amount of fame might linger in the limited circle of the fashion world, but new designers arrived each year. Franc would soon outstrip me in fame, though in a slightly different field. If I gave up, Franc could move into my office and the next prizewinner would have his room. The world would go on without me.

'These were my down moments. Fortunately I had brighter ones to chase them away. Lou brought about one of these when she and Robert invited us to see his manor house one weekend. When I say "us", I mean Albert, Pierre and me. She had only once referred to the disastrous back-handed compliment that Franc had offered her that day. To salvage her pride I had managed to angle things so that we had both been put in our places. We laughed ruefully over the knowledge that we would never rival Jeanne-Marie, and Lou had ended by saying, "Ah well, there's always dear old Robert."

'"You can count on him," I said in English. She got it and laughed. Then I remembered how Dougie hated puns. It's funny how things come back to you at odd moments, isn't it, Jessie?

'I looked forward to that trip. I would spend the entire day with Albert and no one could think it less than *comme il faut*. I had never paid much attention when Lou talked of the place, so it was a bit of a shock to find that it was not all that far from Vaucresson and its memories of Georges. Could I endure seeing the masterpiece which had occupied so much of his thoughts and had united us in a common interest?

'The morning of our departure brought me a different problem when Pierre phoned to render his apologies. It was Lou who took the call. I heard her offer elaborate sympathy. Then she put the phone down and hooted with laughter.

' "What is it?" I asked.

' "It's Pierre," she chortled. "He can't come. He's got a boil on his bum!" She was off again in fits of laughter.

'While I chided her through my own chuckles for her cruelty, my mind was elsewhere. Lou and Robert would automatically be absorbed in each other, throwing Albert and me together. One half of me rejoiced in this but the other half, the sensible half, said, "Be careful. Hide your feelings or you will be sorry."

'I sat beside him in the train and then, later, in the carriage, aware all the time of his nearness but behaving normally. Lou was outrageous, referring time after time to Pierre's complaint. I was relieved to see Albert laugh too but he did point out to her that it was a very painful complaint and could incapacitate a person for quite some time. "You may miss that keen, financial brain, dear Lou. His was the driving force behind your successful enterprise, remember!"

'I had noticed Lou gradually change since she became involved with Robert, but it was most entertaining to see how she behaved when we reached Robert's domain. It was clear to me that she had already thought herself into the part of the countess. The servants were deferential, though they would, by then, know of the liaison, I was sure. Perhaps they judged things differently when their lord and master was involved and anyway, the simple country folk are pragmatic if Lou is anything to go by – not that Lou is simple! She showed a keen interest in what was going on in the estate and it wasn't long before Albert and I were left to entertain ourselves.

'"I think you would be cooler in the shade, Elise," he said. "Shall we walk towards those woods?"

'The coolness was welcoming but quite a shock. I gave a little shiver. Albert looked at me sharply as he took my hand. "Was I wrong in suggesting this? You are thinly clad. Perhaps . . ."

'"Oh, no, it's lovely here," I assured him. "It was just the sudden change – so warm . . . and then . . ."

'"I am glad the weather is like this for our outing, giving you the opportunity to wear such a pretty dress. You always make a picture, Elise."

'I felt myself blush and tried hard to control it. Albert did not mean me to take the compliment that way. It was just his good heart which prompted his speech. Then I stumbled on a tree root and he was offering me his arm. I could not very well refuse, but was sure that he must feel the tremor which shot through me at his touch. If he did, he contented himself with covering my trembling hand with his free one. I did not dare look up.

'Soon the cool clean scents of the woodland had worked their magic and I could be rational again. We sat down on a log in a clearing. Albert started to ask me about the scenery round my home in Scotland. I was startled and then I remembered that I had told him my story right from the beginning, the first day I met him. He would form *some* sort of picture then. Hesitantly I started, "Well, the Renfrewshire countryside is quite varied. We have some high moorland hills with heather and gurgling streams. There is one called the Brandy Burn which flows down from the Gleniffer Braes – these are hills – towards Kilbarchan, my village. That means 'the place of St Barchan'. He was a Celtic saint. The Brandy Burn is called that because it picks up the earth colour as it flows steeply down. Then we have sheep grazing on the lower slopes and cattle in the lush fields further down."

'"You get a lot of rain?"

'I laughed. "You could say that. The local joke is that the people of the town of Greenock all have webbed feet. We are less than twenty miles from the Firth of Clyde – that is the west coast. The word 'firth' is the same as 'fiord', an arm of the sea. There are lovely islands floating off the coast, some of them mountainous, like Arran. When you look at its peaks from the mainland, they form the Sleeping Warrior. The people from the industrial towns round about go to all these coast places for holidays. Some people have little rented cottages or flats that they can use all the year round, if they wish."

'"It sounds a pleasant place, my dear Elise, and yet you never speak of it; you never think of returning?"

'"Oh, I've thought of it often enough, Albert," I said, "but you know my story. I disgraced the family. It was a scandalous thing for a girl to run away with a man."

'"You married him . . ."

'"Oh, yes, I made him wait." I could hear the bitterness creep into my voice. "And you know the reward I got for that!"

'Albert was all contrition. "I have hurt you, my dear. I had no right to tell you what to do. Now, the sun

260

is finding us out again. Shall we walk further in the shade?"

He was offering me his arm. I had been abrupt, ungracious, but he was blaming himself. I could think of nothing to say as we set off again. Then Albert remarked on some of the trees and asked me about the trees in my part of the world.

'"I love the Harz mountains in Germany," he said. "Some day I must . . . I mean," he corrected himself quickly, "some day you must see them." His face had flushed suddenly. I found myself blushing too. Was he confusing me with Anna? Had he been about to say, "Some day I must take you there"?

'"Tell me about them," I said quickly, to ease his confusion.

'"Well, they stretch for many miles, thick-wooded right up to the upper slopes. In the summer the clearings are full of the sound of bees feeding in the Heidelbeeren – I cannot think of the French name." I couldn't think of it either, but I knew what he meant. We laughed as I struggled and tried a few sounds. I could remember the French names for brambles, raspberries and cranberries, but . . .

'"In my country they are called 'blaeberries'," I said.

'"Ah, well, we are now united in our ignorance," he laughed. "We speak in tongues."

'"These same little berries are devils for staining your clothes," I said.

'"Ah, yes," Albert laughed, "but it keeps the young lovers on the straight and narrow path." Then he flushed again. Was he forgetting that I was not Anna?

'"Well, apart from your Heidelbeeren and the thick trees," I said, "what could I expect to see?"

'"Ah! your guide is remiss," said Albert. "To continue! There are many little towns nestling in those mountains. One you would love is Goslar. It has quaint old houses with texts printed round them, just under the roofs. The women of Goslar are very houseproud – Anna declared once that, if you stood still, they would dust you down. You never saw so many snowy lace curtains. Their gardens, too, are ablaze with colour all summer long. The Kaiser's hunting lodge is there, right in the heart of the town. Everything is so solid, so old, so sure of itself."

'He stopped suddenly. "Maybe I am talking too much. You are so patient and understanding, my dear Elise, I impose on you, perhaps?"

'"No, no," I assured him. "You paint me a delightful picture. There are so many things I have not seen in this world – so many things I long to see but never will."

'"Why not?" he said. "You are young enough to visit many lands before you die."

'"But what would happen to my work?" I asked him. "I've already lost a lot of time this year . . ."

'I could have bitten off my tongue as soon as I said it. Albert would think I was grumbling. "Please don't think . . ." I started.

'"My dear!" Albert took my hand, "I know the sacrifices you made for me and mine and, before you say any more, I know that they were made most willingly and that makes them doubly precious. What I was trying to suggest is that you have worked hard, have reached a pinnacle in your own world of fashion. Don't you think that you are now entitled to enjoy some of the fruits of those labours . . . to travel and see the world?"

'The thought which I dared not express came to my

mind, "If only I could travel with you," but I was saved from any reply by the arrival of Lou and Robert.

' "There you are," she said. "We did not think you would have walked so far. You did not stick to the straight path."

' "No! there were no Heidelbeeren," said Albert. Lou grew impatient with us when we could not explain the joke.

' "You'll have to march back quickly," she said. "Lunch is ready and our cook is not in the best of tempers." I noticed the "our" and, glancing at Albert, saw his eyes twinkle, though he managed to keep his face straight.

'My dreams that night were full of Albert. He kept saying, "I must take you there," and his arms were round me as he said it and a little old lady was trying to dust us down and I wriggled out of her reach and woke to find my bedclothes tangled like a bird's nest. I got out of bed and straightened them again. Then I walked to the window and looked out on the sleeping city. I longed for Albert but tried to put the thought from me. If I gave one hint of my true feelings I could embarrass him and end a friendship that had come to mean the world to me. Yes, that was true. A world without Albert would be desolate indeed. What if he married again some day? It was possible. A widower could always marry someone much younger. A pang of jealousy shot through me at the thought of the unknown bride. Yet, what right had I to feel that way? No right at all. I had no claim on Albert at all except that of friendship, and I would soon lose that if I weren't careful.

'Slowly I walked back to my bed and composed myself for the rest of the night. But sleep would not come. I felt unbearably guilty. I was desiring Anna's husband. I ran my hands down my aching body and groaned with despair. I was sullying Anna's memory. What would she think of me? What would Albert think of me if he knew? My tears started to flow at that. As I gave myself up to the relief of tearing sobs I was glad that Lou always slept soundly in her room along the corridor.

'I was calling for Albert, again and again; Albert who spent his life in the relief of suffering but could do nothing for me.'

Chapter 18

'As you could guess, Jessie, by morning I had wept myself into a state of exhaustion but my mind was made up. I knew the danger and I would avoid it. Nothing must be allowed to spoil my friendship with Albert and, if he *did* marry again some day, well, I would learn how to deal with that too. I needed comfort but I must be careful where I sought it. The obvious safe place was the convent and its peaceful little chapel. I was in the position to give generous donations to their funds now, and this salved my conscience a little. Nobody ever asked me questions there. I did not have to be on the defensive.

'A group of Albert's friends were going to the opera and they asked me to join them. I hesitated and then thought, "Why not?" I was not of Anna's family. These people would think it odd if *I* stayed in deep mourning. But it would be an effort for me, I knew. The way to counterbalance that, I felt, was to concentrate on a new outfit – something outstanding that would give me a feeling of achievement and, of course, attract more clients. Lou never lost an opportunity to advertise our wares and that would not stop if she became a countess, either! It seemed a little odd that she was dilly-dallying about taking that final step towards the title when one remembered her "our cook". I wondered if Albert had any theories about that one. Yet I would have to be careful what subjects I introduced into our conversation. I could so easily give myself away!

'My new opera outfit . . . what would it be? Something that showed up well under their lamps, that caught a little light – enough to brighten my complexion and bring out the tawnyness of my hair – but not too much or there would be unflattering shadows and I would look pale. I studied myself carefully in the privacy of my bedroom. My neck and shoulders still seemed to be able to stand close scrutiny so something that set them off could be a start.

'By the time I reached the office my thoughts were crystallizing. Eagerly I sat down, fixed a fresh sheet of paper to the board and lifted my pencil. I wished to be dignified but not stiff, so a stand-away neckline with something to soften it was demanded. One of the new fabrics I had fallen in love with was a sort of beetle's-wing shot taffeta: its blues and greens wavered tantalizingly in front of my eyes. That could form the frame for my neck, but its folds would be softened by little chiffon flowers which picked out the varying shades of the shot fabric. The flowers themselves could be edged and veined in silver thread. That would supply the delicate softness and gentle glitter I was seeking. Soon I was engrossed and Albert was forgotten.

'Lou and Robert had also been invited to join the opera party and, at the last moment, Pierre too. "I expect someone called off," he said to me with a rueful grin, but it didn't stop him from dressing elegantly and kissing his hostess's hand with exquisite charm. Like Lou, Pierre knows which side his bread is buttered on!

'"We should get a few orders out of that one," had been her comment when she saw me in my full glory. Then her face had broken into its sunniest smile. "My cool anglaise, you will have every male heart in the opera house a-flutter tonight. How I wish I had your height, your elegance, your *je ne sais quoi*."

'"The trouble with you, Lou," I said, "is that you know it all. It is my innocence that preserves me."

'She laughed at that one, then said reflectively, "I have the feeling that Albert still sees you as the innocent, the wronged woman. That may be part of your attraction for him."

'This was a dangerous subject as far as I was concerned, so I contented myself with laughing. Later, at the opera, there was no doubt that my gown was a success. I saw it in eyes, sometimes admiring, sometimes envious, and heard it in the appreciative buzz as I passed by. There was no getting away from the fact that I was a leading figure in Paris now. The thought brought its own kind of compensation. Then I began to wonder, "Compensation for what?" but put that to the back of my mind.

'It returned later at the end of what had seemed a very long evening to me. I hoped that my host and hostess had been unaware of that as I sparkled through the protracted supper which followed the performance. Lou had looked as fresh as a daisy when she bade them a gracious good-night but had been glad to kick her shoes off in the hall when we got back and to mount slowly and thankfully barefoot to her room.

'I lay in bed re-living the evening. The compliments on my arrival had been many; the performance had been excellent – everyone said so, though I had found it hard to concentrate; something had been missing and I was well aware of what that "something" had been. There was only one man I wished to attract with my beautiful dress. The thought made me feel guilty.

"It will be lovely when Albert can join us again," the hostess had said to me at one stage. "It won't be long till the year is up now – August, wasn't it?" I could think of nothing to say but, "Yes".

'When that year of mourning was up, what would happen? Would it mean a farewell to those intimate little dinner parties which had come to mean so much to me? Albert had seemed content with them – especially when the other guests went home. Perhaps it was my wishful thinking, but he had looked like a man at home, relaxed by the fire. Then, when he reluctantly decided it was time to return to his lonely house, he would kiss me on both cheeks instead of on the hand as he had formerly done. The progression had been so natural, almost absent-minded, but I treasured it. When he returned to a wider social world I would have to share him. The summer air was heavy with the scents that always made me feel discontented, longing for love. On my way to the convent I would walk the long way round to see the flowers in the Tuileries. At least, that's what I told myself, but my eyes always sought *that house* where Albert was busy caring for his little patients during the day and enduring the loneliness of the long nights.

'It was quite a relief when Lou proposed another visit to Robert's manor. "Poor old Pierre missed it last time and the rose gardens are a dream just now," she said. Albert accepted his invitation with unfeigned eagerness. It wouldn't be difficult to keep the conversation general with Pierre there, I told myself. As it turned out, Pierre wasn't there all that much – Lou saw to that. I had suspected at times that she might be throwing Albert and me together, but could never be sure. In a general way she was more sympathetic to people these days. I put that down to Robert's influence. And she had always thought highly of Albert since his treatment of little Alain. But, on that trip, I became sure of her intentions and dreaded Albert seeing what she was about.

'The spacious rooms were cool after the journey and the wine we were offered was of the highest quality. I could see Pierre revelling in his surroundings. This was the next best thing to Paul's château to a boy born into poverty who had pulled himself up by sheer hard work and intelligence. It was kind of Lou to give him this chance, I thought. I should have known better than to accept the simple explanation where Lou was concerned. When we had cooled down sufficiently she proposed a visit to the rose garden. "It's the finest I've seen anywhere," she was assuring Pierre, while I wondered just how many rose gardens the little minx had bothered to study in her life.

'We had almost reached the walled enclosure when she suddenly drew us up. "Oh, Pierre," she said, "could you give us the benefit of your advice? There's a tricky piece of business that Robert was puzzling over last time we were here. I said that where finance was concerned you were a wizard. It wouldn't take long. Albert and Elise can go on. We'll catch you up in the wood – where you were last time," she said to Albert, not daring to look me in the eye. "Visit the rose garden first. I'll look forward to hearing your opinion later." She had manoeuvred Pierre round towards the house and Robert was meekly following. I felt I didn't dare look at Albert.

' "Well, I suppose we must do what our hostess tells us," he said, "though I have never claimed to be an authority on rose gardens. Did you have many in your garden in Kilbarchan?" It was funny to hear the name of my native village pronounced – and correctly – so far from home and in that setting. Had Albert sensed my discomfiture? Did he know what Lou was about? If he did, he wasn't letting it bother him! I controlled my voice.

'"Yes, all the gardens there had roses, but simple ones. We had a large bush of very sweet-scented white ones which buzzed with bees all summer long. The petals used to shake with their efforts and there was always a carpet of white on the ground. My father kept bees. Their hives were in niches in the stone wall."

'"It sounds peaceful," he said.

'"Yes, it was," I agreed, "but I was always longing to see far-away places."

'"Yes, you must have the opportunity to satisfy your questing spirit, my dear Elise. You must not make your life one long cycle of work, exquisite though that is. Pierre tells me I missed a vision of loveliness at the opera one night recently. He described it beautifully for me. But I am embarrassing you. This archway is the entrance to the finest rose garden that Lou has ever seen. Let us enter paradise." I managed a shaky laugh.

'If there was one way of making me break my promise to myself, Lou had found it. The high stone walls contained the heat which brought out the scent of thousands of roses. I felt faint instantly. This was the most powerful drug anyone could ever have devised for Elsie Allen! I wanted to drown myself in it, forget the rest of the world in that enchanted place. I wanted Albert to take me in his arms, wanted . . . but he was talking.

'"I wasn't wrong. It is indeed paradise. Perhaps our little Lou is a better judge than we had thought."

'I gave a shaky smile. What did he mean? Had he been aware of Lou's intentions? Surely he would be shocked? Or did he make allowances for Lou because of her upbringing?

'"I think it *would* take an expert to appreciate this place to the full," he went on. "There are so many types, so many varieties. My dear, with that pergola behind you, you make a picture. I wish I were a painter. You have never had your portrait painted? We must remedy that. The one who did Marianne's portrait made a wonderful job of it, you must agree."

'I did not know what to say. It was his kind heart speaking, of course. I mustn't read any more into it than that, I told myself. Surely after living with Lou so long I could act the cool anglaise in all circumstances.

'"I think I am a little elderly for that," I said.

'"Nonsense," said Albert. "You are in your prime, younger than I am. But perhaps I seem old to you?"

'This was awful. "No, I didn't mean that," I assured him. "It is just that I think the time for portraits is before you find the first grey hair." This was worse. Albert had gone white since Anna's death and looked handsome with it. I sought desperately for the words that would put things right, but Albert was going on, "I don't think a painter would necessarily agree with you. A mature face tells more of a story; there is more he can draw out from the results of experience . . . suffering and the understanding it brings. But I think I am embarrassing you, and in this lovely paradise too. You are feeling the heat? Shall we adjourn to the woods?" He was offering me his arm and I took it wordlessly.

'The coolness of the woods did not ease my agitation. Though clear of the devastating scents, there was the secrecy, the opportunities. I tried to put them out of my mind. No one would know if Albert took me in his arms here. Georges would have found it the ideal spot. Georges! What had his love for me done for Georges? It had ruined a marriage which could, perhaps, have been patched up as they got older; when desire ceased. When *does* desire cease? Perhaps, with some people, never! In the end, his desire for me had cost Georges his life. Here was I wishing Albert to desire me. How could I wish anything so dangerous for the finest man in Paris? I walked on in a sort of dream, saying nothing. Albert, too, was quiet. We sat down in the little clearing we had discovered on our previous visit. I had the feeling that Albert was trying to think of something to say but I could not help him. Every subject I could think of carried its own danger for me when I was in that mood.

'It was almost a relief when I heard the voices approaching. I glanced at Albert. It was difficult to read his expression. "We are discovered," he said, helping me to rise. For the rest of the day I answered automatically when spoken to. Luckily Lou was animated in her talk about the manor. The word "our" figured frequently, I noticed. If anyone had told me even ten years earlier that Lou would become a connoisseur of rose gardens, I would have laughed with scorn. Now she seemed genuinely interested in Albert's opinion. I gave him top marks for effort. "My dear Lou," he said, "I have never seen anything to match it, in France, Austria or Germany; so many varieties! So many scents mingling like an orchestra to play on the senses. Our dear Elise looked quite drunk, I assure you."

'This brought a laugh and I was glad to join in to ease

my discomfiture. Had Albert interpreted my reaction? Was I discovered? "Mingling like an orchestra to play on the senses," he had said. Perhaps he understood me only too well and was mocking? No, not Albert . . . never! There could be another answer. Did the scents play on *his* senses too? He was always calm, in control of the situation, but his training could account for a lot of that. Perhaps the scents affected him in the same way as they affected me. Was he a passionate man? Did he, like Georges, know how to lead a woman to heaven with his love-making? Anna had always looked happy. The hot blood rose to my face as I realized the impropriety of my thoughts. Albert would be shocked if he knew. I glanced at him but he was laughing at Lou who was telling outrageous stories of my drunken exploits. Nobody believed a word of it, of course, but it gave me time to regain my composure. "Ah, I have made my cool anglaise blush," she finished. "That is not easy."

'It was becoming only too easy to make Elise blush, I thought later, because Elise had much to blush about. All these thoughts and longings were affecting my reactions to the simplest statement. Albert and Pierre had come back to rue Cardinet for some hot chocolate at the end of the evening. Then Pierre had taken his departure, closely followed by Lou and Robert, who were off, no doubt, to their favourite hotel. Albert seemed to be lingering, and I wondered how I was going to keep my composure for much longer, but about ten minutes after the others had gone he took his departure. "May I call for a few minutes tomorrow evening?" he asked just before leaving. I gave a polite, "Of course," trying to hide my puzzlement. It seemed that he lingered a little over his goodnight kiss but then he was gone and I began to put it all down to my imagination, longing, wishful thinking, or whatever it was that caused this turmoil in me whenever Albert and I were alone.

'In bed I chewed over his request before doing my usual review of the day's events. "A few minutes" was what he had asked. If what he had to tell me was only going to take a few minutes why had he postponed it till the next night? It didn't make sense. I reviewed the day. Albert had welcomed the chance of a repeat visit to the manor. Obviously he enjoyed my company. If I had given myself away on a previous occasion he would not have wanted to risk being alone with me again. Of course, he would have been counting on Pierre's presence. Had he realized what Lou was up to? She hadn't been all that subtle. How different a request for "a few minutes" could have been in other circumstances. I drifted into sleep. In my dream Albert was leading me into the woods but they were full of the scents of roses. He was saying, "Only a few minutes, my dear Elise. There are no Heidelbeeren." Then I was in his arms and we were crushed together. When we broke apart my beautiful dress was stained with blaeberry juice and my sister Jean was scolding me beside the white briar rose in our little garden in Kilbarchan. I woke groaning, "I couldn't help it, I couldn't help it." I was aching with longing for Albert. I felt hot. The room seemed stifling and yet one window was open. I stood up and slipped my silk nightdress over my head. The pier glass in the corner gave me a rather ghostly picture of my naked body. I moved towards it, stretching out imploring arms. If Albert could see me like that, what would he think? My skin was still soft and silky though I was "mature".

Slowly I turned and stretched out on top of the bed. "Oh, Albert," I groaned.

'It was a while before I relapsed into a troubled sleep and again morning found me weary-looking. Impatiently I splashed cold water again and again on my skin. "It serves you right, Elsie Allen," I told myself. "You are a disgrace to your upbringing and unworthy of any decent man." In the fresh morning air it was easy to renew my resolution to behave carefully, lest I lose Albert's friendship. I would try to put him out of my mind till evening. Then I would surely get the answer to his mysterious request.

'That evening I spent the time before he arrived concentrating on flower arrangements for the small drawing-room. The sounds of carriages floated in through the open windows but my flower scents created a feeling of the country. Albert was always appreciative of my efforts. I glanced round to check every detail . . . some wine was cooling in the corner . . . that was fine . . . Then I heard the bell and found myself shaking. Hastily I sat down.

'When Monique ushered Albert in, I was able to rise smoothly and with the right sort of smile. "You have given me something to puzzle over," I said. "I am eager to have the mystery solved."

'He accepted the wine I offered and waited till we were sitting down. "There is no mystery but I was reluctant to mar a perfect day. You were looking so beautiful in that setting and happy too, I think."

'I found myself blushing but said nothing. There was silence for a moment then Albert spoke again. "You know that the anniversary of Anna's death is in a few days' time. Marianne and I plan to visit her grave. She still feels aggrieved that she was not at her mother's funeral. I think this visit may help her to settle. She will weep and pray and remember and, hopefully, be strengthened in her capacity as wife and mother. My son, Heinz, has rented a large villa in Royan for the month of August. We shall go there with the children and their nursemaid. Some other members of the family hope to join us at the villa. It will give the little ones the chance to meet their cousins. Marianne and I shall travel alone to Austria." He paused to sip his wine.

'"How long will you be away?" I asked.

'"In Austria, only a few days. The children wish me to stay in Royan for some time when we return. They do not like the idea of my being lonely in Paris. I know what unhappy associations graves and graveyards have for you, my dear Elise. That is why I waited till tonight. I did not wish to spoil the memory of a beautiful day."

'"When do you leave?" I asked, hoping he would not notice the tremor in my voice.

'"The day after tomorrow. I have many notes to write up in case my substitute should need the information. I felt I *had* to tell you . . ."

'"Certainly," I said. "I think you are right that the visit will make Marianne more settled. You will enjoy playing with your grandchildren."

'He gave a rueful smile. "I think I may well feel outnumbered. I have grown used to quiet evenings. It is not reasonable to suppose that I shall experience many in Royan."

'There was nothing more to be said. After he had kissed me, he took my hands between his and held them for a few moments. "Take care of yourself, my dear," he said.'

*   *   *

276

'I looked round the empty drawing-room which had seemed so welcoming a short time before. I was alone. Lou would be out till late. I might well get a telephone call saying that she would not be home at all. Albert and Marianne were off on a journey that I could not share, had no right to share. When it came to the bit, I was not important, only a friend, even if an admired one. Marianne had her brothers too. A solid family. Albert spoke of her capacity as wife and mother – important roles that were denied to me. Nobody needed me. I had helped Pierre build our business but Franc would easily take over my job in a few years' time. Lou would have her Robert and her position to uphold at the manor. She was a natural businesswoman; did not wear herself out in useless longings for what could never be.

'Would I ever be content, I wondered. Had I ever been content? My life seemed to have been one long attempt to find something that had never truly belonged to me. Even when Georges and I were living out those honeymoon days in our enticing retreat, I had known that I was being false – false to all I had been taught as a girl and false to Marguerite in encouraging Georges' wooing.

' "What is truth?" Pilate had said. Where could I find a truth that would satisfy me? Worldly success and even a measure of fame had come to me in those last years but I had to face up to it! I envied Anna, a dead woman; envied her with all my heart!'

Chapter 19

'I was finishing breakfast when Lou returned. "We were so late last night," she said, yawning. "We met some friends Robert hadn't seen for years. We had such fun – Patric has a wonderful sense of humour. They have a villa at Nice and have invited us to go there. It sounds heavenly – parties every night."

'I found it difficult to feign enthusiasm for such a prospect but Lou was rattling on about Aimée being thrilled to hear that she knew the famous Elise and having declared it was a pity that we closed our department during the month of August and why didn't we open an elegant store in Nice; so many people went there now. I told her I would suggest that to you, Elise, but I realize that we have as much as we can cope with at the moment."

'"More than enough," I said fervently.

'Lou looked at me carefully. "What did you do last night?" she asked.

'"Albert called for a few minutes," I said. "It is the anniversary of Anna's death in a few days' time and Marianne and he are going to visit her grave. He thinks that Marianne still resents the fact that she was not at the funeral."

'Lou made a face but confined her remarks to asking when they were leaving. "The day after tomorrow," I said and went on to outline the details that Albert had given me.

'"So, he'll be away for quite a while," Lou said, looking troubled. "I thought when I agreed to go to Nice that Albert . . ." she broke off. "What will you do? Shall I try to get an invitation for you to Nice? Aimée would be thrilled, I know, and Patric would keep you in fits."

'Believe me, the last thing I wanted at that time of self-doubt and despondency was someone who would keep me in fits. I wanted peace, forgetfulness, but it would be difficult to explain that to Lou.

'"While the department is closed," I said, "would be a good time to get on with my portfolio. It is always better to have some in hand. You never know when . . ."

'"Yes! And when Albert comes back," she said, "the year's mourning will be up."

'I couldn't see the connection but Lou seemed to feel happy at the thought and I was glad to let the matter drop. We went off together to the store to decide which of our model garments Lou would take to Nice. "I'll see that nobody spills wine on them," she said, "and that they know where to buy them."

'I managed to wave Lou off with quite convincing cheerfulness, I think, and turned back to my empty house. Everything seemed empty; Pierre had gone to Italy with a friend, so Lou had told me with much rolling of the eyes; Franc had gone home to his village and his little love; and Albert had gone, Albert with Marianne to join the rest of his big happy family, Anna's family which she had created for him. I had no one.

'Well, Jessie, from previous experience I knew that work was the best antidote to self-pity. Jean taught us all that, didn't she? In my big empty office far above the roofs of Paris I studied the notes I had made on some of my regular clients and set to work. This was something I *could* do, and do well. It was no use longing for what I could not have, I told myself. All my dreaming and scheming had only brought trouble and made normal relationships difficult. If I did not take myself in hand, Albert's visits would become something to dread. Soon I was fascinated by my busy pencil, so fascinated that I forgot about lunch. It was about three o'clock when I rubbed my aching back and decided that I had done enough. I would adjourn to one of my favourite little cafés and then go to the convent.

'This formula worked quite well for the first few days. The handful of designs which I had felt obligatory were now completed and I had started to work freely as my imagination dictated. I was amused to see that a trace of Franc's style was creeping into my work. I stopped to study this, comparing my new creations with some I had done two years earlier. With a cup of coffee at my elbow I found myself doodling while my mind wandered. Then when I lifted the empty cup I looked at the pad. My doodle, beautifully executed, was of Notre Dame. I sat down and stared. I had not been in Notre Dame since the break up of my relationship with Georges; had taken care to avoid it, in fact. Why had I started drawing it now? For a long time I sat still, staring out of the window, then slowly I tidied away my tools, put on my hat and gloves and walked towards the lift.

'It was something akin to sleep-walking, that journey. I looked neither to right nor left, kept to a slow steady pace along the streets, baking in summer heat, and walked without pausing across the vast area of

paving and into the cathedral. I dropped the money
in the box, lifted my candle and lit it. Then I knelt,
staring, remembering, and thinking. Albert's reference
to graves had stirred up thoughts that I always tried
to subdue. Since Alain's body had been moved to the
ossuary I had found it impossible to re-create his presence in that cemetery. On his birthday each year I had
returned and placed a wreath among the others there,
but there had been an emptiness, a futility about the
whole thing. His going had left such a gap in my life.
But it was despair over his going that had brought
Georges into it. I tried to see a meaning. Nothing
came.

'I knelt on, unaware of time, snatching at glimpses
of ideas which fled before I could put meaning to them.
Then I began to feel tired and found the slow tears
running down my face. I couldn't be bothered to check
them and, anyway, in this place people were used to
seeing raw emotion. The list of my shortcomings
seemed to be endless. I never seemed to be able to love
a man without lusting after him. There was something
wicked in me. I couldn't accept Albert's wonderful
friendship without wanting more. I wasn't strong
enough to face up to the temptations of this world.
The only place I was truly at peace now was in the
convent. That was true. Success brought its thrills –
the fame that went with the Pierre-Elise Award, the
flattery, the adulation. But that could stir up envy, turn
people like Marguerite to near madness. My influence
on the world was not a good one. I could not be com-
pared with the homeliest looking nun in the convent.
They knew their goal and had the discipline that would
keep them on the path towards it. Of course, I had
been brought up on those lines too, but it was only

now that the truth was getting through to me. I would have to be strong. Nothing less than a complete break with the world would keep me safe from my passionate nature. There was only one thing for it, Jessie – I would have to take the veil.'

I jerked up in bed. 'What did you say – take the veil? Become a nun! No, never! Not when we've just got you back!' My arms went round Elsie and I held her fiercely.

She was quiet for a little while, then she spoke slowly and wearily. 'You're not the first one to react that way, Jessie, but if you could just hear me out . . . you've been so patient . . . it won't take long . . .'

I let go and rolled away a little. 'Right! Carry on, love,' I said. 'I'll try not to interrupt.'

Elsie started quietly. 'I continued to make my way to the office every morning. A bulging portfolio was a debt of honour to Lou and Pierre. That was essential. Each afternoon saw me make my way to the cathedral and each afternoon I found my resolution strengthening. In the evenings I busied myself in little domestic matters, going through my wardrobe and replacing missing buttons, putting the odd stitch in a damaged hem. These clothes would be given away, of course, so they must be in order. When the bell rang on the Saturday evening I was startled. Who would call at this hour? Because of my almost monastic life I had given Monique permission to go out every evening. Dark was falling . . . Then curiosity got the better of me. I lifted one of the fire-irons and made my way through the inner hall. After a moment's hesitation I unlocked the heavy outer door and opened it a crack. "Elise?" It was Albert's voice.

'He stared at me standing there with the fire-iron in

my hand. "My dear Elise, did I frighten you? Where is Monique?"

'My explanation was rather breathless. Albert took the fire-iron from my hand, supported my elbow and led me into the little drawing-room. "This will not do. You have allowed yourself to become nervous. Where is Lou?" Again I launched on a breathless explanation.

'"So you have been all alone in Paris? That is dreadful."

'"Well, there are plenty of people on the streets," I began with an attempt at a smile.

'"But no one of your own," he said.

'"I *have* no one of my own," I blurted without thinking. Albert jumped from his chair and joining me on the sofa took my hands in his. "Never say that. You are the dearest . . . you have many friends who love you dearly."

'"I meant no one of my own blood," I said.

'"Of course," he said. "Well, tomorrow you will not be alone. I propose to take you out to lunch."'

'I gasped. A lunch *à deux* with Albert with me in that state! I would be sure to give myself away. He saw my discomfiture. "You seem to be very nervous, my dear. If you prefer, I could come here. Bread and cheese would be quite enough; I'd bring some wine."

'This would be even worse. Lunch – just Albert and myself; the stuff of dreams. How could I ever get through it without showing my feelings? I thought back to those sessions in Notre Dame. I would have to be strong. But Albert was looking at me, looking hurt.

'"I see that you would rather not, my dear. We shall not speak of it again."

'There was an awkward pause before I rallied. "I did not expect you home so soon," I said. "Did Marianne not wish to stay longer in Royan?"

'"Oh, yes, she is still there – they all are, but I wanted home," he said.

'"Was the visit to the grave an ordeal? – it would be, of course." I was gabbling.

'"No. That went very well. Rid your mind, Elise, of a place like St Ouen. Anna rests in the little graveyard of the village where her father was brought up. She spent all her childhood holidays there and climbed those hills at an early age with her father. Two of the women who were at the funeral had played with her then, and now they take turns to tend her grave. They do it in love. Marianne was much restored, I think, when she learned of this. She will settle now."

'"Didn't you like Royan?"

'"Oh, yes, it is a fine place. The children are happy as the day is long. I just felt . . ." he paused. "I missed my quiet evenings with you. Also I felt that they were too anxious about me – too anxious to please me. It is better that they enjoy themselves freely."

'I sat quietly for some time. Albert regarded me with his clinical look. "I think you wish to be alone, my dear. I shall wish you goodnight." He rose as he spoke. I had hurt the finest man I had ever met, even if it was for the best of reasons. "A moment, Albert," I said.

'I started haltingly to tell him of my struggles and worked my way through, omitting my feelings for him, of course, but ending with the decision I had come to. Albert, who had probably never missed Sunday Mass in his life, stared at me in horror – just as you did.

'"Never! Never!" was all he could say.

'"I cannot see any other way," I said.

'He stuttered for a moment or two. "Why have you suddenly felt like this? You are at a peak of triumph in your work. I know what it is – you have been working too hard, that's what it is! That is the only answer possible. I shall tell Pierre and Lou that you must have a rest, a complete change. You must get away from the atmosphere of the store. It has taken over your life. It is sapping you, my beautiful Elise."

'"*My* beautiful Elise," he had said. I felt my breathing tighten. If only I could be *his* beautiful Elise! But no! If I were, I would only bring him sorrow and that was the last thing I would wish for Albert.

'"I have watched the nuns, Albert. They are so serene," I tailed off.

'"You could be serene too . . ." He swallowed and tried again. "You have the most wonderful gifts . . . you have not said this thing to anyone else? Good! Please do not say anything till we have considered it well. I think you have not been eating good meals, looking after yourself. I shall be here tomorrow at lunchtime. We shall drive into the country to a little inn where no one knows us and you will eat and we shall enjoy the sunshine and you will see the folly of your idea. Nun, indeed! Really, Elise! Promise me you will be ready. I know you will not break a promise."

'It was easier to say "Yes" than "No" when he was in that determined mood. I dragged myself up to bed, dreading the part I would have to play the next day.

'That journey could have been heaven if I had not been watching every word I said, every look I gave. Albert was sitting beside me, often taking my hand in his and pressing it to his side. The waitress at the inn obviously took us for a married couple, but Albert showed no embarrassment. He calmly ordered for me.

When the girl had gone he said with an apologetic smile, "I know what you like, you see."

'The food was lovely but eating was not easy; my heart was too full. Here was Albert giving yet more evidence of his kind heart. "When we have relaxed for a little while after the meal, I think we should take a little walk," he said. "The wild roses may not be up to Lou's standard but they will be good enough for us." He was trying to make me laugh and I did my best to respond. Walking in a country lane with all the country scents around me was not the way to control my feelings but I must make the effort. Albert was doing his utmost for me.

'It was a beautiful afternoon. The fields were golden, the birds singing, the sky blue. "You would not like to be confined to a convent on a day like this, would you?" asked Albert.

'The only answer I could think of was the true one, "No."

'Then Albert's arm came gently round my waist. "My dearest Elise," he said, "you must know what I wish to ask you. I have admired you for so long. You were a dear good friend to Anna and you are an adored aunt to Marianne. This last year your presence has comforted me as nothing else could have done. The year of mourning is up and I dare to ask you. Will you be my wife, my dearest? I shall see that you are never lonely again."

'I felt myself start to tremble. Albert was offering me my dream, my guilty dream. I was being pressed closer to him. I felt my body responding in the way it had done to Michel . . . to Georges. That had brought nothing but disaster. I shook violently and Albert crushed me yet closer to him, murmuring, "You will have nothing to fear, my lovely, nothing at all . . ." His lips were on mine, Jessie, and I was helpless as a jelly. I was in heaven because it was all I had dreamed of, but I was in hell too. My body ached to be closer still, to be as I had been with Georges. Georges!

'I struggled free. I was evil and I must not bring disaster on Albert. That was all I could think about.

'He was surprised, hurt and then apologetic. "I am sorry if I have offended you, Elise."

'"I mustn't let you, Albert," I said. "I will only bring disaster on you as I have done to everyone. I sinned against my parents, running away like that. That was wicked of me. Michel died because he was drunk. I wouldn't sleep with him till he married me. He didn't want to marry anyone. That made him unhappy and so he kept getting drunk. And Georges! He might have settled down with Marguerite if he hadn't been in love with me. It was his kind heart . . . hearing of my distress . . . that's what started the affair. He was too good for me. I am not worthy to be anybody's daughter, wife or mother. God knew that when he took away my lovely little Alain."

'Albert gave a loud groan at that. "My dearest, what can I say when you talk such nonsense? I know how you cared for your lovely little son. Anna has told me many times of the wonderful work you have done at the convent. This last year you have given me so much support with Marianne, made your lovely home a haven for me. Now," he said briskly, putting my arm in his, "I must get you home. Have no fear that I shall trouble you with my attentions."

'It was a funny mixy-maxy sort of day when I think of it, Jessie! There was Albert acting almost like a keeper, seeing me home in the early evening and ordering me to change for dinner and to be ready by the time he returned. I had no wish to go anywhere, but he seemed scared to leave me alone. "Where are we going?" I asked.

'"A decent restaurant."

'"But people will see us . . ." I began.

'"Good!" said Albert. "They'd better take a good look if you're going to hide in a convent for the rest of your life."

'After dinner in an elegant restaurant – I can't for the life of me remember what I ate, Jessie – he saw me back to the house in rue Cardinet. I expected him to make his farewells then. At the back of my mind was the feeling that I might never see him again, yet I was in such confusion that it didn't seem to matter. But he came in with me. The night was a little chilly. Without asking me, he put a match to the fire in the small drawing-room and drew our chairs nearer. I had no energy for speaking, but Albert started in a low voice telling me all the reasons why I should not think of joining a convent; how my gifts were meant to be shared with the world and I could serve God in a much wider field by using my talent for creating beauty. It was soothing to hear the deep voice rumble on. A lot of it washed over me. My mind kept going off at a tangent, to Alain's grave, to Anna's grave, to my parents' grave that I had never seen . . . the parents I had so wronged. I must do penance. If I took the veil there would be no temptation for the flesh, no men, no Albert with his distinguished head of white hair, his bushy grey brows and the piercing blue eyes which were watching me; watching me and trying to work out the best way of curing me. Poor, dear Albert! If only I could enter the heaven he was holding open for me!

'It was late and Albert was still sitting in the small drawing-room when Lou returned that night. "Ah, you're back, Albert," she said. "I thought Elise might be alone."

'"And did you cut your holiday short because of that?" he asked.

'Lou made a face and laughed. "I can go back any time I like. Cut it short and keep them keen is my motto."

'"See, Elise," said Albert. "Another friend has cut short a holiday to be near you. And you think you are not loved!"

'"What's this?" asked Lou.

'"This silly girl is talking of becoming a nun," said Albert.

'Lou hooted with laughter. "And Pierre's the next pope, I expect," she chortled. Then she stopped abruptly. "You're not teasing?"

'I said nothing. Albert looked from one to the other. It was Lou who spoke. "I thought you said your family would be horrified because you married in a Catholic church. What would they say to this little scheme?"

'Albert seized on it. "Yes, my dear. You must not take this step without consulting your family."

'"And how would I get in touch with my family now?" I asked, not expecting an answer.

'"You said you felt guilty, must do penance. I have the feeling that till you lay flowers on your parents' grave and pray there you will not find peace. We must get you strong first, fit to tackle the journey. When you reach there, I feel sure you will find some way of getting in touch with your family. Your sister who married a priest . . . surely someone in his Church would know . . . Now! You have a good portfolio ready. The young Franc will work hard when he returns after the holiday. This is an excellent time for you to make a journey. No more work for the next few days. We will go walking in the Bois; we will sit in the garden at my house; you will rest and I shall take you out for good meals. Yes! We will have you fit in no time. What do you say, Lou?"

'"Sounds better than having your hair cut off to me!"

'"What do you mean?" I asked.

'"You take the veil and they'll cut off all your hair, I tell you."

'I laughed, Jessie, thinking she was being funny.

'"Don't laugh," Lou said. "I swear by the Virgin . . ." She was crossing herself as she spoke. My face must have showed my horror.

'"You didn't think of that, did you?" she snapped. "And you get no choice where they put you. Don't think they all work in civilized places like Paris, for they don't."

'"You could always come and feed me through the bars," I said.

'"Don't count on it," said my faithful little acolyte. "You'll deserve all you get if you throw up Albert . . . and to think Robert and I have waited . . . I mean all the things he's done for you – and Pierre, the business, the Pierre-Elise Award. Remember Marguerite and the horror *that* could have been if Albert had not taken things in hand." She paused, breathing heavily.

'"Lou, it's because of Marguerite and people like her, all the people I have hurt through my selfishness, that I think I ought to . . ."

'"Bury yourself behind a high wall with a lot of man-starved old pussycats . . ." She caught sight of Albert's face and quietened down.

'"Elise will do nothing irrevocable till she has seen her parents' grave and, we hope, some of her family, Lou. If you are meeting Robert tonight, I shall stay here with Elise for a little while. We shall discuss the journey." I saw Lou glance at him quickly. I'm not sure if she had arranged to meet Robert that night at all, but she soon departed.

'"Now, my dear, we can talk a little more quietly. Lou *does* become rather heated but she loves you dearly, you know that."

'"You think she *would* feed me through the bars?" I asked.

'"That's better," said Albert. "Well, the journey, we must plan. It is a pity you have to be alone."

'"I *must* be alone," I said. "I have so many things to think out – how much to tell my family if I should get in touch, for example. So many of the things that have happened in my life would shock them."

'"Well, you know my feeling, Elise. Absolute truth is simplest and safest. Now! Tomorrow. I shall arrive here at ten o'clock and we shall go walking. Yes? Do you have a sleeping draught? I think you should take one tonight. I can see how bewildered you are. And Elise," he turned at the door, "never fear that I shall press my unwelcome attentions on you. I had misunderstood your feelings; that is why . . ."

'He kissed me gently on both cheeks and was gone.

'Lou returned to the attack over breakfast next morning. I had had a good sleep thanks to the draught that Albert recommended and felt more able to cope with her. "Did Albert propose?" she asked. I nodded. "And you turned him down because of some crazy longing to be a nun!! I think it's time we had you locked up!!''

' ''I thought you didn't want me to lock myself up,''
I said just to annoy her.

' ''What in hell's name do you think you are doing?''
she shouted. ''It's time you thought of other people
for a change. Robert and I have waited . . .''

' ''You said something about that last night,'' I said.
''What are you on about . . . Robert and you
waiting? . . .''

' ''We knew Albert would propose as soon as the
year's mourning was up and Robert was going to buy
your share of this house when you went to the
Tuileries.''

' ''You *knew* Albert would propose?''

' ''Everybody knew. Marianne kept saying how
wonderful it would be if Papa married Aunt Elise, and
when we saw how often he stayed on here when the
others had gone, we took it for granted that he meant
to do just that. Pierre was sure it would happen, and
he's not exactly without perception, is he? Anybody
less like a nun, I can't imagine. I thought you found
him attractive!''

'My eyes filled with tears. ''I do,'' I whispered.

' ''God! I'll never understand you, my cool *anglaise*.
Robert and I are going to the manor today and we'll
stay overnight. Have a nice healthy walk with Albert.
That's what an attractive man is for.'' She gave a snort
as she flounced out.'

Chapter 20

'Well, Jessie, we had our brisk walk in the Bois and a fine lunch in a quiet little restaurant. We looked like a married couple and I couldn't help pretending. This would be my last chance. I might as well make the most of it. I dressed for dinner that night with great care, wearing the spectacular dress which Pierre had described to Albert. When he saw me, he gave a funny little gasp that was almost a groan. "I must revise my idea of a restaurant for this evening. Only the grandest will match that beautiful dress, my dear Elise. It is a sight to remember."

'My feelings were so mixed, Jessie. Heads turned when we entered the restaurant. This was the picture I had seen in my happiest dreams. Was Lou right? Was I crazy, I asked myself. Yet I knew that when I was away from all the glitter of the occasion and looked into my heart, I would feel that I was unworthy of Albert.

'Back in the rue Cardinet we sat calmly talking like an old married couple. He parted from me with a gentle kiss on each cheek, promising to pick me up at the same time the next morning.

'I wondered just how long this regime was supposed to last, but over lunch the next day Albert surprised me. "I've been thinking, Elise. You have been worrying for a long time about betraying your parents. I think it would be better to get the penance over with.

I think you should leave tomorrow without any more procrastinating. It is worry that is affecting your health and emotions. I feel sure that you should take the bold step."

'I'm sure I must have looked like the village idiot, Jessie, sitting at that table with my mouth open. And yet, what was the alternative? It *did* seem to make sense to try to get in touch with my family before I took the final step. I couldn't think what to say. Albert was being masterful. "I do wish you could take a maid with you, but I understand your difficulty. I shall see you to your house now and you can instruct Monique about your packing while I see about your tickets. I think that it might be better if you went to bed early tonight."

'I couldn't believe it was all happening, Jessie. Then, all of a sudden, I seemed to catch his mood. I had dithered for so long. This was a step I had to take and I might as well do it properly.

'Monique was startled but soon set to work. I found it so difficult to know what to take with me. Obviously comfortable clothes for the journey were a must, but what else? What would I be doing, apart from visiting the cemetery? I was pulling out this hanger and that when I heard Lou let herself in. She was talking to someone. I wondered whether I should go down and then decided that it was probably Robert and she was hardly in the most communicative mood with me anyway. I'd tell her at breakfast if I didn't see her before. The less time she had to argue with me, the better! In a few minutes I heard Lou run upstairs and then her bedroom door banged. Shortly afterwards it banged again and I heard her hurry downstairs. I suspected she had done one of the wonderful quick changes she had practised in the theatre and which always left me gasping.

'Monique had had her instructions and was deftly packing when I wandered downstairs feeling at a loose end. I got a shock when Albert rose to greet me at the door of the small drawing-room. "How did *you* get here?" I asked.

'"I met Lou when I was returning with your tickets," he said. "She is off in a hurry somewhere with Robert."

'"Does she know I'm going?" I asked.

'"Oh, yes, I explained." He looked at me hesitantly. I put him out of his misery.

'"I take it she is still angry with me?" I said.

'"With both of us, I think," he said with a bit of a smile. "Now, here are your instructions for the morning. I have engaged a taxicab which will get you to the station in plenty of time. The driver says there will be no difficulty in engaging a porter – he guarantees that. Tip generously, my dear. They signal to one another at these departure points. Anything which smooths your journey is worthwhile. Now, I don't think you should trouble to dress up tonight. Let us have a little stroll along the Seine and we can have a light meal in any little café we fancy."

'It was such a lovely warm evening. I felt I was teetering on the edge of a precipice somehow and I could so easily do the wrong thing and ruin a time of magic. Then we walked across the courtyard of Notre Dame. As usual, many people were drifting in. I wondered if Albert would suggest that we follow them. Then I worked it out that he did not want to put any thoughts of the cloister in my head. We were on the threshhold of a café before I realized he was leading me into the one which Georges and I had frequented. "It's pretty busy," he said, "but they all are on a lovely evening like this."

'I wondered how I would feel in the familiar surroundings, but somehow they were so different with Albert. Perhaps because there was nothing for him to feel guilty about. Even if one of our social group had come upon us they would have seen nothing amiss. If Lou was to be believed, they all expected Albert to propose. And they all took it for granted that I would accept. Was I indeed mad as Lou suggested? He had promised not to embarrass me with his attentions and I knew I could depend on his word for that, but his determination to keep me out of the convent seemed to indicate that he had not entirely given up hope. The sudden decision to send me back to Scotland was probably intended to break those associations which were having the wrong effect on me as he saw it.

'It was not an easy parting for either of us that night. Albert kept giving me another little piece of advice that he thought might be helpful but the hands of the clock finally chided him. "I wish you joy with your family if you find them," he said, "and strength to face the sad visit to your parents' grave. You have never lacked courage, my dear Elise and it will not fail you now." He walked slowly towards the door, then turned suddenly. "I know I said that I would not worry you with my attentions again, but it may be that I frightened you . . . gave you the wrong impression . . . if you would bear with me a few minutes longer . . .

'"I want you to consider this on your journey and during your holiday when you are far away. I would not wish you to marry me out of pity or to take Anna's place. That would not be right for either of us. We both have much love to give. If you were to accept my offer, the house at the Tuileries would be at your disposal to alter and recreate to your desire. We would choose a different bedroom. It would be your home as this lovely one is. I do not offer you companionship – you would have that automatically – I wish to make you my wife in the fullest sense of the word. Anything less would be impossible for me. I am being frank for nothing less would be fair and I wish you to know exactly where I stand. Take time to consider these things while you are away. If I am fortunate, you will put your sorrows behind you and step into a new life, a life of love and joy. I shall go now."

'He was moving quickly, Jessie. I followed him to the outside door. He unlocked it, then kissed me tenderly on both cheeks. Suddenly he pushed the door to again. His arms were round me and I was crushed to him in a fervent embrace. I felt faint, with no will of my own. At last I was released. "Forgive me," he whispered, and was gone running down the steps.

'I stood for a long time with my back against the door till my pounding heart steadied. Again I had been at the gate of paradise but dare I enter into it? These sessions at Notre Dame showed me to be a very different person from the one that Albert hoped to marry. What would happen if I did yield to the temptation and he found out later he had made a mistake? A desperate weariness came over me. I had no wish to share this with Lou. Yet Lou with all her courtship skills had noticed signs I had been too blind to see. That was a new thought.

'In bed I turned and tossed for hours. In vain I reminded myself of the long tiring journey ahead, the sea crossing, the noisy railway stations and the ordeal which awaited me. I needed sleep. "If only", the words kept pounding in my head but somehow I could not finish the thought. The first glimpse of dawn on the curtains made me throw myself despairingly against the pillows. At last I slept and the dreams started. I was in Albert's arms, he was kissing me passionately, and then he would suddenly change into Georges. Anna was watching me, her hands clenched. Time after time I woke from a variation of the same dream, consumed with guilt. I had lusted after Albert for so long and now when I had the chance of happiness my conscience would not let me be.

'Even though breakfast was an hour after my usual time, I felt washed out. I hoped that Lou would not be feeling too perky. My nerves couldn't stand it. I needn't have feared. Lou was far from being at her brightest. In fact, I hardly got a word out of her. I was surprised to find that she intended accompanying me to the station. In her sullen state I would as soon have done without her, but I couldn't be bothered saying anything. If she chose to be like that I would just ignore her.

'The cab arrived on time and we duly set off. I tried addressing a few civil remarks to Lou. After all, it might be some time before I saw her again. But when I started to discuss the new season's outfits she nearly snapped my head off.

'"I don't know why you bothered to come." I retaliated.

'"You can blame bloody Albert for that!" she said. "I'd have let you stew. I owed you an obligation, he said. You picked me up out of the gutter, he said."

'"Albert never said that!" I gasped.

'"Good as did," she said bitterly.

'"You've misunderstood him then," I assured her. "Albert knew my story right from the beginning. He knew that you practically saved my life – and Alain's. Remember Anna said how lucky I was to have a friend like you, that day we took the baby carriage back!"

'I saw Lou's mouth quiver and a tear rolled down her face. I was used to her tempestuous tears when she did not get her own way but this was a different matter. "Lou, dear, no sister could have been kinder than you have been to me. Albert knows that. I can't imagine what made him say things like that to you. You must have misunderstood."

'Lou sniffed. "Perhaps it's because you've given him a hell of a disappointment, but I don't see why he has to take it out on me."

'"Come on, Lou," I urged, "What exactly did he say?"

'"Oh, I don't know . . ." she started, "something about you travelling alone and he had promised not to press his attentions on you so you wouldn't want him to see you off. I was mad angry about Robert not being able to get the house at rue Cardinet and I said you could damn well . . . something or other . . . and he said that was no way to talk about a lady who had given me her friendship, a lady anyone in Paris society would be glad to call a friend; said I would never have got any further than the chorus line and furtive liaisons or something like that – made out I would have been a prostitute all my days and Robert would never have dreamed of proposing if he hadn't associated me with your world . . ."

'I put my arm round the wee soul, Jessie. She was really upset. "I think Albert must not have been feeling himself when he said things like that," I assured her.

"You are both upset and disappointed in me and it makes people unreasonable. You have been my dear, dear friend for many years, Lou, and nothing will ever change that." She hugged me as she gave a little sob. I've never seen her gently sorrowful like that before. Then she dabbed her eyes and got out her little mirror and applied her *papier poudre* and sat up straight again. "That's my Lou," I said.

'She soon had porters dancing attendance on me and after the inevitable noisy bustle I was comfortably settled. As the train drew out of sight, I looked back and my tough little peasant had buried her face in a handkerchief.

'Well, Jessie, that's my story. You know the rest. All the time on the boat and on the trains on this side of the Channel I was thinking, thinking, thinking. I booked in at the hotel at Glasgow. I was exhausted but didn't get much sleep. It was noisy and I suppose the noises were different, but I made up my mind to go to Kilbarchan in the morning. It had to be done. And then, Jessie, you met me.'

She was crying gently as I held her in my arms. I don't know which one of us fell asleep first.

It was Beth's tap on the door which woke me. She came in quietly. 'Are you all right, Mother? It's lunchtime. I looked in earlier but you were both dead to the world. Aunt Elsie still looks far away. I've got tea and toast on the landing here, if you would like it, and I'll prepare anything you like for lunch.'

My throat felt parched. I got Beth to put the tray on a little table near the bed. As she poured me a welcome cup of tea, Elsie stirred. When she heard about Beth's offer she said she would try to come down for some lunch. We sat up in bed together saying nothing but remembering the revelations of the night before. 'We never have toast,' mumbled Elsie. 'I'd forgotten how nice and comforting it is. Croissants seemed marvellous when I first went to France but I must try this for a change . . . perhaps their bread is too dry . . .'

When she left for her bath I carried the tray downstairs. 'Did you write that letter?' I asked Beth.

'Yes. Father took it to post on his way to work.'

'It struck me afterwards,' I said, 'that if Elsie had taught Lou to speak English, you didn't need to write it in French at all.'

'Well, I knew that,' said Beth, 'but it would be quicker for her and she might want to read it to the Great Albert over the phone. Her translations might be on the free side from what I've made out.'

'The Great Albert might not get a squeak out of Miss Lou,' I said. 'He seems to have blotted his copybook there . . . it's a long story.'

'I could write to him in German,' Beth offered.

'Ooh, aren't you the little show off,' I said.

'Just good practice, Mother. You wouldn't like my expensive education to go for nothing now, would you?'

'It might not be a bad idea, come to think of it,' I began.

'Done!' said Beth.

I reasoned that Albert and I were allies in keeping Elsie out of the convent. He was bound to be anxious for her safely apart from anything else. He had browbeaten Lou into taking Elsie to the station, but a caring man like him would be thinking of all the transfers she had to make from train to boat, boat to train and train again. Yes! He was bound to be worried, and if Beth wanted to practise her German, I'd let her.

Beth had set a lunch table in the snug and the salad was decorated beautifully in Elsie's honour. The door to the conservatory was open and the sun streamed in on us. Suddenly we were both hungry. 'I'd forgotten what Ayrshire potatoes tasted like,' said Elsie. 'It's a different flavour entirely.'

'Sandy thinks it's because they put seaweed on the land as a fertilizer,' I offered. 'It's got a lot of iron in it. Somebody else said it was all to do with the variety of the potato – I don't know, but they always seem perfect at this time of year . . . home-boiled ham and salad and Ayrshire potatoes . . . well, they just answer each other.'

'Ooh! Cold lemon pudding. That takes me back many a year,' she exclaimed when Beth reappeared. 'I seem to have got my appetite back.'

'Good! I'm sure Albert would be pleased about that,' I said.

She looked startled. 'Yes, he would.' Then murmured softly, 'The dear man.'

Beth had placed comfortable chairs in a shady spot in the garden. I had a good idea what was going to happen when I saw Elsie yawning and found myself copying her. Before I fell asleep I remembered what Beth had said about having finished her preparations for next term. She would be dying to go north to join up with her cousin Isobel who was already at Ardgrian. Sandy, too, hoped to be finished by the evening. I knew that my big sons would be itching to get off on holiday. Sandy wouldn't leave without me, but Elsie still had to get to that grave in Kilbarchan . . .

Again it was Beth who woke me. This time she was offering a sumptuous afternoon tea. I had no compunction in waking Elsie. Paris had nothing to offer in the way of competition to this, I knew. The scones were crisp on the outside and soft and golden inside. Beth had spread them with my home-made lemon curd. My gingerbread, rich with fruit, was spread with the fresh butter which came from a farm a few miles away. The light sponge which Beth had whipped up oozed cream and raspberry jam. No! I was sure that Paris could not compete and Elsie confirmed it as she carefully wiped her hands on her napkin. 'I don't know why you aren't all huge – eating all that lovely stuff. Oh, I do feel much better!'

'That's good,' I said. 'Sandy and the boys will be finished by tonight – I told you we would normally be up at the castle by this time. Once you have been to Mam and Faither's grave we'll be able to take you up north to meet the others.'

'What's this about a castle, Jessie?' she asked. 'You *did* mention something about it before but I was too confused.'

'Well, we've been trying not to confuse you, Elsie,' I said. 'It's really Bella's story and she'll want to tell you it anyway, so I'll just give you the outline. Her husband, Arthur, was head gardener to the laird at Ardgrian Castle. Together they turned the grounds into one of the showplaces in Britain. People come from all over to see the rare plants. Well, Bella's two eldest boys fought in the Boer War. Walter the second boy was a gentle soul, very artistic, and he followed his big brother George. They both landed at the siege of Ladysmith and Walter died of dysentery. George came back a changed fellow. He blamed himself for

Walter's death; was bitter and cynical about the war; seemingly there were a lot of traitors over there. Anyway, he made life a misery for them all before he went off to Australia. Bella had nursed the laird's wife when she was dying and when the old laird died he left the castle to George, who had been a great favourite of his. I think he maybe thought it would bring him back home. It did, but his young wife didn't like our climate and Bella was scared they would sell the place and Arthur might lose his job. It was my clever Sandy who gave the boy the idea of turning the main part of the castle into a hotel for garden lovers. Then he showed George how the two turreted wings could be turned into holiday flats for the family to rent. Bella's son-in-law manages the hotel. One of her daughters helps her run the garden tearoom which is open in the summer. You'll love it, Elsie. It's absolutely beautiful.'

'I still don't know how I'm going to face them all, Jessie,' she said.

'Well, you've managed to face us and we haven't eaten you yet.'

She gave a wee smile at that but still looked troubled. 'It's the cemetery I'm dreading most.'

'The sooner that's over the better,' I said. Actually I was thinking as much of Sandy as I was of Elsie. He needed his holiday and, though he hadn't said as much, I could feel that he wasn't quite so sympathetic to Elsie as I was.

I was right about the boys wanting off on holiday. After checking that my laundry was up to date, they informed that they were leaving early in the morning. Sandy would be keen to get away too. He never says much but he usually manages to get his own way. And he did that night. He suggested taking our coffee into the conservatory. The scents of the garden were all around us and he sat back relaxed.

'Well, Elsie,' he said, 'you're looking fine. I think you should get to Kilbarchan tomorrow. Beth is quite happy to go with you – I've had a word with her – and it'll make it easier for Jessie and you.'

I wondered if Elsie would deduce what I did from that remark. He was making sure that I wouldn't have to cope with a hysterical Elsie on my own. I looked at her, but her head was held proudly and she gave no sign of having been slighted. I had half expected that Beth would leave with her brothers in the morning. She probably had had the same idea but Sandy had only to say a word to her usually . . . They had a great respect for each other, those two. Sometimes they ganged up on me. I resented it but I knew it was meant for my own good.

'What I would suggest,' Sandy said, 'is that you set off from here by cab about noon tomorrow. When you get to Kilbarchan folks will either be making their dinner or eating it – not that many of them would know you now anyway. The weavers have nearly all gone. It'll give you time to have a nice long lie in the morning too, after all the sleep you've been losing.' That was for my benefit too, I knew! 'I'll see Maggie off on her train just before lunchtime. You'll not be needing her while you're packing and we can be off early the next morning. Now, Jessie tells me you're dreading meeting the sisters. I think it would be better if you got that over with in one go. They'll all want to know your story, but they'll all be talking at once so you can select which bits you like and toss those at them. If you feel something awkward is coming up, just ask Bella a question. Once that tap is turned on . . .'

We all laughed. Elsie looked bemused. The Parisian society lady wasn't used to being manipulated like this – except maybe by Albert, and that seemed to be a recent development! Before she knew what was happening, Sandy was suggesting a stroll round the garden before we turned in for an early night; the boys would probably be banging doors early in the morning so we might as well get peace while we could. He suggested she might like to have a good look at the plants available if she wanted to make up a bouquet in the morning. It was all done calmly and slowly but Sandy as usual had got his own way!

Daylight was still filtering through the curtains when Sandy drew me into his arms. 'And it's about time you were back in your own bed, Mrs Forbes!' he said.

I walked round the garden with Elsie after breakfast. I had no idea which flowers she would choose but I was confident that there was a good variety. Roses seemed an obvious choice and it didn't surprise me when she stopped by one of the beds. 'I see the ones I want,' she said, 'but I need a wiry frame . . . I know – pink escallonia!' She snipped away, placing the strands carefully in the trug. Then we were back by the roses. She chose one of my favourites – a beautiful creamy white with a firm, graceful centre. The only thing they lack is a strong scent. I mentioned this and Elsie said, 'I'll get that from the purple pansies. I need lots and lots of them. I'm glad you have so many.'

'Good!' I said, 'less dead-heading for me. Sandy says he leaves me that job because I'm nearer the ground than he is. Remember that's what they used to tell me when we were young?' Elsie laughed, but I thought I saw a trace of a tear on her lashes. She was being brave about this visit but it was still an ordeal. Beth brought us some coffee to the conservatory while Elsie got on with her creation. First of all she made a sort of hoop with the escallonia; then she criss-crossed strands of it to form a lattice background. The roses were carefully measured and trimmed before being inserted through the spaces till they formed a cross. Then she painstakingly pulled the stems of the pansies through till the roses stood out from a purple cushion. The misty pink and green of the escallonia made a lovely soft background. It was exquisite! The sort of thing I would never have thought of.

We wore our veils, Elsie and I. Beth kept her aunt chatting about Paris most of the way to Kilbarchan. Elsie stopped suddenly when the cottage came in sight and I saw the muscles tighten on her cheek, but I said nothing. The cabman had had his orders from Beth and took us right to the gate of the cemetery. As Sandy had foreseen, there was no one about. We walked slowly to the grave. Elsie stooped and laid her flowers in the centre, then suddenly dropped to her knees. Beth's hand had shot out to catch her but I signed and she stepped back. Then I pulled my skirts out a little and Beth followed suit. Anyone passing by the railings would not see Elsie's face. The tears were streaming down immediately, then she started whispering. The prayers were in Latin and French. I found myself staring at the gravestone; at the inscription I could never forget: *He died that another might live.* That was Dougie, the big brother I had hero-worshipped, the brother who had tried to share his learning with his sisters. It was thanks to Dougie that Elsie had known enough French to scrape through on her own when Michel deserted her. Dougie had not approved of Elsie and her social climbing. What would Dougie think of her now, I wondered? What would Dougie's answer to her problem be? Somehow I didn't think he would recommend the nunnery. 'Let's get things in proportion,' had been one of his favourite phrases. He would work out what Elsie could do best. Her artistry with a needle had impressed him. My imagination boggled at the idea of Elsie as a nun – rough shapeless clothes, her hair cut off, no perfume, no beautiful furniture and elegant hangings; in short, nothing that I could ever associate with Elsie.

I lifted my eyes from the stone. The sky was blue with a few fluffy white clouds making a picture. The larks were singing so clearly. Kilbarchan was such a bonnie wee place I couldn't understand why Elsie had always been so keen to leave it. Come to think of it, she seemed to have painted a lovely picture of it for Albert. Maybe her values had changed. I felt drawn to her Albert. He sounded a bit like my Sandy – calm and controlled most of the time but capable of deep anger too. And he could be devious in a good cause! Now, Albert had manipulated that reporter after Marguerite's attack on Elsie. Sandy would have thought it out like that too.

Elsie had lifted her veil and was dabbing at her eyes. I found I had to do the same. Would I ever get over Dougie's death . . . Dougie – young, handsome and with so much to offer? Beth helped Elsie to rise and we walked slowly to the cab, supporting her. All the way back to Paisley we listened to her stifled sobs. Beth immediately made for the kitchen to get the kettle on while I walked slowly upstairs with Elsie. We were no sooner in her room that she started howling. I found myself shivering. It was awful. I eased her over to the bed and took her shoes off. She seemed as helpless as she had been the morning she arrived. Beth came bounding upstairs and hurried in without knocking. 'Father said you might need help,' she said.

'If you could help me get her dress off, Beth,' I said. 'Then a cup of hot tea with some brandy in it might be a good idea.' I sat beside the bed while Beth was getting the tea. I heard her come upstairs and thought I heard Sandy too. Beth signalled from the door. Sandy was waiting on the landing.

'I managed to get Bill Walker,' he said. 'I knew it was his golf afternoon so I had to hurry. He says to give her a couple of her pills – no brandy. He thinks this may be the watershed; he'll look in this evening but thinks she should be all right by morning. I'm all for Beth getting away for the train this afternoon.'

'But she'll be late arriving,' I said.

'I'll phone Duncan at the castle,' said Sandy. 'He's pally with the minister up there and could borrow his trap, I'm sure, to fetch her from the station. Isobel would probably go with her father. She's always longing to have a pow-wow with Beth anyway. Elsie should stay in Duncan and Meg's flat, I think. They have plenty of room and if Jean gets jealous we can say that Elsie needed the minister for spiritual comfort. That'll shut Tam and Jean up. Tam's a bit of a bible thumper and might get on to Elsie about the Catholic business. Duncan's got more in his head and your Meg was always good at calming people down – the ideal wife for a minister.'

That was Sandy! Everything was organized. Beth didn't take long to pack her things and they were off to the station. The pills soon landed Elsie in a deep sleep and I wandered downstairs to the snug. All of a sudden I was missing my bairns. What if Elsie had a relapse and I was stuck at home? Sandy needed his holiday and I knew he wouldn't go without me. I voiced my fears when he came back from the station. 'Well, the doctor thinks this should be the end of it,' Sandy said wearily. 'He says that if she *does* persist in her tirrivees – no, he didna put it like that so you can stop looking horrified – he says that if she is not much improved by the time he looks in tonight, he could see about getting her into a nursing home where they could sedate her for a little while.'

'But after all these years,' I protested. 'I couldn't do that to her.'

'Lassie, lassie,' said Sandy, 'I've got to think of *you* for you'll not think of yourself. The bairns will be waiting to see their mother. Aunts and cousins and things are fine for a wee while but wee Madge especially will be thinking you have deserted her if you stay away much longer.'

He knew how to get at me, though I still felt I couldn't bear to part with the sister I had lost for all those years.

Elsie was fast asleep when Sandy and I sat in to our supper. So I still did not know what was going to happen. When the doctor arrived, though, he didn't seem surprised that she had slept so long. 'That's a good sign,' he said; 'a good cry and a good sleep could bring her back to normal now she's got over the thing she was dreading. Let's hope so.'

She was still asleep when we walked into the bedroom, but she stirred when the doctor started to take her pulse. Her eyes opened and she looked surprised

for a little while. Then she gave the doctor a slow smile.
I watched the tawny eyes glow, her mouth curve in
the attractive way she had. Elsie was getting back to
normal.

'Well, I don't think you have much to worry about
now, Madame Blanchard,' the doctor said. 'Your pulse
is strong and steady and all you are needing is a breath
of Highland air. I envy you going up there. It's a
wonderful part of the world. I don't think you should
have any further trouble, but there will be plenty of
friends to look after you, I'm sure.'

Sandy was standing at the foot of the stairs and I saw
the doctor wiggle his eyebrows at him before saying in
a matter-of-fact way, 'Everything's fine; no reason to
put off your holiday any longer.' I could sniff an air of
conspiracy but I knew I would never win any battle of
wits with these two! Besides, I had all the packing to
do with an early start in prospect.

I watched Elsie's hands on that journey. They told
me that her erect head and calm posture were being
maintained only by a great effort of will. She twisted
her rings round and round, plucked at her handkerchief and her cuffs, then went back to twisting the
rings. Sandy was performing manfully, his deep gentle
voice went calmly on, drawing her attention to this or
that point on the landscape. It's such a glorious journey, I always love to share it with someone seeing it
for the first time, but I could see that Elsie's mind was
counting the time till the worst obstacle would be over
– meeting Jean. It was no use telling her that Jean had
mellowed with the years and that none of the younger
generation had ever been scared of her the way we
had been. Elsie's memories of reprimands were vivid

311

and she knew that those reprimands had been sparked off by Jean's concern for our Mam. None of us had ever let Mam down as Elsie had, and she was only too aware of that. It was as if her years of triumph in Paris had never been when it came to facing up to her eldest sister!

As we sat in the cab which would take us the last lap of the journey I slipped my arm through hers and she smiled gratefully. 'Beth will have told Meg and Duncan,' I said, 'but it will be a surprise to the others. Don't worry. they'll be too happy to see you for any embarrassing questions.'

We had decided to remove the travel stains in our own flat before taking Elsie to Meg's. Propped up on the hall table were Beth's instructions and an envelope. The instructions read,

> Younger fry off to a fair in Oban – back sixish. I've subsidized their pocket money. Father please note! Commencement time of party has been given to Lilias as 2.45 p.m. because she is always late. Your cards are in the envelope. Beth

I drew out two cards, one in Elsie's name and one in mine. We stood there giggling helplessly till Sandy took my card and read it out loud.

> High Class Caterers, Williamson and Forbes, invite you to a party in the flat of the Rev. Duncan and Mrs Williamson at 3 p.m. sharp. Entry by invitation card only. Spare handkerchiefs recommended. Dress – best bib and tucker.

'Well,' said Sandy, 'you'd best get bibbed and tuckered, girls. I'm off to see what Arthur's up to in the garden.'

It was Beth who opened the door of Meg's flat. I saw Isobel standing in the kitchen doorway anxious to catch a glimpse of her French auntie. Beth opened the sitting-room door and stood back. I looked at my sisters. Lilias uncurled her slight body from the depths of an armchair and looked questioningly from Elsie to me. Bella gave a funny little gasp. Her face went white and then crimson. Meg smiled calmly but her eyes were moist. It was Jean, the martinet, who made the first move, stumbling forward with arms outstretched. 'My lassie . . . at last . . .' she said.

Glossary

douce	gentle, well-behaved
piaf	a little sparrow, street urchin
rackety	unsure
skelpit leathering	good spanking
stookie	a plaster cast
swithering	dithering, undecided
tackety	studded
thirled	bound by bonds of affection
tippeting	prancing nervously
tirrivee	tantrum